"Marriage! again before

But who could b woken up never expecting to see Rashid again. This morning, she woke up in his bed.

"Of course. I took your innocence."

"You didn't 'take my innocence,' I gave it to you. And will you stop being so archaic and so—so… Azmaharian?"

"You're refusing to marry me?"

Her heartstrings shook at the darkness in his rumble. "I'm refusing to introduce the concept of 'marriage' at this point."

And if displeasure could take form, it would wear just that face. "Marriage between us now is not a concept, it's a necessity."

Dear Reader,

When Rashid Aal Munsoori walked into the DESERT KNIGHTS trilogy's first book, *The Sheikh's Redemption,* and hijacked the spotlight during his scenes, he intrigued me the most of all my Mills & Boon® Desire™ heroes to date. With each glimpse he revealed of himself, I knew I had my darkest, most tormented, most ruthless Desire hero yet. I couldn't wait for him to tell me his whole story. And for a heroine to undertake the seemingly impossible task of soothing this scarred beast and laying his demons to rest.

But I knew I had my work cut out for me. For what woman could see through his armor of disfigurement and distance, let alone persevere until she'd uncovered the passionate, forever-man he could be?

Then I discovered I had already created that heroine. Laylah Aal Shalaan had appeared in *To Tame a Sheikh,* the first book of my previous trilogy, PRIDE OF ZOHAYD. And she told me she'd loved Rashid all her life. Did *that* turn the unapproachable Rashid inside out!

What followed was a roller coaster of emotions as Laylah unraveled the bands around Rashid's soul and replaced them with those of her love, only to discover at her happiest that their relationship had all been a lie. Or was it?

Read on and learn the truth behind the secrets that wrap up DESERT KNIGHTS among the upheavals that the lovers have to survive to reach their happy ending. I hope you enjoy reading their story as much as I did writing it.

I love to hear from readers, so email me at oliviagates@gmail.com. And please stay connected with me on Facebook at my fan page Olivia Gates Author, and on Twitter @OliviaGates.

Thanks for reading!

Olivia

THE SHEIKH'S DESTINY

BY
OLIVIA GATES

Published in Great Britain 2013
by Mills & Boon, an imprint of Harlequin (UK) Limited,
Eton House, 18-24 Paradise Road, Richmond, Surrey TW9 1SR

© Olivia Gates 2012

ISBN: 978 0 263 90463 5
ebook ISBN: 978 1 472 00083 5

51-0213

Harlequin (UK) policy is to use papers that are natural, renewable and recyclable products and made from wood grown in sustainable forests. The logging and manufacturing processes conform to the legal environmental regulations of the country of origin.

Printed and bound in Spain
by Blackprint CPI, Barcelona

Olivia Gates has always pursued creative passions such as singing and handicrafts. She still does, but only one of her passions grew gratifying enough, consuming enough, to become an ongoing career—writing.

She is most fulfilled when she is creating worlds and conflicts for her characters, then exploring and untangling them bit by bit, sharing her protagonists' every heart-wrenching heartache and hope, their every heart-pounding doubt and trial, until she leads them to an indisputably earned and gloriously satisfying happy ending.

When she's not writing, she is a doctor, a wife to her own alpha male and a mother to one brilliant girl and one demanding Angora cat. Visit Olivia at www.oliviagates.com.

To the one who inspires all those
powerful, ultra-romantic, luscious heroes.
Thank you for being you.

One

Laylah Aal Shalaan felt a shiver burn down her spine.

It wasn't the below-zero Chicago December evening. That would have caused ice, not fire, to shudder through her veins.

This sensation had scalded through her so many times during the past few weeks, it was as if she were having hot flashes. Which would be some record at age twenty-seven. But then she held other unwelcome records. Like being the only female born to her family in forty years. Why not throw in premature menopause, too?

Not that she really thought abnormal hormones were at work here. An outside influence was. One she couldn't detect when she'd tried to investigate it, though she'd been certain of its cause for some time.

Someone was watching her.

This felt nothing like having the security detail she'd once had breathing down her neck. Those men had never tried to hide themselves, and to hell with her personal space. Though she shouldn't have resented them. They'd been doing their job. Of course, with her safety no longer among anyone's priorities for the past two years, there were no more guards dogging her steps.

Not that she thought that she needed protection. She observed normal safety protocols, like anyone who lived in Chicago did. And since she'd exiled herself from Zohayd and come to live in the Windy City, she always had.

Until tonight.

Usually she would go home with Mira, her business partner and roommate. But Mira had left to see her father, who had been taken to the E.R. in another state. So here she was, alone at night for the first time in more than two years, leaving the deserted building from the back exit that opened onto an equally empty back street.

Not that *that* had anything to do with what she now felt.

She'd entered the building accompanied by the sensation of being enveloped in that watchful force field. She'd stepped out only to be caught in its electrifying embrace again.

Strangest part was, she didn't feel threatened by that unwavering intent. Just burning with curiosity and…excitement?

She looked across the street at three parked cars. The nearest had a man slamming the hood, getting inside and driving away with the exhaust firing. The next one, also nondescript, was pulling away from the curb, too. The farthest one, a late-model Mercedes with dark windows, looked empty.

Before she could decide where the influence was radiating from, the second car suddenly floored its engine.

Before she could draw another breath, the car screeched to a halt beside her and its doors burst open. Four men exploded out. She'd barely taken two running steps when they swarmed her.

Hulking bodies and coarse faces, distorted with vile intent, filled her vision. Blood and time thickened, hindering her heartbeat and reactions as hands sank into her flesh, each dig creating a bolt of outrage and terror.

Dread exploded in her chest, fury in her skull as she lashed out with everything she had, even as shards of dialogue lodged into her brain.

"Iz only one, man."

"Tom said there'd be two. You better not pay half now."

"Iz the one we want. Ye'll get yer dough."

"You said she'd fall at 'ur feet sniveling but she ain't no pushover. She almost kneed me."

"An' she might've scratched m'eye out!"

"*You* quit snivelin' an' stuff 'er in the car."

Each word sank a talon of realization into Laylah's brain.
This wasn't a random attack. They knew her routine.

No. They couldn't be the presence she'd been sensing!

They dragged her closer to the car. Once they shoved her
inside, it would be over.

She exploded in another manic struggle, drawing blood and
shouts of pain and rage until a jackhammer collided with her
jaw. Agony turned her brain into shrapnel.

Suddenly, through the vortex of crimson-blotched darkness, one of her attackers seemed to be sucked away as if into
a black hole. He slammed into the side of the building with a
sickening crunch.

A second assailant turned away, but a hair-raising crack sent
his blood arcing inches from her face. His terrified gaze bored
into hers before his body slammed into her as if from the impact of a speeding car. He took her down with him.

She struggled under his dead weight, fear pulsing through
her disorientation. Who had come to her rescue? Would they
turn on her once they had finished off her attackers?

The body pinning her down was heaved away. She wriggled up frantically on the freezing sidewalk and saw…saw…

Him.

A fallen angel. Huge, dark, ominous. Frightening in his
beauty, radiating power and menace. Almost impossible to
bear looking at, yet equally impossible to look away from.

And she knew him. She'd known him all her life.

But it couldn't be him. Not only had he changed almost
beyond recognition, but what would he be doing here? Now?
When she'd been certain she'd never see him again?

Was her jolted brain conjuring up an imaginary savior?

If so, why not one of her cousins who were as well equipped to fill the role? Why him?

Why Rashid Aal Munsoori?

But with her senses stabilizing, no doubt remained. It *was* Rashid. A remote, if steady, presence in her life during her first seventeen years. The man she'd had a crush on since before she could remember.

He was now facing the remaining two attackers like a monolith, his one-of-a-kind face carved from the coldness of the night, majestic head almost shaved, juggernaut body swathed in a coat that flapped around him like angry creatures from the abyss.

The men recovered from their shock, charged him, snarling, slashing switchblades at him. Dread deluged her.

Unfazed by her shout or their attack, Rashid maneuvered like a matador fielding raging bulls, harnessing the mindlessness of their charge against them. His arms and legs lashed out in a choreography of deadly precision, his methods merciless, flawless, as second nature as breathing was to her. He looked like an avenging demon reveling in vanquishing the loathsome quarry he lived to prey on.

By the time she pulled herself to her feet, Rashid had the two men plastered against the building. One had lost consciousness. The other hung in the air, feet kicking feebly.

Over the night's moaning wind, she heard rumbles issuing from Rashid. They didn't sound human.

For a crazy moment, she thought they might not be. That he did have some…entity inhabiting him, one that wouldn't be satisfied with anything less than taking those men's lives.

That conviction broke her paralysis. "You'll kill them!"

At her choking protest he turned his head and…*ya Ruhmaan.*

Merciful God—what had happened to him? He barely resembled the man she'd obsessed over all her life. The eerie blankness in his eyes, the serene viciousness baring his teeth. Like a beast in killing mode.

And that *scar*...

"And?"

She shuddered. His voice. It completed the impression. That some demon occupied him, had taken him over, was metamorphosing his body to suit its nature and needs, was using his voice to transmit its darkness and danger.

This man who'd once been Rashid was serious in his question. He had no compunction about killing in principle, and none at all about snuffing out the lives of the thugs he'd conquered.

There was no way to appeal to the mercy of this creature. He had none. Of that she was certain. She couldn't use fear of consequences, either. She was as sure he felt no fear of any sort. He seemed to feel nothing but violence and vengeance. It was as if he'd stepped in to punish the criminals, not to save her, the victim.

Only appealing to his logic remained.

"*And* there's no need." She could barely form words in her frozen, constricted throat. "You've already beaten them—to a pulp. None of them will be out of intensive care anytime soon."

"Putting them back together will be a gross waste of medical resources. I should spare society the cost of their continued existence." He turned his eyes to the man wriggling and whimpering in his hold. "Scum like this don't deserve to live."

She ventured closer, feeling as if she was interrupting a lion's kill. "A death sentence is over the top for their crime, don't you think?"

Still looking at the struggling man, Rashid said, "The ones they've committed so far, you mean. They would have probably ended up killing you—"

"No, man…" The man choked, terror flowing from his eyes. "We were only…goin' to hold 'er…for ransom. A bro recognized 'er for a princess…from one o' those filthy rich oil kingdoms…said we'd get…serious dough…for 'er. We weren't going to hurt 'er…*or* touch 'er…" he spluttered the qualification when Rashid squeezed his throat harder. "I…*swear*. Danny got carried away when she hit him…and you probably killed him for it…but I didn't do anything to her…don't kill me…*please*…"

In spite of everything, she pitied this flimsy creature in the body of a brute. He'd been reduced to blubbering in the grip of a force the likes of which he hadn't known existed.

The imbalance of power should have been in their favor, four hulks versed in violence. But Rashid had overpowered them like a superior feline would a pack of rats.

But it was as if he didn't even feel her there, had been debating with his inner demon the actions he should take, finding only approval from it.

She had one last shot before this situation passed the point of no return. Give him, and that demon, something to appease their merciless convictions.

She ventured a touch on his arm, flinched. Even through the layers of clothes, electricity arced from the steel cables he had for muscles to strike her to her toes.

She swallowed a lump of agitation. "Wouldn't you rather they live to suffer the consequences of their crimes? You've probably given them all some permanent disability."

When his dark gaze turned to her again, it felt as if he was seeing her for the first time, letting her and her words breach the barrier of his implacability.

Suddenly, he unclenched his hands. The men, both unconscious now, thudded to the ground like sacks of bricks.

Relief shuddered through her, the freezing air filling her lungs. Rashid had killed before. But it had been as a soldier in three wars. Here, it would have been different. And she couldn't have even those thugs' deaths on her conscience.

As he stood appraising his handiwork, she sensed his demon scratching at its containment to be let loose to finish its job. But Rashid seemed in control of their symbiosis again, back to being the ultramodern desert knight who had the world at his feet and everyone in it at his disposal.

He produced his cell phone, called the police then an ambulance. Then he turned to her. "Did they hurt you?"

At his question, she suddenly felt the imprint of their hands all over her arms and back. But the epicenter of pain was the left side of her jaw. Her hand flew to it instinctively.

He urged her below a streetlight. She stumbled at the feel of his hand on her arm, then again as he kicked one of the thugs in the head when he began to stir. The contrast between his violence with her attacker and his gentleness with her was staggering.

Once within the circle of light, his hand moved hers away from her face so he could examine it.

"Maybe I will kill them after all."

She almost flinched at his verdict, attempted to make light of it. "For a right hook?"

"That was the beginning of the abuse that would have left you scarred for life, if not physically then psychologically. They do deserve to die." She grabbed his arm as he moved, feeling she had as much chance of stopping him as she would a hurricane. His muscles eased beneath her frantic fingers. "Relax. I'll only make them wish I had killed them."

"How about you leave it to the law to deal with them?"

His hooded eyes grew heavier with disapproval. "You'd rather let them get away with it?"

"Certainly not. I just believe in appropriate punishment."

Those lethal eyes flared ebony fire. "What would be appropriate for abusing and kidnapping a woman, putting her through hell fearing for her life, before maybe ending it?"

She bit her lip at the terrible scenario that could have come to pass if not for him. "When you put it that way, a death sentence doesn't look too extreme. But that didn't happen."

"Only because I stopped them."

"And now we can't punish them for what could have been, only for what actually was."

"That's according to the law—here. Where I come from only *hadd'al herabah* is appropriate punishment for this heinous crime."

She shuddered again as she imagined the ancient punishment

sanctioned in their home region for those caught red-handed in major crimes like this—amputating an arm and a leg from opposing sides.

Deeming the subject closed, he turned to the fallen goons. And she saw it. A glistening wetness below his coat.

Sick electricity forked through her as she grabbed his arm, jerked him into the light. He pulled away from her frantic grip, made her grasp him to restore her balance. Her hands sank into the unmistakable warmth of blood.

She tore them away, looked down at her crimson-stained palms before looking up at him in horror. "You're injured!"

His gaze moved from her upturned hands to his midriff before travelling up to hers. "It's nothing."

"Nothing?" she exclaimed. "You're *bleeding! Ya Ullah!*"

Something like…annoyance? Impatience? simmered in his eyes. "It's just a scratch."

"A scratch? Your whole left side is drenched in blood."

"And?" There he went again with that *and* of his. "Are you squeamish? I hope you won't faint."

"Squeamish?" she exclaimed. "It's you I'm worried about…"

Dread clogged her throat, more suffocating than anything she'd felt on her own account. His nonchalance had to be shock. His wound had to be severe to bleed that much, to not have registered its pain yet. Adrenaline and cold must be all that was keeping him on his feet. By the time the ambulance arrived, it might be too late…

Stem his bleeding. Buy him time.

Tearing her scarf from around her neck, she lunged at him, pressing its creamy softness against the tear in his sweater. He stiffened, his hands covering hers as if to push them away.

She threw her weight at him, pressing him back against the side of the building, panting now. "We must apply pressure."

He stilled against her, stared down at her, his face a mask. Was he on the verge of losing consciousness?

He undid her hands, replaced them with his. "I'll do it." She sensed that he would, not because he believed he needed it, but to keep her away. "You can go now."

Huh? He didn't only want her to stay away, but to *go* away?

She shook her head, hands smeared in his blood trembling. "I have to be here when the police arrive."

He reached for her hands, wiping them clean with the other end of the scarf. "I'll say they attacked me. Those lowlifes will welcome my adjustment. A jury will give them a lesser sentence for attacking me rather than you."

"But you wanted them to get the harshest punishment possible."

"Whatever sentence the law passes won't be that. I am bound by no such limitations, and I'll make sure they'll never think of doing this to anyone else ever again."

"You mean you want them to get off lightly so you can administer your own brand of justice…?" She threw her hands up in the air. "What are we talking about? You're *injured.* And I'm going nowhere but to the E.R. with you."

"Since I'm not going to the E.R., the only place you can go now is home." At her head shake, his voice hardened. "Take my car and drive a few blocks away. My guards will come to escort you back home. They'll come up with you to make sure the coast is clear and will stand guard until we make sure this abduction plan had no contingencies." When she didn't move or answer he exhaled forcibly. "Go *now,* before the police arrive. You've been through enough on those scums' account. Walk away and forget this ever happened."

"I can't and won't leave you. And you *will* go to the E.R. Is that your car?" She indicated the imposing Mercedes.

He nodded. "I stopped to send a file from my phone."

"And that's when you saw me being attacked."

He didn't nod again, his gaze growing incapacitating.

"Give me your keys." A formidably winged eyebrow told her what he thought of her demand. "I'm driving you to the E.R."

"As you pointed out, I can't leave the crime scene. The police will be here in minutes."

"They can take *our* statements at the E.R. You might succumb to hypothermia and shock in those minutes."

"I will succumb to nothing. I've had injuries a dozen times worse, endured them for *days* in conditions that make these pleasant in comparison."

She knew he wasn't exaggerating. She couldn't imagine what he'd endured in war, couldn't bear to think what kind of injury had given him that blood-curdling scar that slithered like an angry snake from his left eye down to his jaw, neck…and below.

Noticing her eyes on his scar, his lips compressed. "As you can see I've survived far worse. Don't concern yourself over this glorified paper cut."

Retorts fired in her mind, froze on her tongue. What did he think her? A selfish twit who'd grab the easy way out and run away?

But if he thought so, then… "You don't recognize me?"

That eyebrow rose again. "I need to know someone to come to their rescue?"

"That's not what I meant." She knew he'd defend to the death anyone in need of his superior powers. He'd once made a career of it as a warrior. He'd clearly never stopped being one.

He just as clearly hadn't recognized her.

Then he said, "Of course I recognized you. Just like the one who sent those goons did. You're more recognizable than you evidently think you are, Princess Laylah."

So he *did* recognize her. Which actually shouldn't have been a sure thing. There'd been far…less of her when he'd last seen her, and she'd been wearing glasses back then, too. He'd always made her feel he'd never *seen* her, the way he'd look through her, like he had everyone else. Even now, nothing in his demeanor indicated that he knew her. The reticent Rashid she'd known had become impenetrable.

"I saw you many times around the city before tonight."

Would this man stop surprising her? "Y-you did? Where?"

"I have offices in this building. You also frequent the restaurants I do."

He had been the presence she'd felt!

Now *that* made sense. As did the fact that he hadn't thought of acknowledging her until he'd been forced to, to save her life no less. She'd always known Rashid had been a far-fetched dream, but he'd become an impossible one after he'd turned from her closest cousins' best friend to their mortal enemy.

"You clearly don't recognize me," he added.

"I'd as soon not recognize myself, Sheikh Rashid."

Everything in him seemed to hit Pause. The wind, the whole world followed suit.

Okay. That *had* come out too…revealing. Another attack of what her mother called her "crassness affliction." She'd thought she had it under control, but it seemed she couldn't control her brash candor any more than her mother's family could their crooked ways.

So be it. She'd never be able to give him anything of equal value to what he'd given her tonight, so she'd at least give him the truth. He could do with it as he wished.

It appeared he was at a loss what to do with it. Her confession had clearly stunned him.

His response, when it finally came, was to pretend he hadn't heard it and to pursue his previous point. "Back my statement, that they attacked me and not you, and I will go to the E.R."

He was trying to spare her the postattack ordeal, from the investigations through to the trial.

Still… "I can't let you bear the burden of this mess."

Those daunting shoulders barely moved in dismissal. "In comparison to the messes I deal with daily, this is a breeze."

She'd bet. Rashid had created his IT development empire from scratch in record time. He must have dealt with endless obstacles and adversaries to remain at the top of such a cutthroat field. And it *would* be a mess for her, sabotaging the peaceful life and low profile she'd struggled to create since she'd left Zohayd.

"Okay." The tension gripping the night eased, until she added, "But only if you let me drive you to the E.R."

"You think I won't keep my word?"

"I think you'd keep your word even if it meant your life."

Another long, empty stare greeted her statement, which she now realized signified surprise. "Why this stipulation, then? You think I can't drive myself?"

It was her turn to shrug. "I'm taking no chances."

His grimness deepened until she was certain he'd say no.

Suddenly, he handed her the bloody scarf. She fumbled with it as if with a hot coal as he fished inside his coat for a pen and a notebook. He scribbled a few lines, tore the paper out, bent and tucked it onto a thug. A calling card on gifts for the police?

The thug stirred as Rashid whispered in his ear before slamming him into the ground, snuffing his consciousness again.

Calmly rising, he retrieved the scarf from her limp fingers, turned on his heels and crossed the street to his car.

He was leaving?

She watched him go, at a loss for what to do.

Instead of taking the wheel, he walked around to the passenger's side. Then, leaning over the car's top, he looked across the distance at her. "Coming?"

Her heart gave a thunderclap of relief as she stumbled into a run, her four-inch stilettos a staccato of eagerness on the asphalt.

In seconds she was inside the posh car, heard faint sirens in the distance as the door closed behind her with a muted thud.

Trembling with the urge to throw herself at him and hug him, she turned to him. "Thank you."

He ignored that. "Are we waiting for them after all?"

"Oh, no." She fumbled for the ignition, discovered that the car was running, the motor so smooth it didn't produce sound or vibration. The car was such a dream to handle that even in her state, she drove to the nearest E.R. without incident.

As she parked, he turned to her. "Now drive home. I'll have the car and a driver at your disposal from now on."

He was almost out of the car before she flung herself after him. "I'm coming in with you."

His stare was even more spectacular in close quarters. "The deal was to drive me here, not escort me inside."

She clutched his arm tighter. "New deal, then."

"You have nothing to thank me for."

Now he answered her earlier thank you.

"I wasn't thanking you for saving my life, since I figured you'd have an allergic reaction to that. I was thanking you for letting me bargain with my safety for yours. Don't revert to being an aggravating superhero and insist on walking into the night alone."

After yet another long stare, he turned and exited the car.

Her heart constricted with disappointment and anxiety. If she persisted now, she'd be imposing on him.

Well, tough. That big, bad warrior would just have to use his endless stamina to put up with her concern.

The moment she was out of the car, her heart gave that boom that only he provoked. He was standing at the E.R. entrance, his pose worthy of the superhero she'd likened him to, one hand braced on his lean hips, the other still gripping her bloody scarf.

He was waiting for her.

She ran toward him, her heartbeat overtaking her feet.

Before she reached him, those cruelly sensuous lips twitched. Was that a smile? She wouldn't know. She'd never seen him smile.

Before she could make sure, he turned and strode inside.

He had her running to keep up with him, demonstrating that her concern was needless. *And* that he wouldn't make it easy for her to see her purpose through.

Once she knew he'd be okay, she'd show him exactly how much she'd put up with to be with him. That, if he let her, she would follow him to the ends of the earth.

Two

All through the admission process, Rashid felt Laylah's presence a breath away.

He couldn't take one without it mixing with the scent and heat of her body and her worry.

He found himself barely breathing so both wouldn't deluge him further. But rationing that involuntary act turned out to be easier than stopping another supposedly voluntary one. In spite of his intention to demonstrate that her presence was unnecessary as well as unimportant, his gaze kept going back to her like iron filings to a magnet. When no one, certainly never a woman, had ever commanded his unwilling response.

But Laylah Aal Shalaan wasn't anyone. There was no one else in the world that he remembered from the day of their birth.

He'd just turned eight when she was born, the first female offspring in the Aal Shalaan family in forty years. It had only been a week after he'd met her maternal *and* paternal cousins, Haidar and Jalal, and begun a friendship that had lasted for the next two decades.

She'd grown up under his gaze, always in his orbit, glowing

brighter every day with a radiance that had progressively dismayed him. He'd thought it so unfair, for her to be so matchlessly beautiful on the outside, when she could possess no beauty at all on the inside. Not when she was the daughter of a house of serpents.

Now that she'd matured, the injustice had been exacerbated.

His gaze returned to her again and again, documenting her every nuance. Hair and eyes the color of the richest chocolate and brushed with sunlight, skin of honeyed velvet and warm sunsets, a body of lush vitality and femininity and a face of a peculiar brand of splendor and harmony. But it was what those most unusual features radiated that perplexed him.

How could they transmit such…sweetness? Such…genuineness? The woman was descended from ruthless bitches and hardened criminals. There was no way any of that could be real.

Yet he was forced to believe one thing was real. Her concern for him. Its purity and intensity singed him.

But that could be explained away. By gratitude. To her lifeline in this harrowing experience. Once fright and shock drained away, so would her simulation of humanity and good nature.

Then he'd be free to resume thinking the worst of her. And treating her accordingly without the least remorse.

For now, he had to get out of her range. He needed to get his act together. To plan his next step.

"I'm coming with you."

At her blurted-out declaration, Rashid turned at the door of the treatment room. That eloquent eyebrow of his made her feel like an illogical species in the presence of a Vulcan.

He'd so far let her accompany him through the admission procedure. When the police had arrived, he'd fielded doubts about her being involved in the attack, lying with spectacular smoothness when they'd asked about her bruise.

According to him, it had been a basketball to the face during a one-on-two match with Mira—whom he'd always seen with her in the times she'd only sensed him—who'd back up anything she'd say. Just like the thugs would back up anything *he* said.

Not that those policemen would investigate any further. She had a feeling they realized the truth but seemed to appreciate his motivation for adjusting it wholeheartedly. They'd behaved as if they realized they were in the presence of a superior force who'd taken the pursuit of justice far beyond their level. The bare bones of his background had left them—and her—awed. They'd left the E.R. shaking his hand for what he'd done to those repeat offenders and slapping his back for how ruthlessly he'd done it.

It was the female E.R. doctor who answered her. "Only family members can accompany patients." She turned her awed eyes to Rashid. "Or if the patient specifically asks for your presence."

And you'd rather he didn't ask, Laylah almost retorted.

She tried cajoling, something she was abysmal at. "You've come this far. Might as well let me go all the way."

His eyes confirmed that she *had* failed to learn that survival mechanism as an endangered estrogen-based species in her family's testosterone jungle. Then he presented her with that unyielding back as he preceded the woman into the treatment room.

By the time thirty minutes had passed and more and more doctors had rushed into the room, she was certain they'd discovered his injury was catastrophic, and they'd been trying to contain the situation—and failing...

"I can't believe your luck, lady."

Laylah started, her nerves jangling. It was the E.R. nurse who'd first met them. She was exiting the treatment room.

Nurse Norma McGregor smiled widely at her. "Not that you were almost kidnapped, but that this god happened by and swooped in to save you."

She barely remembered Rashid's version in time. "Uh...that isn't what happened..."

"Oh, I know what he *said* happened, but I've seen the men he ripped apart. That had to be to punish what he'd consider a far more serious crime than attacking him. Attacking *you*. I also don't buy that story about your bruise. You two don't feel like you know each other enough for basketball. But don't worry. The boys in blue will swear on his version, so *we* can discuss the truth."

Laylah released the air trapped in her lungs. "You're uncanny at reading people."

Nurse McGregor tinkled a laugh. "Comes with the territory."

"I didn't want him to give the police a false statement…"

"But he insisted," Nurse McGregor put in. "And it makes him even more of a god. Shouldering this for you will save you no end of aggravation."

"Yeah. And he'd already saved me from far worse. If not for him, I would have been somewhere in the underbelly of Chicago by now, wondering if I'd survive. Instead, it was he who…who…" She had to stop as the tears finally began to flow.

Nurse McGregor frowned. "Hey, easy, girl. This is going to hit you hard when you process what happened and what *could* have happened. So don't fight it. Seek help."

Laylah wiped away her tears. "This isn't about my reaction. It's his wound…"

"Seeing that much blood disturbed you, huh?"

She shook her head. "I was a volunteer paramedic in my country. I've dealt with all kinds of injuries. But to see him hurt because he came to my defense…"

Comprehension dawned in the woman's blue eyes. "So it's because he's your knight in darkest armor that his superficial injury is making you so upset!"

"What superficial injury takes this long to take care of?" Laylah cried.

The woman waved. "Oh, his wound is long taken care of."

Laylah frowned. "So why are doctors rushing in there and not coming out?"

Nurse McGregor grinned. "That has nothing to do with *how* he is and everything to do with *who* he is."

"Huh?"

"You can't tell me you didn't notice the women fighting to take his case?"

She hadn't. With Rashid around, everything else in the world became inconsequential, almost invisible.

Nurse McGregor chuckled. "Well, they did, when normally they wouldn't be caught dead with such 'first-year-intern' injuries. Then Doctor Vergas threw her weight around as E.R. director and snapped him up." Laylah had noticed *that*. "Boy, did he give us a hard time, ordering us to get *him* sutures, saying he had more experience suturing wounds than all of us combined. But Doc Vergas convinced him to let her do it using the one thing she figured would get through to him."

"And that was?"

"You, of course."

"Huh?"

"She said if he didn't let her suture him, she'd have you come in to talk sense into him. He allowed her to sew him up without further resistance."

Oh.

He'd conceded only when threatened with the prospect of seeing *her?*

Was that good, bad or terrible?

Nurse McGregor sighed dramatically. "Even when he caved, he wouldn't take his sweater off, just raised it. But the inches we saw of him were…*whoa.*" A hand frantically fanned her face. "Maybe we wouldn't have survived seeing the whole package, after all."

TMI, Laylah almost blurted out. *TMDI. Too much* distressing *info.* She could do without more stimulation of her fantasies starring Rashid. Coupling concepts like "'all the way'" and "'the whole package'" with him wasn't good for her psychological health.

The woman went on. "Man, it's like he isn't human. First

that body, and then he didn't make a sound as we stitched him up when he'd refused local anesthesia or painkillers afterward. Then there's that *presence,* even when he didn't look at us or say a word."

Layla was intimate with Rashid's influence from lifelong experience. But… "All E.R. personnel *have* come out, including you. So who are those people who keep pouring into the room? What's going on?"

"That's what I meant when I said it's all about who he is. After we were done, he said he'd make a donation to the department. Then he mentioned a number. That's when we E.R personnel stampeded out, to spread the word and investigate him on the internet And we found out exactly *who* we have in there."

That must have been a shock. Rashid was worth a few dozen billions. Men of his caliber had entire hospitals at their beck and call and health insurance that would airlift them anywhere in the world if they sprained their ankle. It was actually odd that he'd consented to go to a regular E.R., even for a "glorified paper cut."

Nurse McGregor flicked her head toward the room. "So those illustrious figures you saw storming in there? They're department heads, each trying to sell him on a project that needs funding."

He was in there talking *business?* Leaving her out here going out of her mind?

With a smile that must be as brittle as her nerves, she said, "Thanks for the recap and everything else, Nurse McGregor."

Then she marched into that till-now off-limits room.

Sure enough, Rashid *was* swarmed.

Not that he appeared concerned. Even surrounded by people like a rock star by groupies, he towered a head over everyone, that vast energy he emitted engulfing the scene. He was wearing only his bloody slate-gray sweater. His coat was hooked carelessly from a finger over his back.

She'd thought that coat had made him more imposing. But stripped of its obscuring folds, the symmetry and strength that infused his every line, the power and perfection that filled and strained against the cashmere, ruined as it was, were…

What had the nurse said? Yeah. *Whoa.*

No wonder *god* had been the only word the woman had found to describe him. He did look the part, presiding over his worshippers with all the contained might and forbearance of one.

He saw her the second she entered. In fact, his gaze had been pinned on the door.

Had he been expecting her to disobey hospital rules? But that wasn't what had kept her out. It had been his unspoken, and this time non-negotiable, demand. So had he been expecting her to disregard his wishes? And had he been watching the door so intently because he'd been worried she would? Or only as his means of escape from those who would devour him whole?

There was no way to read the answer on that heart-wrenchingly gorgeous face he wore like a mask. But she let him read her own thoughts in the gaze that clashed with his.

His response was to raise that eyebrow in a calm, *Still here?*

She folded her arms over her chest, letting him know he could spend the night holed up in here, wheeling and dealing, and she'd stand right here and wait for him to be done.

A glint in his fathomless eyes acknowledged he was aware of her intention.

Then he turned his gaze to the man standing closest to him. "Mr. Hendrix, please send your proposal to my corporation's email with E.R. in the subject line. I'll get back to you within two weeks." Voices rose, trying to get the same offer. He cut them all short. "Give Mr. Hendrix your proposals. I'll do what I can."

Without one further look at anyone, he walked away. She could see they wanted to cling to him, but there was no way anyone could stand in Rashid's way once he'd made up his mind. They parted for him like the Red Sea for Moses.

He didn't slow down as he reached her, only inclined his

head at her as he exited the room, his earlier silent inquiry now a statement. "You didn't leave."

She hurried after him, stumbling on legs that felt mismatched as his scent, even over the overpowering hospital smells, filled her lungs. "You thought I would?"

He spared her a sideways glance from his prodigious height. "You should have."

"Yeah, right." Her gaze flitted to the pristine white bandage peeking below what now looked like viscous ink on his sweater. She felt nauseated that his flesh had been torn, again, this time for her.

"Are you all right?" she asked. Her breathlessness had nothing to do with almost running to match his endless strides.

He gave her a look that pointed out that she was the one having trouble keeping up. "I don't look it?"

You look more than all right. You look divine.

She barely bit back the words. "Looks can be deceiving. Especially yours."

Both eyebrows rose this time. "I wish I'd known I had chameleonlike powers before. That would have come in handy during my black ops days."

So after being a war hero he'd veered into ultimate warrior territory. A natural progression, really. Only the most formidable soldiers made it and survived in that utmost-skill, maximum-peril world.

Had that been what had shaped him into this force of darkness? He'd always been complex, but his current depths must have been forged in experiences she couldn't even imagine. The brutal demands and dangers of a black ops life fit the bill.

She cleared her tightening throat. "I meant your skin. It's so…" *Polished and bronzed and tough, so touchable…so lickable…* She clamped down on the overheating thoughts. "Tanned. Anyone less…opaque would be pale as a ghost from blood loss by now."

His eyes moved dismissively away. "It's clear you've never seen what blood loss looks like."

She quickened her steps to capture his fixed-ahead gaze. "I do now. I was a volunteer paramedic through college in Zohayd."

Had she managed to stun him again? That she could decipher a flicker in his eyes meant that she had. And then some.

Did it surprise him that much that she'd volunteered, and in such an occupation? Was he surprised to discover she wasn't what her mother had tried so hard to make her—a pampered pawn?

"Then you must know all this blood only looks dramatic. I've got liters still circulating about, doing its job, and the loss is merely an incentive for my body to produce a replacement, something I've always found revitalizing."

Her jaw dropped. "You find blood loss *revitalizing?*"

"It does jog my body out of a rut. Before you wonder, I don't have proclivities for inflicting it on myself for kicks, but when it does happen, I look at the bright side."

She and Nurse McGregor had been right. There *was* something more than human about him.

"You're still not convinced, even when your paramedical experience is telling you I'm right."

He was. But… "I—I just can't stop thinking how much worse it could have been…"

"But it wasn't. You can stop guilt-tripping."

He was wrong about *that*. It wasn't guilt. It was this…fear for him, even when she knew that danger had been averted.

He sighed. "What will convince you that I won't keel over? I assure you I don't intend to for roughly the next fifty years."

The out-of-nowhere flashes of his dry-as-tinder sense of humor amazed her.

Her lips quivered. "I'll hold you to that."

Another sideways glance, longer this time, and even more unsettling. But he said nothing more as he navigated out of the hospital and into the freezing night.

She fought the urge to take his hand as they crossed the road. Driving him here and escorting him inside were two things he'd grudgingly consented to. Literally holding his hand was another level of infringement altogether. And she'd rather not be exposed to more eyebrow action.

But she was, in response to her rushing to take the wheel.

He reinforced that eyebrow's censure by remaining outside, his bulk blocking the passenger-side window.

A button wound it down. "Get in already."

He only stood there, uncaring of the icy wind as his coat flowed around him like a magician's cape. "You'd rather drive yourself home instead of giving me directions?"

She thought of saying yes, just so he'd get in from the cold. But even if she didn't suffer from advanced candor, she wouldn't bargain with him with anything less than the full truth.

She looked up at him with her unequivocal intention. "I'm driving *you* home."

Widening his stance, he shoved his hands in his pants' pockets, evidently having no problem with haggling over this all night. "Our deal wasn't open-ended. It ended when you heard with your own ears that my injury was trivial."

"So the injury wasn't as bad as you're used to, and the blood loss turned out to be a kick. But the stitches must be hurting like hell, especially since you went all Rambo and refused anesthesia *and* painkillers. Even if you have an inhuman pain threshold and feel nothing, bottom line is, I'm still driving. *And* I won't just drop you home and leave. I'm coming in with you."

That silenced him. For at least thirty seconds.

Then he leaned down, looked straight into her eyes, the night of his own eyes deep enough to engulf her whole.

Slowly, distinctly, he said, "I've been in three wars, princess. I forget how many other lesser scale, if sometimes even more vicious, armed conflicts. Not to mention all those missions I undertook with one-way tickets because coming back at all, let alone in one piece, was a one in a hundred shot at best. I've seen and done and had done to me some of the absolute worst things imaginable. Two-dozen stitches actually feels nostalgic now that I've left the battlefield behind for the boardroom. I assure you, I can tuck myself into bed."

That image filled her with heat. How many women had fought for that privilege, had had that pleasure…?

She bit her lip at the disconcerting projections. "I'm sure you can also lug the whole world on your back, Sheikh Atlas. But that doesn't mean that you have to, or that you have to do it alone. No matter what, you're not alone tonight. You got those stitches in my defense, so that makes them mine, too, and I have an equal right in deciding how to view them. You think they're negligible or nostalgic, I think they're premium grounds for fussing. You evidently find being fussed over an alien concept, but you'll have to suck it up, since fuss over you I will. So you might as well give in, get in and let me take you home."

Judging by the infinitesimal widening of his eyes, she'd definitely flabbergasted him. She'd bet no one had ever dared talk to him like that.

When he finally spoke, his voice was an octave deeper, if that was possible, "I really don't need—"

"I know you need nothing from anyone." Now that she had him miraculously off-balance, she had to strike the red-hot iron of his indecision and get the obdurate man in from the cold. "It's a given you can take care of yourself at the absolute worst of times, having done so all your life. But you won't tonight. Tonight, I take care of you."

Three

She'd pushed her luck too far.

From the way Rashid was looking at her, as if she were an alien life form, she feared she'd done worse. Instead of persuading him to get into the car, she might have convinced him to walk home on foot.

What the hell. Might as well go all the way.

She leaned farther so she could look up at him. "If you're thinking of calling a cab, I'll follow it. If you decide to walk, I'll cruise along beside you. Or I'll get out and walk with you and you'll have my hypothermia on your hands and your conscience."

He clearly couldn't believe his ears.

She grinned up at him. *Stick around and, according to my family, you'll hear plenty of pretty unbelievable stuff.*

Before she could utter another word he was in the car, and she sat back quickly into her seat, stunned by how fast he had moved.

She blinked at him. How could someone of his height and

bulk flow so effortlessly? It was as if he had a stealth mode and tricked her senses into not registering his movement.

Had they taught him that in black ops training? Or were those powers of undetectability why he'd been sought for the position in the first place?

After closing the window, he presented her with his profile. Not even his horrific scar detracted from its hewn perfection.

Ya Ullah, but he was utter beauty.

Her one complaint was that he'd almost shaved off his hair. She'd once made a profound study of how its lush silkiness framed his masterpiece of a face, how its virile hairline outlined his lion's forehead, how it captured light only to emit it in glimmers of raven gloss. She'd been grateful when he'd kept growing it so there'd been more of it for her to delight in. When she'd been twelve or thirteen, he'd worn it in a ponytail midway down his back. She'd lived for the times when he'd unbound it.

Even when he'd joined the army, he hadn't gotten a military cut. But now he had barely half an inch to adorn his warrior's head. That was an injustice of massive proportions.

Burning to ask why he kept it so ruthlessly cropped, she waited for him to say something. Like where to drive.

His continued silence told her she should figure out what to do with the rest of her one-sided plan. *He'd* contribute nothing more.

She started the ignition, cranked up the heater, turned back to him. "I'll need directions."

Without a word, he set the GPS then resumed his position.

So. The silent treatment. Two could play at this game.

Twenty minutes later, cruising the powerful car down almost-empty streets on the outskirts of the city, she'd long realized that *that* was easier bragged about than achieved.

She'd spent a lifetime yearning to talk to him and failing. Now she wanted to make up for all of those frustrating times. She wanted to deluge him with a thousand questions, yammer on about all the things she'd longed to say to him all her life.

But his silence was like a barrier. It made her awareness of him highly distressing. She felt as if his every breath expanded in her own chest, as if every impulse powering his magnificent body quivered through her nerves.

Then she felt him slide a discreet glance her way.

She tore her gaze from the road to his face. For a fraction of a second she saw something...unguarded.

It was gone before she could latch on to it, but she felt he was wrestling with something. Irritation? Humor? What?

"You understand that was blackmail."

All her hairs, perpetually at half-mast around him, stood on end as the velvet night of his voice poured into her ear.

Her lips wobbled. "I choose to call it persistence. In response to your pointless resistance."

"My resistance wasn't pointless. Just useless."

Her grin widened as she returned her eyes to the road. "That it was. But pray tell, what *was* its point?"

"That you shouldn't be with me. That it's inappropriate."

"Oh, no. You're not pulling our region's traditions on me, of what's 'appropriate' behavior for women, especially the variety stigmatized by spinsterhood."

"You're not a spinster."

Her laugh dripped in sarcasm. "Tell that to my family, especially my dear mother. I've been a spinster in her eyes for over ten years."

"Ten years ago you were a child of seventeen."

He knew her age!

She tried not to grin like a fool at the discovery. "And I was already past my prime then. You know girls in our region are expected to interest men in acquiring them earlier than that."

Instead of debating her, he only said, "Any reason why you don't find this situation inappropriate?"

Was he for real? "Because we're not in Azmahar or Zohayd?"

"Our behavior shouldn't change based on geography. Wherever we are, we remain who we are. You—more than anyone from our region—should always observe said 'traditions.' As you realized tonight, they're not only set to limit your freedom, but to protect you."

"You're *not* saddling me with the responsibility for tonight's attack. Tonight was a fluke…"

"You can't afford flukes. Or to think that guards would 'cramp your style.'"

"Is that why you think I don't have guards? Seems you haven't kept abreast with the latest developments."

"Why don't you update me?"

"Sure. Where did you last leave off the soap opera that is my family life? You know the basics, how the whole mess started. Two brothers marrying two sisters to unite two kingdoms, and instead of being satisfied with their enviable lots of wealth, status and healthy children, becoming each others' worst enemies."

His gaze plunged into his own realizations. "You discovered how things stood between your parents, and your uncle and aunt."

"Only from the time I knew who they were."

That she'd always known seemed to interest him. At least she thought that was what that last heavy-lidded glance signified.

She sighed. "Then it all came to an inevitably explosive end when my mother and aunt plotted against their husbands and got caught, divorced and exiled. That's where the part about my guards comes in. All my life, until her exile, my mother was obsessed with one thing. That she, the lofty Princess Somayah of Azmahar, not end up as a second-rate princess, known only for being sister to Queen Sondoss of Zohayd and married to King Atef's brother. She had me hounded by a platoon to safeguard the asset she hoped would bring her an alliance that would elevate her to her sister's higher royal status, and rid her of dependence on my father's family. My father, who's always been mired in gold-digging mistresses, only sent guards after me to evict hers in his petty feud with her. Once their toxic relationship was thankfully over, they dismissed me from their minds, the one thing they'd rather forget bonded them forever. So, I've been guard-free since I left Zohayd."

His jaw hardened. "Why didn't you ask your uncle Atef or your cousins for replacements? Why don't you hire some yourself?"

"I never ask anyone for anything, let alone round-the-clock protection. And while my software development business is taking off, my liquid assets are tied up in its operating capital. Most important, I really felt I didn't need protection. I came here to start a new life as just another single woman living in the city. I paid attention to my safety. This was the first time I ran into any trouble."

"It only takes once."

She exhaled. "True. But it didn't happen because I was negligent. Someone was determined to hurt me. They would have found a way no matter what I did. And I'm grateful you happened along."

A long moment of silence followed her statement.

At length, he exhaled. "As a princess of Zohayd, you must never be without protection. And you should never be with a strange man, let alone offer to drive him home."

Oh, man. He *was* going all protective and disapproving on her. As if she needed to find him any yummier.

"You *are* strange—" in a uniquely and incredibly exciting way, her grin told him "—but not a stranger."

That majestic head inclined in delicious curtness. "Not a *total* stranger, granted, but still one."

"Oh, come on, Rashid. Next you're going to say I need a *mehrem*." In other words, an adult male of her kin whom she couldn't marry to chaperone her in the presence of males she could. "How about you stop behaving as if we don't know each other?"

"We don't."

A huff of incredulity burst out at his emphatic declaration. "Yeah, right. I've known you all my life."

"You've seen me from afar for a portion of it."

"Yeah, a portion comprising its first seventeen years. And the 'from afar' bit was your doing. It sure wasn't for lack of trying to come closer on my part."

There. Her crass candor was getting into gear. But boy, had she tried to come closer.

She'd tried to be everywhere he was while he'd been in Zohayd, had found every reason to be in Azmahar when he'd been there, striving for a chance to talk to him. Yet no matter her ingenuity, she could count on one hand the quasi-exchanges they'd ever had. The one thing ameliorating her disappointment had been that Rashid was like that with *everyone*. Not that he'd been *that* reserved with others. And not that she'd ever given up.

After he'd joined the army and his appearances had become more sporadic, she'd obsessively done everything she could to be around for the rare visits. But war between Azmahar and Damhoor had erupted mere months after he'd enlisted. Then he'd been reported missing and thought dead….

Ya Ullah, she'd never known such desperation. Or such relief when he'd turned up weeks later, alive and leading his squad back to civilization. She'd almost died of frustration when she hadn't been able to go with Haidar and Jalal to greet him at his return. But she'd gone to the ceremony where he'd received Azmahar's highest medal of valor. She'd still had to ambush him to congratulate him, tell him how thankful she'd been for his safety. But he'd been more aloof than ever before.

He'd drifted farther away from then on until he'd seemed to disappear off the face of the earth. He'd resurfaced almost three years ago, just as the upheaval in Zohayd had erupted, as her closest cousins', Haidar's and Jalal's, enemy, and subsequently the enemy of her whole family.

No one knew what had happened between the former best friends to tear them apart so viciously. She didn't even know if it was the same thing that had alienated Haidar and Jalal themselves. All she'd known was that she had to be resigned that *she* would never see him again. That she'd never had any chance with him, anyway.

Now fate had brought him exploding back into her life, only for her to find he'd become this exhilarating delight of a man who was still making her struggle for every inch closer…

The GPS announced that they'd arrived at their destination.

Bringing the car to a stop, she squinted up through the windshield.

He lived in a…warehouse?

His next words confirmed it. "Now that you've driven me home, I'll have someone tail you to yours."

She took the key out and handed it to him. When he wouldn't take it, she placed it on his lap and took off her seat belt. "Which part of 'I'm taking care of you tonight' didn't you get?"

His gaze bathed her in such calm contemplation it had blood fizzing in her ears. "This comes from being one of the two prized female Aal Shalaans, right?"

"Uh…what does?"

"The expectation that men will do your bidding. You're used to saying 'jump' only for your male kin to ask 'how high?'"

One thing for sure, *she'd* jump if only he said to. She'd stay in the air until he said down, too.

No need to tell him that just yet. For now, she'd let him believe she was an old hand at getting her way. If he believed she was more effective than she really was, it made it more likely she'd sway him, too. Good press was everything, after all.

She smiled. "Invite me in, Rashid."

"That's an ill-advised demand, princess."

"Will you stop with this 'princess' business? You'd better, if you don't want me to 'sheikh' you."

"'Sheikh' away. Boundaries are essential."

She rolled her eyes. "Whatever. Can we take our boundaries inside? I'm dying for a cup of tea. I promise to make you one."

"I don't drink tea."

He didn't, huh? She might just discover he didn't eat food, either, his sustenance being evil souls. And he'd already gorged on four for dinner.

"You must have other beverages in your place."

"Tap water."

Her lips twisted. "You won't put me off, you know."

"I'm stating facts."

"Next you'll say you have nothing to eat but dried dates."

His shrug should have been immortalized on video as the template for nonchalance. "It's not far from the truth."

Water and dates, huh? The sustenance of desert nomads. It actually fit that he, having lived years in survival mode through hardships and deprivation the likes of which she couldn't imagine, would be programmed to exist on the bare necessities. Even now that he was a billionaire, he hadn't gone soft or become dependent upon modern comforts and conveniences. He might drive a car only his kind of money could buy, but he reverted to his adversity-thriving true self in a heartbeat.

We remain who we are, no matter where we are.

And who he was, was the best thing she'd ever known.

She grinned into his brooding eyes. "Water and dates work for me."

"Fine. You can come in." Not much of an invitation, but she'd take it. She was sizzling with eagerness to. At least, she was before he doused it. "Until your escort arrives."

Before she could object, he was out of the car in yet another impossibly effortless move.

Her exit wasn't as graceful, nor was her progress to catch up with him at the door of what looked like a deserted warehouse below an equally empty, old, industrial-looking brick building.

As he pointed a remote at the huge steel door, she nodded at the deserted area. "See this? There's no one around like there always is in our region. No malicious eyes to monitor my visit or wagging tongues to weave it into a scandal. Why are you worried?"

"Why aren't you?"

"Because I can't worry about anything with you around. Because I feel safer with you than I ever did in my life. Why else?"

Another episode of inertness descended on him. She was quickly learning that indicated astonishment. Even shock.

His next words reinforced that belief, his eyes narrowing a fraction. "You believe I pose no danger of any sort?"

"Definitely not to me." The words were out before she realized he might mean a different kind of danger...the sexual kind.

If only. With this avenging archangel, she was safer in that arena than she was in her currently all-female environment. A depressing thought if any ever was.

He pressed the remote and the door opened with the whirr of a perfectly oiled machine, belying its weather-beaten appearance.

Before he turned away, he belatedly commented on her wholehearted assertion. "Interesting."

You can say that again, she thought, watching the receding streetlights paint shadows across his back as he forged deeper into the darkness, a sorcerer becoming one with his lair.

He left the lights off. On purpose, she was sure, to rattle her. Punishing her for behaving so "inappropriately"?

Too bad for him it wouldn't work. Not only did she have no fear of darkness, it was true she'd fear nothing with him by her side. Maybe they did lack some knowledge of one another that closer interaction would have fostered, but she did know the essential him. His essence had touched hers so profoundly that he starred in her very first memory.

Deciding to call him out on his efforts to intimidate her, she said, "Let there be light, Rashid. Only so neither of us breaks a toe against a cabinet or something."

At her mockery, there *was* light. Not a sudden burst, but a dawning of golden, sourceless illumination so gradual her vision didn't have to adjust to take in her surroundings. A vast, 50-foot-ceilinged warehouse-to-loft conversion. There was one word for it: Spartan. She now truly knew what the word meant. It was this: a warrior's dwelling. Sparse, utilitarian, austere. It was also more. A piece of ancient Azmahar, before oil and technology had transformed its distinctive heritage into yet another twenty-first-century Westernized hybrid. Every line and surface, and what little furniture there was, was steeped in Azmahar's history, bearing the stamp of its authenticity in a muted palette of desert-inspired tones.

"Of course." She realized she'd said that out loud when he turned to her. "Now that I've seen this place, I realize nothing else—and nothing less—could have suited you. Or…contained you."

"Contained me?" His gaze swept the place before he leveled that bone-melting stare back on her. "Quite the bottle, isn't it?"

A laugh burst out of her. "You do fit the genie profile. Especially with the way you materialized out of thin air tonight."

Shrugging out of his coat, he moved deeper into the huge space. "I'm sure that satisfies your sense of dramatic license far more than the mundane explanation."

Removing her coat as well and following him farther into the room, she faced him as he stopped before a fireplace and held out her arms for the logs he'd picked up. "I'll do that. You sit down."

"So it's not 'jump' this time, but 'sit,' eh? What next? Roll over? Beg?"

A chuckle bubbled out as she tried to imagine him doing any of that. But the funny actions only turned to licentious images in her head. Oh, the *images*.

Trapping a moan, she grinned. "Maybe. And maybe I'll ask you to jump to that mezzanine. I bet you can jump tall buildings in a single bound. But even superheroes need to put their feet up once in a while. As you're going to do tonight."

Without a shadow of a smile in return, he handed her the logs and left her to start a fire. He sank down on top of a woolen *kelim* woven in Azmahar's national colors and motifs. Leaning on one of two huge complementing cushions, he proceeded to watch her like a black panther would contemplate a contrary gazelle.

His gaze made her more distressed with each breath; its touch unleashing impulses she'd believed would be forever banked with him forever out of her life.

As he would be after tonight.

But tonight was still here. As was she. And she would make the most out of this windfall.

With the fire going, she turned to him. "You're hungry."

"I am?"

"Judging by your size and muscle mass, you must require quite a lot of sustenance frequently. It's been almost four hours since you came to my rescue. So yes, you're hungry now."

It could have been the play of firelight. But she could swear an obsidian flame started flickering in the depths of his eyes.

He inclined his head, casting his face in deeper shadow, depriving her of closer investigation. "So you don't just order your males around, you tell them how they feel, too."

"'My males?'" A laugh overcame her. "*Ya Ullah,* what a concept." His intensity ratcheted up until she had to look away, had to walk to the open-plan kitchen at the far end of the gigantic space. "So…food. Please tell me I'll find something more than water and dates in there."

"I can still call someone to follow you home now rather than later."

"No, thanks." Arriving at the kitchen, she looked around. "You weren't exaggerating, were you? No fridge? So how do you eat? Out? Or do you exist on takeaway? Or have a cook come in regularly?"

"No cook. I get fresh ingredients delivered daily, use them up, rinse and repeat."

That actually sounded like a very healthy way to live. He *was* the picture of vigor and virility, so he was doing it right. Very.

She leaned across the island, luxuriated in watching him coming closer. "So where's today's consignment?"

He stopped before her. "I intended to have dinner out."

"Until me."

"Until you."

The way he said those words… Was there tenderness in his tone, or was it her imagination again?

She cleared her tight throat. "So how am I supposed to feed you? You don't even have dates, do you?"

"I have all kinds of dried fruits." He pointed toward the cupboards behind her.

"I can use those. For dessert. For the main course, I bet you can get anything delivered at any time."

He brooded at her for what felt like an hour.

Her gaze began to waver. He was going to outstare her and...

He suddenly looked heavenward, as if asking the fates just what they'd thrown in his path tonight. Then he inhaled sharply, exhaled as forcefully.

Wow. She'd done it. She'd dragged a full-blown reaction out of him. A *human* one, to boot.

Her internal celebration hiccupped as he recaptured her in the crosshairs of his focus. "Fine. I'll have whatever ingredients you require delivered. What do you want to feed me?"

She barely managed not to jump and pump a fist into the air.

Another minibattle won!

Her smile was so wide she doubted her lips would revert to their former size. "What do *you* want to eat?"

In response, he produced his cell phone, called someone named Ahmad then handed her the phone.

As he walked away he said over his shoulder, "Surprise me. You're superlative at it, after all."

Four

Surprise had long given way to ever-expanding disbelief as Rashid watched Laylah prowling all over his place, "taking care of him." She was now in his kitchen again, preparing him dessert.

This was not going according to plan.

Why was he *letting* her do this to him? He should be the one setting the pace, calling the shots.

Yet, since she'd pounced on him with her scarf and concern in that alley, he'd been letting her steer him. And this alien experience of being taken care of only got more…incapacitating.

No one had ever done anything like this for him, to him. He'd never let anyone near enough to even try. Not even Haidar and Jalal. He'd once rejected all their efforts to impose their brand of caring on him. He'd since lived happily alone.

Zain. So "happily" didn't apply. He had no idea what happiness was. He'd heard people describe it. He'd observed them living it. It was what Haidar and Jalal appeared to be eyeballs-deep in now, with their brides. He'd never experienced anything remotely resembling their conditions and he'd been fiercely thankful for that. They'd been…compromised. Their power was no longer their own; their priorities forever messed up. He'd been unwavering in his belief that he wasn't equipped to succumb to anything like that so-called happiness, that there was nothing to jog his ironclad order and intentions. Happiness, and everything else that people wanted, was for other men. Men with no mission.

Then tonight had happened. *She* had happened.

Laylah Aal Shalaan. This…*shock*.

Instead of the self-centered and self-serving spoiled witch he'd expected her to be, a budding edition of her black-hearted mother and aunt, there was this…being who seemed to exude a pristine nature and an overwhelming generosity of spirit. He'd spent the past hours looking for chinks in her act. He'd found none.

So he was floundering. Not only because she was not following the script he'd had in mind but because *he* wasn't.

He kept doing the opposite of what he'd intended to do. He kept doing everything in his power to sabotage his own plans.

Instead of grabbing this opportunity that had hurled itself at him, he'd found himself shaking it off as if it burned him. He'd done everything to push her away, when he'd been following her for weeks, planning how to get close. She'd had to push him and pull at him until he'd let her come here. When he should have suggested it, or at least not fought against it with all he had.

But he *had* fought her every step of the way, his resistance becoming fiercer the more she'd clung. He'd tried all he could to talk her out of giving him what he'd planned to manipulate her into.

So no, nothing was going as planned. Everything was going *far* better than anything he'd dared hope for.

And that more than disturbed him.

He'd never been in a situation like this. He always had a plan, then followed it to the last meticulous detail. Whenever he seemed to be improvising brilliantly, he was only following one of the contingencies he'd made allowances for.

The only time he hadn't done that to the letter, he'd almost paid with his life. He *had* paid with his mutilation.

Even then, he hadn't veered off his planned course that far. He'd never let anything or anyone sabotage his plans that much.

But she was doing so by setting his plans on hyperdrive. What he'd hope to achieve in weeks had been condensed into hours. He hadn't needed a strategy to get her where he wanted her. He was the one who needed to come to terms with how fast his plan was working when he hadn't even meant to initiate it. He was the one who was wondering what had hit him. The one who had to struggle to catch his breath.

Her enthusiasm might turn out to be as deleterious to his plans as her flat-out rejection could have been. Being so uncharted and unpredictable, it could prove even more catastrophic.

His heart thudded as she flashed him a smile before resuming her work, humming some merry tune.

Maybe he was overthinking it. Maybe he should not question his good luck.

But how could he not? Nothing like this had ever happened to him. He'd never been exposed to anyone like her. Was it any wonder he had no skill set in place to handle it or her?

And *that* was why he was succumbing to her coddling. He kept searching through his head for a method to regain control of the situation. But he found no precedent with which to deal with her.

The paradox was that she was overriding him with the sheer force of her…openness, her guilelessness. Her eagerness. Three qualities he had no experience with.

He should be using her willingness to do anything for him, her unwillingness to leave him, to his advantage.

Yet said advantage was the last thing on his mind. Thinking at all wasn't among his capabilities right now. His faculties were all engaged in surrendering to whatever she wished to do, for him, to him. In dreading the time when she had to leave.

These unknown reactions could be due to blood loss after all. Or the brush with resurrected insanity.

He watched her move toward him, her undulations the essence of femininity, yet not in the least studied, as spontaneous as everything else about her. Her face was open for him to read, the smile that spread those full, flushed lips transmitting something he'd never thought to see. Pure pleasure at being with him. And it wasn't gratitude. It was far more. He couldn't think how this could be.

But why think? Or analyze why she wanted to be here, why *he* wanted her here? Why everything was going so perfectly? It *was* an alien concept, but maybe he should just go along with it.

Maybe this time, having his original plan destroyed wouldn't end in disaster.

"I've discovered one thing you're *not* superlative at!"

At her triumphant declaration, Rashid raised his eyes in utmost deliberateness from the bowl he'd just wiped clean.

Anyone would have quaked under the impact of his gaze.

Laylah did quake. With an excitement that was getting harder to contain. Being with him was like being hooked to a source of inexhaustible energy. Like being infused with a narcotic, an upper. She did feel high. On him. On life, now that he was near.

Her delight had soared as she'd engaged him in repartee until the delivery of her requested items, then as she'd prepared them. When he'd sauntered into the kitchen and started working alongside her, she'd run to fetch a cushion, placed it where she'd have the best view of him and patted it. He'd stood there staring at that cushion, the picture of disbelief.

When he'd finally grumbled that this was worse than black ops conditioning, she'd spluttered in laughter. Hilarity had become fierce sweetness as that indomitable force had sat down where she'd indicated, letting her have this pleasure.

And pleasure it had been, the likes of which she'd never experienced. She'd never enjoyed cooking as she had for him, never enjoyed eating as she had with him. And then there had been the delight of watching him devour everything she'd prepared, and listening to his rumbles of enjoyment as he'd demolished the honey-glazed salmon, sautéed vegetables and avocado-based salad.

He'd just finished the *khoshaaf* she'd made soaking dried fruits in honeyed water and topping them with toasted almonds and spices. He'd scooped the last drops of syrup as if he'd coax the bowl to give up more, showing her how much he wished there was. He'd been vocally appreciative of her effort and not a little stunned at her skill. He'd admitted he'd thought he'd have to suffer ingesting whatever she'd imagined passed for cooking and be done with it. As it was, he could have eaten ten times as much. Not that he'd accepted second helpings. He'd insisted he never ate that much at a time, nor that elaborately.

Every word, no matter how it betrayed his preconceptions of her, had been a caress to her heart.

Now he was waiting for her to qualify her statement that there was something he wasn't perfect at.

"Math," she elaborated. "You counted the 'prized female Aal Shalaans' wrong. I've been one of *three* for a while now."

Those divinely sculpted lips curled on that pout/twist combo that made her inside quiver. Her fingers itched to explore their dips and swells, her lips their...

He interrupted the cascade of imagery. "*Aih,* since discovering that Aliyah, now queen of Judar, is one. I hear she, too, had perfected the art of twisting untwistable men around her little finger."

That, too, made her smile widen. "If you mean King Kamal, the twisting is mutual, I assure you."

His gaze was dismissal itself. "Whatever you say."

She took the bowl from his relaxed hands. "Why count on my word? One look at them would tell you they're both equally smitten."

Leaning back against the wall at the dining area—another floor arrangement with only a *tubbleyah*, a one-foot-high, unfinished-wood, round table, another *keleem* and a couple more megacushions—he crossed now-bare feet at the ankles. "Women of Aliyah's caliber can wreak untold havoc. But she must have her hard life to thank for her ability to rein in her lethal potential. Her family's indulgence was so misguided that it almost destroyed her body and mind. After struggling to overcome the damage they did, she must have learned control, not to mention compassion for others. That makes Kamal one lucky wretch."

His eyes challenged her to find a credible answer to his evaluation.

Instead, she held her hand down to him.

His gaze moved to it but he did not take it.

Not willing to accept a hand up from her? Guess she'd pushed her luck again, this time right into his comfort zone.

Hand prickling with the letdown, she withdrew it—only for it to be snagged in a vise of sheer power: his warm, beautiful, tough hand.

A thousand sensations coursed through her. Tears prickled behind her eyes at the exquisiteness of each.

Earlier, he'd *had* to touch her. This was his first voluntary touch, an answer to her request to let her closer. An acceptance she'd only dreamed of having. Every impulse strained to pull that hand that had been bruised in her defense to her lips, to worship every knuckle and callus.

A gasp escaped from her throat, as without tugging on her, just by tightening his grip, he was on his feet, towering over her. He was so close—his heat and scent flooded her, his aura cloaked her. For a haywire series of heartbeats she thought he'd…

He only stood there, looking down at their joined hands.

Then he raised them along with that delightful eyebrow. "Where do you want me now?"

Anywhere. Everywhere. As long as you're in my life.

Good thing she wasn't *that* candid. Not yet. No need to scare the poor man this early on.

Showing him where she wanted him for now, she led him back to the fireplace. Once he was seated again, she ran to the kitchen and brought him a mug of hot hibiscus tea, which he accepted with a direct gaze that she now knew meant he found no point in resisting anymore and would let her run her coddling routine with no more objections. If he'd had hair for her to ruffle, she would have ventured to do so.

She settled for a teasing smile as she sat beside him. "I've heard of being damned by faint praise, but you damn by the fervent variety. You included me when you mentioned women of a certain 'caliber,' right? And analyzing why Aliyah didn't become a weapon of mass destruction was your roundabout way of telling me that because *I* was spoiled rotten, I remain deadly?"

He raised his mug to her in salutation of her accuracy. "If the roundabout way offends you, my apologies."

Her head pitched back on a laugh. His wit, what he let her see of it, tickled her. What would it be like fully unleashed?

"Apologies will only be accepted if you stop burning calories skirting issues. It's all I'll ever ask of you, to be truthful with me. Always. I will never be anything but that with you."

It was a long moment before he raised his eyes from the steaming depths of his drink. "If you think you can handle it."

"Oh, you have no idea what I can handle." She gave him a quirked eyebrow. "I hope you can take it as well as dish it out?"

"What do you think?" Those black lasers he had for eyes told her exactly what to think. "But I attempted a watered-down approach for my own sake. I hear your species subsists on a steady diet of fawning and flattery, and I wasn't up to saving you again if an injection of the truth sent you into anaphylactic shock."

At her hoot of delight, he continued watching her over the rim of his mug, taking more tranquil sips.

Wiping away tears, she rose to her knees, facing him. "Sir, you misjudge my species. Understandable, since it's undocu-

mented with me as its only member. The fluke female Aal
Shalaan. Of which you know nothing, according to you. I guess
all knowledge *is* on my side. I bet you never noticed I existed
before tonight."

A bolt of black lightning arced from his eyes.

Did that mean he *had* noticed her? When? How hadn't *she*
noticed, when she'd been analyzing his every nuance, scaveng-
ing for any sign of interest or attention?

She let out a choppy exhalation. "So you noticed me? And
still think I was indulged? What on earth did you observe in
my family's treatment of me that could have been mistaken for
indulgence? You thought my mother keeping me practically on
a leash was that? Or my father making any excuse he could
think of to escape giving me five minutes of his time? Or both
using me as a pawn in their maneuvers with everyone else or
a weapon in their own ongoing war?"

He frowned. She hadn't seen him do that when he'd been
about to kill her attackers; then, she had only seen that scarily
empty expression.

But now she felt something emanating from him, far dead-
lier than the rage he'd exuded earlier tonight.

Wow. Was this in response to her account of how her parents had treated her? She hadn't meant to sound bitter, but in
reality, she'd "watered things down." Not that she'd thought to
appeal to his sympathy. Whatever she'd suffered at her parents' self-serving hands had been nothing compared to what
he'd suffered.

Needing to lighten the mood, she infused her voice with
extra lightness. "Or maybe you believed I was indulged because my legions of cousins didn't rough me up like they did
each other? That had nothing to do with my being female, just
being the youngest."

As if consenting to play along, his lips twisted. "I didn't
see those who succeeded you to that position being spared,
since these were disappointingly male. You can't deny the Aal
Shalaans' situation goes against everything our region believes

in. Instead of valuing males above females for offspring, having nothing but sons made the Aal Shalaan males a dime a dozen, and a female a treasure. Your aunt Bahiyah was that for decades. Then came you."

Her hairs stood on end at the way he said those words. It got worse when he leaned closer, and she was hit with another wave of his vigor and virility.

He only placed his empty mug on the floor between them. "It's the one thing that made your family tolerate your Hydra of a mother. That she managed the miracle of giving the Aal Shalaans a female child."

She grimaced. "Hydra, huh? Ouch." Then she laughed. "But, yeah, apt description. Though in anything else, you must be talking about an alternate universe. In this one, I never noticed any tolerance toward my mother. Not that I blame anyone for that. My mother, as you so bluntly noted, *is* intolerable. I also never had any evidence that I was such a big deal to the family for achieving the feat of being born female. In fact, I mostly experienced the opposite. Being the lone estrogen bubble floating in an ocean of testosterone was no fun."

A contemplative look greeted her words. "I expect it must have had its drawbacks."

Her laugh was mirthless this time. "For my first decade I couldn't understand that I wasn't a boy, then I *wouldn't* accept I wasn't, tried my best to be one, so I'd fit in. My mother did her best to flog me, emotionally and sometimes physically, out of my efforts. Then puberty hit and I began to feel some good sides to being a girl." *Like growing a whole new appreciation of his masculine wonder.* "But those did not outweigh the bad. I was such a disappointment to everyone. Not male, so couldn't be shoved into the roles in need of a steady supply of Aal Shalaans, and not the type of female they had in mind. The older I got, the more disgusted with me my mother and aunt became for not inheriting their refined genes, for manifesting the looks and temperament of the Neanderthal-like Aal Shalaans. I was 'tainted' by my Aal Shalaan blood, as my mother put it when she was trying to 'cleanse' me of its disadvantages. And though I cleaned up good when they had their way with me, when left to my own devices, I slipped back into my graceless, disgraceful self. Not that they gave up. They kept hoping that through constant pressure they'd prove the ancient proverb right."

"Which proverb is that?"

"Ekfi'l edrah ala fommaha, tet'la el bent l'ommaha."

"Set the cauldron on its face, after mother the girl takes."

She whooped. "And it almost rhymes, too."

He tutted. "Almost doesn't count. Either it rhymes, or it's lame. That *was* lame."

Another man would have accepted her praise of his translation. He'd accept nothing he hadn't fully earned. The self-made, self-sufficient entity that he was would care nothing about others' approval, anyway.

She waved his dismissal away. "Details. It was good enough. And clever. Not to mention instantaneous."

Not one to continue a subject he'd already dismissed, his gave her what felt like a mind and soul scan. "So your mother and aunt couldn't 'turn' you."

A chuckle overcame her. Yes, he was disparaging her family, but he did it deliciously, not to mention accurately. "Like vampires would, huh? Another spot-on analogy, sorry to admit. And nope. To their escalating frustration, I remained an inferior human with loads of abhorrent failings that made them break out in hives. The worst of it was the traits you had a demonstration of tonight."

Was that teasing that simmered in the blackness of his eyes? Was it even possible?

"Being overriding and unstoppable?"

"*Hah.* They'd have a stroke if they heard anyone describe me as *that*. Their dissatisfaction with me was based on what they said formed the foundation of my character. In their words, a 'total lack of discretion, insight and shrewdness and a genetic absence of poise, presence and influence.'"

Yep, she'd memorized the slurs. They'd been said in too many variations often enough.

His eyes told her he'd made a note of that fact. "It's clear they didn't know you well."

Her lips relaxed, as did her heart. "Do you mind if I take that as a compliment?"

A perfectly formed hand—strength, skill and command wrapped in bronze and adorned by raven silk—waved her a *knock yourself out.* What she'd give to know those hands better.

She sighed. "Then I began to mess up their plans for me and was exposed to the full measure of their ruthlessness. Just when I thought things couldn't get any worse, their conspiracy to depose Uncle Atef and take over Zohayd was exposed. Not only didn't I see any of it coming, when I was the closest anyone ever got to either of them, I never realized they were capable of such…malevolence. Guess they were right about my lack of insight and shrewdness."

"You feel guilty that you didn't realize what they were planning."

As usual, he was right. "I felt almost responsible. It's one of the main reasons I left Zohayd." She gave a self-deprecating shrug. "And here I am."

"Here you are."

The words hung in the warm air like intoxicating incense. They sounded as if he was glad that she was.

Okay, so a man like Rashid—though there were no men like him—didn't do 'glad.' But there'd been an emotion, as powerful as everything else about him, attached to those three words. Whatever it was, it warmed her, contented her.

Silence enveloped the gigantic space, enfolded them. She soaked up its peace and profundity. She couldn't believe she'd shared with him things she hadn't even told her best friends. How he'd listened, become involved, interested, letting her unburden herself, letting her come closer.

If only he'd reciprocate.

For now he was giving her what she'd never hoped to have.

The pleasure of basking in his nearness and communion, the sense of being isolated with him in a world that contained no one but them. She felt sequestered from everything—the past, the future, existing in a sheer state of presence, in *his* presence.

Then poignancy passed from soul to senses, took hold...and wrenched. The need to smooth her hands down his scar, over that glorious head and shoulders and chest became an ache. But it was the expression on his half-turned face that had tenderness sweeping through her. It was as if he'd forgotten to put on his mask, as if he couldn't hold it in place.

"What are you thinking?" she whispered.

The expression was gone. "Nothing."

"I think it's a fourth impossibility that your mind isn't in high gear every single second you're awake. I bet you're thinking even when you're asleep. It feels as if you're perpetually observing, analyzing, concluding and deciding how to use each and every detail of what's going on around you."

Both eyebrows rose. But he only said, "And the first three impossibilities are?"

"You don't know? But it's a very common saying."

"In Zohayd, I assume. Contrary to common belief, Azmahar was never an extension of Zohayd that splintered into oil-fueled if ill-fated autonomy. It wasn't destined to return to the motherland's bosom begging to be annexed back. Not until ex-king Nedal, that is."

"Whoa. That's a huge nerve you got exposed there. But sheathe your claws, Rashid. I, of all people, don't subscribe to any of that. With said king being my uncle, I'm half-Azmaharian through the side of my family who're responsible for Azmahar's decline. I can do nothing about anyone's actions or what they led to, but I've always loved Azmahar and am proud to call it my second home."

His gaze stilled on her face.

Was that welcome news? Or was he only adjusting another misconception in that fathomless mind of his?

He finally exhaled. "You wouldn't be faulted if you didn't.

Azmahar, as it stands today, doesn't have much to it to love or to be proud of. It was mismanaged and misrepresented by its rulers and constrained and condescended to by its allies for decades. Most of its people have either forgotten what it is to be proud to be Azmaharian, or never learned it was possible to be so."

That urge to touch him, hug him, almost overwhelmed her. "But not you. You're Super Azmahar Man who'll rectify all that, now that you're a candidate for the throne."

His expression changed as if a steel door had slammed shut. It made her realize how much he'd opened up. Another off-limits topic?

When he answered, it seemed she'd imagined all the tension. His shrug was easy. "Candidacy means nothing."

"Only winning does, huh?"

Again he didn't pursue the subject she'd introduced. Which she was burning to know more about.

Since her uncle had been forced to abdicate the throne after a long reign of gross "mismanagement," and his heirs had been rejected for succession, Azmahar had called for a new king. But the country was now divided into three fronts, each supporting a different candidate.

The other two candidates were Haidar and Jalal, her paternal *and* maternal cousins. They'd been dubbed the Princes of Two Kingdoms and so many said they were perfect for the throne of Azmahar.

Which was ridiculous. Though she loved them and they were incredible men and businessmen, she couldn't see how anyone would consider them, or anyone else, when Rashid was in the picture. Apart from being beyond compare as a man, in her own humble opinion, he was full-blooded Azmaharian and a war hero many times over, and the wealthiest, most successful businessman in Azmahar's history.

Rashid's deep-velvet voice interrupted her musings. "You still haven't told me what the first three impossibilities are, according to Zohaydan folklore."

"I do know it's not known in Azmahar, but I thought with

you once spending so much time in Zohayd you'd be as versed as any of us in local colloquial nuances."

"That one must have slipped my omni-awareness."

She couldn't stop herself from laughing out loud. He kept surprising her. That combination of corrosive humor and straight-faced delivery was lethal. Like everything about him. It didn't help to discover he was fun as well as hot as hell. As if she wasn't already in enough trouble.

Feeling as if her smile would never fade, she said, *"Al ghul wal anqa'a wal khell'lel waffi."*

The ghoul, the phoenix and the faithful friend.

His lips curled. "I don't know about the first two but the impossibility of that last one is certain."

That was what he believed? About Haidar and Jalal? The three of them had once been inseparable. More. Bonded beyond even brotherhood. What could have happened to shatter their vital connection?

Dared she ask?

No. She'd stepped on too many of his privacy toes for one night. Something of that magnitude had to be reserved for later.

If there was a later.

With dejection setting in, she sighed. "Both our issues are tied to those who should have been our closest friends."

That again seemed to stun him. "Are you suggesting we have something in common?"

Her astonishment equaled his. "I'm not suggesting. I'm stating."

"It seems more than two years of living in Chicago has dimmed your memory of who you are, princess. And of who I am."

Her eyes rolled. "We're back to princessing me, huh? Please don't tell me you're even suggesting that when it comes to status, I'm the one standing on higher ground!"

"I'm not suggesting. I'm stating."

She almost snorted. "Please! You've overcome unimaginable adversity and are now a phenomenal self-made success story, with a kingdom begging you to be its king. And what am I? While I made enough money to set up my business, and it's beginning to take off, it will never be anywhere near as huge as yours. And while my family might have thought they *were* 'prizing' me—what they actually did was hold me back and almost break me down. I've barely recovered from a lifetime of emotional abuse. At least when your guardian and his family abused you, you had the comfort of knowing they weren't your flesh and blood. So no, there's nothing higher about my status."

Again she felt that vast...wrath percolate inside him. It made her shiver, even when she knew it wasn't directed at her.

"You're still a princess," he finally said.

"A minor one."

"The only daughter of the Aal Shalaans is anything but minor. Your parents are siblings of monarchs. You're next in status only to those in line to the crown of both kingdoms. If that doesn't make you a major princess, I don't know what does."

"Take heart. I'm no longer royal on one side, since my mother's family was ousted from Zohayd and Azmahar. And with Uncle Atef relinquishing Zohayd to Amjad, having only a cousin on the throne distances me from it and diminishes said lofty status."

"Whatever the political developments, you're still royal on both sides going back a few dozen generations."

She threw her hands in the air. "*Ya Ullah*...now I know why dates are *my* fourth impossibility. My statistics make me sound so...stuffy. Not to mention scary. Who wants to go out with a woman with all this ancient blue sludge clogging her veins? And all the minefields that come with it?"

"Any man would do anything to...date you, even if it would jeopardize his very life."

Was *that* a compliment? That doozy? Would "any man" include him? Or was he just saying men would overlook the dangers of associating with her for supposedly unimaginable privileges?

Before she could ask what he meant, he was already asking another question. "You don't date?"

"No." *Because you exist, and any man compared to you is predictable, disappointing and...well, non-existent.* Out loud she qualified her response. "I start nothing I know won't work."

"How do you know it won't work out until you try?"

"One try is enough to tell me it won't."

Ugh. She'd made it sound as if her M.O. was a string of one-night stands, ditching guys who didn't wow her the morning after.

Before she could rectify this massive miscommunication, she found him on his feet.

She blinked up at him. "You gotta teach me how you do that."

An empty glance answered her as he produced his phone. After he again ordered his right hand man to come over, he turned to her.

"It's time you went home, princess."

She found herself on her feet, too, her heart almost uprooting itself in dismay. "But I don't want to go yet."

"It's 1:00 a.m. That woman who seems joined to you at the hip must have already reported you missing."

"Mira had to fly to Tennessee—her father was taken to the emergency room. That's why I haven't called her yet, and why I was going home alone tonight. I was also much later than usual because I had to stay behind and finish things for her."

"So her father forced her into one E.R., and you forced me into another."

Her lips quivered on a mixture of humor and rising anxiety. "As if anyone could force you into anything."

"I once believed no one could. After tonight, I stand corrected. Look what's happened to me since I let that lowlife nick me. I've been dragged to the E.R., pushed into the hands of doctors who had anything but work on their minds, blackmailed back into my car, taken home like a minor, informed how I feel, told to sit and where, and fed and pampered like an invalid. Now I can't even go to bed because you want to fuss over me some more."

No longer sure if he was teasing or fed up, she blurted out, "I promise to stop fussing over you, if you let me stay the night."

And she finally did it. She'd shocked him mute.

When she thought he wouldn't speak again, he exhaled. "Coming here was inappropriate. 'Staying the night' needs new adjectives."

Still not sure what to make of his mood, she ventured a smile. "Unacceptable? Outrageous? Shocking as hell?"

"How about 'out of the question'?"

"C'mon, Rashid, this *is* twenty-first century Chicago."

The hardness settling in his eyes told her no argument would work this time. He'd send her away then tell himself he shouldn't see her again. Tonight was all she could have.

She caught his arm, her voice shaking then breaking. "You can't send me home to an empty condo after what happened tonight."

The frown furrowing his forehead along the lines inflicted by his harsh life was one of bafflement this time. "You're that afraid of being alone? You didn't seem worried before."

"Just because I'm not a mess doesn't mean I'm okay." Which was true. "Only being with you has stopped the whole thing from sinking in and ripping at my insides." Which was also true.

His eyes widened that fraction that told her something major was going on inside him. This was the moment she had to seize, when he was teetering on the verge of relenting, before he talked himself out of softening.

She did. "Let me stay with you. Please, Rashid."

Her insides were quivering for his verdict when he suddenly let out a long breath.

Before she could gauge if that was exasperation or capitulation, he turned and walked away.

As she struggled with worry, he threw her a cool glance over his shoulder. "One thing for sure, princess. Your mother and aunt were clueless about you. You could influence the dead."

She hurried after him, needing confirmation. "And since you're very much alive, this means I can stay?"

"At your peril, princess."

Five

Talk about false advertisement.

Despite Rashid's thrilling warning about her spending the night, nothing had happened.

In fact, what she'd feared most had occurred. He'd treated her like an inapproachable charge in his custody.

This gigantic residence turned out to have separate areas, even though none had any doors since the place was made for one person's privacy. One area was in the mezzanine, behind a partitioning wall, which was used as his bedroom suite. This was the space he'd given her for the night.

The huge room was even sparser than the rest of the place, with only a skylight, a built-in wardrobe and a nine-by-nine-foot mattress spread in dark sheets on the floor. But to her delight, the connecting bathroom was decadent. It was good to know that although his living and sleeping quarters were a throwback to his life as a survivalist, where hygiene was involved, Rashid had succumbed to state-of-the-art luxury.

He'd offered her some of his clean clothes to wear. But since he had nothing to replace her stilettos, he'd encouraged her to go barefoot, assuring her he kept the floors spotless. Then, without so much as a good-night, he'd left her.

And here she was, sitting on his "bed," flooded to the knee in his sweatshirt and unable to sleep.

Not because he'd let her stay the night with him, but not really with him at all. But because now that she'd had time to think, she realized the real reason behind her earlier desperation to stay. She'd sensed something was very wrong. With him.

She *had* felt it, heard it and seen it while he'd been ripping her attackers apart. That volcanic rage that had incinerated his reason. Far beyond anything an ordinary man would feel about scum who preyed on a helpless female. Something uncontrollable, consuming. Damaging. Terrible.

The effort she'd felt him exert to bring his violence under control, the volatility she'd felt him struggle with so he could appear stable under her scrutiny, had singed her with its intensity. This hadn't been a new reaction ignited by tonight's events. This was old. And immense. She could not begin to imagine what had spawned it. But she knew whatever it was continued to prey on him. That demon she'd felt possessing him, body and mind, was just beneath the surface.

And even before she'd analyzed all that consciously, she hadn't been able to let that demon consume the man she loved any further, not when it *had* manifested in full force this time on her account.

Oh, yes. Love. There was no use calling what she felt for him anything else.

So what if he was no longer the same man she'd had a crush on all her life? He was now far more than anything she'd ever imagined. Darker, larger-than-life, more complex and intriguing than anyone she'd ever met. Even under normal circumstances, she would have been disturbed at the prospect of allowing herself any emotional involvement with this highly upgraded Rashid. But she saw no reason for caution or trepidation now when she never had before. She wouldn't have to deal with the consequences of emotions that would no doubt remain unrequited. Rashid was driven, self-contained and off-limits. He had no place in his life for a woman or in his heart for love.

But it didn't matter. It brought her peace to accept her emotions, even revel in them. To know the one man she could love existed, and why exactly she loved him, and would never be with another.

It wasn't as pathetic or melodramatic as it sounded. She'd even call it wise, since *that* was learning from others' experiences and mistakes. She'd seen too many marriages that had been made without love and how disastrously they'd ended, or worse, continued. She also had the example of those marriages that had flourished because they'd been based on the kind of love that came once in a lifetime, and thrived against all odds. *That* kind of love she'd feel only for Rashid. It was unwise, even self-destructive, settling for less. But what were the odds he'd reciprocate her emotions? Negligible, really.

He might have let her "influence" him tonight, but only as an extension of his chivalry. Maybe the old times he'd discounted did count for a man afflicted by a gargantuan sense of honor. After all, he'd once gone to unimaginable lengths to pay the debts of a man who'd abused him, to repay that man for the shelter he'd given him when the already motherless Rashid had become a complete orphan.

Suddenly, that familiar chill moved through her.

She now knew the feeling was a Rashid proximity alert. Could he be approaching? If he was, would it be because he…?

She wished. He must be coming to check up on her after she'd misled him about the nature of her turmoil. But what if…

Reality check, moron. He probably just wanted something from the bedroom she occupied.

Breath bated, she expected him to walk in any moment.

He didn't. Had she imagined it?

No. Something had intensified her awareness of him. This might mean… Something was wrong!

Who knew where that scumbag's switchblade had been?

That wound Rashid had dismissed might be starting to fester. He'd probably refused antibiotics like he had analgesics.

She shot to her feet. At the mezzanine's railing, her streak came to a stumbling halt as if she'd slammed into an invisible force field. From the far end of the hangar-sized space, something reverberated in her ears, her bones. It felt and sounded like the erratic, furious pounding of a distant, gigantic heart.

She hadn't heard the sound in the sequestered bedroom area. But it must have been what had sent anxiety skewering through her.

She ran down the stairs, almost slipping on the slick stone. Once her feet touched rougher floor, her dash resumed. The force of the sounds ratcheted up with every step as she approached a wall partition at the far end of the loft. Beyond it, the pounding felt as if it would bruise her insides.

Her own heart thundering in response, she walked around the wall. And she saw the sound's origin. *Rashid.*

Stripped to the waist, barefoot and barehanded, he was kick-boxing a punching bag in a constant barrage of viciousness that had almost destroyed its supposedly indestructible form. Those punches and roundhouse kicks could bring down a wall. A single one would have killed anything living. It made her realize he'd actually held back when he'd dealt with her attackers.

It was as if he was venting surplus anger, tearing the bag apart as he hadn't a chance to do to them. Or was he imagining striking out at those who'd given him his ghastly scar?

Ya Ullah—that *scar.*

Continuing on a path of mutilation from his neck, it widened as it ran down his back. At his waist it snaked around to his front, as if to shackle his body, slithered up over his abdomen to his chest in a passage of livid disfiguration. Where it ended, its very tip, sharp and jagged, seemed to plunge beneath his skin to skewer into his heart.

It certainly felt as if it had plunged into hers. What he must have suffered!

B'Ellahi—how and when had this happened to him? And

more important, what had it done to him? How deeply had that scar sunk into his psyche, into his soul?

It sank talons of anguish into hers.

Yet as she neared, fascination began to replace the anguish that gripped her insides. He was moving so fast, she hadn't been able to make out what that darkness staining his skin around the scar was. She'd at first thought it was charred flesh, making her almost want to retch. But now she realized what it was.

A tattoo. Weaving around the scar as if to ward off its advance, stop it from spreading its damage.

Then she was close enough to fathom its complex configuration, to realize what the shapes enveloping the scar were. An ingenious pattern made of the symbol of the noble house he belonged to, a distant branch of her maternal family, of which he was the last surviving member.

She stood for what felt like hours, mesmerized, watching that powerhouse display of heart-wrenching rage and mind-numbing might. His skin, flawless apart from the scar that marred it and that he'd so boldly outlined, glowed as if real flames fueled his fury. Sweat accentuated the polish and definition of every formidable muscle, spraying crystalline droplets with each swing. His every line and move was sheer poetry of power and perfection.

What kind of training and drive fueled this level of expertise and endurance? He didn't even seem to be breathing hard. Or seem to show that he'd ever slow down or stop.

Suddenly, he did, his arms falling to his sides. Fists clenched, he remained rock-still, feet planted apart, primed for reeruption into full-blown aggression, staring at his handiwork, every muscle bunched on the precarious control that momentarily contained the demon driving him to such excesses.

She'd never seen anything so absolutely magnificent.

Even unaware of her presence, lost to his inner struggle, his aura flooded her. It felt mystical, limitless. A knight with might enough to bear mythical burdens, determination enough to forge legends. She had no doubt she was looking at the only man who could restore Azmahar to its now-distant glory. He might have lived as an orphan and an outcast, but he was born to be a king.

He'd always been king of her heart.

And she couldn't bear witnessing his turmoil. He'd suffered enough. She'd give anything so he wouldn't suffer ever again.

"Rashid."

At her tremulous whisper, he swung around, his face a mask of surprise, his slanting eyes widening, the flames beneath his skin blazing brighter.

"Laylah…"

It was the first time he'd ever said her name. *Just* her name.

Hearing it in that incomparable voice of his, darkness and magic made audible, shot liquid fire from her heart to flood her limbs. Her feet almost tangled around each other as she approached him. The field of agitation enveloping them tightened, choking her as she stopped before him.

Surprise deserted his face, harshness replacing it, hardening its hewn angles. "Don't you know curiosity always backfires, princess? Now you have to live with this sight polluting your mind's eye forever."

Her gaze darted to where his exercise pants hung precariously low on his muscled hips. She forced it back up to his drenched face. "Your all-out revenge on the punching bag?"

Those obsidian flames lashed out from his eyes again. "Are you pretending that this—" he made a sweeping gesture to his tattooed scar "—doesn't horrify you? I thought you had enough courage and candor to spare me the damned political correctness. Everyone struggles to pretend my scar doesn't exist, when it's all anyone can see anymore, and they're torn between cringing, curiosity and the unreasoning worry that it will somehow infect them. But to a perfect woman used to perfection in everything, especially in men, I know it must revolt you, princess."

"Rev—?" That zapped any languidness his nearness provoked. "Now listen here, *Sheikh* Rashid. I've put up with your misconceptions, since I realized you know nothing about me, and I was willing to educate you. But this is where I won't try to convince you. This is where I'll *tell* you." She grabbed his arms, stood on tiptoes, to make up for the disadvantage of being dwarfed by him and his sweatshirt, to inject her posture with authority. "*You* have always defined perfection to me."

His eyes shot wider, as if she'd punched him in the gut.

Shocked? How much more shocked would he be when she touched him where his flesh had been sundered and sealed along that terrible rift?

Her hand trembled as it fulfilled her overwhelming need.

It stopped midway, caught in the iron vise of his hand.

Raising her eyes, she found his face gripped with a ferociousness that would have scared off anyone else.

It only made touching him a necessity. Her heart felt it would stop if she didn't.

Her other hand rose, met with the same fate, made her almost whimper. "Please, Rashid. Let me touch you."

"Why? Even if I believed your wild claim, my alleged perfection is a thing of the past, from before I was almost torn apart and so sloppily put back together. So don't you dare placate or pity me. I don't take kindly to either offense."

This needed taking care of, once and for all.

Hands gripped in his, she forced her lips to quiver into a smile. "Fine. Just remember, I tried to spare you. You now have only yourself to blame when I give you my uncensored opinion."

His hands convulsed around hers before he let them go. Then, face empty of expression, he stepped back.

Her heart twisted. It was as if he needed to hear it from a safe distance. He believed her true opinion would hurt.

She bridged the distance he'd put between them, taking his hands, insisting on keeping him in place. "When you were younger and softer and in one pristine piece, you more than defined perfection for me. You filled my 'mind's eye' with your impossible example and made anyone else fade into nothing."

She clung to his hands harder when he again attempted to jerk them away. "But that scar, what you've been through to have it, only to come out stronger—how you wear it as a tribute to your family and ancestors, making it the very embodiment of your noble house—it makes you indescribable. And infinitely more irresistible."

Judging that the time to reach out again was now, when she had him boggling at the audacity of her confessions, her hands released his, making another attempt to reach his scar.

His hands caught them before she could blink. "You can't really want to touch…this."

"Did *indescribable* and *irresistible* have too many syllables for you to understand? I would find you both even if you were scarred all over. I don't only *want* to touch you, I've been waiting all my *life* to do it."

This time, his stupefaction was almost tangible.

Pouncing on the opening it afforded her, she persisted, "Will you let me touch you? Please?"

A full-scale war seemed to erupt within him.

Then, with his gaze the darkest it had ever been, he let go of her hands.

Her first instinct was to pounce on him. But that starving-woman-at-a-buffet routine would be too much for him at this point.

Instead, she reached out, hands trembling as they made that first contact. With the scar at his heart.

The moment her flesh met his at that mark of old and severe pain and damage, her whole being seized, as if her essence flowed through her fingertips into him. She would give endlessly of it, if it would only erase his suffering, past and present.

On the verge of breaking down, her voice wobbled on the question that seared her. "Does— Does it still hurt?"

"No."

The monosyllable conveyed how much and how long it *had* hurt.

"What does it feel like?"

A shudder coursed through him. Or it might be she who was shaking so hard. She couldn't tell where the tremors originated.

"People stop asking when they know it's not painful anymore." His voice was thicker, impeded. "They don't think any other sensation but pain matters."

Empathy tightened her throat. "I'm not people. I'm me. And anything that you feel matters to me. Matters, period." Unable to hold back anymore, one hand curled around his nape, urging his head down so her lips could follow her fingers in exploring that scar that made her only far more appreciative and protective of his every other inch. This time, there was no mistaking the jolt that passed through him as her lips traveled from the edge of his jaw down to the root of his powerful neck. She held him closer, insistent against his damp, hot skin. "Tell me, Rashid."

Letting her discover every inch of his scar, his voice ragged, he said, "If I'm totally still, I can convince myself it doesn't exist. But at the slightest movement, it feels as if the ruined skin no longer belongs to me. It sometimes feels like a chasm into another reality, a fault line where something malicious seeps into my body, infects me with its poison."

So he *did* feel possessed. She'd do whatever it took to make sure he didn't feel that way ever again.

Slipping around him, her lips followed the scar as it flowed from his neck to his back, as if she *would* kiss it better, suck all the negative energy into herself.

"How do you feel when it's touched?" she whispered.

She felt his tension spike before it resumed buzzing through him like high voltage through a maximum-resistance cable. His voice was a hoarse rasp when he answered. "The few times it was touched, it felt like a jolt of acute discomfort and revulsion. It made me feel…violent."

Her lips stopped over his shoulder blade, along with her heart. "Do— Do you feel like that now?"

"No."

Her heart clanged at his instantaneous negation.

When he didn't qualify it, she resumed her exploration, bolder now. "Then how do you feel when I do this…?"

A finger joined her lips in their sweep through the ridge.

When nothing but his slow, deep breathing answered her—which to the über-fit Rashid constituted panting—she nudged her head against his arm. He raised it, letting her follow an uninterrupted path up his abdomen to where the scar ended over his heart.

At the very tip, she slipped her tongue out to taste it and him. The voltage coursing through him almost electrocuted her.

She raised her gaze, panting. "How does that feel, Rashid?"

His face looked like a force of nature roused. His voice did sound like muted thunder when he answered. "Your every touch, your every breath triggers everything I can feel at once. It's as if every sensation is amplified within the scar's confines only to shoot out to my every nerve ending."

Her hands stilled over the scar's tip as she wet lips so dry she felt they'd crack. "Sounds…distressing."

He followed her tongue's movements, something deliciously scary smoldering in his eyes. "It is. Overwhelmingly so. It's pleasurable to the point of pain. And arousing to beyond madness."

His fingers were suddenly digging into her hair, twisting into her long tresses, tilting her face up to his. Her lips opened on a gasp of shock and pleasure at the spikes that shot from every hair to her toes, pooling in between in her core in a heavy, liquid throb.

She swayed into him, feeling the sensual whirlpool he generated tugging her under. At the touch of her length against his, his steady grip trembled once before firming again.

Holding her eyes, he singed her with intensity. "Is this what you want me to feel, princess? Is this what you want me to do?"

And his lips crashed over hers.

At the impact of his passion, a cry burst from her, laden with surprise, relief, delight and a dozen other emotions. He swallowed it, poured his own groans into her. Her lips opened wider, begging for more of his taste and ferocity.

She needed this kiss, this man she'd been waiting for all her life, more than she needed her next breath.

"Is this what you want?" He tore his lips away from hers to growl against her cheeks, her forehead, her neck, roaming over her with demand, owning her. At her frantic nod, he swept up the sweatshirt he'd loaned her, cupped her buttocks in the warmth of his large, calloused hands. Pressing her against the wall, he opened her thighs, grinding against her core with the massive hardness his pants barely contained. "Is this what you've been after as you pushed me and pulled at me and exposed me to your inexorable temptation? Do you want me to lose every shred of restraint, every spark of sanity and devour you whole?"

He accentuated his last words by thrusting against her in an explicit mimicking of possession. She could only moan her consent, going limp in his arms.

"Be absolutely sure it's what you want, princess. I would have taken nothing, but if you say yes, I'll take it all."

Was he trying to scare her off? For her own good?

She had to convince him her only "good" was to be with him.

She struggled to wrap her legs around his hips, but was quaking so much, her legs slipped off him. She moaned in thankfulness when he scooped them up and held them around him.

Her hands trembled over his head as she transmitted her conviction into his eyes. "I am an all-or-nothing kind of person myself. And make no mistake, Rashid, I want it all with you."

He pressed harder into her, as if testing her claims. "*You* make no mistake, give me one more intimacy and I'll take everything you have. *Everything,* princess."

The misguided man still thought the idea of his ravishing her could scare her away.

She decided to stoke all that ferocity higher. "You mean if at any point I say stop, you won't?"

His eyes blazed in imperious confidence. "You will not want me to stop."

She dragged his head down to hers, opened her lips over his scar, grazed it with her teeth. "Yet here I am still trying to convince you to start—"

She trailed off on a yelp. In another of those magical moves, he swept her up in his arms.

She snuggled against his muscled shoulder, soaking up the momentous feeling. He was striding across his domain, taking her to where she'd thought she'd spend the night alone then leave to never see him again. Could it be that everything she'd ever dreamed of was coming true instead? She would finally be with Rashid?

Her fingers dug into his arm, making him slow down. "I want *you* to be clear on something, Rashid." He smoldered down at her, awaiting her conditions. "You will give me everything, too."

After a protracted, unreadable glance, he gave a brief nod.

He accepted her terms, would abide by them.

Elation fizzed in her blood even as arousal thickened it.

And that was before he said, "Just remember, when I give you everything, it was you who asked for it."

Promises, promises, she almost said.

But teasing Rashid would come later. When he opened up to her more. Hopefully soon. And fully.

For now, she would take one miracle at a time.

Six

The miracle wasn't unfolding as Laylah had anticipated.

It had played to her expectations till Rashid had lowered her onto his bed. Then it had diverged onto a totally unexpected path.

Instead of continuing his seduction, he'd risen to his feet. He now stood brooding down at her.

"Rashid, *arjook*..."

Was that her voice? That thick, covetous rasp?

But who could blame her? The man she'd fantasized about all her life was standing before her, proving her most extravagant fantasies of him modest.

Instead of answering her plea, he was turning away, tossing words over his shoulder. "You won't appreciate me all over you sweaty like this." Before she could cry out that she *loved* him sweaty like that, would want him all over her even slathered in mud, he dragged his blunt fingernails down his face, producing a scratching sound that deluged her in a fresh bout of tremors. "I've also grown some industrial strength sandpaper."

Next second, he disappeared into the bathroom.

* * *

The moment he closed the bathroom door, Rashid bolted into the shower, turned it on cold and plunged beneath its freezing spray.

Gulping down air, he squeezed his eyes shut, leaned his flaming forehead against the cold tiles, willing the icy needles to pummel arousal's hold on his senses.

What was he *doing?*

This had progressed so fast. Too fast. Too far.

Even when he'd been doing everything in his power to sabotage his own plans, it had only accelerated them.

Now she was out there, the woman he'd meant to eventually have in his bed, begging him to take her, now, not later. When he hadn't done a thing to seduce her, had done the opposite, trying to ward her away, giving her every reason to back off.

It would have been an ingenious strategy had he meant it, pulling away so she'd be the one to pursue him, but he'd genuinely tried everything he could to dissuade her.

Now that he'd failed, he couldn't go through with it. For she *wasn't* the woman he'd meant to seduce. *That* woman existed only in his preconceptions. The real Laylah was something he hadn't known existed. A being pure of heart and magnanimous. And she wasn't seeking him in response to a maddening challenge.

She truly wanted him. And had for all her life, she'd said.

He shouldn't have let her touch him.

Her hands and lips on his disfigured flesh had… *Ya Ullah*…

He'd never known there could be sensations like that. They'd bolted from his flesh to his psyche, tearing into him, detonating his barriers, his brakes. Nothing had mattered after that first touch but that she kept on touching him. As she had.

Then she'd told him she wanted it all with him. He had no idea how he'd stopped himself from dragging her to the ground right then and there and driving inside her, assuaging their mutual need.

But he couldn't take what she was so fervently offering. Not after the past hours' experiences and revelations. Not now that he knew she wasn't who he'd thought she was.

He now owed her far better than that.

Yet how could he deny her, after he'd promised her himself?

He would give her one last chance to make sure. If being with him in ultimate intimacy was as necessary to her as it was to him, and not a reaction to tonight's turmoil, he'd have to succumb.

Laylah stared at the bathroom door, worry preying on her.

When the door finally opened, it felt like it had been ten hours instead of just ten minutes. The scent of the musky soap she'd used earlier preceded Rashid. Bonded to his own scent, it smelled different, intoxicating. The flames that hadn't dimmed in his absence roared higher.

What if her absence had doused his? What would she do?

But…what was she *doing,* asking him to do…*this?*

Her fantasies had never taken her so far. They'd been so tentative that the most they'd dared contemplate was a kiss. Now…this.

Did she even have any idea what *this* would be like? What it would lead to? Or wouldn't lead to? Was this how she wanted to have him? Because she'd thrown herself at him until he couldn't resist anymore?

He came to stand over her again. Clean-shaven, head and skin still gleaming with wetness, his beauty twisted a spear of longing through her gut. She leaned limply against the wall, her legs tucked beneath her, hands folded over her heart, as if to stop it from beating its way out of her chest.

He finally murmured, "Your beauty is incomparable." She gaped at him. "But this must have been the first thing you learned about yourself, princess."

She'd learned no such thing. Not that she was about to debate it. If he thought so, even if it turned out he only needed glasses, she wouldn't jar him from his illusion.

"I could see your potential from the time you were six. I

knew your beauty would become so overpowering, men would fight over you and kings would fall at your feet. I was right. The list of the royals who have begged for your hand is as tall as you are."

She cast a deprecating glance down her body. While not short, she was the shortest in her family at five foot six. "Not really tall, with a sum total of seven such 'royals.' And none was after my 'overpowering beauty' but rather my 'overwhelming connections.'"

"If that was true, then the only explanation is that they're not into women. What heterosexual male would not want you?"

"Uh…off the top of my head, I know of eighty-eight such males."

He shook his head. "Your relatives don't count."

But she hadn't counted as a desirable female to any man that she knew of. Whatever her personal assets, they'd always been nullified by her family's. Men had either wanted her, or hadn't wanted her, based on those. Not that she'd ever cared. Not when Rashid was the only man she'd ever wanted.

His gaze, sliding from the feet tucked beneath her to her face, felt like a full-body caress. "It almost…hurts to look at you."

Her smile wavered. "I'm hoping that's a compliment."

"It's the truth." He was suddenly on his knees, facing her on the mattress. "You're an impossibility. I don't believe in perfection, but here you are, against everything I believe. And against anything I *can* believe, you say you want me."

Her heart kicked so hard it brought her up on her knees, too, looking fervently up at him. "I *do* want you. I always have."

The brooding look gripping his face deepened. "You said I defined perfection to you. So now I ask—how? What is it about me that you ever found perfect, let alone now?"

A drop of water streaked down his chest and caught in the groove of his scar, making her tongue ache to lick it off.

She dragged her gaze up to his. "It would be easier to count the things I don't find perfect about you. Like how you were always so distant, as if in a world of your own. But then, that's not an imperfection, just a frustration." Giving in to the need, her fingertips swept a trembling path down his scar. "The thing is, you might not be perfect per se. But you are perfect to me."

A large hand covered hers, pressed it to his six pack of steel. "I had time to reconsider in the shower."

Oh, no! He'd say he'd lost his head under her temptation, reprimand her for being inappropriate again and end this. Then in the morning she'd leave and never find her way back to him again.

But she'd taken this as far as she could. Anything he decided now, she had to abide by.

She waited for his verdict, her teeth starting to chatter.

His eyebrows furrowed as he documented her reaction. "Whatever I said before, you must not think it's too late to change your mind. You're free to reconsider."

The letdown felt like the two-floors'-worth fall from this mezzanine onto the stone ground below.

She gritted her teeth on a sob that almost escaped, forced steadiness in her voice. "If you want to take back everything you said, *you* feel free. You don't have to let me down easy."

His eyes narrowed. "You mean you still feel the same way?"

Her shoulders slumped. "It's not important what I feel."

"It's all-important. But what you feel now could be PTS."

"Post-traumatic stress? From the attack, you mean?"

"It's common to need to reaffirm life through uncharacteristic, uninhibited acts after surviving a life-threatening experience."

"And you're an expert in that, right?" His gaze dropped, his whole face becoming inanimate. Beyond trying to analyze his reaction, she had to resolve this. "Since I detailed my lifelong crush on you, you know this isn't spur of the moment on my part. If you want to give me a way out of looking like a pathetic fool by pretending it was the stress talking, go ahead, be chivalrous to the end."

Without raising his eyes, he murmured, "The last thing I am is chivalrous."

She sagged back on her heels. "Then it's even worse. You succumbed to an 'uncharacteristic and uninhibited act' because *you're* stressed and had a hormonal surge due to a woman throwing herself at you and pawing you all over. Now that the urge has subsided, you want to end this on a not-too-sour note."

His eyes rose then, bored into hers again. "Does it look like my 'hormonal surge' has subsided?" His gaze lowered, dragging hers with it and... *Whoa.* His clean sweatpants showed that...nothing had subsided. Not in the least. "And women have thrown themselves at me and pawed me before, and none has caused even a hormonal blip."

Her heart thundered. "You mean you still want...want..."

Desire surged in his voice and gaze again. "Everything. But I needed to be sure I wouldn't be taking advantage of your vulnerability."

So. Moment of truth. Setting him, and herself, straight. She wanted everything with him, whatever it led to.

She leaned into him, spread her hands over his formidable chest, moaning at feeling his vitality and power quiver beneath her touch. "If another man had saved me tonight, I would have made sure he got medical attention and promised to be there for him if he ever needed my help. But I wouldn't have gone home with him, and I certainly wouldn't be in his bed now. From the E.R. onward, everything I did was because it was you. Everything I feel is for you. All I want is *you.*"

He suddenly severed their contact by standing up.

At her choking disappointment, he said, "To do your unrepeatable offer of everything justice, I've revised my approach of gulping you down whole."

Biting her lip on the yo-yoing agitation and excitement, she whispered, "So what will you do?"

He undid the drawstrings of his pants ever so slowly. "I'll savor you within an inch of your sanity."

She wanted to tell him she was already a few miles beyond sane. That when he let those pants drop, she might suffer a coronary. Then he did.

Finding black silk boxers beneath didn't ward off the mini heart attack. The potency tenting it, those muscled thighs and legs encased in the perfect amount of black silk, and imagining what all that would soon be doing to her, was enough.

Then, muscles rippling, he knelt before her again. He skimmed his lips over her face and neck, inhaling her, groaning his delight at her scent. The conqueror she'd expected him to be had turned into a seducer bound on driving her out of her mind.

Tears stung her eyes as she tried to wind herself around him. "Don't savor me, Rashid. *Arjook,* I can't wait…"

He gently disentangled himself, groaned deep inside her mouth, "Don't rush me, *ya ameerati.* Let me do all this beauty and generosity justice."

It was only that she realized he was in as much torment as she was, that made her concede and suffer his pace.

His hands trembled as he released her from the few clothes she had on, which though loose had become suffocating. She writhed and moaned, caressing his head, drawing him closer, wishing there was hair for her hands to convulse in. At the first touch of those electrifying hands on her breasts, she scraped her fingernails across his scalp. He groaned in equal suffering, but wouldn't hurry.

By the time he had her naked, she knew what erotic torment truly was. It was still worth it, just to see his face as he looked down at her.

She cried out at the savage hunger in his eyes. He closed them instantly, opened them again with it under control. Still afraid for her alleged fragile state of mind?

But he couldn't control the raggedness in his voice. "*Anti akthar menn kamelah*—more than perfect. You're beauty incarnate."

Her head thrashed in protest. "That would be you."

He caught it in gentle hands, pressed a fierce kiss on her lips. "You honor me with your approval, but let me show you how much I hunger for every inch of you…"

And he showed her. He drank her lips dry, then moved to her neck, her arms, her hands. When he drew one of her fingers inside his hot mouth, pleasure forked through her, lodging deep into her core. She hadn't *known* that it could be like this. That he could do this to her, just sucking a finger. Then his lips pulled—hard.

She bucked off the mattress. The throb between her legs squeezed another rush of molten agony. *"Rashid...arjook, daheenah..."*

She was coming apart, needed him now...*now*...

But he had other plans, deeper levels of torment. He exposed her to all forms of sensual stimulation, plumbing every response she hadn't known her body was equipped with, taking every intimacy as he'd warned, creating erogenous zones wherever his hands and lips landed, or his tongue and teeth followed.

He was everywhere. Kneading, kissing, licking. Nibbling, nipping and suckling. Her feet, down her back, all over her stomach and breasts and buttocks, the insides of her arms and thighs. All the time coming up to plunge deeper and deeper kisses into her mouth, along with more aroused, arousing confessions. She lost count how many times she begged for him.

When he finally drew away, she thought he'd at last remove the only remaining barrier between them and join his body with hers. She rose to hurry him, welcome him...

Next second she was flat on her back with her legs over his shoulders. Surprise and consternation warred inside her as a wave of contrary shyness overtook her. She'd been begging to share the ultimate intimacy with him, but had qualms about letting him have a lesser one? Stupid, but no less cripplingly real.

Panting, she tried to sit up. "I want you, Rashid, *you*..."

"You'll have me, all of me. But first I feast on all of you."

He drew her legs wider apart, flattened on his stomach between them, cupping her buttocks, opening her core fully to him. Before one more neuron could fire, he blew a hot breath on the knot where it felt every last nerve in her body converged.

The sound that she made was one of alien hunger. Coherence

seeped out of her, nothing remaining but craving and sensation. The emptiness inside her was spreading, engulfing her...

Her head thrashed, her face tangled in her hair. "You're killing me..."

"I'm worshiping you, *ya ajmal an'naas.*"

Hearing him call her "my princess" before, not just princess was one thing. But "most beautiful of all people"? That he thought such a thing, the way he said it, only made her state more acute. Then he slid a rough, careful finger between the molten lips of her core.

She screamed, bowed up, her whole body quaking. Her breathing stopped, her heartbeat stumbled.

One trembling but insistent hand soothed her down, kneading her breasts, rolling her nipples as his other hand stroked her liquefied flesh in tight circles, just the right speed, just the perfect pressure. She writhed and begged for him more and more. He only quickened his ministrations, and quakes started, radiating from where his fingers played her flesh like a virtuoso. Her hips undulated, moving with his fingers, ripples of delight hurtling with frightening speed toward something far more intense than she'd ever felt or imagined...

He rubbed his now-smooth face against her tender inner thighs, like a lion nuzzling his mate. He sounded like one when he growled, "So hot and fragrant, so ready for me. Now to taste you..."

A shriek tore out of her at his tongue's first plunge into her, drinking her pleasure at the source. Tightening his hold over her bucking buttocks, he swept its firm, slick heat through her trembling flesh to the pinpoint of torment. She imploded, collapsing back on herself.

Then he sucked her flesh into his mouth, unleashing every spark of accumulated sensation.

She ceased to exist, dissipated in wave after wave of white-hot release...

The shudders racking her finally eased, her vision returned

to the sight of his regal head between her thighs, still suckling her, drawing out her aftermath.

Closing her eyes, she melted back into his cossetting, surrendered to his ministrations.

Suddenly, her eyes snapped open. Pleasure wasn't subsiding, it was building, the screaming tension for release back in full force. He went on and on until she was heaving and keening again, in the merciless grip of an even fiercer climax.

Afterward, inside a body that was no longer hers to command and a mind she felt she had no access to, she saw him rise to prowl over her numb body, sweeping her with soothing caresses. Her eyes stung again at his generosity, his restraint. She couldn't believe a man could deny himself so long when he was as agonizingly aroused as Rashid evidently was.

But instead of moving on top of her, he tugged her into the curve of his great body, stroking her quivering flesh gently, murmuring praise and passion in that voice that spoke to her soul.

"Laylah…the taste and sight and sound of your pleasure, everything about you—is beyond perfect, beyond belief…"

What was beyond belief was that he was arousing her again, when she suspected he was trying to lull her to sleep, too. When she'd thought he'd drained her of sensation, maybe forever. Now that her body knew what kind of pleasure he could provide, his merest touch and breath had it clawing its demand for his.

She twisted in his arms, wound herself around him, arms and legs. "You promised me yourself."

Something almost frightening erupted in his eyes. His voice couldn't hide his state, either. "Don't pour more fuel on the fire now, *ya ameerati*."

"I will if it's the only way you're going to stop worshipping me and give me what I need—you, inside me." Catching his face between her hands, she rained kisses all over it before sliding to his scar, suckling and nibbling it in abandon, moaning against his burning flesh, "Come inside me, Rashid, *arjook*. I feel my heart will stop if you don't fill me…now, Rashid, *now!*"

Those roughened hands whose touch drove her out of her mind and ignited every last one of her senses, tightened on her arms as he turned her on her back, loomed over her.

"My condition is reversed. My heart beats thirty beats a minute." Wow. Now *that* was fitness! "At maximum exertion it reaches seventy. Feel it now." He clasped her trembling hand to the pulse point below his scar. The artery leaping beneath her touch was doing so at much higher than seventy beats a minute. "That's what needing to be inside you is doing to me. Holding back is taxing my system more than the toughest survival test."

Her teeth caught at his magnificent cleft chin and nipped. "Serves you right for holding out on me."

His lips twitched as he repaid her nip with a nibble that traveled down to her breast. By the time he was suckling one nipple with his fingers tormenting the other, she had tears of arousal pouring down her cheeks.

She dug discharging fingers into his shoulders. "You misunderstood my condition. It's the same as yours. My heart will stop because it will run out of beats."

Obeying her desperation at last, he rose above her, caressed the thighs that spread in eagerness for him.

Moving between them, he leaned his daunting bulk over her. "I *will* stop your heart. With pleasure."

His sandpaper growl made her swoon, and her hands fumbled with his boxers, needing this last barrier out of the way. His lips tugged in approval of her frenzy, letting her free him. But her hands lost all coordination the moment she released what she'd been begging for. The sheer beauty and size of him was…was…

Her core clenched with intimidation, only to flood in a surplus of readiness.

All she could do now was lie there, open, panting, need tearing at her. "*Arjook,* Rashid, *arjook*…"

And still he didn't plunge inside her. Holding her gaze with an intensity she felt would singe her retinas, he groaned, "Look at me, at us. Look what I'm going to do to you."

His gaze lowered, taking hers with it to where he held his shaft in his hand. Then he leaned, put the head of his erection to her engorged folds. She cried out at the sensation, her back bowing in a steeper arch of surrender, her core opening to him in total offering.

Growling something indiscernible, one of his hands secured her buttocks while the other moved his shaft against her flesh, bathing himself in her desire. At each nudge, sensations shredded through her, tightening the coil of desperation more with every grind.

Soon he had her on the edge of unraveling again, almost but not quite breaching her. She keened, her undulations fevered, her breathing fractured, her frenzy complete.

Then, holding her by her tresses and by his tempestuous gaze, he growled, "Now look—at us, as I take you, as you take me."

The moment she obeyed, he slid inside her.

The power of his thrust forged through her barrier, tore it apart, before his shaft stabbed past into the depths that yielded for him.

A scream welled somewhere deep within her, but it couldn't pummel through the barricade of total shock to her system, to her soul. Everything inside her converged on the part of him that was embedded in her depths like a red-hot lance.

Time stretched before blindness started to part. Harsh breathing, inside her, around her, filling her ears. Her reigniting vision filled with his face. Dark, frozen. His body was bunched over her, still. His eyes ferocious in their focus, unreadable.

But the pain was retreating like a rushing out tide. In its place an unbelievable feeling of fullness was taking over her, an unknown mindlessness rushing in. Her body knew what it wanted. For him to *move*. To fill her over and over and assuage that maddening ache.

But he didn't move. His gaze bored into hers until she almost screamed, this time in frustration. Why wasn't he moving?

"You should have told me."

Her teeth clattered at the way he said it. At the realization that she hadn't told him she was—had been—a virgin. She'd been so far out of her mind that she hadn't considered that fact. Hadn't realized that was why his invasion had felt like it had ripped her apart until he'd brought it to her attention.

What did he feel about it? Concerned? Worried? Angry? Would he have taken her had he known? Would he stop now?

It was next to impossible to think of anything but being overstretched with his potency, invaded, delirious with the carnality, with the completion. She felt she'd die if he withdrew.

Then he was withdrawing, making her claw at him. "Rashid...don't leave...don't stop...*arjook*—give me..."

When he hesitated, her legs clamped around him, pulling him back into her deepest reaches. This time the cry that escaped her was one of exultation, of ecstasy.

She'd thought he'd filled her on that first thrust. He now felt as if he'd never hit bottom, as if he'd forged all the way inside her to her womb, to her heart. She trembled all over, inside and out, as if with the advance tremors of a major quake.

She arched into him, begging for what would unleash the sensations that would disintegrate her if they accumulated more.

His face clenched on what looked like suffering as he raised himself on his arms. "Stop...I'm hurting you..."

She clung harder. "Only at first—now—*ya Ullah ya* Rashid—the pleasure of you inside me—I never knew anything could feel like this—that I could ever feel so much pleasure. But I need more, everything, as you promised me. Give it all to me, Rashid...*arjook*..."

"Anti sehr, j'noon..." His growl, declaring her magic and madness, was that of a man at the end of his tether. It zapped through her with its ferociousness, its desperation, with the hope he would finally give in, give her everything.

And he did. He drove back all the way to the recesses of her essence. Then, holding her gaze, his own as feverish as she knew hers must be, he began to move.

Each glide layered pleasure upon pleasure, burying her

under an avalanche. With each stretching of her slick tissues around his invasion, she fell further apart, her surrender to *his* magic and madness deepening. Needing even more, her demands for it rose until his gentleness caught the fire of urgency, then ferocity, until everything was condensed into one pinpoint of absolute existence where he was plunging deepest inside her. Then it exploded.

She came apart, unraveling on shrieks of his name. She shattered then reformed around his thickness with every discharge, her core straining to drain all the pleasure he was driving into her body. He roared her name, stiffened in her arms, plunged deeper, breaching her completely as jets of his seed filled her. She writhed and wept from the sheer pleasure inundating her, with feeling his release surge against her intimate flesh, his weight and feel as he anchored her in the storm completion itself.

With her body replete to its last cell, lips open on labored breaths and his scar, the world spiraled down into a dark, safe place of contentment—the depths of his embrace....

In a dream state of pervasive bliss, sensations coalesced. She was lying on top of something hot and hard but so perfectly comfortable. And emanating steady, restrained booms.

A roughened caress swept down her back to cup her buttock. No dream had ever felt so bone-meltingly good, so mind-messingly arousing. She opened her eyes, met his.

Rashid. The best thing she'd ever woken up to.

Lying beneath her like a sleek black panther, it was evident he'd been long awake. And watching her.

Delight blossomed at the sight of him, spreading her lips, weighing down her lids, melting everything else. "I'd say good morning, but it would be the understatement of the millennium."

His caresses continued, igniting every inch they smoothed. "A new adjective has to be coined to describe it, yes."

Joy quivered in her heart. He thought the same in the cold light of day. He didn't regret it.

But that look in his eyes…it was new. Nothing she understood…

"I have an adjective for last night, though. Life-changing."

On that, too, they agreed. Though she was surprised he thought so. He wasn't the one who'd been saved by the person he'd loved all his life then ended up begging her to take his virginity, which she did while teaching him what ecstasy was.

But she wasn't about to look that gift miracle in the mouth.

She stretched languorously over his great body, delighting that he was big enough to sleep on, that he seemed to derive as much pleasure from being slept on.

Her voice came out a purr when she said, "And then some."

"*Aih.* Neither of our lives will ever be the same again now that they will be forever entwined."

She raised her head, stared at him. The way he'd said *that*. And that intent look. He couldn't possibly mean…

In the next moment, he ended speculation. "Through marriage."

Seven

"Marriage!"

Laylah's incredulity echoed in the huge room as she scrambled up from Rashid's embrace.

She gaped at him as he, too, rose to a sitting position, totally uncaring of his nakedness, or the fact that he was still gloriously aroused. Or maybe he always woke up in the morning like that...?

Focus, moron. Not the time to be drooling over his assets or reliving what he'd done to her with them when he'd just said...said...

"Marriage!"

The word rang out again before she could hold it back.

But who could blame her? Yesterday, she'd woken up never expecting to see Rashid again. Today she woke up in his bed, and he was already talking...

No! She *wasn't* going to squeak it out again.

His hand reached out to smooth a long tress off her hot, damp cheek. "Of course. I took your innocence and I don't—"

"Don't." His words hit her like a bucket of ice water in the face. Embarrassed at her nakedness all of a sudden, she groped for the covers she'd kicked to the bottom of the mattress a lifetime ago. "Just don't even start on *that*."

Having Rashid in her life at all was a miracle. Having Rashid as her husband was beyond imaginable. But she was damned if she'd let this progress to a bona fide offer based on *that* reason.

"You didn't 'take my innocence', I *gave* it to you. And will you stop being so archaic and so—so…Azmaharian? Innocence, indeed. So now I'm, what, because you've 'taken' it—wicked?"

The eyes that had hardened and cooled with her every word suddenly softened, heated. "Indeed. But then, you were already that as an innocent. Now the mind boggles at what levels of devastation you'll attain in your…newly forged wickedness."

Heat splashed through her as she remembered in detail how *he'd*…forged said wickedness inside her…

Catching her swollen-from-his-passion-and-stinging-for-more lip in her teeth and letting the cover go, she leaned to rub her face against his chest. "Why don't we find out?"

He caught her by the shoulders as her lips strayed over his flesh, held her off, his smile filling with indulgence. "We will. We have a lifetime to make extensive explorations of every iota of your potential for sensual mayhem."

There he went again, talking about lifetimes. Nothing she wanted more than to have several of those entwined with him, but *not* if it was prodded by his outdated sense of honor.

She pulled back, this time wrapping the cover around her. "Listen, Rashid, I already told you in embarrassing detail how I had this hopeless passion for you. It turns out I didn't have a clue what passion was all about, something you've rectified with enough clues to fill this place. If I thought I wanted you before, now I *know,* and just how fiercely and totally. If you want me with anything approaching that ferocity and totality, then there's nothing more that I want than to be with you. Just not 'through marriage.'"

And she realized the real meaning of yet another word. *Ominous*. That had to be what defined that scowl.

"You're refusing to marry me?"

Her heartstrings shook at the darkness in his rumble. "I'm refusing to introduce the concept of 'marriage' at this point."

And if displeasure could take form, it would wear just that face, and lash out with that solar-flare-level glare. "Marriage between us now is not a concept, it's a necessity."

"Oh, please, not the 'innocence' thing again. I wasn't saving it for an eventual groom and you did not come and 'take advantage' of my 'vulnerability' and now you don't have to offer yourself at the altar of honor and propriety!"

"You *were* saving it. If you don't subscribe to our region's values, why else are you—*were* you—still a virgin at this age?"

"*Gah*…at *this* age? *Et tu,* Brute?"

"Laylah!"

His warning growl was the essence of deliciousness. She grinned into his stern eyes. "I do subscribe to some regional values, but certainly not this one. So I'll refer you to my previous confession for the answer to this question and every other you have now or might have in the future."

"What confession?"

"Do you forget it every time I say it? That I wanted *you* all my life, of course. What other confession did I make?"

"I remember a night-long medley of revelations."

She nudged him playfully in the ribs. "Admit it, I'm entertaining." A twitch almost undid his lips' disapproving rigidity. Her grin widened. "As for finding me in mint condition at this advanced age, it's only because I wasn't about to jump in bed with anyone else when all I wanted was you. You could say I was pointlessly saving it for you. So when fate provided both you and a bed, well—you have firsthand experience with how things progressed. Terminally chivalrous, you did your level best to ward me off, to make me back down. But I left you nowhere to run."

"I've beaten back armies, pulverized my way out of sieges

in war zones—on front lines, in boardrooms and in the market. The only reason I didn't 'ward you off' was because I didn't want to. Because I wanted you so much, I didn't even stop when I found out you were—yes, here it comes again—an innocent."

Her heart tap-danced at the momentous confession. That she'd been the one thing Rashid hadn't been able to resist, and his desire for her the one thing he hadn't been able to conquer.

Her grin grew teasing, even as her eyes filled with joy. "Take heart. By the time you found out, I was no longer any such thing. But how can you compare me to armies and adversaries? Their attacks only made you stronger, made beating them that much easier. Against my desire, you didn't have a prayer."

His grimness deepened as he exhaled. "You got that right. I was never exposed to anything like you. I didn't know anything like you existed. You…overpower me."

She fell back on her heels, rocked to her core. That confession was more than huge. It was historic.

But the way he'd said it… "You—you resent that?"

His focus sharpened on her. *"No."* The force of his denial defused her rising anxiety. "But…it's something I have no experience with. I could never abide accepting anything from anyone. Then you come along…" His hand traveled up her arm to her neck then her cheek, cupping it. "The way you want me, what you give me and how much I want it and you—it's so unknown, I have no idea how to handle it."

"You've handled it all flawlessly so far." She threw herself at him, hugged him with all her strength. "But if you feel as shaken to your core as I do, are no longer sure if you're coming or going like I am, that's all the more reason to take it slowly and not jump into something as big as marriage." She raised her face to his. "How about we take it one day at a time? And after a reasonable time—let's say a month, if you can still stand me—you can bring up marriage again?" She pinched his hard cheek. "And if that comes to pass, I'd appreciate an offer, not a decree."

He arched an eyebrow adamantly. "I won't wait a month.

Not even a day, if it means I won't have you in my bed in the interim."

"Bed? What bed?" She chuckled at the lion's rumble that reverberated in his gut and melted back against him, indulgence turning her to goo. "Down boy. I wouldn't dream of staying out of your…mattress. In fact, after last night, you just try to keep me off it. And if it was as incredible for you as it was for me…"

Those scrumptiously serious eyes became solemn. "I might not have been an innocent, but what I experienced with you *was* a first. I meant it when I said last night was life-changing."

Delight gripped her heart so fiercely she feared it might pierce it. "Then it would be downright self-destructive if we didn't indulge in this activity as frequently as humanly possible. But there are many more areas where we need to see if we're *that* compatible."

"Last night proved we are, in all areas that matter. You were right when you said we are not strangers. That has to be why we connected so smoothly and deeply."

She laughed. "Sure. Connecting my tentacles deeply into you sure went smoothly. You've set a new record for Male Struggles Against Female Advances."

"My struggles were a misguided attempt at chivalry, as you so correctly diagnosed." His eyes lost that gravity, grew heated, hungered. "No more struggling, ever again."

"That's better news than anything I ever dared hope for. So can't you let me, let us, savor this?" She smoothed out his gathering frown. "What's the rush?"

She caught a relenting glimmer in his eyes, something she was starting to realize meant he was softening inside. "The rush is that your power, which your mother and aunt clearly knew nothing about, is so overwhelming, you shredded my ironclad control. I took you without protection. You might already be pregnant."

The wish for that to be true was so intense, she couldn't breathe.

When she could draw air again she said, "That's still not a

reason to rush into marriage." Even if it was the struggle of her life not to jump on his offer. "I have to admit *you* were right. We don't know a lot about each other."

"We know enough. All the important things."

Feeling herself on the verge of giving in, she tried again. "Why not take the time to know all the unimportant things, too? I hear those are usually what make people turn each others' lives into hell and end up breaking them apart." She ran a teasing finger down the cleft in his chin. "Maybe in a month's time I'll find you an incredible bore and you'll find me an unbearable pain in the neck, and we'll both be glad we didn't rush into anything."

His arm tugged her closer, pulling her into his rock-hard body. "Wanting like this would counteract any boredom you might feel. And it would relieve any neck pain I might suffer." Before she could argue more, he had her spread and open beneath him. "But though I believe we don't need it, you can have your month. As long as I have you all through it. And it's not one day longer."

Then he took her lips, took her. She welcomed him back into her body, her heart soaring.

She only hoped that by month's end, his insistence on legitimizing their passion would no longer be driven by any hint of honor, commitment and duty. She wanted the passion itself to be the only reason.

Though what she really yearned for was that he would come to love her. As much as she loved him.

One miracle at a time, she reminded herself, as she drowned in his passion and pleasure again.

"Can we have a bed?"

Laylah stretched her arms up in the air, savoring the soreness in her every muscle as she walked back to Rashid. He was awaiting her return on that mattress where he'd been taking her to heavens she hadn't known existed for the past week.

"Not that I don't love that mattress. Literally the best time of my life has been spent on it. I just want some…variation."

He caught her hand, brought her down on his lap, ensconcing her within his great body. "We can have anything at all that you want. If I don't anticipate your wishes, just ask."

Which would be impossible to do. Since their first night together, he'd not only been anticipating her wishes but doing things for her she hadn't even known to wish for. Like taking her on a surprise flight on his private jet to visit Mira in Tennessee. And surprising her with an ingenious analysis report that would see her business jumping to a whole new level.

He seemed to be thinking of her every minute of the day, and what he could do for her. In his own unique way, he was doing something she'd never dreamed he'd do. He was courting her.

As if she needed to love him more. But she did as he wooed and watched over her, as he pleasured and possessed her. With every word and touch and action, he kept dragging her deeper in love with him. Every moment she shared with him, every breath and glance, was every dream she hadn't dared believe would come true.

And he hadn't kept her just to his personal time and domain. He'd shown her his business side, letting her see how a master negotiated deals and waged war, teaching her tricks she couldn't wait to implement in her own business, tutoring her in the methods of maximum efficiency with minimum effort and time. He let her in on his every secret method, thought process and strategy. He was intense about everything, brilliant in every way.

But what surprised her most was how sensitive and caring he was, in his own subtle, practical, effective way. Not only with her, in and out of bed, but with his people. His right-hand man, Ahmad, had told her yesterday that Rashid's army of deputies and underlings worshipped the dirt under his feet, would walk into an inferno for him. She believed it.

It was a validation of how right she'd been about him all her life. He was everything she'd ever admired and respected. He was her hero in every way.

She couldn't imagine how anyone could contemplate anyone else for the throne of Azmahar. In her opinion, no king in history had ever been more qualified.

"I just want a bed," she said, coming up for breath from his last kiss.

Passion blazed in his black eyes, but his voice betrayed some lightness. "I just gave you carte blanche. Do it justice, *ya ameerati,* use it well."

"I did tell you I'm no good at asking for or accepting stuff. I'm no good at *wanting* stuff. I really want nothing else. So… I'll just keep this carte blanche to use well in…other areas."

"In *those* areas, you already have carte rainbow. But in *this* area, I'm ahead of you. I've already ordered everything that will turn this place into the sensual wonderland where I can do your voluptuous magnificence justice, with all the props that will give me every…variation to pleasure and service you into oblivion."

If he was already redecorating his place for her, this had to be serious, and long-term. Oh, sure, he'd already asked her to marry him. But that had been driven by honor as much as passion.

This was all passion.

Overwhelmed with joy, she whispered, "I want one more thing."

"Name it."

She ran hands trembling with longing to and fro over his head, the dense, cropped silk covering it feeling like velvet beneath her aching palms. "Grow your hair back."

His caresses stilled, his expression shuttering closed.

Had she tripped one of his proximity sensors? Did he find it easy to give her material things, let her come as close as could be sexually, but when it came to emotional intimacy, he balked?

Just as she was kicking herself for presuming too much, too

soon, he pulled her closer, flattening her breasts against his chest, his eyes searing into her soul.

Then he said, "Done."

Forgetting her decision to never again make such demands of him, she whooped, jumped in his arms, deluged him in kisses before pulling back, letting her greed take over. "Mid-back? In a ponytail?"

His lips twisted. "How about we take it an inch at a time?"

"That's payback for my 'day at a time,' isn't it?"

He wouldn't admit to it, but she knew. He wasn't thrilled about waiting. But it thrilled her that he wasn't badgering her into an early acceptance. That he was letting them experience this phase of their relationship, enjoy its wonders.

He rose, swinging her up in his arms, making her feel weightless. "Let's explore some of the new props."

"You mean you already have some here?"

"You mean you didn't notice the new additions? I thought they'd stick out in the void downstairs."

"With you meeting me at the door and taking me against it, before hauling me here semiconscious with pleasure? I wouldn't have noticed if said void had been engulfed in a meteor crater."

"Now that might not be a bad idea. A crater I'd fill with perfect temperature water." Somehow holding her with one arm as he descended the stairs, he smoothed his knuckles against her cheek tenderly. "Would you like an indoor swimming pool?"

Afraid she'd pour through his arms, she sighed. "A huge tub with you in it? Well, duh!"

He sat her down on what she realized was a swing.

As her imagination flooded with erotic possibilities for *that* "prop," he gave her lower lip an approving nip. "Duh it is, then."

"So why is Laylah not staying with you?"

Mira's question caused Laylah to look at Rashid intently as he drove all three of them back from an excellent dinner out.

For the past three weeks he'd been sharing something new with her every day. Picnics, hikes, business trips, museums, shows. Intimate rendezvouses at his place and then at secluded hideaways while the pool had been installed. Tonight he'd taken her—and Mira—to an incredible restaurant for another unprecedented experience.

"I mean," Mira went on from the backseat, her voice half an octave higher as always in Rashid's presence. "You return her so late every night it's always after I go to sleep."

Rashid looked at Mira in the mirror with that tranquility that Laylah knew indicated unending patience with her for being *her* best friend. It still amazed her that there wasn't the least bit of male appreciation in his eyes for the fiery and statuesque beauty who turned heads wherever they went.

He inclined his head in gallant apology. "I am sorry if I've been the reason for disturbing your sleep."

"That's not what I meant!" Mira spluttered, as always out of her depth around Rashid.

Laylah could sympathize big-time. Rashid's larger-than-life vibe could mess with anyone's balance. Especially those with XX chromosomes. It had to be loving him that much, and his unlimited indulgence with her, that made her function somewhat normally around him.

Mira elaborated, "Hey, I've been having the time of my life with you guys these past weeks. I love the ride home every day from work in this wonder car, and in the company of my favorite couple in the world. And I can't tell you how much I appreciate all that wish-fulfillment stuff you keep pulling— flying me in private jets, getting round-the-clock medical attention for Dad at home and taking me out with you to places I didn't know existed, not to mention the magic wand you've touched our business with. I'm just wondering, since you've been condensing your working hours to the bare minimum to make more time for each other, why not stay in the same place to have even more time together?"

"According to Laylah," Rashid said, "it's because I'm terminally archaic and can't evolve beyond my Azmaharian programming."

Yeah. She'd told him that. And a few more elaborate frustrations. He would be with her only during "appropriate" hours. But he wouldn't hear of her spending the nights at his place, or her reputation would evidently disintegrate to ashes. The only time she'd spent the night with him had been that first night.

But that paled in comparison to another matter.

Tonight was their one-month anniversary.

At least it had been. Now after midnight, the day had passed.

And Rashid hadn't asked her to marry him again.

She'd remained on pins and needles all day, thinking he'd say something during their late lunch. He hadn't. Then at dinner, he'd invited Mira along and had so far said nothing.

Because Mira was around? Why invite her if she'd cramp his style? What did it all mean?

Had he rethought his offer? Decided it had been rushed and rash? With her being so free with her favors, maybe he thought he'd been wrong to worry about her "honor" when she wasn't worried about it herself. Maybe he thought he should just enjoy what they had.

She'd want that, too, as long as it was long-term. But what if his change of heart meant that whatever he thought they had wouldn't last long? What if he started winding down gradually to an inevitable end? Maybe he'd made that decision early on, and that was why he'd been adamant about her not moving in or even staying the occasional night. Maybe he didn't want to cloak their intimacies in any kind of permanence.

She tried to shake off her doubts, listen to the almost one-sided conversation between Mira and Rashid. She couldn't.

He pulled up to their building and said good-night to Mira, who responded with the self-possession of a starstruck schoolgirl, before she exited the car, murmuring for Laylah to take her time.

She didn't. After a kiss that she initiated and he ended too soon, Rashid said that he had to rush away.

She stood on the sidewalk watching him drive off, feeling a chill that had nothing to do with the weather creeping into her bones. She hadn't thought twice about what it meant any other night when he'd dropped her at her place and driven off. But tonight…

Could it be he didn't realize what tonight was?

No. No way. Rashid forgot nothing. And since he'd said nothing, maybe he just had nothing to say.

It was a long time after he'd disappeared that she'd dejectedly turned and entered the building.

Unable to face Mira again, she waited outside their apartment, struggling with tears, until she heard silence inside.

Once in her room, she rushed into the shower, dissolved the hot tears she could no longer hold back in hotter water, as suspicions overtook her thoughts.

Why had he insisted on Mira's presence tonight of all nights? Had he needed her as a buffer against any possibility of intimacy? Today *had* been the first day without any form of that. Had he considered today, instead of being the beginning of a new phase in their relationship, to be the beginning of the end? Had her prophecy come to pass? A month in her company had been more than enough, and she'd started to grate on him?

But last night he'd made love to her with as much hunger as ever. Was that not enough anymore, and being the chivalrous knight that he was, he was trying to find a painless way out of this mess? What would she do if this was true?

After a night in a hell of uncertainty, morning brought with it the searing light of realization. Why Rashid was pulling away.

It had to be because she'd told him she loved him.

At first, it had been in the throes of passion, then gradually afterward she'd said it at every opportunity. She hadn't worried when he hadn't said it back. She'd thought it had been too soon for him, but she had been certain it was coming.

What if, instead of being truthful with him about her emotions, as she'd thought she should be, she'd only pressured him? And his response to her fervor, when he believed he couldn't reciprocate it, was to pull away?

Unable to hold back anymore, anxiety and urgency eating

through her restraint, she snatched her phone up, dialed his number.

He picked up on the second ring. She recognized the background sounds. He was in his car.

"Laylah—"

She cut him off before he could say anything more. "I didn't…didn't mean anything when I said I loved you. Please, just forget I said it."

Eight

A cacophony of sounds was all Rashid heard after Laylah told him to forget she'd told him she loved him.

It wasn't until a policeman knocked on his window that Rashid realized the noise was a storm of honking.

He'd braked in the middle of the street.

He didn't remember ending the call with her, or what exactly he said to the policeman. He only knew he found himself parked in front of the entrance of her building, staring up at her window, one thing pummeling through him.

She'd come to her senses.

He'd been dreading she would. Almost waiting for her to.

He shouldn't have waited. He should have pushed for marriage sooner. But he'd been terrified he'd scare her away, yet it had been hell trying to pull back. But it had also been a heaven he hadn't known existed, being with her. Being loved by her.

For she *had* loved him. Her love had been so pure and intense, had permeated him from her every touch and word and action, he'd basked in its unbelievable blessing with every breath. He hadn't known how or why she'd loved him, but she *had*.

He'd been trying to tell himself that, with Laylah being so overt about her emotions, when she agreed to marry him, no one would suspect that their marriage was not for the right reasons. That it would serve his purpose, get him everything he'd planned.

But with every hour in her company, every other consideration had ceased to exist. Nothing mattered anymore but her. Everything from her, with her, had overwhelmed him, undone him. With her he'd finally understood what happiness was.

But he'd left it too late. Even when he'd done everything in his power to stop her from realizing the truth about him, time had exposed him to her for what he was. A damaged, dangerous monster.

What had he expected? He shouldn't have been in her heart in the first place. He didn't deserve to be there.

Without knowing how, he found himself on her apartment doorstep just as she opened her door.

A huge gasp escaped her at the sight of him, the streams of tears already pouring down her face thickening.

Feeling sorry for him? Regretting that she had to let him down?

He couldn't bear for her to feel bad. Never on his account. He'd sacrifice anything for her to never shed another tear.

Before he could say anything, she dragged him inside, her eyes all over him before she hugged him with all her strength, smothering her face in his chest.

"Rashid, *ya Ullah,* Rashid…you're okay, you're okay…"

Struck to his core at feeling her against him again, he stood, unable to move in her embrace, everything inside him demolished.

"I went insane when I heard that commotion and the line went dead and I couldn't call you back. I thought you had an accident…"

Her voice broke on a sob that fractured his muteness, made him choke, "I'm sorry I scared you."

"What matters is that you're okay." Suddenly, she undid her frantic hold on him, embarrassment in her every line as she moved away. "I—I meant what I said, Rashid."

That she wanted him to forget that she'd said she loved him.

He owed her the complete truth, if only in this. "How can I ever forget the one real honor and profound joy I ever had? The memory that you once loved me will fuel the rest of my life, and at its end, will be my one worthwhile achievement."

Confusion then stupefaction gripped her loveliness.

Then she blurted out, "What do you mean 'once'? You think I...? Oh, no, Rashid, I only meant I wasn't pushing you to reciprocate when I said I love you. I had no other purpose behind it but telling you how I feel. I thought you felt pressured by my confessions because the month I asked for is up and you didn't—didn't..."

It was his turn to be flabbergasted.

"You thought..." He stopped, hope too joyous, too brutal. "You thought your declarations of love made me *reconsider my proposal?*"

Delightful peach invaded her honeyed cheeks. "I didn't know what to think, so I thought the worst. Y-you must know what yesterday was."

"It was the one-month anniversary of the attack. But this morning, this *hour,* is the one-month anniversary of my proposal."

Her eyes rounded on still-fragile hope. "Y-you mean...?"

"I mean I was coming at the exact time I proposed last month, this time to ask...to *beg* that you consider marriage. Not because I want you and because my honor dictates it. But because my life would mean nothing anymore without you."

Suddenly, his arms were full of hurtling, clinging love and eagerness made flesh and blood. And he wrapped himself around her, containing her, vowing to never let her go again.

Those minutes when he'd thought he'd lost her had hurt far more than the injury that had left him scarred, had been more desperate than any time he'd thought he'd die.

Deluging him in kisses, Laylah buried her fingers in the hair he was growing back for her, her voice a throb of silk and night and hunger. "My life would mean nothing without you, too. It never did. I love you with everything I am, Rashid…"

Reeling with disbelief that this perfect being continued to love him, he carried her where he could seal the magic of those moments with that of their passion and turn the once-impossible fantasy into reality.

What felt like a lifetime later, but what was actually only a couple of hours, still overcome with Rashid's last possession and the echoes of the aborted scare, Laylah stretched luxuriously against his hot, hard body.

His beloved face was flushed a marvelous copper tone. His whisper, when it came, spread its dark compulsion inside her. "Do I take it all that was a yes?"

She snuggled into his body more securely. "You mean you didn't hear any of the hundreds of yeses I said? I must have raised Chicago's noise pollution levels to an all-time high."

"Just give me one now that your blood has cooled."

She rubbed her thigh against his. "You mean you don't know yet that you and cool blood are mutually exclusive?"

His arms gathered her into his body with such tender reverence, trembling with the same emotion that blazed in his eyes. "Laylah…give it to me. One yes. Total and final."

And she gave it to him. Her irrevocable pledge. "Yes, Rashid. As total as my whole being and final to my life's end."

His groan was one of relief and elation as he took her lips, sealing their lifelong pact.

As she surrendered her all to him yet again, it felt different this time. She'd always been his, but this time, in her very essence, she became his wife.

* * *

Before Mira returned from work, Rashid took Laylah back to his place. It was evening when he took a break from branding her with his most tender lovemaking ever, carried her to the shower, then to the kitchen, where they now delighted in cooking together.

He was handing her the pesto he'd prepared to add to the pasta she had made when she said, "Do you have a preference for how exactly we should get married? Me, I'd like a tiny ceremony."

His hand froze midway with the pesto. Then he placed it on the island, pulled her to him. "We can't start thinking of the ceremony yet. Accepting me is only half the battle won."

She squinted up at him, perplexed. "What do you mean *half?*"

"Now I need to go win the other half. Your family."

"What do *they* have to do with anything between us? The most involvement they'll have is to get stuffed in their fineries and come to our wedding. Those I'll *let* attend. *If* they behave." His hands cupped her face. For the first time ever, she removed them. "You're not talking me out of this, Rashid. My family stays out of our lives, and that's final."

His eyes grew watchful, as if he was gauging how to handle her sudden volatility. "If it were up to me, I would have vowed myself to you in absolute seclusion. But you are a princess..."

"Oh, no. You're *not* princessing me again!"

He coaxed her into his arms again, caressing resistance out of her a nerve at a time. "I know you want it not to matter, but it does. Tradition is important, even when it's infuriating. But this won't only be about us. It will be about our children." The concept of children, his and hers, liquefied something inside her. "I want there to be peace and acceptance surrounding our union from the start, for you, for them. What makes things a bit more complicated is that I'm not a prince..."

"You're worth a thousand of every prince who ever lived!"

Pride and pleasure glittered in his eyes, softened his lips. "Your approval and allegiance mean *everything*. To me. But I need to get theirs, too. Your family includes some very powerful individuals, and I'm not on their right side to start with. I don't want them to bother you with their disapproval or attempts to come between us. I need to…defuse their danger."

"And how are you supposed to do that?"

"As per tradition, your family tribunal will make demands of me and put me through trials, as outrageous as they can make them. They'll agree to give me your hand in marriage only once I pass all their tests and meet all their requirements."

"Shades of Antarah ibn Shaddad when Ablah's father asked for a thousand red camels to stymie him! I'm all for defusing their danger, but I draw the line at hurtling back in time to the eleventh century to do it."

"That's what tradition is—age-old practices."

"I have nothing against those when they're about innocuous stuff like food or design or celebrations. But I'm damned if I bow to traditions that delete centuries of progress and make me some prize to be won for the right price. I might as well throw away my master's degrees in business management and information technology. How would I be different from any tent-bound maiden bartered to whomever haggled with her elders for her, before carrying her away as one of his possessions, a bit above his goat, but certainly beneath his horse and sword?"

"In my case, it would be private jets and multinational corporations." She rewarded his teasing with a rib nudge. His eyes softened as he gathered her more securely against his hard body. "We'll just play along to save headaches."

"You really intend to submit to such a…*ridiculous* practice?"

"I will, *ya habibati*. Like I will worship you with my body and serve and protect you with my wealth and strength, I will submit to anything to honor you before your family and the world. I want there to be no doubt to what lengths I would go to, to have the privilege of your choice, the power of your love."

And what could she say to *that*?

Resistance almost gone, she tried one last thing. "But according to this moronic tradition, if ten percent of *awleya'a el amr*—the elders—refuse you, you won't be able to marry me."

Something inexorable came into his eyes. "I will have zero percent refusals. Failure is not an option."

Nine

For years, Rashid had considered returning to Zohayd an impossibility. Now he wasn't just back in the country, he was in a limo heading to Zohayd's royal palace, a place he'd sworn never to tread again.

But then he was sitting right next to another impossibility. Laylah. Who loved him. Who wanted him. Who believed in him.

Having her by his side made returning to Zohayd…bearable.

This was the land where he'd spent too many years watching Laylah from afar, unable to return her glances or reciprocate her interest. Where he'd found and lost those he'd thought of as brothers given to him by fate in exchange for taking everyone else away from him. Where he'd suffered the betrayal that had left him mutilated.

Then, claiming the kingship of Azmahar had become his life's goal, and he'd known he'd be forced to return to Zohayd one day. But even when he'd started his plan, he hadn't imagined this would be how he'd return. With Laylah as his world, not his pawn.

The supple hand entwined with his tugged him out of the darkness of his memories and worries to the sunniness of her smile and reality. "So who's waiting for us at the palace?"

"I informed King Atef. I assume he'll tell everyone else."

Her grin widened. "Word of advice. Don't use the word *king* around Uncle Atef. He hurled the title at Amjad and seems to want to forget the decades when he was one."

"He's been King Atef to me since I can remember. It'll be very difficult to think of him as plain Sheikh Atef now. And of Amjad as king."

"I know what you mean. Amjad is such a virtuoso in infuriating everyone and pulverizing rules and protocols, I thought he'd bring Zohayd down in a week when he became king. But though he's taken being outrageous to a new realm, he's now head-to-head with Aliyah's Kamal for the position of best king in the region's history." She snuggled deeper into him, her smile catching the fire of adoration that he now felt he needed to sustain his vital functions. "Of course, the region hasn't seen *you* as king yet."

His heart trembled at how he'd come to depend on her esteem and belief. At how he felt he didn't deserve them. "You always talk as if becoming a king is a sure thing for me."

"I can't see how it isn't. You're the absolute best man for the role, ever. Apart from my opinion, you're a pureblooded Azmaharian, a decorated war hero and your success in business has surpassed even Haidar's and Jalal's. *And* you're an Aal Munsoori."

"Azmaharians hate that name now."

Her expression became adorably serious. "They hate only one branch of the family, but still think of the Aal Munsooris at large as their rightful monarchs." Her smile dawned again as her eyes devoured him. "And if anyone ever looked the part, it's you." Her hands strayed all over his shoulders and chest… and lower. "They must have coined the adjective *regal* for you."

He caught her hands, his gaze shooting to the partition between the limo's compartments. Even though he knew Ahmad couldn't see or hear them, he didn't want to start something he might not be able to stop. And he'd made a decision that, while in their region, he wouldn't do anything to compromise her image.

It was still almost beyond his ability to deprive them both of the needed pleasure. He was almost panting when he said, "You're clearly not in the least biased."

She lay back against him, her hands captured in his, her eyes gobbling him up. "I am the essence of impartiality. If Azmaharians know what's best for them, they'll choose you."

"If they do, how do you feel about becoming their queen?"

Her blink was surprise itself.

Would *she* ever stop surprising him? "You didn't think of it?"

She sat up, her smooth forehead furrowing. "Uh...thinking wasn't among my priorities this past month. But then I not only didn't connect the dots between you becoming king and me becoming queen, I never contemplated being one, when it was all my mother thought of making me, too."

His heart contracted at what *he* hadn't contemplated. "It would be an unwelcome burden? A life you wouldn't want for yourself or our children?"

The eyes that always shone with appreciation and humor grew somber. "It *would* be a huge responsibility and a radical change. It would take as drastic an adjustment." Before he could blurt out that he would never disrupt her peace, that he would forget his kingship ambitions, her eyes glowed with conviction. "But I'll share your choices and your life's developments no matter what they are. If it's your destiny to become king, then it's my destiny to become your queen."

And he forgot his abstinence resolution. His arms convulsed around her, his lips mashing to her forehead, to her cheeks, her lips, his heart overflowing. *"Habibati..."*

A rap on the limo's window jerked him out of his surrender to poignancy. It had Laylah starting out of his embrace, too.

They both turned to find Amjad Aal Shalaan, Laylah's oldest cousin and the infernal king of Zohayd, smirking down at them through the window.

Rashid hadn't realized they'd been nearing the palace let alone that they were already there.

Shielding her from Amjad's eyes, giving her time to rearrange anything he'd mussed, he opened the door and glared up at the man whose alliance he was supposed to court.

Even before Amjad's transformation into a manipulative, borderline insane son of a bitch after his first wife had nearly poisoned him to death, he'd always rubbed Rashid the wrong way. There'd always been something about Amjad that reminded him too much of himself.

Against all expectations, Amjad had married again. Maram Aal Waaked, the daughter of the ruling prince of a neighboring emirate, Ossaylan. Amjad had tried to use Maram to force her father to return the Pride of Zohayd jewels, which, according to Zohaydan law and legend, conferred the right to rule the kingdom. It had turned out Maram's hapless father had been blackmailed by the ex-queen of Zohayd, Sondoss, Laylah's aunt, into helping her steal the jewels. Reportedly, Amjad had fallen flat on his face in love with Maram. Now after he'd been dubbed the Mad Prince, he'd become the Crazy King—crazy in love with his new wife.

That Rashid had to see to believe.

All he saw now was Amjad's provocation as he met those startlingly emerald eyes on the same level. Not that he needed more than Amjad's rude interruption of his tender moment with Laylah to guarantee his hackles wouldn't subside for the foreseeable future.

"King Amjad," he gritted between clenched teeth in lieu of a punch in the nose.

"Sheikh Rashid." Devilry danced in Amjad's eyes as he inclined his head. "Rumor has it you're here on a bid to cure my cousin's chronic spinsterhood."

Before he could respond to that insolence, Laylah squeezed his arm, no doubt to stop him from putting his fist through her cousin's and king's smirking face. He'd been insane if he thought he could ally himself with this incorrigible creature.

"It's so good to see being a harassed king and a henpecked husband hasn't defanged you, Amjad," Laylah said merrily.

Amjad continued talking about her as if she wasn't there. "But then she's been trying to catch your eye since she could toddle. Oh, yes, we all noticed. And cringed. It was excruciating watching her pant after you. Made me hyperventilate. So how did she suddenly succeed in curing *your* blindness to her splendor?"

The wily wolf was skeptical. Rashid had known he would be. Amjad had suspicion for blood. It was why he'd originally hatched this whole plan. To pass Amjad's maximum-distrust inspection.

Amjad continued, "It *was* weird, how determined you were in not noticing her. It got so fishy, I asked Haidar and Jalal if they knew which team you played for."

Against his better judgment, Rashid said, "There were years when speculation about *your* team loyalties ran rampant, too."

Amjad's grin grew more goading, delighted that he'd gotten a rise from him. "*I* didn't have a smitten angel hero-worshipping me for years."

"I hear Queen Maram did just that before you rethought your…predilections."

Amjad's eyes blazed greener. The bastard loved this. "Those were only put on hold after my monster bride slathered me in arsenic. That's a good enough reason to swear off women for a few years, don't you think? What was your excuse?"

It was no use. This would develop into a full-scale war.

So be it. And to hell with his alliance. "While you were getting over your self-pitying and preserving neurosis, I was serving my country and putting my life on the line for the region's safety. I didn't think it fair to involve a woman in a life that could end prematurely."

Laylah's convulsive dig into his arm transmitted how horrifying she found the what-if scenario.

He squeezed her hand, warding off the imaginary dread, re-assuring her that he was here, would always be here, with her.

Amjad, not missing a thing, continued his inflammatory interrogation. "But that heroic existence came to an end a few years ago. What reminded you of my worshipping cousin all of a sudden? And made you not only look her way this time, but decide to take her off the shelf, and in record time, too?"

He decided to tell both of them the truth about this at least. "The reason I never looked at you—" he turned his eyes to Laylah, whose eyes filled with tears and wonder as she heard his confession for the first time "—wasn't because I didn't notice you, or wasn't interested. I was, painfully so. But I wasn't worthy of looking in your direction then."

Amjad let out a deriding guffaw. "And you think you are now?"

Laylah stepped between them. "Are you two gigantic boys done chest-thumping, or do you need to release some more testosterone? Why don't you just beat each other black and blue and get this 'who's the bigger, badder alpha' thing out of your systems?"

Rashid watched as Amjad looked down with extreme amusement at Laylah, who cared not a bit that he was one of the most powerful men in the world, smacking him in chastisement, as if he was only her exasperating—and younger—relative and not her king.

Jealousy radiated up Rashid's spine. Cousin or not, he wanted her to smack no other male, wanted no other male to revel in being smacked by her.

Amjad gave her a mock bow. "For knock-down, drag-out fights, and any other physically expressed stupidity, I'll refer you to Harres. Or Jalal. Me, my wit is my lash, my tongue my sword."

Fighting the need to shove him away from Laylah, Rashid said, "You imagine you wield such weapons, when it's your status that stops people from showing you their real worth in a fair fight."

Amjad pretended shock. "You mean you're holding back in respect for my status?" He wiggled his eyebrows at him. "I hereby decree you're free to do your best. Or is it only your worst?"

Again Laylah came between them, this time one palm flat on each of their chests, keeping them apart. "Down boys. In your corners."

Amjad sighed. "Okay. Just because Rashid is an endangered species and we need him alive and able to breed. I don't think we'd find you another mate if he expires."

Laylah dug her elbow in Amjad's gut, her smile so radiant as she looked up, asking Rashid to share the joke. He only wanted to poke Amjad's green eyes out.

Turning to Amjad, she asked, "Is my father here?"

"You expected him to be?" Amjad scoffed. "That deadbeat? And I thought you were above such sentimental tripe. If you haven't yet, it's time to face it already, Laylah. In *that* generation only one apple didn't turn out rotten. *My* father is all we got in the way of a parent around this place."

An incensed step brought Rashid slamming into Amjad chest-first. "Even if she knows the truth about her father, it doesn't mean it doesn't still hurt her. You don't have to be cruel."

"Oh, I assure you, I have to." Amjad's eyes suddenly smoldered with something besides mockery. Fury. "It's called tough love, and she's better off considering *both* her parents as dead as my mother or your parents. Just remembering my uncle makes me want to kick his useless ass, or anyone's who mentions him."

Before he could punch Amjad's lights out, Laylah growled, "I swear, one more word out of either of you, and I'm putting each of you in a corner at the ends of this palace. *Ya Ullah*— now I remember why I left. I was drowning in male posturing and hormones. Are there any buffering women around here?"

"All the women who've invaded the Aal Shalaan male maze will be here tomorrow," Amjad said. "For today you can seek the feminine amelioration of my Maram, of course, and Johara."

She whooped. "I can't wait to meet the phenomenon who's put a collar around your neck. And see Johara again. And the children. You know, some sensible, age-appropriate-behaving individuals."

Amjad pulled another of those inciting expressions in his arsenal and shooed her away. "Skip along, then. Rashid and I have more juvenile silliness scheduled before we're through. I have to drive him to within an inch of his sanity before I even look into his application to acquire our last remaining—if long-stored and fraying around the edges—Aal Shalaan treasure."

Laylah grinned up at Rashid. "Guess you were right about my code name here." She turned her best demolishing glance on Amjad. "Not that anyone can accuse you of knowing how to hang on to your treasures, as evidenced by what happened to the Pride of Zohayd, your foremost one. So hang on to *your* sanity, Amjad. Rashid is a world-renowned authority in sanity extraction, among other...extractable things. I leave you to his not-so-tender mercies, *taal omrak.*"

Amjad let out a spectacular snort at her tagging the king's hail of "may you live long" to her irreverence. Then she stood on tiptoe and pressed a clinging kiss to Rashid's lips.

Before he forgot Amjad and the watchful eyes of the palace dwellers and crushed her to him, she drew away with a smile that lit his existence before almost dancing away.

Feeling bereft already without her, his gaze clung to her as she receded. And he registered where they were for the first time.

The royal palace of Zohayd was right up there with the Taj Mahal in splendor and intricacy of design, and even more extensive. The mid-seventeenth-century palace that had taken more than three decades and thousands of artisans and craftsmen to build had once been his playground and domain along with Haidar and Jalal from age eight to twenty. He'd taken as much pride and pleasure in it as they had before his stays here had declined until they'd stopped altogether, around ten years ago.

It felt so strange to be back after everything that had hap-

pened since to pollute his memory. Nostalgia was like a wave
that crashed down on him as he walked through this place
again, felt its history and the grandeur saturating its walls,
permeating his senses with bittersweet memories. On account
of its being Laylah's home, not the stage where chunks of his
life had been played. It had been mostly here where he'd seen
her and dared not dream of her. Now she was here *with* him. It
made being here again so...poignant.

Amjad, the self-appointed poignancy disperser, flicked a
hand at Laylah as she disappeared around a bend. "Are you as
viciously intelligent as you look? Did you latch onto Laylah
when you thought you were 'worthy' of her for the right reasons? Do you realize what a miracle she is? The product of Me-
dusa and Narcissus should have been a man-eating gorgon, not
the most sensitive, selfless being to walk the earth. That she's
female, too, makes her a veritable impossibility."

Now that Amjad was singing Laylah's praises, Rashid no
longer felt like wiping the palace floor with him face-first.

Still looking where Laylah had disappeared, as if to bask in
her echoes, he sighed. "Just what I was thinking. Before your
insufferable, inflammatory intrusion on our privacy."

"Insufferable, inflammatory intrusion? Can you say that
five times in quick succession?" Amjad suddenly slapped him
on the back. "So how did you do it?"

Struggling not to rearrange the king's well put-together face,
Rashid gritted, "Not choke you for all the insensitivities you
poured on Laylah's head? You're only still breathing because
I need you to do some talking on my behalf."

Amjad's guffaw was all enjoyment now. "I may like you yet."
Another back slap. "And by do it, I mean Laylah." At Rashid's
growl, Amjad held up his hands. "To quote Laylah, 'down boy.'
I *mean*—apart from her sharper-than-I-remember tongue—that
was a woman fathoms deep in love. I know the symptoms well.
My Maram looks and sounds like that around me."

"It must be the era of impossibilities."

Amjad laughed again. "Yeah, I still can't figure out why

Maram loves me. But I always figured Laylah's obsession with you stemmed from your unavailability. Now you're all over her, not to mention a far deteriorated version of your younger self. What's keeping someone like her interested in someone like you?"

"If you mean my scar…"

"Please. That's your one interesting feature. Provides you with character. Also proves you're human, since there have been major doubts about that. Nah, it has nothing to do with what you look like, and everything to do with what you *are* like. You're one dour, ruthless, unstable son of a bitch. Don't get me wrong, it makes you *my* kind of guy, but how can Laylah, that perpetual ray of sunshine, stand you?"

He forced out a breath. "How does your Maram stand *you?*"

"She does because we're alike. When you take away all the human traits I lack, she's got a razor for a mind and a scythe for a tongue, too. I don't believe in this opposites attract thing."

"Laylah and I are not opposites. We're very much alike, too."

Amjad snorted again. "Now I've heard it all."

"Think about it. As you pointed out, she is practically as parentless as I am. She has felt alone and out of place all her life, as I have. She's felt responsible for other people's crimes and punished herself for them."

"Her mother's crimes and your guardian's, huh? Now that you point it out, yeah, I can see the resemblance in all the major stuff." Amjad gave him an assessing glance. "So what's your real plan?"

Ten

Rashid's heart slammed against his ribs.

Amjad still suspected him? How, when he no longer *had* a plan?

He only had the truth to contribute. "I plan to dedicate my life to honoring her, to serving and championing her."

"Not to loving her?" Amjad tsked. "Women are fond of this part almost to the exclusion of all else."

And he did something he'd never thought he would: appealed to that maddening man. "You're a man in love, Amjad. Look at me and tell me you don't see *your* symptoms all over me."

After another protracted glance, Amjad let out a laugh. "And how. The trappings of *eshg*—extreme and unremitting love, though they clash on you like a pink dress on a grizzly bear—*are* all over you. But you have something against saying the words, right?"

"The words don't do justice to what I feel for her."

Amjad huffed again. "Been there, done that. And you'll invent new ways and words to transmit the enormity of your feelings. But those simple words, with the truth of your emotions behind them, have a way of transmitting exactly how you feel to your loved one. So word of advice—don't leave it too long without saying them, or she might have trouble getting comfortable hearing or believing them when you finally do."

It was Rashid's turn to scoff. "Now *I've* heard everything. You, giving me romantic advice?"

"That's for the cousin and sister who was the only beacon of brightness in this gloomy place for over two decades." Amjad suddenly made a hurrying gesture. "C'mon. Grovel already."

Giving Amjad a look that said he would make *him* grovel someday, Rashid said, "I ask that you gather the Aal Shalaan family tribunal to sanction giving me Laylah's hand in marriage."

A "gotcha" smile split Amjad's face. "You really are stuck in some desert knight folktale, aren't you? 'Tribunal', indeed."

Rashid counted to ten. "It's *your* family tradition."

"Tradition bladition. I'm King of Zohayd, pal. I play chess with those tribunal members. Just wait until I'm making them jump three diagonal moves ahead then back."

"So it's your decision that counts. *Zain.* Make your demands."

Amjad poked a finger at Rashid's temple, rapped it three times. "*Any* rudimentary sense of humor in there?"

Rashid swatted his hand away. "I'll snark your head off, *Ya Maolai,* as soon as Your Majesty approves my proposal. Or knock it off if you refuse it."

Amjad raised his arms up theatrically. "He lives!" One of his arms suddenly came around Rashid's shoulder, leading him toward the main palace hall. "Just because I now have hope that you won't bore Laylah to the point where she'd plot to be rid of you, I'll consider your proposal. But first, about those seven tasks..."

He knocked Amjad's arm off his shoulder. "No wonder your ex-wife tried to off you."

Amjad's grin was as unrepentant as ever. "She did when I had some propriety. Imagine what she would have done now."

"Shoot you, most probably."

"Is that what you feel like doing?"

"I would gladly kill anyone who would stand between me and Layla. Or at least make him wish he was dead. Care to try?"

Amjad pretended horror. "You'll add me to your inventory of revenge? Will I tail the list after Haidar and Jalal?"

"Come between Layla and I, and you'll reserve your spot at the top."

Amjad stuck his face into his. "You think you can take me?"

"I don't think. I know. And there wouldn't be much left of you once I'm done. And you know it."

Amjad's guffaw boomed again. "And he wins himself a doll."

"I swear, Amjad, if you don't stop yanking my chain, *taal omrak* won't be a concept that will apply to you anymore."

"You know, Rashid, I would have kicked you out on your ear with the first sign of kissing up. But you threatened to kill me instead, so I think I'm in love. Yep, rejoice. You passed." His arm was over Rashid's shoulder once more. "How about we go pretend that family 'tribunal' of mine actually matters?"

Still afraid to rejoice, Rashid hissed, "Didn't you say your word is everything, O king of all you survey?"

"It is. But you'll be king of the headache-inducing but inevitably inseparable Azmahar soon. You will be the one constant partner in my political bed. I'm doing myself a favor showing you the ropes of kingship. Yeah, I'm into training allies to my preferences. I'm charitable like that."

Rashid stilled. That was totally unexpected. That Amjad would bring up the idea of Rashid becoming king of Azmahar. And in this way. What was his game?

He probed, hoping to gain more insight. "It's strange that you'd assume I would be king with your two brothers running against me."

Amjad gave a dismissing wave. "Haidar and Jalal would make decent kings, I guess, but their hearts aren't really in it.

Yours is. You have more at stake in Azmahar and that is why you'll reap the votes."

Digesting this unforeseen development, Rashid put all his cards on the table, even if it was for a game he no longer cared about in the least. "I wouldn't without your alliance. Which *they* have in full."

Amjad gave a masterful imitation of affront. "Because they're my brothers? Nepotism? *Moi?* Tut-tut, shame on you. Have you forgotten they're only my *half* brothers? With Sondoss's blood running in their veins, actually half demon. Considering you're only half oaf, you win in that context, too."

Rashid looked heavenward. "Do you ever stop?"

"No. Maram won't let me."

Rashid tried one last time. "Are you *ever* serious?"

Those impossibly green eyes smoldered with a complex intelligence that had Rashid realizing this man saw and understood everything. "I'm *always* serious. I say what others are too shy or cowardly or merciful to say. Think back and you'll find I said nothing but the whole truth all through this bracing encounter." He clapped his hand once. "Now, from a full-fledged king to an embryonic one, let me give you an introductory course in dealing with pompous asses."

Rashid let Amjad put an arm around his shoulder this time. "You must be an authority on your own species."

Amjad chuckled. "I *can* still give you a hard time, you know."

"Knock yourself out. Name whatever price or mission. I'll surpass any so there won't be any shadow of owing you a thing."

"You can never repay what you'll owe me. Your eternal happiness with Laylah. Face it, Rashid. I own you."

He shrugged Amjad's arm off again. "Tell you what. Save it. I'll take Laylah up on her offer and elope."

Amjad's considering glance lengthened this time. "She's your Achilles' heel, isn't she?"

"You're all Greek mythology today, aren't you?"

Amjad gave a mock serious nod. "I've expended the Indian

and Middle Eastern myths on Haidar and Jalal in the past two days."

After that, Amjad remained miraculously silent as they passed through the majestic marble corridors adorned in the most intricate and magnificently designed colored mosaics toward the palace's great hall.

As they approached the hall's twenty-foot gilded double doors, Amjad suddenly spoke again, continuing his previous point seamlessly. "It balances you, grounds you, being so totally vulnerable to her." He winked. "It makes you a man at last." At Rashid's exasperated exhalation, Amjad added, "It's not a slur on your manhood. *This* time. I think a man can't call himself that until a woman has him totally whipped."

Unbelievable as it was, this Amjad was turning out to be one insightful and romantic fellow. "Like Maram has you?"

The smile that wreathed Amjad's face was the very essence of longing and indulgence, as if he was transmitting it to his wife. Rashid somehow believed Maram *would* feel it. "And then some. I gave up everything I had and was for her. I would give up far more if she'd let me. You'd do the same for Laylah, wouldn't you?"

"I would."

At his nonnegotiable answer, Amjad patted Rashid on the back as they entered the grand hall. "Then there's no rush with those seven tasks, Hercules. You'll be spreading them out throughout your lives together." He suddenly shuddered. "Just seeing her in labor is going to teach you the meaning of terror and take you to the limit of your endurance and beyond." They'd stopped in the middle of the expansive hall, below the hundred-foot central dome where Laylah's male kin were gathered in rows like a Roman senate, when Amjad gave him a playful punch. "You lucky bastard."

It was a marvel watching Amjad in action.

As he informed the Aal Shalaan elders that Rashid was going to marry Laylah, Amjad did the opposite of what kings, or anyone sane, should and had been known to do. In the past twenty minutes Rashid had watched him put down, make fun of and alienate everyone in the hall, including his father, in lieu of courting their favor. It was staggering how fluently and inventively he did it. But what was truly flabbergasting was that everyone loved him for it. They not only obeyed him, they practically invited him to walk all over them some more.

Maybe he should take private lessons in Amjad's School of Kingship, after all.

Suddenly, every thought in his mind dispersed as they walked out of the hall, only to be filled with one thing. Laylah.

She was striding toward him from the other end of the grand corridor, her dress's looseness only emphasizing her lethal curves, its cream color accentuating her sunlit hair, skin and eyes.

She had a taller woman with her. Maram, Amjad's wife and Queen of Zohayd. But though Maram's flawless complexion and silky hair approximated Laylah's hues, they didn't strike anything inside him like the burn of appreciation Laylah's did.

The moment it took to register Maram dissolved, everything gravitating to the center of his universe again. It struck him again how pleasurable it was to behold Laylah, how beautiful he found her. How terrified he was that this miracle wouldn't come to pass.

Suppressing the need to run to meet her halfway, he watched her and Maram approach, weighed down by the worry that kept ambushing him—that it would be impossible for everything to keep going so smoothly, incapacitating him further with each attack.

Maram flowed into Amjad's arms as if slotting into her other half. Then Laylah, flaunting tradition and inciting kingdom-wide wagging tongues, did the same with him. It was frowned upon for married couples to indulge in physical affection in public. It was unheard of between the unmarried.

Most likely presuming his stiffness was caused by his sense of propriety, Laylah grinned up at him. "Did those fossils agree to let you take me off the shelf or do I have to go in there and show them what the last remaining, if fraying around the edges, Zohaydan treasure will do if they snap her last decaying nerve?"

Maram groaned. "Those expressions reek of Amjad."

Laylah giggled. "Discipline him for me, will you?"

"It'll be my pleasure." Maram chuckled. "Though I suspect it will be his, too. I think he misbehaves on purpose."

Amjad pulled his wife deeper into his embrace. "Like any love-slave worth his salt, I live to provoke my next punishment."

As Maram laughed her pleasure, Laylah prodded him. "Well? Any need for drastic action on my side?"

Before Rashid got his constricted throat to work, Amjad produced the phone his *kabeer al yaweran*—his head of royal guard—had handed him as they'd exited the hall.

He gave it to Laylah. "I thought you should have an audio memento of me kicking our family's ass as I acquired for you the groom who's going to save you from a fate worse than death."

"You recorded the meeting?" Laylah exclaimed as she pounced on the phone and a chill assailed Rashid when she let him go. Then he once again heard the medley of abuse Amjad had exposed his family to. Amjad hadn't even introduced Rashid's proposal, had only pulverized everyone to their true size before announcing the upcoming marriage as a fact, and announcing that he'd be passing the royal decree documents for everyone to stamp with their house seal.

After gaping through the playback, Laylah squealed, "Amjad! You insane, incredible man, you!"

Amjad waved her delight away. "I don't do presents, so consider this my gift for the duration of your dual lifetimes."

Laylah gave him a squeezing hug. "Oh, Amjad, I love you!"

Amjad pushed out of her arms, a stern finger raised at her. "Don't do or say that again. And I mean *ever*."

Laylah winked at Maram. "Your mistress/owner will sanction the occasional hug from the universal kid sister around here."

Amjad's head jerk indicated Rashid, who'd taken an involuntary threatening step closer. "It's someone twice her size and who packs the wallop of a weapon of mass destruction that I'm worried about. Explaining this kid-sister thing to that monolith you brought home might not work. Or it might, and he'd still take my head off just because I'm male and you came in contact with me."

Laylah laughed, her whole face alight with elation as she looked up at Rashid. "Don't worry. He needs you in one piece."

Amjad tutted. "Not a good enough deterrent with that berserker. So let's play it safe." He pulled Maram back into his arms, shared with her that look of total allegiance that Rashid had unbelievably found with Laylah. "I have a wife and kids who'd like me around for half a century or so."

With the trio indulging in more banter, Rashid walked with them to Amjad and Maram's private quarters, still struggling with the ominous sensation settling deeper in his bones. It just didn't seem right that everything would go so wonderfully.

When would the other shoe drop?

It did, partially, in the evening.

More Aal Shalaans kept showing up to congratulate them, with their delight and acceptance only setting him further on edge. Then he announced the wedding would be in Azmahar a week later.

It was then that everything went wrong.

Maram and Aliyah led the women in insisting there was no way they'd put together another royal wedding in a week, like they recently had Jalal's. They'd take a month. And that was final.

When Amjad corroborated his wife's desire, and Laylah herself didn't protest for long, Rashid felt that if he did, they'd wonder why he was so nervous about postponement, and grudgingly succumbed.

From then on, he felt each moment as if it were counting down to an explosion that would go off and destroy everything.

Eleven

"You know, there's this age-old invention. It's said to have endless merits."

Rashid gritted his teeth as Laylah whispered in his ear. It had been ten days since they'd come to Zohayd. All the wedding preparations on the Zohaydan side had been concluded. They'd move to Azmahar in a couple of days to start the preparations there, where the ceremony would be held. A couple of days when Laylah wouldn't be with him.

She'd played a ruse on her companions to get him into her private quarters alone. Normally he would have objected, even refused. Not this time. He had to talk her out of her potentially disastrous decision.

He stiffened when her arms came around him from behind, her hair spilling its fragrant silk over his shoulder as she leaned over the couch where he sat in her old bedroom suite.

She nipped his earlobe. "That invention is called a smile."

Unable to hold back, he swung around, took hold of her and swept her over the couch and onto his lap.

Giggling, melting in his embrace, her fingers traced his tight lips, tried to spread them. "You do it like that. C'mon, you can do it. I promise you, your face won't crack."

He caught her hands. "It's not the right moment to ask me to try this trick."

Her face lost its impishness as she sighed. "I'm going to visit my mother, not going on a suicide mission."

"You mean there's a difference?" he asked, feeling himself spiraling out of control.

"You were the one who insisted I bring my family into this."

"I meant the nonvenomous ones only."

She chuckled. "I *am* one-quarter serpent."

"The gene bypassed you."

"But it might be a good idea to keep in touch with its literal mother lode, just to keep abreast of how to manage it. Said gene might not miss the next generation."

"It will. That gene stops with your mother and aunt."

She cupped his face in her hands. "And you know what? I almost believe you'd will that to happen."

"I would."

"You'll make an incomparable king, you know that?"

The fist around his heart squeezed. This subject of king-ship had become the one thing he dreaded thinking or hearing about. "Let's not put me on a throne just yet." He caught her face in urgent hands, needing to defuse this catastrophe in the making. "Don't go, *ya rohi.* I don't want anything to poison your mood, *ya hayati,* not now, not ever."

She flushed in pleasure, her eyes filling with joy.

Amjad had been right. The words of love, as deficient as they were, had come to mean more, just because he said them to her, poured his emotions into them. She delighted in hear-ing him call her his soul and life. As she was.

After pressing a fiercely tender kiss on his lips, she with-drew. "It's why I'm going, *ya habibi.* Because there's this lin-gering bitterness that I want to get rid of. It will only go away if I see my mother again, talk this out with her." She sifted her fingers lovingly through the inch of hair he now had. "I also have this unstoppable need to brag that I not only amounted to something when left to my own devices, but I'm getting myself a husband worth millions of the men she tried to set me up with."

Struggling with the urge to bundle her up and hide her away, preferably forever, so nothing and no one could hurt her, he mumbled, "Icebergs will tumble in Azmahar's desert before she shares your opinion of me."

Her laugh tinkled over his overstrung nerves. "She might not admit it at peril of her life, but she must appreciate the hell out of what you are today, bless her power-hungry soul." She wrapped her arms around his neck. "But no matter what she's done to me, it *has* been her own misguided way of loving me. And no matter what she is, she's my mother...and I love her."

What could he possibly say to that? That she shouldn't give her mother any of her love because the woman didn't deserve it? When he didn't deserve it, either, yet wanted her to give him all the love she had?

He found himself groaning, "Don't go, if you love *me*."

He winced at how petty that had come out. How desperate.

She caressed his scar, deluging him in tenderness. "That's going to be a problem, since I don't 'love' you. You're just the sharer of my soul, and so far the owner of my heart."

His heart squeezed. "So far?"

"I'm assuming little Rashids will share your status one day."

The concept of children with her muted him.

Her touch ameliorated his upheaval, boosted it. "My mother won't attend our wedding, won't be able to practice her saboteur tricks. I'll see her in the safety of her exile and be back in less than forty-eight hours. And no, you can't come with me. I'm not so foolish that I'd put you in her range. And you have much to do. I know. I'm the one who set up your schedule."

He couldn't stop her without admitting what he would take to his grave. How this had started. And why he would prefer a worse scar than what he had to having her mother near her, and therefore them, again.

So she'd go. And he'd spend forty-eight hours going insane. More insane than he already was.

He heaved to his feet, taking her up in his arms, rushing to her bathroom. "If you must go, then I must have you first."

"I should punish you for the celibacy you imposed on us," she teased as he locked the door. "But I'm just too hungry for you."

He took her lips, his tongue thrusting deep into her eager warmth. "Not as hungry as I am for you."

He dragged her down to a fluffy cream mat, tore her clothes out of the way, freed himself. He was heavy and hard and maddened for her molten depths. Ten days since he'd last been with her, inside her, had driven him to the edge.

He entered her in one full thrust, forging into the inferno of pleasure that was her welcoming flesh.

Her cries of pleasure drove him into a frenzy. He buried himself in her over and over, each plunge a shockwave of mindlessness from his loins to his every nerve.

Too soon the friction and ferocity drove them over the edge of insanity and into ecstasy. He poured himself into her depths, transfigured yet again with the power and totality of her desire, with the purity of passion she bestowed on him.

As she trembled and keened her satisfaction beneath him, blind possession overcame him. For a mad moment he wanted to force her not to leave him. He could keep her his willing prisoner...

Her lips opened over his scar, crooning his name, her love. Heat blossomed behind his eyes, burning away the instability.

Nothing would ever mean a thing if she didn't give it freely, breathlessly. He had to let her go.

As he took one last kiss, as if he could transmit his unspoken plea to never stop wanting him, he prayed.

That nothing would ever come between them.

Rashid had been right. She shouldn't have come.

Laylah was realizing that with every second. Her mother

was even more difficult than she'd remembered. Somayah's exile, though it was a luxurious one in Jamaica, had brought out the worst in her.

As majestic as ever, looking more beautiful than she remembered, her mother had received Laylah in full regalia, her hair blonder now but still in that signature chignon. She hadn't even pretended any pleasure to see her daughter, let alone to hear her news.

The news her mother had already known.

Somayah now looked down the four inches between them, disdain rising. "You think you'll…what? Impress me? Show me how you've succeeded against all my expectations? You think you did?"

Laylah's heart squeezed. She would have given anything to have what most people had. A mother who was on her side.

"My business is taking off, and I'm marrying the man who'll be your motherland's king. I'd say I did."

Her mother's glance grew more irritated. "You know what burns me? Since you were born, an Aal Shalaan female anomaly, I dedicated my life to making the most of this miracle, while trying to cure you of your Aal Shalaan defects."

Laylah's shoulders slumped further. "Yeah, you wanted to excise my Aal Shalaan half, turn me into a pure Aal Munsoori."

"I certainly wasn't after *that*. Though the Aal Munsooris are my father's house, the mundane, inept genes in our branch of the family are abundant. Just look at your uncle Nedal and his moronic sons. I always belonged body and soul to my mother's family and I wanted to polish you into an Aal Refa'ee gem. I wanted to raise you from the second-class princess I was to a queen. I worked tirelessly to plan you a marriage that would put you on a throne."

Laylah's lips twisted. "Then you should appreciate the irony here. Though you failed to set me up with those useless weasels whose only asset was their royal blood, I ended up with a man who will be king, because he deserves to be."

"There's irony in abundance here, indeed. For you to reject

all those men because they wanted you for your Aal Shalaan blood, only to *choose* a man who wants you for just that."

Laylah's heart stumbled. Her mother was assuming...

Of course, she was. She believed that blood was Laylah's only asset, believed everyone would think the same.

"But those men were honorable enough to declare their intentions. *This* leftover of the lowest branch of the Aal Munsooris, who is festering with hostility toward anyone higher than he is, is manipulating you, not even leaving you the dignity of knowing you are the chip he needs to become king."

Laylah's heart slowed down, as if afraid to take every next beat. "What—what are you talking about?"

Her mother's gaze grew incredulous. "I always knew you had no insight *or* foresight. But that you didn't even *suspect* him is too much. Let's review history, shall we? For your first seventeen years Rashid Aal Munsoori didn't look your way as you followed him around like a lost puppy, begging for a pat on the head." At Laylah's sharp intake of breath, her mother let out a bitter laugh. "Of course, I noticed. Everyone did. You were so obvious, it was painful to watch. That constituted the major part of my frustration with you. Especially as I watched him take his pleasure in pretending you didn't exist, and it only made you humiliate yourself more as you begged for smaller crumbs, until a glance your way was the height of your aspirations.

"Then, like all inferiority-complex-ridden breeds, the first thing he did once he could was bite the hands that offered him friendship and support. He did everything he could to destroy your kin, but being the pathetic thrall that you are, I bet you convinced yourself he must have good or even noble reasons."

"You know nothing about him, in the past or now."

"I know far more than you do, you stupid girl. Didn't you even ask yourself why, after you lived without incident in the United States, you were suddenly targeted for kidnapping? When you were no longer a good candidate for ransom, with half your family in exile and the other half off the royalty A-list? Didn't you wonder how he happened to be there to save you?"

Her mother's insinuations sank into her brain. "No…"

Her mother barreled on. "Let me guess what happened next. You were so grateful for his saving you, so thankful for the opportunity to be with him, you clung to him. Did he pretend to reciprocate your feelings right off, or did he dangle the bait of reluctance to stir you into a frenzy? How long did he make you pant after him before he deigned to let you closer? Knowing you, I expect you offered him everything, if only he'd take it. And he ended up taking it all, didn't he?"

Suddenly her legs lost all cohesion. Laylah collapsed on the nearest couch, feeling like the little girl who used to suffocate under the barrage of her mother's censure. But the way her mother wielded her contempt now was beyond any cruelty she'd inflicted on Laylah before.

And she wasn't done. "So how soon did he play his hand? Ask to marry you? I expect he made you sweat it first." That was the only part her mother had gotten wrong. It was as if she'd been with them, only putting alternate, horrifying interpretations on the actual events. "You didn't find any of what was happening strange? That after a lifetime of shoving your irrelevance in your face, and after he declared war on your family, he'd explode into your life out of the blue and risk his life for yours? Then, in record time, ask to marry you? What reason did he give for this? What's the reason *you* told yourself? That he wants you for you, not like all those 'weasels' you so righteously and shrewdly rejected?"

Mute with pain, coming apart with dread, that her mother still had worse to say, Laylah stared helplessly up at her.

"Let me tell you why he's swallowing your abhorred pill," her mother hissed. "Because you're the only remedy for a major ailment he has. A severe lack of Aal Shalaan blood. Only a blood bond with the king of Zohayd through marriage will put him on the throne of Azmahar. And the only available female Aal Shalaan is you."

That "you" felt like a direct hit to Laylah's heart.

Her mother bent over her as if to make every word a harder blow. "But he couldn't come to you with a proposition to use you to forge an alliance with Zohayd. Knowing you, you would have agreed to anything he asked, but he probably couldn't risk the Aal Shalaans, especially that paranoid madman Amjad, suspecting his motives. So he had to make you think this was real. Since he knows everything about you and your infatuation with him, a little act was all he needed to have you thanking fate for bringing him into your life and blindly swallowing his bait. As you did."

"Please...stop..."

At her bleeding whisper, her mother straightened. "I have nothing more to add. You can now go sacrifice yourself at the altar of your obsession with this psychopath, let him step on you to the throne of Azmahar then kick you aside once he sits on it. Or maybe he'll keep you until he uses your womb to create a permanent source of Aal Shalaan blood, one he actually wants."

Laylah stared at her mother, wounded to her core that Somayah would think nothing of mutilating her own daughter to "cure" her of her "obsession" with Rashid. But...what if anything she'd said was true...?

No. It wasn't. It couldn't be...

Her mother interrupted her chaotic thoughts. "Go ask him, Laylah. Look into his eyes as you ask, as he answers. If you're certain in your heart that nothing I said is true, then just forget about it."

With that, her mother turned, leaving the cloud of her exclusive fragrance behind as she exited the room.

Impending loss consumed Laylah. Whatever the outcome of confronting him, she'd lose something vital irrevocably. If her mother turned out to be wrong, Laylah wouldn't forgive her, losing her forever.

If her mother was right, Laylah would lose everything else.

Twelve

"What's your game this time, Rashid?"

He groaned at the sound of that voice. Haidar. His once-best friend. Rashid hated him now as much as he'd once loved him.

But he had no time to continue their battles. The pilot of his private jet had said he'd be landing in an hour. Rashid had to be at the airstrip to meet Laylah. She'd said not to come, that she'd be at the palace in half an hour. But he could not wait a half hour longer to see her.

He turned toward Haidar. He was blocking the door of Rashid's suite in Azmahar's royal palace where he'd be staying while the wedding preparations were being made.

His careless glance answered Haidar's black scowl as he passed him on his way out of the room. "Schedule a duel with Ahmad on your way out, Haidar."

His arm was snagged in Haidar's grip. "Is marrying Laylah part of your war on us?"

Rashid swung around to face Haidar, snarling. "She has *nothing* to do with any of that."

"So what will you have me believe?" Haidar hissed. "That you fell in love with her and that's why you're marrying her?"

He shook off Haidar's hand. "I care nothing about what you believe. Will you see yourself out, or do you need help?"

Haidar blocked his way again, furious, urgent, entreating. "Whatever it is you think you have against me and Jalal, do whatever you want to us. *We* can take it. But Laylah has always loved you, and if you're using her, it will destroy her."

"You think I need to use anyone to trounce you?"

"Then is this about the throne? If you're trying to complete the last corner in your campaign through her, I'll save you the trouble. I'll make the battle unnecessary. I'll withdraw from the race. I can make Jalal do the same. Just don't do this to her."

Something snapped inside him. He hefted Haidar off the floor, slammed him into the wall, a beast's snarl issuing from his depths. "I will say this once, Haidar. I have always wanted Laylah, but now I find no reason and no way to exist without her. I would rather die, or worse, than hurt her. So if you dare insinuate otherwise, I won't fight you anymore, I'll finish you."

Haidar's fingers dug into his hands hard enough to penetrate his red haze of aggression, extricating himself from his rabid grasp, his eyes narrowing, as if to gauge Rashid's sincerity.

Seeming convinced, Haidar exhaled. "With you turning all Comte De Monte Cristo on us, I feared there might be no line you wouldn't cross. I also thought you'd never fall in love. *B'Ellahi,* the only girlfriend we ever heard about turned out to be fictional. For years you misled us into thinking you picked that inferior college to be near said girlfriend, not because it was what you could afford. And then, Laylah kept trying to get you to notice her, and you never showed any indication you even saw her."

"Just as I couldn't afford a better college, I couldn't afford to look at her." His heart convulsed. "I still can't believe I have her now."

Exasperation filled Haidar's face. "This pride of yours— this pathologically huge sense of honor—it stopped you from taking everything that was yours. Our support, Laylah's love. And it made you saddle yourself with your bastard of a guardian's debts, so that you derailed your whole life to pay them off, without help from anyone."

"But when I *really* needed help, and it clashed with your best interests, you didn't care if I lived or died." At Haidar's bewildered glance, he plowed on. "So don't think I will spare you now because you're Laylah's cousin."

Still looking confused, Haidar smirked. "Not even if she asks you to? If you love her as much as you claim, you'll do whatever she wants. Like I would, for Roxanne."

"I am bound to obey her, even if it means my honor and my life. But if she does ask, I might tell her the truth about you. She would withdraw her intervention if she knew what you did."

Haidar exploded. "And what the hell *did* I do, damn you?"

"You damned *me*."

At his bellow, Haidar's stupefaction felt real.

Was it possible Haidar didn't know what Rashid was referring to?

No. No time to dwell on the possibility of anything this disturbing, this huge. He had to get to Laylah. Only she mattered.

He pushed past Haidar, making it clear there would be no detaining him this time. "Now my salvation is waiting for me, and you're keeping me from her. I'd decimate you for that alone."

The moment he cleared the door, his heart stopped.

Laylah. A dozen feet from his door.

After the first drench of unreasoning horror that she might have heard anything, he ran to sweep her into his arms.

"Habibati..." he groaned against her temple, her cheeks, her lips. "How are you here already?"

"We landed earlier."

"And Zaaher didn't tell me!"

"At my insistence, so don't you dare take this up with him."

His heartstrings vibrated with the delight of having her in his arms again. *"To'moreeni*—as you command."

"It's creepy how you have Rashid doing your bidding, Laylah." Haidar stopped by their side, dropped a kiss on her head and met Rashid's incensed gaze with a calm glance. Rashid's fury rose as Laylah returned Haidar's smile and kiss. "It's like seeing a shark doing tricks in a swimming pool. Who knew you had it in you? But keep up the good work, *ya bent al amm.* Holding the reins of such an unstoppable force can come in handy. For us."

Rashid bit back something demolishing. He'd never expose her to tension. Which might mean sparing Haidar and Jalal, after all.

He'd think about that later. All he could think of now was that he had her back.

Uncaring anymore that the palace dwellers would see him taking her to his quarters, the moment she said goodbye to Haidar, he rushed back there with her in his arms. He told himself he'd never let her go again.

Laylah clung to Rashid as if she'd never let him go, feeling reclaimed from the hell of doubts and dread.

Before she could say anything, he opened his mouth on her neck, suckled her as if assimilating her into himself, growling those extravagant endearments he'd been deluging her in of late.

Fireworks exploded in her blood as he put her down, ground the steel of his erection into her belly, showing her she only had to wrap herself around him and he'd fill her emptiness.

She forgot everything but this, him, them, like that.

"Rashid, take me…"

At her urgency, he snatched her dress up, spreading her thighs around his hips. He pressed her against something that rattled as he freed himself, tore her panties out of the way then slid her up to scale his length. She felt the hot hardness of him at her entrance, keened, disintegrating with the firebomb of hunger he'd detonated inside her. Obeying her plea for hard and fast, he let her crash down on him as he thrust up, impaling her.

It took no more than feeling him inside her—filling her beyond her capacity, embedding at the gate of her womb—to shatter her. She screamed as an orgasm unleashed all her tension, squeezed her around him inside and out.

Igniting with her, he fed her convulsions with thrust after thrust, mingling his growls with her shrieks. "*Aih, khodeeni kolli, eeji alai*—take all of me, come all over me."

Pleasure raged on until he roared and slammed into her, the pulse of his release wringing her of sensations. She sobbed, her flesh quivering around him.

Possessing her slack mouth, he filled her breathless lungs with his ragged breath, rocking gently inside her, satisfying her to her last tremor.

"*Awhashteeni...bejnoon...*"

I missed you...insanely...

Her head flopped on his shoulder as she tried to get her nerves to spark. She needed to hold on to his reality, his magic, to ward off the doubts. "It's been...less than...two days."

"*Kateer. Tw'hasheeni wenti gossad aini.*"

Too much. I miss you when you're right before my eyes.

Could all this...sincerity be a lie?

He strode with her wrapped around him to the bathroom. He lowered her gently on pristine white marble before reluctantly, carefully, withdrawing from her depths.

She moaned at his beauty and caring as he kneeled in front of her, taking care of the evidence of their lovemaking. Then he rose to his feet, muscles rippling under his shirt as he struggled to stuff his erection into his pants, his emotions an open book for her to read in his eyes.

But how could *that* be the truth? The mainstay of Rashid's character was his reticence. How could he have become so... uninhibited? Because of her overwhelming effect on him? Or because it was easy to say and pretend what he didn't feel?

Which explanation sounded more plausible?

The answer, validated by the evidence of history, was so incontrovertible, her stomach heaved. The dream she'd been living in quivered on the verge of plunging into a nightmare.

It was no use trying to ignore this. Doubt was poisoning her, snuffing out her life. She had to know for sure.

What if he denied it? Would she ever feel secure again? Would the doubts ever go away?

Yes. They would. Her mother had no idea who Rashid was. She was projecting her own end-justifies-the-means beliefs on him.

Rashid would tell her the truth. And she'd believe him.

She urged his head up as he rained kisses and words of worship all over her face and neck.

His glazed-with-passion, heavy-with-indulgence eyes met hers.

Feeling like she was about to jump off a cliff, she asked, "Do you need to marry me to become king of Azmahar?"

His face shut down. But not before she saw it.

The alarm. The dismay. Of premature exposure.

Everything her mother had said was true.

Rashid stared at Laylah, feeling his heart had burst.

So this was it. What he'd been dreading. The catastrophe that would end everything.

Every shred of control he'd been struggling for years to muster suddenly drained away. The chaos that was always hovering at the edge of his awareness crashed into his mind, unraveling it...

No. He couldn't afford to surrender to the volatility that threatened to swallow him whole. He had to contain this.

Then he opened his mouth, and his voice sounded like he felt, desperate, out-of-control. "Is...is that what your mother told you?"

Her eyes, for the first time ever, were a void, expressing nothing. "I want *you* to tell me."

His hands dug into her shoulders, feeling if he didn't cling to her, she'd disappear. "I don't care about the throne anymore. I only care about you. You must believe that."

He had no idea if that helped or hurt his case. There was nothing in her expression to guide him.

"But it's true that, no matter if you're the best candidate, without an alliance with Zohayd, you won't claim the throne?"

She needed the truth, and he'd give it to her. He'd explain how things had started, how they'd changed. She'd understand.

Maybe it was for the best this had come out, so he'd stop self-consuming with worry, so total disclosure would leave no possibility for anything going wrong or coming between them.

He still couldn't breathe due to anxiety. "Azmaharians believe they need Zohayd's alliance to survive. I always believed this dependence on Zohayd was toxic, and intended to make Azmahar fully independent if I became king. But I was left in no doubt that to become king I had to form a connection with Zohayd. The only way I could rival Haidar's and Jalal's blood relation to Zohayd's king was to form one of my own with him."

"And the only way was through marriage." Her voice was as expressionless as her face. "Since I am the closest thing Amjad has to a sister, and I happen to be the only available female Aal Shalaan, anyway, you had no choice but to marry me."

Hearing her analyze the plan he'd once weaved turned his stomach. And that was before she went on.

"So you planned to hunt me down, pretend you didn't find me as abhorrent as you did my family and con me into marriage. Once you impregnated me and your heir replaced me as a perpetual blood bond, you'd discard the worthless creature you believed me to be."

The accuracy of her projections drenched him with desperation. "Whatever I thought or planned, everything changed from that first night. That first *hour*."

A faraway look came into her eyes, as if she was looking back into that time. "It was no coincidence that you were there that night. I felt your presence for weeks before that." His choking silence corroborated her assumption. "You were studying me, like a hunter would his prey, finding out my habits, my haunts, to use this knowledge and my obliviousness to get to me. Once you made 'accidental' contact, you used the data you gathered to manipulate me into entering your trap willingly, even eagerly. As I did."

Hot needles invaded his heart. "That was true, until you were attacked. Everything changed from then on. *Everything*."

"You mean the attack you planned? The rescue you enacted?"

He almost doubled over with her accusation.

This was beyond his worst fears. That she'd think…think…

Her next words had protests recoiling in his chest, hacking into it. "The ironic thing is, you didn't need to set me up. If you, of all people, had offered me a marriage of convenience, I would have jumped at the opportunity. That was how much I wanted you. I would have agreed to your cold deal and dreamed of one day melting your heart, of making you see me as more than a means to your end. I would have probably realized the mistake I had made sooner rather than later, but you would have gotten what you wanted by then. Just think about it—the truth would have served your purpose far better than this charade."

"There was no charade," he groaned, desperation taking over. "Every moment with you was the only real thing I ever had…"

Her eyes suddenly filled with tears, suffocating him. "But you couldn't risk my family, especially Amjad, suspecting your motives, so you had to make me believe in your authenticity. But even with an heir binding you forever to the Aal Shalaans, you wouldn't have risked a falling-out with them when you discarded me." Her reddened eyes seemed to melt. "Did you plan another attack to get rid of me after I'd served my purpose?"

He'd taken a bullet in the gut before. He'd been showered in shrapnel. He'd been tortured beyond the limits of endurance and sanity. Her projections hurt, damaged him, far more.

He couldn't even shout his denial, could only choke his horror. "*Ya Ullah ya Laylah, laa*—don't even utter such ugliness…"

Those eyes that had bathed him in the balm of their belief, drilled into him now with bitterness and betrayal. "Ugliness is what you did to me, what you plunged me into. Now I'll never feel anything untainted by its sordidness again."

Disintegrating with the need to ward off the pain he'd inflicted on her, he extended a trembling hand to her. "You won't believe anything I say now, but when you're over the first rage and disillusion, remember what we shared…"

"We shared *nothing*." Her voice was thick with disdain. "Nothing but your deceit and exploitation. But I can't even blame you. I'm the one who threw myself at you. You only obliged and jerked me around. I deserve everything you did to me."

And it was as if a dam broke. Sobs racked her body, tears ran in torrents down her cheeks.

"Y-you want me to remember? I *do*. Every thought and emotion as I loved you…craved you…and longed to be there for you. Every sensation as I touched you…as you touched me, moved inside me…until I felt you were part of me. How you must have despised me for…how easy I was, how cheaply I came…"

Her pain crushed his heart.

But his pain didn't matter. Only hers did. He wanted to absorb her agony.

At his imploring touch, she tore herself away, quaking on sobs he feared would tear her insides apart. "I spent my *whole life* looking up to you… I thought you were made of honor, of integrity…that if there was a haven in this world for me… it would be you. But not even those who I thought would have raped and killed me could have…*debased* me like you did."

He fell to his knees before her, insanity clawing at his mind, begging. "Don't let pain take you that far, *ya habibati,* I beg you. Rage and rave and slash me apart…but don't make me a demon when I'm only a pathetic fool. I did devise the plot, but I didn't see it through…"

"You did," she wailed. "That first night—*ya Ullah*—how did you *do* it? Anticipating me…adjusting your response on the fly to keep me hurtling…deeper into your trap. You had me in your bed in hours…thinking it was at my insistence. You stayed up

all night, didn't you? It was the only time you forced yourself to stay beside me…burning to close the deal. You must have wanted to strangle me when I…forced you to pretend to court me before I returned with you to Zohayd so ecstatic, I managed to fool…even Amjad for you. You would have seen it through to the end…if I hadn't found out the truth."

"That's *not* the truth." His protest strangled as she stumbled away from his begging hands only to collapse a foot away, ending up with her streaming face pressed against the wall, her whole body quaking. "But whatever else you think me guilty of, I beg you, believe I had nothing to do with the attack."

"Do you know that my earliest memory is of you?"

He doubled over with the surprise confession.

Her sobs subsided by degrees. "It was my fourth birthday. You were standing behind Haidar, wearing light blue jeans and a black T-shirt. I thought you were the most wonderful thing I'd ever seen. As I blew out the candles I made one wish, for you to be my friend. I've made no other wish since.

"I idolized you, saw a wealth of beauty in everything about you, even the way you kept your distance. I thought we shared so much, both of us outsiders, with no one who loved us most or put us first. I lived dreaming of our being each other's allies against all odds. Now all my memories are contaminated with the truth, and my past wasted in loving a figment of my imagination. My future will be consumed in regret over every moment and emotion I wasted on you."

He crawled toward her, the ground burning him worse than the sands he'd once dragged himself over for days to a salvation that kept receding. Her feeble resistance died as his arms shook around her, taking her drenched face against his heaving chest.

"Don't say that…don't think it and make it real in your mind. Don't do this to yourself, to us. I *never* lied about my feelings…"

Her head rolled against his shoulder, her eyes meeting his. For seconds he saw his Laylah, felt he might reach her again.

Then she whispered, "I would have laid my life down for you, Rashid. Now I would rather die than see you again."

She pushed away from him, stumbled up to her feet.

Looking down at him as he remained on his knees, demolished, her eyes were as dead as her voice. "Wishing you the heartbreak you inflicted on me wouldn't work when you have no heart. So I'll settle for crippling you like you crippled me. I'll make sure you lose the only thing that matters to you—the throne."

Thirteen

"So how *did* you manage to lose that girl?"

Amjad's sarcasm scraped across Rashid's every screaming nerve.

He turned slowly toward Amjad. He'd been doing everything slowly since he'd followed Laylah back to Zohayd less than a day after she'd left him in Azmahar. Any sudden moves might set him off.

His trigger quivered as Amjad sauntered toward him from his office on the ground floor of the royal palace of Zohayd, his signature mockery hitting him between the eyes.

"You must have committed some nuclear-level stupidity to blast through her immutable worship of you."

"Listen, *King* Amjad," he snarled. "I have only been in anything approaching this state once in my life. I was cut open and my life was bleeding out. And I still managed to kill all my torturers. There were eight of them. I am now far more desperate."

"Whoa. Are you aware you just threatened to kill a king right in his own palace? Or are you really as out of it as you look?"

"That threat is a few more words from becoming reality.

And don't think your royal guard can help you. I can end you all without breaking a sweat."

"You know what?" Amjad gave him the once-over. "I believe you can, Super Soldier-man. But what next? You massacred your previous tormenters, who I assume gave you this delightful souvenir—" he flicked a hand at Rashid's scar "—and escaped to live long and prosper. I don't see a similar scenario here, as there'll be no living long and prospering for you now. Not without Laylah."

Hearing her name slipped another notch of his control. "I am at the point where I don't care what happens next. If you don't get out of my way, I'll kill you for the pleasure of it."

Amjad smirked. "Was that why Laylah canceled your wedding? She discovered your homicidal tendencies?"

Rashid didn't even try to hide the truth. "She believes I want to marry her only to have an alliance with Zohayd. With *you*."

"That's not true. Sure, being Laylah's husband will sweeten the deal when I take you under my wing. But that's just collateral damage. You really love her."

"Love? Love is a conditional emotion tainted with self-serving. I've been using the word, making believe it means what I feel. But I can't describe how I feel for Laylah. There is right and wrong and honor and disgrace, until it comes to her. Then there is only her. There's nothing I wouldn't do, nothing I wouldn't endure or sacrifice for her."

Amjad held up his hands. "Hey, I'm not the one you should swing that sales pitch at. *I* believe you. It takes one colossal fool for love to know another. I almost alienated Maram forever, too. Good news is, those women of ours love once and all the way, no matter what. Yeah, Maram told me as much, after she nearly killed me, before taking me back. So even if you think your world is over and Laylah lost to you forever, if you grovel creatively enough, strip yourself to the bone until there's not much left, she'll relent, fish you out of hell and dunk you back in paradise."

Amjad's assurances did nothing to dispel Rashid's despair.

"Maram discovered you used her to get the Pride of Zohayd jewels back. But your goal looked noble, as the conspiracy could have resulted in war. Laylah discovered I planned our engagement to become king, which looks purely self-serving. And while you kidnapped Maram under the pretext of a sandstorm, Laylah believes I approached her under the pretext of a kidnapping attempt."

Amjad scowled. "Okay, that's where you not only lose all my sympathy, it's where I might have you thrown in the dungeon. I might even let you sit on that throne just to squash you on it."

"If you think me capable of something like that, feel free to treat me like the criminal it would make me."

After a contemplative second, Amjad waved. "Nah. One thing I'm infallible at is reading people. Especially men. You have some terminally honorable syndrome, wouldn't scare any woman like that, not even for a throne. So, where did she get the idea?"

"Hasn't she already told you everything?" he gritted.

"She informed us the wedding was off, wouldn't be persuaded to say why, adding only that she never wanted to see you again."

This bewildered him. "She said she would stop me from becoming king. I thought she would tell you what she believes happened, ending any chance of an alliance between us. Why didn't she carry out her threat?"

Amjad's lips twisted. "See? A sign that she still cares."

"I know how much she cares—*cared*. Her agony and disillusion now is as absolute."

"Yeah, I know." At his exasperated growl, Amjad tsked. "Seems I'm going to have a perpetually pissed off lion for an ally."

"You won't have *anything* if you keep condescending to me."

"No condescension. *This* time. I told you, been there, done that, with Maram." Amjad grinned. "Tell you what. I'll work on Laylah. I'll exasperate her until she has to talk to you again."

The hope that Laylah might speak to him again caused Rashid's throat to almost close. "You'd do that for me?"

"Yep. I'm magnanimous like that."

"You get her to speak to me again, Amjad, and I'll hand you my neck on the end of a leash."

Amjad winked at him. "*That's* how I like my allies. Done."

Then with one more smirk, Amjad turned and walked away.

Rashid watched him leave, thoughts of tearing through the palace looking for Laylah roiling like thunderclouds through his mind.

But what would he do when he found her? She was no longer his Laylah, but the woman who'd told him no one had hurt or degraded her like he had. What could he do to atone?

Before he could make a move, Haidar and Jalal exploded through the palace doors. He watched them stride toward him, their steps and expressions laden with fury.

Haidar almost slammed into him, did punch him in the chest. "You lied to me."

Jalal wrenched him around. "You did plan to use her to get the throne, didn't you?"

Haidar jerked him back. "And you're here looking like a madman, to what? Beg for Amjad to *still* endorse you for the throne of Azmahar? Yeah, we know he thinks you're the number one candidate. That weasel. But he turned out to be a stupid one. You had even him fooled."

Rashid shoved the twins away. "You two and the throne can go to hell. I'd send you all there if I had time for you. But I don't."

He stormed away. Haidar and Jalal caught up with him on the first floor, dragged him into an empty meeting room.

"You're not walking away from us again," Haidar hissed.

"We're getting everything out in the open once and for all." Jalal turned from closing the door. "And I mean *everything*."

Images of cutting them both down where they stood, something he could do in his sleep, deluged his mind.

Suppressing the mindless aggression with the last tatters of control, he glared at them. "You're still pretending you don't know why I hate you? You're still trying to slither your way out of any responsibility, you sons of a serpent?"

"Shut up, you exasperating son of a..." Haidar jerked his shoulders uneasily. "I have no idea what your mother was, but I sure as hell won't call her names so I can insult *you*."

"Calling your mother a serpent is a terrible insult—" he bit off "—to the worst human snake who ever lived. But you want my version of what happened? So you can have a complete picture? Fine."

And with four years' worth of anger and agony and betrayal churning up his insides, he told them.

As they gaped at him throughout his account, one thing became indisputable. They *hadn't* known.

They'd had no hand in what had been done to him.

He'd lived for years poisoned by the belief that they'd brutally betrayed him, for nothing.

Finally, a shell-shocked Haidar said, "*Ya Ullah ya* Rashid— you spent all these years thinking we did that to you? And we're still in one piece?"

Jalal, seeming as stunned, nodded. "That's what I'm wondering, too. That you believed what you did, and only tried to destroy us in business, gives me a whole new insight into your character. You must be part saint."

Rashid couldn't bear another word. "I don't care about what happened or who did it or why anymore. I only care about Laylah."

Haidar approached him tentatively. "But if you tell her what you just told us, she'd—"

"No." His shout went off like a gunshot. "She will *never* hear anything about this. I'm not getting her back at this price."

Jalal approached from the other side, as if helping his twin contain the volatile quantity that was Rashid. "It might be the only price that's good enough, Rashid."

"I said *no*. And if you tell her, I will stop at nothing this time to punish you for breaching my confidence."

Haidar ventured a hand on his shoulder. "Settle down, will you? We won't say a thing." He squeezed his eyes. "*Ya Ullah*—what I really want is to wipe everything you said from my mind. But then, a mental scar is nothing compared to what you suffered."

Any other time, Rashid might have felt relief that the scar of losing them would heal, that he could have them back in his life and heart. But now that he no longer had Laylah there, nothing meant anything.

Haidar leveled his gaze on Rashid, anguish and regret gripping his face. "I can't tell you how powerless I feel that I can neither change the past nor punish the culprits. But I will put this right if it takes the rest of my life. You're my other twin, Rashid, and I've been…bereft all these years without you. I swear to you, we'll make up for lost time."

Jalal joined his twin in his pledge. "That goes for me, too. But you're right, Rashid. What matters now is Laylah. I swear to you, we'll do everything to reunite you with her."

Everything hadn't been enough.

It had now been eighteen days in a hell worse than anything he'd known, sinking deeper in the quicksand of Laylah's rejection.

Amjad had given him quarters close to hers so he could "stalk" her, or they'd do a "pincer" on her, with everyone herding her toward him until she was forced to confront him.

She didn't. She'd let them push her to within inches of him, only to pass him by as if he didn't exist. A punishment for his present transgressions and past avoidance. Feeling nonexistent to her, no matter if it was on purpose, was excruciating.

So he'd written his confessions in what had amounted to a small volume, which had been fated to the bin.

And he'd been forced to do what he'd thought impossible.

He'd poured his heart out to anyone who'd listen. That ultimate exposure *had* felt like he'd "stripped himself down to the bone" as Amjad had said. Not that it had any effect.

She'd treated the explanations everyone transmitted with the same disdain she had his written ones. She'd had to grudgingly believe he hadn't orchestrated the attack on her, under the deluge of proof he'd provided. But she believed his withdrawal from the race for the throne to be another convoluted plan to gain more sympathy and strengthen his position.

He'd hit rock bottom when he'd realized how completely she'd lost her faith in him.

"There is no line you won't cross, is there?"

His whole being seized in shock. In delight. Laylah. Here. His heart boomed so hard it swung him around to her.

"Laylah…"

She was closing the suite's door and turning to him, indescribable in a floor-length silk turquoise dress that offset the perfection of every inch of skin it didn't cover, intensified the burnished gloss of her hair.

Brutal longing paralyzed him as she stopped two feet away, her eyes those of a stranger.

"It was almost embarrassing, watching how far you went in 'exposing' your 'inner self' in your damage-control efforts. But what really surprises me is how totally you've taken my family in. I thought they, especially Amjad, were shrewd. I guess no one is immune to your powers of emotional manipulation."

"They are shrewd people," he rasped. "That's why they recognize my sincerity against all damning evidence."

Her laugh was mirthless. "You know, I was delusional to think someone with your life experiences had any emotions left. Logically, you can't be faulted for that. The first thing you must have learned in order to deal with your personal situation, then your life as a soldier, was to turn off your emotions. It only makes sense that you feel nothing but ambition and hunger for power now."

He reached an aching hand to the thick lock of hair undulating over her breast. "If only that was true."

She stepped away, making the silk slip through his fingers just as she kept doing. "Please, stop the pretense. I'm not angry at you anymore." She wasn't? "Actually, most of my anger was directed at myself. For believing what I so fiercely wanted to believe. Nothing you did ever added up, but I was so desperate for you, I silenced my disbelief that you could fall for me at all, let alone that fast, that you'd tie yourself to me for life. Disillusion and damage were the only possible outcome for my stupidity."

He took her by the shoulders, wouldn't let her shake him off this time, his grip gentling until she let him hold her.

"Laylah, you have to listen to me. Not so that I can beg your forgiveness or exonerate myself. You need to listen for *you*. What pains me most is that this has reinforced your belief that no one has ever wanted you for you, when the reverse is true. You are valued and loved by everyone who knows you. You are worshipped by me. Even if you choose to never forgive me, please be secure in that, and that my crimes are a reflection on me, never on you."

For a long moment, as the setting sun struck russet in eyes that gazed at him as if realizing something profound, he started to hope that at least he'd succeeded in this endeavor.

Then they filled with cool disdain as she removed his hands with utmost tranquility. "That's your latest strategy? Feed my need for validation and heal my fractured self-image? Sorry, but I've beaten you to it. I've come to terms with the fact that my worth has nothing to do with how others see it, starting with my parents and ending with the queue of men like you. *I* value me. If others don't, no matter who they are, screw them."

"I'll do anything to solidify your certainty. Ask for the impossible, impose any punishment…"

"It's me who'll be punished. When I marry you."

Was his mind disintegrating at last? He'd thought he heard her say…

"I've already told my family that the wedding is on again."

He could only stare at her.

"I'm pregnant."

Power drained from his body, coherence from his mind, beats from his heart.

The wall suddenly slammed into his back. He'd staggered under the blow of shock. Of joy. And grief. At the way she'd said it. As if it was the worst thing that had ever happened to her.

"Laylah, *habibati*..."

She warded off his embrace. "I'm not sharing the happy news with my adoring groom, I'm informing my ingenious manipulator that your plan has worked to the last detail."

"It was *not* a plan—"

"I don't care what you call it. But you were not only right in predicting the outcome of me 'shredding your ironclad control,' but in anticipating what I'd do, even if I discovered your plot prematurely. You knew me well enough to realize that even if I kept saying I don't care about my family, I do. Even if I don't care about tradition, they do. Especially when it comes to legitimacy. I won't impose illegitimacy on my baby, when there's a father so eager to put his claim on it, even for all the wrong reasons."

Could he have destroyed her love so absolutely he'd become so unredeemable in her eyes?

Her cold stare said he had and was. "Go ahead, Rashid, don't struggle to keep a straight face. Your charade is out in the open and it won't hurt your agenda anymore to celebrate your success. An Aal Shalaan blood bond, and after the masterful lovelorn, honorable knight act you plied my family with, a sure path to the throne of Azmahar. If the baby turns out to be male—and I bet it will, since you seem to will fate to obey you—you'll even get the heir you need right away."

"None of this has any truth to it anymore."

"The only truth here is that history is repeating itself. I was the result of a toxic marriage of convenience and I swore no child of mine would ever suffer anything like that. And here I am, repeating my parents' terrible pattern. But I'll be damned if I'll live a life filled with hostility and resentment. I'll play into your hands willingly. I will give you the one thing you wanted from me and suffer through this wedding, *only* so that it will legitimize the baby in our society's eyes. This ordeal will assure that our baby gets all its rights from you, no matter what happens, so after we announce my pregnancy and convince people the baby was conceived within wedlock, this travesty of a marriage ends."

Leaving him suffocating on her rejection again, she turned and walked away. The need to rush after her, catch her back, kiss her and melt her almost had him roaring.

Two things held him back. Knowing that he could swear and beg and produce a thousand proofs, and she'd remain immovably distant and irretrievably injured.

And that in spite of everything, she was going to marry him.

That she would, for any reason, was a miracle. That she carried his child was beyond imagining.

This cold, finite arrangement she'd made was still more than he'd dreamed he would have.

It was another chance.

Fourteen

"Have I told you lately how much I hate you?"

Laylah gazed at Aliyah, her cousin and that third precious Aal Shalaan female. Aliyah was scowling at her after wheeling in a hanger teeming with wedding dresses for Laylah to try on.

Laylah sighed. "In the last hour? No."

The other women in the room chuckled. The wives of her cousins had all been recruited for the emergency wedding preparations. It was surreal to be home among so many women, with whom she had so much in common, from age to education to temperament.

There was one thing, however, she didn't share with them. They all had the unequivocal love of their men, and they all ranged from being ecstatically pregnant to delighted mothers many times over.

Johara, whom Laylah had helped prepare for her wedding to her cousin Shaheen almost three years ago, grinned. "Give it up, Aliyah. Every time we say we're never going to put together a royal wedding on short notice again, we end up with even less time in which to do it. Maybe next time we should say we'll do it in hours, and we'll end up with months on our hands?"

The women looked among themselves then snorted a collective, *"Nah."*

Roxanne, Haidar's wife, chuckled. "Those men of ours end up crowding us for time no matter what we do."

Lujayn, Jalal's wife and the most recent bride, though she had a two-year-old with Jalal, raised an eyebrow at Laylah. "But for a change it was Laylah who squeezed us for time."

"Two days is not a squeeze," Aliyah lamented. "It's cruel."

Maram laughed. "Talk about leaving it to the last moment, then wham." She gave Laylah a shrewd look. "Don't get me wrong, I'm all for making those impossible and impossibly luscious men sweat it. It can only do their overriding souls good. But you *could* have given *us* some advance notice so we could restart preparations discretely while he stewed—as he needed to."

Laylah sighed, deciding to come clean. "I couldn't really. Strictly between us please, ladies, but the pink strip only appeared yesterday."

Gasps of delight echoed around her room, followed by cooing, if uncomfortable, congratulations. They could see she wasn't happy about the pregnancy, that it made necessary a marriage she didn't want.

All of the ladies had been in varied positions of reluctance during their weddings, too. But the problems and misunderstandings in their relationships had been resolved. Hers wouldn't be.

From then on, the women did all they could to reinstate the cheerfulness of the proceedings and lift her spirits.

She cooperated, pretended interest as they talked color coordination, bridal procession dresses and table trimmings. She kept up her pretense until they took her around the royal palace of Azmahar, deciding decorations.

Knowing this place, and the power it signified, was what Rashid really wanted and not her was suffocating, literally, and the world started to fade. Cries rang out in the dimness before everything turned to black.

Exiting a dark tunnel filled with sounds of distress, Laylah opened her eyes to see beautiful faces coated with concern.

She'd fainted. And the ladies had taken her back to her room.

"How are you feeling now, Laylah?" Maram asked, her voice soft and soothing as she continued to massage her hands.

Laylah tried to sit up, found Johara and Aliyah helping her. "I'm fine. Sorry for that."

"That first trimester can be a pain," Roxanne said, shuddering, no doubt remembering her own. "Good news is, you'll feel the best you ever did during the second one."

Not wanting to inform them her fainting spell had nothing to do with her pregnancy, she went along. "Can't wait."

"Wait until you see what we came back to the room to find!" Lujayn exclaimed as she rushed away.

Laylah's eyes widened as she saw what she came back holding.

Johara sighed. "You remember when Shaheen did this for me? Rashid, even though you're not ready to forgive him yet, is certainly as thoughtful and his choice is as perfect for you as Shaheen's was for me."

Laylah gaped at Rashid's "choice." A creation the likes of which she'd never imagined.

A one-piece Arabian/Indian masterpiece, it had a sleeveless bodice that nipped to a waist she was certain was the exact size of hers, with a décolleté that would emphasize her breasts and expose her neck and most of her shoulders and any necklace she would wear. With its base a golden mahogany the exact color of her hair and eyes, it was almost covered in breathtaking hand-embroidery of sequins, beads, pearls, crystals, semi-precious stones and appliqué, from the lightest coral to the deepest vermillion to the most vivid crimson, all intertwined with gold.

A skirt in hues echoing the top's embroidery cascaded in multiple layers of tulle and chiffon over a shimmering mahogany silk taffeta lining, its embellishments in the range of gold and russet, with ingenious scalloping at the hemline. A veil with heavily embellished borders was crimson where it would rest on her hair, gradually transforming to a luminescent golden-brown where it would trail on the floor.

But it was the patterns covering the whole outfit that robbed her of breath again. Those of Rashid's house.

It was as if he was…putting his *brand* on her with that dress, just like he had branded her body and soul.

The ladies interrupted her heavy-hearted musings, clamoring for her to try on the outfit at once. Just as she'd expected, it fit her perfectly. Rashid always knew exactly what he wanted, down to the last detail.

As Maram and Aliyah contacted their husbands to demand jewelry that would match the outfit, from Zohayd's and Judar's royal collections no less, Laylah watched the other ladies flipping through catalogues to pick their complementary dresses, and wondered.

If she felt this terrible just preparing for this farce, how would she feel on the day itself?

The day was here. The *minute* she had to marry Rashid. And not really marry him.

The distinctive percussive music of her *zaffah*—her bridal procession—was already reverberating through the palace. Hundreds of voices were raised in the traditional congratulatory songs.

Aliyah and Maram were adorning her neck, arms and head in legendary jewels while Johara, Talia, Roxanne and Lujayn fussed with her veil, hairdo and makeup. They all looked stunning with their glowing beauty and bright spirits, their lithe bodies wrapped in sarilike dresses as exquisite as they were, in reds and golds to complement her own gown.

She almost didn't recognize the splendid creature staring back at her in the mirror.

Rashid knew just how to package the royal acquisition he'd flaunt to the world tonight. The last piece in his master plan.

Her heavy-hearted musings halted as everyone rushed her out to lead her procession to the ballroom where the ceremonies were to be held. She hadn't seen any of the preparations as she'd been holed up in her quarters for the past two days. Now she felt she had entered a fantasy setting from Arabian Nights.

Brass lanterns and torches blazed everywhere, infusing the palace with a mystic ambiance. Every other decoration, from banners to veils to flowers, was color-coordinated with her gown and jewelry. Not that she could find any pleasure in her surroundings. Not when she couldn't forget why Rashid had "rented" the palace for their wedding. Not so that she could reclaim that part of her heritage, as he'd claimed, but so he could rehearse being its liege.

Even in her previous obliviousness, it had pained her knowing so much would be missing on this day—her mother there for her, her father giving her away. Now she knew her groom didn't really want to receive her, and this wedding was a charade, a sacrifice of her heart and dignity for the one thing that would mean more to her than her very life—her child...

Suddenly, her heartbeat drowned out the thundering music, and air, the world, disappeared.

Rashid stood alone at the wide-open gilded doors of the ballroom, shrouded in shadow even in the blazing illumination, as if he'd absorbed all light.

In spite of herself, her starving senses rushed to devour his grandeur.

His outfit matched hers, only in darker, muted shades. Another detail he'd orchestrated to perfection. A mahogany *abaya* hugged his Herculean shoulders, adorned in embroidery echoing her gown's patterns, before cascading to his ankles like a cloak of enchantment. Underneath, burnt-sienna silk stretched across his formidable chest and abdomen, tucking into skin-tight same-color pants that gathered into darkest brown leather boots. A bronze metal belt hung around his powerful hips, anchoring a ceremonial dagger sheathed in a scabbard worked in bloodred and gold enamel.

This was a man whose legacy was rooted in fables, the embodiment of this harsh, magnificent land, a personification of its might and majesty, a shaper of the world around him.

He *was* born to be king.

If only he hadn't used her to claim his destiny.

If only he'd come clean. She would have done anything for him. Would have still had her heart and illusions intact.

But he hadn't. And she now only survived for their...*her* baby.

He stood there now, with those darkest-night eyes, searing her with his fake longing, his counterfeit entreaty.

"Laylah..."

The pure passion and anguish he made of her name nullified the din, quivered through her bones. How could it feel so real? How could she still want to throw herself into his arms?

Then those arms were coming around her. Feeling they'd singe her, she bolted. He let her stride ahead down the royal-red carpet that cut through the ballroom all the way to the *kooshah.* Intertwining gradations of red and gold chiffon veils undulated from Arabesque woodwork that embodied the gilded cage of matrimony, she guessed. He was beside her once more as she climbed a dozen crimson satin-covered steps to where they'd preside over the proceedings.

The *ma'zoon,* an imposing-looking cleric, was sitting in the middle of a pale gold sofa, with scrolls spread before him in triplicate. Haidar and Jalal flanked the sofa like bodyguards.

They would be *al shohood,* the witnesses of the marriage. She didn't know how Rashid had gotten them to consent to this, let alone to plead his case with her, when they'd been mortal enemies till recently. But she wouldn't put anything beyond his powers of manipulation. She'd refused her uncle's and cousins' offers to be her *wakeel,* her proxy. She wouldn't let them take a bigger part in this sham. She'd gotten herself into this, and she'd shoulder the sticky parts to the end alone.

As soon as they reached the platform, the music stopped. Almost plopping down beside the *ma'zoon,* desperate to look anywhere but at Rashid, her gaze swept the ballroom, where a hundred tables were set in the luxury level only someone of Rashid's means could attain. Around them sat a thousand of those who moved and shook the world. That was the kind of power Rashid wielded already. He probably wouldn't wield more as king.

Then he was leaning nearer behind the *ma'zoon.* She pre-empted him. "Shall we get this over with already?"

After failing to capture her gaze, Rashid exhaled, directed the *ma'zoon* to proceed.

After a while, he murmured, "*Habibati,* give me your hand."

Her gut wrenched. Her hand in his for the duration of the ritual was bad enough. But it was that *habibati* that scraped her nerves raw. Who was he still acting for?

She gave him a hand as stiff and cold as a corpse's, and tried not to flinch as that big, calloused hand that had taught her what passion and pleasure meant enfolded it. She kept her eyes fixed as he opposed their thumbs and the *ma'zoon* covered their hands in a pristine white handkerchief and placed his on top, then as she droned back the marriage vows the man recited.

After Rashid had, too, the *ma'zoon* addressed him, "Name your *mahr* and *mo'akh'khar al suddaag,* Sheikh Rashid."

The so-called "price of the bride," or as revisionists called it, the "bride's worth." That was paid in two installments. The *mahr,* at signing the contract, and the *mo'akh'khar,* "latter portion of the agreed-upon"—or in reality a severance payment—at termination of the marriage.

"My *mahr* is this." Rashid produced a box, gave it to her.

She took the scarlet velvet box, opened it.

A simple gold brooch lay against darkest red satin. Another rendering of his house's emblem. Very precise and delicate but by no means worth much in terms of cash value.

"It was my mother's." Rashid's voice numbed her with its fathomless magic. "It was my earliest memory. I was four when she told me it was my father's first gift to her. He was only eighteen when he bought it with his first pay. I slipped into her room the night she died. I kicked and screamed, but they wouldn't let me see her. All I could do was grab something of hers as they dragged me out of her room. It was this brooch. It is all I have left of her. It is the one possession I care about. Just as you are the one person, the one thing, I care about in this life."

"You…bastard."

The *ma'zoon* started at her viciousness.

Rashid's eyes only gentled. "Call me anything, think me a monster, but *arjooki ya roh galbi,* don't make it final. Leave the door ajar. Please, Laylah, take this."

When she only glared at him, her blood boiling, her heart splintering, he took out the brooch, and with trembling hands, he pinned it over her heart. It felt as if he'd pierced it.

Fighting the urge to rip it off and hurl it away, she didn't give him the satisfaction. At any emotional display, he'd only soothe her, appear as the loving, forbearing groom even more.

She glared at him as he signaled to Haidar and Jalal. "And my *mo'akh'khar* is this."

Haidar handed the *ma'zoon* a thick dossier. He opened it, read the first page before raising stupefied eyes to Rashid.

"Do I understand this correctly, Sheikh Rashid?"

Rashid nodded. "Yes. That is all my assets."

She gaped at him.

Then she finally asked, "What are you playing at now?"

"I never played at anything to start with, *ya habibati.* I am all yours, heart and soul. My assets are the least part of me."

"And I don't want them, like I don't want any part of you."

Rashid only exhaled, turned to the *ma'zoon.* "Document this."

The man did as asked, and an oppressive silence descended on them all. Then he invited her and Rashid to sign the three copies, and for Haidar and Jalal to stamp them with their seals.

On leaving the *kooshah,* the *ma'zoon* shot her a puzzled, disapproving glance. Haidar and Jalal gave her an entreating one. On Rashid's behalf. He *had* put them back in his pocket again.

The guests rose as one, toasted them with glasses filled with ruby-red *sharbaat ward,* rose-essence traditional wedding nectar.

As everyone resumed sitting, live Azmahrian music rose with their chatter, leaving bride and groom to their own conversation.

Talking with Rashid had once been all she'd wanted from life, something she'd reveled in and treasured until a few weeks ago. Now, she had nothing to say to him that wasn't bitter. She was done with bitterness. Which meant she wouldn't talk to him.

Suddenly she felt as if her left side had been set on fire. Rashid had slid across the sofa, almost touching her.

He met her cold glance with his soft and coaxing one. "You will have to talk to me at some point. Might as well start now."

She ignored him, pretended to wave to her *waseefat,* matrons of honor. They only shooed her away, urging her to respond to Rashid.

Fuming, she reached for her *sharbaat* and felt she'd touched a live wire. His hand. He'd beat her to the crystal glass.

When she wouldn't take it, he whispered, "Throw it in my face. I deserve far more for even considering my moronic plan."

Refusing to give him the outburst he was after, she took the glass, downed it, still not looking at him.

"Anger makes you thirsty? But this will only dehydrate you more. Also a sugar rush combined with adrenaline isn't advisable."

So. He'd given up the fiercely tender facade and was trying on the bedeviling one. She said nothing.

"That degree of self-control is admirable. I wonder—would it hold if I kissed you?" At her continued silence, he slipped an arm around her waist. "Shall we find out?"

Staring ahead, she said, "Being funny doesn't suit you."

"Talk to me, and I'll spare you my failed attempts at humor."

She flicked him a condescending glance. "You need your high-ranking guests to think we're having a great time? Afraid they'd realize your bride is sitting here under duress?"

"I care nothing about what anyone thinks. Test my claim."

"You're counting that I won't, so I won't upset my family."

His response got drowned out by the first part of the night's entertainment, an ingeniously choreographed and composed medley of beloved folk songs and dances.

As the guests were swept up in the energy of the performance, he pulled her closer. "Those songs are all for you."

She slid him a cool glance. "Thanks."

Tenderness filled his eyes again, poignancy, too. "Even if you say it's not real, I'm now your husband..."

"Only for a while, until the baby is born, max."

The indulgence in his eyes flooded her. "That's seven months from now. Remember what once happened in seven hours?"

"When I was a needy, self-deceiving twit? In vivid detail. What do you think the odds are of my falling for your manipulations again?"

"Beating impossible odds is what I do. I've triumphed over death many times. I'm going to conquer your aversion, even if it takes the rest of my life."

"It *will* take the rest of your life. Plus an hour."

His arm tightened around her. "Take the pound of flesh I owe you, *ya habibati.* Take as many pounds as you wish. Do it here and now." The feel of him against her, his consecutive blows of passion, entreaty and tenderness were chipping away at her control. "I dare you."

She pulled away as a storm of applause greeted the end of the performance, then rose to her feet.

Everyone turned to look at her as she came to stand at the edge of the *kooshah.* "Now to another time-honored tradition that no celebration in our region is complete without. Poetry."

A buzz rose. Her family consulted with each other if that was an arranged number.

"An ode to my new and loving groom," she started, perfect acoustics carrying her voice to the farthest corners of the ballroom.

"Howah kat'tamaseeh, yathreffod' dam'a enda muddgh fareesatuhu

Fahtaresu menhu i'tha arradto'l najjata

La ya'ghorannakom jamala mohayahu

Fama ajmal'l nomoor lakn korbuha ho'wal mammata."

(Like crocodiles he sheds tears when he gnaws his prey

So beware of him if you want to stay alive

Don't be fooled by the beauty of his visage

For how beautiful are tigers you'd never survive.)

Her quatrain was greeted by a shockwave of silence.

Suddenly a whistle pierced the hush, followed by a single pair of lazily clapping hands.

"Thank you, cousin. I was about to provoke an international incident to avoid watching another folklore number."

That was Amjad. Of course.

She couldn't pay him or anyone else attention. Rashid had gotten up to his feet, was approaching her like that stealthy predator she'd just likened him to.

He came to tower over her, his eyes the embodiment of adoration as he raised his voice. "An ode to the barren past when I could only look at my incomparable bride from afar:

Amorro ala'd dyari, dyari Laylah

Oqubbelo tha'l jeddara waa tha'l jeddari

Wama hobbo'l dyari shagafna qulbi,

Walaken hobbo man sakanna'd dyari."

(I pass by those dwellings, those of Laylah.

And I kiss these walls and those walls

It's not love of the place that has taken my heart

But of the One who dwelled in these halls.)

Silence again blanketed the vastness, raging inside her.

Instead of a defense, or an offense, he'd hit her with a quatrain from Qays Ibn Al Mulawah's poetry, the ancient poet renowned as *Majnun* Laylah, or Laylah's Madman.

And he'd used Qays's verses to claim he'd only loved and valued this palace and Zohayd's for her being in them.

Wow. Who would have thought he'd have poetry in his arsenal. But then as an ultimate tactician, he must have an infinite range of weapons. Seemed even now she hadn't realized the scope of his talent for subterfuge.

Before she could think of another unmasking verse, he went down before her on his knees. A collective gasp spread like wildfire around the ballroom. Everything inside her malfunctioned.

Looking exactly like the man she'd thought loved her with all his heart, he took her hands to his lips then, in a now ragged voice, recited the verses.

She gaped down at him long after he'd finished.

In lyrical Arabic, even more moving and exquisite than the famous verses, he'd said:

The bounty that you have given me, strip it not away
The generosity you have shown me, tear it not away
My ugly acts that you came to know, forgive them
I seek intercession from you with you
And I seek sanctuary in you from you
I come to you craving your beneficence
So act toward me with the mercy of which you are worthy
For I am not worthy of your vengeance.

She tried to breathe, failed yet again.

Had—had he just composed *that* on the spot?

He had insta-poetry among his powers of enthrallment?

"*Aaand* since nothing in this suddenly entertaining and memorable evening will top *that,* I suggest we eat."

Amjad again. And naturally, he had everyone following his lead, clapping a rising wave of approval at the unique verbal duel they'd witnessed between bride and groom.

Laylah tore her gaze from Rashid, still kneeling before her, bolted down the steps, and completed the evening's fireworks by running out of her own wedding.

She wanted to keep on running until she left everything be-hind, starting with her heart.

Running after Laylah had been out of the question. He'd al-ready pushed too soon and had only driven her away further.

He'd followed her out of the ballroom, but not to pursue her. He left it to Haidar and Jalal to say whatever they pleased to the guests. He cared nothing about the guests continuing a wedding without the bride and groom when it seemed he was destined to continue his life without Laylah.

Night had deepened by the time he'd reached the seaside villa where she'd once told him she loved him, and which he'd bought for her, for them. He'd sell it in the morning. He couldn't stay here without her. And she wouldn't take it.

He walked across the veranda of the master bedroom suite to the balustrade, lost in thoughts as tumultuous as the sea. He…

"I've made a decision."

His every hair stood on end. *Laylah.*

He swung around to her, his heart thudding in disbelief. She was the last person he'd expected to see here, tonight, or ever.

She'd taken off the wedding gown he'd had made for her, and was in one of those flowing dresses she'd been wearing since they'd come back to the region. It looked as if it were weaved from moonlight. *She* was made of his every dream and was so…missed, he swayed where he stood with the sheer intensity of longing.

Her approach continued until she was flush against him.

His whole being, body and soul, surged at the feel of her. Confusion then hope were as overwhelming as his response. Was she…?

Her hand curled around his nape, brought his head down to hers. Before she took his lips in the kiss he'd been dying for, she ended all confusion. And hope.

She said, "Like you used me, took your pleasure when you felt nothing, I'll use you as cold-bloodedly, for my pleasure."

Fifteen

Her cold words doused the heat of her embrace.

He jerked back. "You can't mean that."

"I do." Her lips opened on his scar, what she'd turned into the trigger of his every uncontrollable desire. "You're fantastic in bed, and you are the man in my life—for now. I'll take my pleasure from you. As is my right."

He tried to hold her off, to hold back from snatching her. "You have every right to everything in me."

Her teeth nipped his chin. "I want nothing else from you."

"But I do. I want your love, your trust."

It was she who pulled away this time. "Sex is all I can give you. Ask for more, and I'll walk out, and you will see me only from afar until it's time to end the marriage."

It was in her face. She meant it.

If he said no, he'd lose her now, not later.

But if he said yes, he might still have a chance. He might still melt her in the inferno of their passion.

There was no choice really. A beggar had none.

Exhaling his defeat, he swept her up in his arms.

As soon as he put her down on the ground by the bed she charged him, climbed him, wrapped herself around him. His senses blazed with her hunger, his heart crumbled now she'd stormed out of it.

He tried to lower her to the bed, but she twisted in his arms, made him change direction, take her on top.

He watched her sweep off her loose dress, ablaze with exquisiteness, revealing another of those mind-messing creations he'd chosen for her in such intense pleasure and anticipation, the scarlet emphasizing the magic of her coloring and worshipping the perfections of her lushness. His hands trembled over her soft stomach where the miracle of their passion was growing, delight and dejection almost rupturing his heart.

Praying she'd reclaim him from the wasteland of her alienation, he opened himself to her possession, let her devour him and dominate him, drowning in her desire as she exposed him to its full measure, even as she withheld the spiritual part he needed most, was withering without. She ignited fever all over him until she claimed the manhood that been created to mesh them together, to give her pleasure.

Thrusting his hips to her ravenous rhythm, sinking deeper into her hunger, his hands shook all over her, his body and heart in her power. After a lifetime of sufficiency and restraint, his dependence on her was devastating, yet vital.

Her fingers dug into his buttocks, demanding his full surrender, what he'd learned to give her. His hand convulsed in her hair as his loins exploded, as she drained him, yet only left him crazed for more, for her.

He tried to snatch her up to his heart, but she took him over again, straddling him, her eyes as mindless as he felt with the need to merge. "I want you, Rashid."

"*Aih, ya hayati kollaha,* my whole life, want me." He helped her position him at her entrance. "Take all of me…"

She took him in one downward stroke.

A whiteout of sensation blinded him as her scorching core engulfed him, his home inside her. His only home.

Senses reignited when he'd forged all the way inside her, felt her shuddering all over him, inside and out, his name a litany of moans on her lips.

He knew how she felt, frenzied, as he rose with her impaled on him, leaned against the wall, spread her buttocks in his palms.

"Ride me, *ya rohi*. Take me and take your pleasure of me."

Hands bracing against his shoulders, thighs trembling, she slid up half his shaft when he engulfed one nipple in his mouth. Her hands slipped off his shoulders, had her crashing down on him, lodging him at her womb, her wail of stimulation tearing through both of them. "Rashid...do it..."

He obeyed, holding her hips and moving her up and down his length to the rhythm of his suckling and confessions. "Do you feel what you're doing to me? I never dreamed pleasure like this existed..."

Her fingers dug into his flesh, for breaching the sex-only stipulation. But he had to try to reconnect with her.

He rolled her around, slid up her moist, silken flesh, stretched her farther around his invasion, fighting to hold back the impending avalanche.

Throbbing in her depths, he rose above her. "Heaven would be nothing compared to being inside you." Her teeth sank in his scar, punishing him. His head pitched back on the excruciating pleasure. "*Aih,* Laylah, punish me and take me back—all of me."

At his plunge all the way into her, she shrieked, her inner muscles squeezing his length in a fit of release. He rode the breakers of her orgasm in a fury, surrendering to the pleasure he'd only ever known with her, jetting his essence into her milking depths, swearing his love as swell after swell of agonized completion swept him. "*Atawassal elaiki suddegeeni—ahebbek, a'ashagek*...I beg you believe me, I love you, worship you. I never loved anyone but you, never lied about this."

She went limp beneath him.

Unreasoning fears crashed on him. He might have been too aggressive, hurt her, the baby...

He tore himself from her clinging depths. "Laylah…"

Her eyes were open and empty. Dread overcame him, until she suddenly moved, removing herself from his frantic grip.

Her voice was as lifeless as her gaze. "I'm only serving my purpose to you. You're serving yours to me now, so it's a fair deal. But if you don't stop saying you love me, I will stop being with you at all."

Unable to look her rejection in the eyes anymore, he rose off the bed, needing to seek refuge anywhere but where she was.

Before he exited the room, he turned to her, announced his submission to her sentence. "I'll agree to anything you want."

What Laylah wanted amounted to hell on earth.

The next weeks set the pattern. She wouldn't let him into her life in any form. Not during the day. At night, she drew him back into the vortex of need. Even with her emotional coldness, their physical passion blazed out of control, scorching his body in satisfaction, and his soul in sorrow.

He'd reached the point where he knew. Though he'd take anything he could have of her at the price of his own destruction, he couldn't.

He'd soon be forced to end this.

"I'm now forced to make a decision."

Amjad sounded serious. For a second. Then he wiggled his eyebrows at Laylah, Haidar and Jalal where they sat side by side in his office. He'd summoned them urgently an hour ago and had refused to say anything until they were all there and sitting before him like an audience.

Amjad went on, "But then I'm the only one qualified to make one around this region."

Haidar, who sat beside Laylah with Jalal on her other side, huffed. "Spare us, Amjad."

"How can I? You can't live without my harassment." Amjad turned his smirk on her. "But I lied. I've long made my decision. It's in your court now, Laylah."

He wanted her to pass her verdict. On Rashid.

Though he'd made his, if she let her personal turmoil dictate an unfair one, he'd obey it.

It was up to her to deprive Rashid of becoming king.

But she'd never been vindictive this way, not even toward her worst enemy. And Rashid wasn't even… Was—was… Whatever he was, it had been heartache talking when she'd threatened that. Even at the height of her agony, even now as she felt her time with him ticking away, her belief in Rashid as the best king never wavered.

"Sorry, guys." She winced at Haidar and Jalal. "But I do believe he's the best man for the job."

"Our Aal Shalaan treasure has spoken." Amjad's sardonic smile grew dissecting. "So…is this your revenge? Pushing him onto the throne you believe he manipulated you to get, when you know you're only shoving him into a pit of thorns?"

Her lips trembled. "You seem to be quite comfy on yours."

"Only because I have Maram on my lap. Rashid no longer has you." So he knew how things remained between her and Rashid. Everyone probably did. Amjad's gaze bored into her. "Sitting on that throne without you will be agony without the ecstasy."

Her heart twisted. "Rashid is nothing like you. He doesn't need anyone."

Amjad huffed. "Did I ever look like I needed anyone? Turns out I do need one person. Maram. Like Rashid needs you."

How she wished that were true.

She rose before the tears that lurked a word away escaped. "I gave you my opinion. It's your decision now who to back."

Amjad had backed Rashid.

Haidar and Jalal, to Laylah's surprise yet again, endorsed his decision wholeheartedly.

Rashid would be king of Azmahar.

His *joloos,* sitting on the throne, was in two days.

This had been what he'd wanted so fiercely. What he deserved. What would he do now that he'd gotten it?

She was giving herself a nervous breakdown wondering when he walked into the suite in his house where he'd left her that first night, and every night since.

He never came to her this early. That, along with the intensity in his gaze, had hope suddenly surging inside her.

She found herself on her feet. He was her man, her soul, and even if he never loved her like she loved him, with all his passion, he must care as much as he was capable of. They would share a tough life, filled with duty and responsibility, but they'd make it if they had each other, and their baby...

Everything came to a stumbling halt as he caught her seeking hands. And the look in his eyes.

It was as if he was saying goodbye.

Then he said worse. "I wish it could have been different, but there's no use wishing. I can't...sleep with you anymore."

She'd thought her heart had been pulverized before. It hadn't been, or it had started to heal. He smashed it all over again. This time she knew there would be no putting it back together.

Agony suddenly poured from her. "You never 'slept' with me. The only time I woke up to find you still with me was that first night, and you only stayed to clinch your deal."

He said nothing. Just kept looking at her as if he, too, was devastated. It made her insane with pain.

"I have no doubt you'll do everything possible to claim the baby when it's born, but I demand my every right to it documented now, not then."

"Laylah..."

She spoke over him. "As for us, if you won't 'sleep' with me, then I have no use pretending this marriage is real. Our deal is over. I want a divorce. *Now.*"

He closed his eyes. Then before her heart could break on one more fractured beat, he turned and strode out.

Collapsing where she stood, she wept until she felt herself coming apart.

The moment he had what he wanted, he'd thrown her aside. Just like her mother had prophesized.

But he wouldn't do it yet. Not before he sat on that throne that meant everything to him.

Like she meant nothing.

The day of the *joloos* had come.

Rashid hadn't.

When Maram had said he hadn't come to the rehearsal ceremony, Laylah thought he'd show up at the last moment. He hadn't. Nobody knew where he was, or what had happened. According to everyone, he seemed to have disappeared off the face of the earth.

She was going out of her mind.

Something terrible must have happened. There was no other explanation for why he'd miss the most important day of his life. And if something had happened to him…

Another storm of weeping wrung her out as she prayed, again and again and again.

Let him be okay, let him fulfill his destiny. It doesn't matter that he doesn't love me. I love him. I always will…

"Laylah."

The deep voice hit her like a blow to the heart.

Because it wasn't Rashid's.

It was Haidar's. Jalal was with him.

She staggered around to them, her eyes and hands rabid as she clung to them, shook them. "Did you find him? Is he okay? *Tell me!*"

Haidar scowled down at her. "What do you care? Don't you hate him now?"

A huge sob tore out of her. "I—I could never hate him. I will always love him…no matter what…"

"That isn't what you've made him believe. He believes you hate him so absolutely, he's self-destructing in despair."

Horror mushroomed inside her. "You—you mean…"

Jalal exhaled. "You need to sit down when we tell you this."

And she wailed. *"Laa...laa...ya Ullah...laa..."*

"He *hasn't* hurt himself." Haidar's assertion broke the rising wave of panic. It rose again as he exchanged a look with Jalal as if agreeing on divulging something terrible before pushing her down firmly on the sofa. "Though he swore us to secrecy, at peril of some creative retribution, you need to know everything."

As they sat down, her soul seeped down her cheeks with the terror of anticipation.

"You know why Rashid joined the army," Jalal started.

He'd joined to pay off his guardian's debts. The army in Azmahar had been offering top recruits lucrative salaries and educational opportunities. Rashid had calculated he'd repay those debts in five years, get a better education than the one he'd been able to afford, and become a soldier, a career he'd always admired.

Haidar and Jalal had tried to dissuade him. Hostilities had been brewing between Azmahar and Damhoor and they didn't want him joining the army in time to be sent to war. But he'd made up his mind. And war had broken out.

On one mission, his squad leader had led his troops astray in the desert. They would have perished if not for Rashid. Using what he'd learned alongside Haidar and Jalal in the harshest survival methods, he'd led his squad to safety. Laylah remembered those weeks when she'd nearly gone mad fearing for him. Zohayd and Judar had mediated peace. But that hadn't been the end. She'd continued to go insane with worry as he'd fought in more armed conflicts.

But Rashid had survived them all, done all he'd set out to do, obtained one degree and promotion after another. Then he'd disappeared.

Haidar continued as if reading her thoughts. "You remember when he seemed to disappear? He'd started working in intelligence. And he discovered the threads of our mothers' conspiracy."

Her heart, having expended all its force, flailed feebly as

she realized that the coming revelation would be worse than anything she'd imagined.

"He went undercover to get proof, told me he got a promotion and would be under the radar. Thinking he didn't want to see me again, I told him I didn't care if I never heard from him again."

A skewer twisted in her chest. How hurt Rashid must have been at the apparent lack of caring from his lifelong friend.

Jalal exhaled. "But though we *both* treated his choice like brats who only cared they couldn't have their friend around all the time, he was hoping that he was wrong about our mothers. Knowing what we do now, I'll bet he considered *you* more in his efforts to find proof *against* the conspiracy. Instead, he only found incontrovertible proof against our mothers. He still decided to give us a chance to do something about it first." Jalal dragged his hands down his face. "But on his way to see us, he was attacked and abducted."

She fell back in a nerveless mass. She'd been right. That first night *had* been like déjà vu for him.

Haidar carried on. "His kidnappers were our mothers' flunkies. They tortured him for the information he'd uncovered as well as for intel he had that our mothers' needed to perfect their plans. At one point, he managed to call me. He was in such bad shape I thought he was drunk. He told me where he thought he was, begged me to help. I rushed over, but found nothing at that address. It was another of our mothers' contingency tricks. They instructed his kidnappers to text me from that phone and apologize for calling me while drunk, before they destroyed it so that I couldn't trace it.

"Rashid thought I didn't come to his rescue because I, and Jalal, were in on the conspiracy. Even though he was almost broken in mind and body, that agonized him so much, he struck back. He killed his captors and crawled across Zohayd's desert to Damhoor's border. The injuries those monsters had carved in his body—which were sliced open every time they started to heal—were so badly infected, he almost died. After spending weeks between life and death, he was stabilized, but no surgery could fix the scars. And I think his psychic scars ran deeper.

"He couldn't do anything about the conspiracy, since he'd lost all the evidence. When our mothers were exposed, he thought *we'd* pretended to abort their conspiracy so we could plot another day. Meanwhile he'd become friends with King Malek of Damhoor, and using his IT knowledge and intelligence techniques, Rashid developed an impenetrable defense system for him. King Malek offered him a ministry, but Rashid preferred to take his payment in hard cash to start his own business. And to pursue what had become his major goal—punishing us, by 'assimilating our ill-earned achievements.' He said he considered this a worse injury than exposing us, but I believe he was still unable to hurt us *that* badly. He's far more mushy-hearted than any of us thought possible.

"Then the chain reaction happened in Azmahar, and he was pitted against us for the throne of what he considered *his* kingdom. He decided he would do anything rather than let either of us take it. The rest you know."

Agony too great to find physical manifestation cleaved into her soul.

Rashid...Rashid...all this time...

"There's more." Her gaze slid sluggishly to Jalal. How could there be more? "There's a reason he didn't make it to his *joloos*."

She'd forgotten about that. She wished she could forget who she was. The daughter of the woman who'd mutilated the one man she'd ever loved.

"He suffered from post-traumatic stress disorder. He'd said it was under control, but he called us just now to say it's back, making him unfit to be king. He told us to toss a coin to decide who will sit on the throne and who will be crown prince."

Jalal stopped, looking uneasily at Haidar.

There could be nothing worse than what they'd already shared.

Haidar let her know there was always worse. "He said he should have never come back, should have died in one of those wars or in the desert, that it would have saved everyone endless trouble. He also said he understands if you don't want him near his child and he'll abide by anything you decide."

Desperation drove her to her feet. *"Where is he?"*

Haidar's face twisted. "The place that means the most to him."

She jumped on that. "I heard he bought his old family home."

Jalal shook his head. "We thought that at first, but we realized that's not where he's been happiest."

"Then *where?*" she cried out.

Haidar exhaled. "His Chicago loft."

During the trip to Rashid's loft, Laylah sank deeper in despair. What if Haidar and Jalal were wrong about his whereabouts? What if they'd been right, but he'd already left? She couldn't dare believe their rationalization of why he'd go there. After all she and her family had put him through, how could he consider the place where they'd started their relationship to be the place where he'd been happiest?

She'd come alone. She couldn't bear for anyone to come with her to the one place *she'd* been her happiest. Where she'd been Rashid's. Before the world had intruded and almost destroyed everything.

A few steps into the vast loft had her battered nerves jangling. With that familiar pleasure that burned through them.

Rashid *was* here.

Then he materialized out of the darkness at the mezzanine.

After staring down at her for an eternity, he started down the stairs. "You didn't have to come. I'll grant you the divorce and anything else you ask for."

"I—I'm not…I'm here to…" She swallowed the jagged lump of agony in her throat. Then she blurted out, "They told me everything."

Harshness replaced the blankness on his face. "I will make them regret telling you."

"*You* should have told me."

"You should never have known any of this."

"I had a *right* to know. It's my *mother* who did this to you."

His face hardened more. "You had enough spoiling your memories and soiling your psyche where she is concerned. There was nothing to be gained if you knew more, and so much to be lost."

He'd been protecting her. When he should have used this to hit back at her, at least to defend himself.

"What she did to me were the misdemeanors of an overbearing mother who didn't know when to let her daughter breathe on her own. What she did to you was an unforgiveable *crime*."

The turbulence in his eyes ratcheted up. "And that's why I didn't want you to know. So you wouldn't feel like this. I never wanted to add this to your disillusions."

And she couldn't bear being away from him for one more second. "Rashid…"

He jerked away from her. "Don't. Don't touch me, don't even come near me. It's not safe. I'm not safe."

A sob hacked her chest. "*Ya Ullah ya,* Rashid…I'm so sorry…"

"Don't…" he gritted. "Don't pity me. Just don't."

She lunged at him, hugged him with all her strength even as he tried to push her away. "It's not pity…*ya Ullah*…it's rage and regret and pain so fierce it shreds my heart with every breath."

Trying to undo her frantic hold, he groaned, "No, Laylah. Don't feel bad about it. You had nothing to do with this."

She clung harder. "It's still my mother who did this to you."

His arms fell to his side, surrendering to her embrace. "It's in the past. Let it go. I have."

She raised her face, seeing him blurred through the tears. "It's very much in your present, in your future."

"I swear to you, it's not."

"I know about your PTSD," she sobbed.

His headshake was adamant. "Memories of that ordeal are no longer what's fueling my instability."

Tears slowed down. "What is then?"

His shrug was forced. It told her he was going to lie. Then he did. "I guess it's self-perpetuating now."

And she had to know. "Is that why you never slept with me?"

His nod was difficult. "It's why I don't have anything around me when I sleep. I used to wake up with things broken, with sheets shredded and mattresses gutted with the shards."

He'd been killing his abusers over and over in his nightmares.

"I couldn't risk lashing out at you as I wrestled with my demons, even when I thought I had my condition under control. Then it was no longer under control, and I even had episodes while awake. I can no longer be around you."

"If memories aren't why your PTSD flared, what is? Was it the stress of seeking the throne, the fear of losing it?"

He closed his eyes. When he opened them, he let her see all the way into him for the first time. "It was the stress of seeking *you,* of having you yet not having you, and the fear of losing even that much of you. And I managed to fulfill my fears. I literally became *Majnun* Laylah, making it imperative to inflict your loss on myself. But then I lost you irrevocably that day you discovered my original plans. I only kept telling myself I might get you back. It was when I faced that I never would that my PTSD crashed back a hundredfold. You were the one who started me on the path to true healing and losing you has plunged me into worse than my worst days.

"I thought everything inside me was long dead. But you resurrected it all, made me discover hopes, emotions and needs I never knew I had. I suddenly found myself dependent on another human being. It was glorious, yet scarier than any mortal danger I had ever been exposed to. Then—everything went to hell. Knowing I'd lost your respect, your love, that I had broken your faith and your heart, being unable to heal you, is something I can never heal from."

And she charged him, deluging him in tears and kisses and pledges. "You never lost me or my love. You never will as long as I'm still alive, since that's all I am—love, for you. I was stupid and hurt and trying to protect myself. But I made that deal with you so I would still be with you, in hope that you'd love me someday, if only a fraction as much I love you. I've loved you forever, *will* love you forever." She pulled away to look into his eyes, her heart twisting. "But how can *you* love me, after what my family, after what *I* did to you? You *should* hate me."

He suddenly sank with her in front of the extinguished fireplace where they'd shared such ecstasies, his face trembling, his eyes filling. "You did far less than what I deserved. And your family made up for everything they'd ever done by having you. I might even love them for it."

A laugh of incredulity burst through the upheaval. "Now don't go overboard. But whatever you do, *I* will never forgive them."

He held her face between those callused hands that embodied tenderness and cherishing. "I need you to believe that one touch, one smile, one moment with you *has* atoned for all their crimes, has healed all my injuries. All I want now is for you to forget this and be at peace. If I have you, I have everything, past, present and future. I want only to be your lover and husband and father of our child."

"And king of Azmahar," she blurted out.

"Azmahar deserves someone unscarred inside and out."

"Azmahar needs *you*. And it's your destiny to rule the kingdom you defended and almost died for, the kingdom you've taken back from the brink of destruction and will now lead to prosperity. And that kingdom chose you. Like I did. Because you *are* the absolute best. Even your rivals think that. Hell, even Amjad thinks that. You *must* take your throne."

"On my life and honor, I will do anything you ever demand. But why not wait and see if I am the best choice for Azmahar?"

As she started to launch into another argument, he kissed her, silenced everything but the need to merge with him.

Not knowing how, she found herself where he'd first made her his as he came on top of her on the mattress she'd made him return after she'd found it far superior to any bed.

The next forever was consumed in finding their way back to each other, body, heart and soul.

What felt like a lifetime of bliss later, he moved her sweat- and pleasure-drenched body on top of his, caressed her all over, paying special attention to the belly that was starting to round.

"About the throne…" she began.

He cut her off. "About the honeymoon we never had. How about you tell me where you want to have it?"

She dove deeper into his embrace. "Right here. But…"

"There are too many reasons not to think of the throne now."

"Your PTSD flared up on my account. It should subside now."

"Even if it does, I can't be king. I need to be with you through your pregnancy and during our baby's birth and first months. I *will* make up for both of our lifetimes of alienation."

She ran adoring hands and eyes down his beloved face. "*Then* you'll consider taking the throne?"

"How about we take this one day at a time?" He gave her back the words she'd given him in what felt like another life. "Let's just savor this. What's the rush?"

"Uh…a kingdom with no king?"

He waved it away. "Haidar and Jalal will hold down the fort. It's good training in case one of them ends up on the throne."

As she opened her mouth, everything inside her stopped. At a sight she'd thought she'd never see.

Rashid's first full smile.

"How's that?" He tickled her out of her swooning. "Am I doing it right?"

She melted even more. "If I thought your scowl heart-stopping, your smile is possibly life-threatening."

And he treated her to another first, his unbridled guffaw.

"Ahh…" She lost all cohesion. "I'm gonna die!"

Still exposing her to the incomparable beauty of his grin, he countered, "You're gonna live. To love me and be loved by me."

Joy inundated her, that true ease had finally entered his heart and made his smile ready and laughter possible.

Deciding not to push for the throne for now, she grinned widely back. "All I ever wanted is to be yours, and for you to be mine."

He illuminated her whole world and being with his delight and devotion. "Done. And done."

Epilogue

Haidar and Jalal scowled at Rashid.

He only raised serene eyes to them, grinning, delighted at how that still fazed them.

Haidar blinked, as if to clear his eyes from a burst of light, and bit off the words, "You said a couple of months."

"And when was *six* months ever 'a couple'?" Jalal added, folding his arms over his chest, looking as unsettled at seeing him smile.

"You were both once intent on taking on the job permanently. What's so difficult about doing so for half a year?"

Haidar huffed. "Since you landed the bid, we rearranged our lives accordingly, and you ran and left us holding the baby."

He shrugged. "I did so *I* can hold my and Laylah's baby. And I'm not holding anything else until I do."

"Just give us a straight answer, damn you," Haidar growled before sitting next to him, grabbing his shoulder, looking deeply into his eyes. "Are you really okay now?"

"Far better than you can imagine." Rashid smiled at him, an act that came so easily to him now. "I have my own miracle. And she's providing me with another one...in about a week's time."

Jalal sat on his other side. "*Then* we can be allowed to have a piece of you? You can be a husband, a father and a friend, too, you know. We've tried it and it works."

Rashid grinned at him. "If I don't expire of happiness when our baby boy is born, I'll squeeze you, and the throne, onto my list of priorities."

Haidar rolled his eyes. "Once we could never get you to crack a joke, now you're almost rivaling Amjad, your biggest fan and our biggest pain in the ass, in being irreverent. Laylah isn't a miracle worker, she's a saboteur."

"You found out my true agenda!"

As Haidar and Jalal turned whimsical gazes to their ribbing cousin, Rashid filled his sight with Laylah as she waddled down the stairs of their loft. She became more beautiful with every passing day.

Firelight beamed off the brooch she almost always wore. His *mahr*. What he considered his mother's gift to her.

He had another gift for her now. One from *her* mother.

He rose, looking at Haidar and Jalal. "It's a good thing you're here to hear this. I just learned this moments before you barged in." His arms went around Laylah, the one being who encompassed the world to him. "I've been reinvestigating this ever since you came back to me. And today I made sure. Your mother had nothing to do with my kidnapping."

Tears surged into her eyes as her whole face trembled. "You're not just—just..."

"I only ever hid things I thought were no longer relevant, but I never and will never lie to you, *ya mashoogati*. It's the truth. You can have your mother back now."

He received an armful of sobbing love and thankfulness in utmost gratitude, before he turned to Haidar and Jalal.

"I'm sorry, *ya shabaab,* but your mother was solely responsible for this." At their pained, resigned looks, he added, "But she didn't order my mutilation, or death, after they extracted

the information. Her orders were to get the information without damaging me, then keep me prisoner until she carried out
her plan. What they did was their own payback to me. I'd been
responsible for their imprisonment or that of their relatives."

Haidar frowned. "Are you saying this to make us feel better?"

"With Sondoss as your mother, I doubt that's possible." At
their grimaces, he grinned, making them do a hilarious double take. "Seriously, she's not as bad as I thought she was. She
has lines she won't cross, which makes her dangerous and misguided but not a hardened criminal. As far as I'm concerned
this—" he indicated his scar "—isn't her doing. So I basically
forgive her. And so should you."

Haidar groaned. "It's a miracle we're so well-adjusted."

Jalal's eyes widened. "You're talking about us?" He shook
his head as he rose, put his hand on Rashid's shoulder. "The
only reason we're not as dangerous as our mother is because we
found you so early on. And before we strayed too much after
you left us, we found Roxanne and Lujayn."

Haidar rose, huffed a mirthless laugh. "That *was* a couple
more catastrophes averted, thanks to the right people at the
right time. So…" He placed a hand on Rashid's other shoulder.
"Right *man,* when will you take your kingdom off our hands?"

"Uh…never?" As they all exploded in protests, he smirked.
"I meant it's never going to be totally off your hands. Even after
I take the throne, you'll share it with me. You pick your titles."

Jalal shook him in mock panic. "Please, not heir and spare.
Harres and Shaheen suffer untold horrors being Amjad's."

"My heir is right here." He lovingly caressed Laylah's round
belly, soaked up her adoration. "You can be anything and everything else."

"*Sokrunn ya rubb*—thank God!" Haidar pretended relief.
"But we'll have to get back to you on that, *after* Roxanne and
Lujayn tell us exactly what we'll be, and what we'll do."

Rashid laughed. "A very wise if terminally annoying king

once told me that a man can't call himself that until a woman has him totally whipped."

Haidar guffawed. "We're the manliest men who ever lived then."

Rashid looked down at Laylah, loving her, thanking the fates for her with every heartbeat. "*No* one is manlier than me."

A contest of anecdotes proving who was manlier followed, after which they settled everything else.

When he returned from seeing Haidar and Jalal off, he came down on the floor beside Laylah as she stretched on the couch, rubbing and kissing her belly soothingly.

Sighing her pleasure, she drew her hands luxuriantly through the hair that now brushed his neck. "Thank you, *ya rohi.*"

"I'm the one who's thankful I could give you this."

"I'm not only thanking you for doing all this in the hope of exonerating my mother of the one crime I would have never forgiven her for, or for giving me the chance to rebuild my relationship with her. I'm thanking you for being you, for being mine."

"You thank me for that every day. You spoil me."

"Tough. I will keep on thanking you. But then you do the same. Now give me the straight answer you didn't give the guys."

"I *am* doing a lot for Azmahar from here. But I will only go back there with our whole family accounted for. Whether to be king or not remains to be seen. This is the destiny I care about—being yours, and our baby's."

"The throne is the other half of your destiny!" She pulled him up to her by his hair. "Didn't you claim to be the 'manliest' man there is? Prove it. Say it is and that you'll take it."

Taking her lips, taking her into his arms and heart, he smiled his pledge. "*Amrek, ya habibati.* As you command, my love. It is, and I will."

Laughing delightedly, she enfolded him back in her arms and heart. "Good man."

* * * * *

"I'm the mother. The legal birth mother. I get to make the decisions."

The eyes he'd been admiring only minutes earlier gleamed in a way that caused the hairs on the back of his neck to rise.

"So I have the final say in who will adopt the baby," she continued, "and it won't be an arrogant, unmarried Russian millionaire!"

"Billionaire," he corrected gently, and watched her smolder even as his own anger bubbled.

"The amount of money you have doesn't change a darn thing. She's going to a couple—a family who wants her, who will love her. That's what I intended when I agreed to be a surrogate for Keira, and that's what I still want for her. End of story."

A challenge had been issued. And he fully intended to meet it.

Ruthlessly suppressing his own hot rage, he murmured, "Well then, it seems I'll just have to get married."

It had been worth the temporary flare of temper. Yevgeny watched with supreme satisfaction as Ella's mouth dropped open.

War, Yevgeny suspected, had been declared.

Dear Reader,

When the year is drawing to a close, but the new year has not yet arrived, Christmas should be the time to spend with family and friends.

But it doesn't always happen that way. And that's the case for Ella, the heroine of *Staking His Claim,* who looks all set to spend the holiday all by herself—yet she hasn't even considered that she will be alone. She's been too busy working to think much about her own happiness.

Then a baby and a tall, dark hero called Yevgeny change everything. And poor Ella faces the hardest choices she's ever had to make.

For Ella and Yevgeny, the holiday becomes a time of hope, new beginnings—and a new life together.

I hope you enjoy Ella and Yevgeny's story as much as I enjoyed piecing it all together.

With love,

Tessa Radley

www.tessaradley.com

PS Don't forget to friend me on Facebook!

STAKING
HIS CLAIM

BY
TESSA RADLEY

MILLS & BOON

Published in Great Britain 2013
by Mills & Boon, an imprint of Harlequin (UK) Limited,
Eton House, 18-24 Paradise Road, Richmond, Surrey TW9 1SR

© Tessa Radley 2012

ISBN: 978 0 263 90463 5
ebook ISBN: 978 1 472 00084 2

51-0213

Harlequin (UK) policy is to use papers that are natural, renewable and recyclable products and made from wood grown in sustainable forests. The logging and manufacturing processes conform to the legal environmental regulations of the country of origin.

Printed and bound in Spain
by Blackprint CPI, Barcelona

Tessa Radley loves traveling, reading and watching the world around her. As a teen, Tessa wanted to be an intrepid foreign correspondent. But after completing a bachelor of arts degree and marrying her sweetheart, she became fascinated by law and ended up studying further and practicing as an attorney in a city firm.

A six-month break spent traveling through Australia with her family rewoke the yen to write. And life as a writer suits her perfectly—traveling and reading count as research, and as for analyzing the world...well, she can think "what if?" all day long. When she's not reading, traveling or thinking about writing, she's spending time with her husband, her two sons or her zany and wonderful friends. You can contact Tessa through her website, www.tessaradley.com.

For all my fabulous readers—
it's always wonderful to write a new book for you!

One

"You've decided to do *what?*"

It was Friday afternoon, the end of a grueling workweek, and Ella McLeod desperately wanted to put up her swollen feet…and relax.

Instead, from the depths of the sofa in her town house living room, Ella bit back the rest of the explosive reaction that threatened to erupt. She hoped wildly that her sister's next words would settle her world back on its axis so that the nasty jolt of shock reverberating through her system might just evaporate.

As if the sight of Ella's swollen belly prodded her conscience, Keira's gaze skittered away and she had the good grace to look discomforted. "Dmitri and I have decided to go to Africa for a year."

Ella shifted to ease the nagging ache in her lower back that had started earlier at the law chambers. Keeping her attention fixed on her sister fidgeting on the opposite end of the sofa, she said, "Yes, I understood that part—you and Dmitri plan to work for an international aid charity."

Her younger sister's gaze crept back, already glimmering with relief. "Oh, Ella, I knew you'd understand! You always do."

Not this time. Clearly Keira thought this was a done deal. It was rapidly becoming clear why Keira had dropped in this evening. And Ella had thought her sister's anticipation about the baby's imminent arrival had driven the surprise visit....

How wrong she'd been!

Gathering herself, Ella said slowly, "I don't quite understand the rest. What about the baby?"

The baby.

The baby in her belly that Keira had been so desperate for. Keira's baby. A baby girl. Keira and Dmitri had been present at the twenty-week ultrasound when the baby's sex had been revealed. Afterward the pair had gone shopping to finish buying furnishings for a nursery suitable for a baby girl.

Yet now that very same baby girl suddenly appeared to have ceased to be the focus of her sister's universe.

"Well—" Keira wet her lips "—obviously the baby can't come with."

It wasn't obvious at all.

"Why not?" Ella wasn't letting Keira wriggle out of her responsibilities so easily. *Not this time.* This wasn't the course of expensive French lessons Keira had grown tired of...or the fledgling florist business that Ella had sunk money into so that Keira would have a satisfying career when the one she'd chosen had become impossible. This was the *baby* Keira had always dreamed of one day having.

When Keira bit her lip and tears welled up in her eyes, a familiar guilt consumed Ella. Before she could relent—as she always did—she said, "Keira, there's no reason why the baby can't go with you. I'm sure you'll find people in Africa will have babies."

The tears swelled into big, shiny drops. "What if the baby becomes ill? Or dies? Ella, it's not as if this is a five-star beach resort. This is aid work in a poverty-stricken part of Africa."

Refusing to be drawn into her sister's dramatics, Ella leaned forward and tore a tissue from the box on the glass coffee table in front of the sofa, then passed it to Keira.

"Do you even know what kind of infrastructure exists? You could ask whether a baby would be safe." But Ella suspected she was fighting a losing battle when Keira failed to answer. She tried again. "If it's so unsafe, then what about your own health? Your safety? Have you and Dmitri thought this through? Do you really want to be living in a war zone?"

"It's not a war zone," Keira denied hotly. The tears had miraculously evaporated without a dab from the tissue that drifted to the carpet. "Credit me with some sense. It's Malawi. The country is stable—the people are friendly. It's poverty and illiteracy that we will be fighting."

So much for Keira's claim that it would be impossible to take a child there. But Ella knew she'd lost the battle; Keira had already made up her mind—the baby was not going with her.

"So what will happen to the baby?"

Silence.

Keira's eyes turned pleading, just like those of Patches, the beloved spaniel from their childhood.

"No! It is not staying with me." Ella made it a statement. A *firm* statement. The kind she used when delivering an ultimatum to opposing counsel.

Keira opened her mouth.

The baby chose that moment to kick.

Ella squeezed her eyes shut and suppressed a gasp at the hard jab against her ribs. Perspiration pricked at her forehead. She rubbed her side.

Thrusting the pain away, she opened her eyes and said to her sister, "Have you spoken to Jo about your new plans?" Ella suspected Jo Wells, the social worker who had been involved in helping arrange the paperwork side of the adoption for Keira and Dmitri, would be as floored as she was by Keira's change of heart.

"Dmitri is right. We're too young to become parents," Keira

said, sidestepping Ella's question. "We haven't even been married a year."

Drawing a deep breath, Ella said slowly, "A bit late to come to the conclusion that you're not ready to be parents."

Nine months too late to be precise.

Ella patted her own swollen stomach and watched mercilessly as Keira flushed.

"This baby is due next week. All your life you wanted to get married, start a family...that's why you did an early childcare course." It was why Ella was now stuck across the sofa from her sister like a stranded whale with a bulging belly. "How can you walk away from your child now?"

She had a nasty suspicion that she knew what—or rather, who—was behind the change of heart. Dmitri's big brother. Yevgeny Volkovoy.

Bossy big brother. Billionaire. Bigot.

Ella couldn't stand the man. He'd been furious to discover that Dmitri had gotten married without his say-so. He'd caused poor Keira endless tears with his terrifying tirades. Only by signing a post-nuptial agreement that allowed Keira the barest of maintenance in the case of divorce, and skewed everything in favor of the Volkovoy dynasty had Keira escaped his ire. Ella'd had a fit when she'd learned about the contract—and her alarm had grown when she read the terms. But by then it had been too late. The marriage was a done deal.

And Keira hadn't asked her for her expertise...or her help.

Of course, Yevgeny hadn't been in favor of the baby plan, either. Ella had known from the moment he'd switched to Russian. Dmitri had gone bright red—clearly he'd been less happy with Big Brother's opinions.

Now it sounded like Big Brother had finally gotten his way and managed to persuade Dmitri that he wasn't ready to become a parent.

Shifting again to ease her body's increasing discomfort, Ella tried to stem the emotions that were swirling around inside her. Disbelief. Confusion. The beginnings of anger. None of this cocktail of emotions could be good for the baby. And, even though Ella had never had any intentions of having her own child, she'd taken great care of this one. She'd eaten well—going to great lengths to cut out her four-cups-a-day coffee habit—she'd even shortened her workday and made certain she'd been in bed by ten o'clock each night. She'd even taught herself to meditate so that the baby wouldn't be contaminated by her stressful workday thoughts.

All because she'd wanted to make sure the baby was perfect. Her gift to Keira.

A gift Keira was now returning. Unborn, rather than unwrapped.

How did one return a baby, for heaven's sake? A baby that was a week away from becoming a live person?

Which brought Ella to...

"You're not leaving for Africa before the baby is born." She made it a statement. "There will be decisions that have to be made before you go."

Panic turned Keira's eyes opaque. "No! I can't."

"What do you mean you *can't?*"

"I can't handle those decisions. We've already booked our tickets. You'll need to make the arrangements."

"Me?" Drawing a deep shuddering breath, Ella went cold. "Keira, this is a baby we're talking about—you can't just walk away."

Her sister's gaze dropped pointedly to Ella's very round stomach. "You're still the legal mother—the adoption doesn't kick in until twelve days after the baby's born. You know that, Ella. Because you told me so yourself."

Of course she knew it. Knowing stuff like that was part of her job as one of the most respected family lawyers in Auckland. But the knowledge was only just starting to sink in that Keira was planning to leave her holding the baby!

"Oh, no!" Shaking her head, Ella said emphatically, "The only reason I lent you my body was so that you could have the baby you always dreamed of having. This is *your* dream, Keira.

Your baby." *My nightmare.* Then, in case it hadn't sunk in, she added pointedly, "Yours and Dmitri's."

"It's *your* egg."

"Only because you can't—" Ella bit off the words she'd been about to utter.

Too late.

Keira had gone white.

Driven by remorse, Ella propelled her colossal self from the sofa and reached for Keira. Her sister was as stiff as a wooden block in her arms. "I'm so sorry, sweetheart, I shouldn't have said that."

"It's the truth." Keira's voice was flat. "I don't have eggs or a uterus—I can't have children."

"So why—" Ella almost bit her tongue off. She tightened her hold around her sister.

"Don't worry, you can ask. No, I'll ask for you. 'Why are you doing this? Why are you going to Africa without the baby?' That's what you really want to know, isn't it?"

Ella inclined her head.

"I'm not sure I can explain." Keira shrugged out of her hold. Given no choice, Ella let her sister go.

While Keira gathered her thoughts, Ella became aware of the stark silence that stretched to the breaking point between them across the length of the sofa. A silent divide. It might as well have been the blue-green of the Indian Ocean that stretched beyond Australia all the way to Africa that yawned between them…because her sister had already retreated mentally farther than the arm's length that separated them.

Then Keira started to speak. "This is something both Dmitri and I have to do." The blank, flat stare she fixed on Ella was a little unnerving. "I have to find myself, Ella. Find out who I am. All my life I wanted to teach little children—and have my own houseful of kids at home." Her eyes grew more bleak. "But things didn't go according to plan."

"Keira—"

"I loved my job at Little Ducks Center—"

"Keira." The pain in her sister's voice was unbearable. "Don't!"

But Keira carried on as if she hadn't heard. "I couldn't work there after the car accident...after I found out the truth—that there never would be any babies."

"Oh, honey—"

Keira ducked away from Ella's enfolding arms.

An unwelcome sense of rejection filled Ella. Followed by emptiness. Instantly she scolded herself for her selfishness. She shouldn't feel hurt. Keira was suffering.

Yet, despite all her empathy for her sister, the most important question still remained unanswered: What about the baby? *The baby I helped create to fulfill your dream?* "But Keira, you will have a baby now—and you have a husband who loves you."

Wasn't that enough?

Eyes softening, Keira admitted, "Yes, I was very, very fortunate to find Dmitri."

Ella hadn't been so sure of that in the beginning. In fact, she'd foreseen nothing but heartbreak ahead for her sister. The arrival of Yevgeny Volkovoy in Auckland had been big news. Not satisfied with inheriting millions from the hotel empire his father had built up, the Russian had expanded the dynasty by building up the best river cruise operation in Russia. In the past few years he'd expanded into ocean cruise liners. With the planned expansion of Auckland's cruise ship terminal, it was not surprising to learn that Yevgeny intended to secure Auckland as a voyage destination. What had been surprising had been learning through the newspapers that the Russian had fallen in love with New Zealand—and planned to relocate himself permanently. He'd sent his brother to New Zealand to secure corporate offices and staff them for Volkovoy Cruising's new base. At first Ella had been less than impressed with the younger Volkovoy. With all the Volkovoy money Dmitri threw around, Ella had considered him spoiled and irresponsible. Nothing fortunate in that. Yet there was no doubt that he loved her sister...and thankfully he'd lost that reckless edge that had worried Ella so much at first. But heading off to Africa without the baby was not the right thing for Keira.

The baby…

Ella's hand crept to her stomach.

Mindful of how much her sister hated it when she nagged, Ella tempered her outrage. "You can't just leave a baby for a few months…or even a year…and hope it will be there when you get back."

"I know that, Ella." Keira's brows drew together. "Don't try to put the guilts on me. I'm not ready for a baby—neither of us are."

Ignoring her sister's unfair accusation, Ella tried to fathom out what Keira's response meant. Did she intend to give the baby up for adoption? Shock chilled Ella. Had her sister thought this through? She would hate to see Keira suffer when it one day came home to her what she'd lost. Perhaps Keira needed to be reminded of that.

"If you're thinking about giving the baby up for adoption, just remember it's not going to be easy to find a surrogate again if you decide you want a baby when you come back from Africa."

She certainly wouldn't be doing it again. She shouldn't even have done it this time. Dumb. Dumb. Dumb decision. That's what came of making decisions with her heart rather than her head.

Keira flicked back her pale silver hair. "We can do what Yevgeny suggested when we first talked about you being our surrogate—put our names down to adopt a baby."

She'd known Dmitri's high-handed brother was behind this!

The ache in her lower back that had been worsening all day, intensified. It wasn't worth arguing with Keira, pointing out that putting down your name didn't guarantee a baby because so few became available for adoption. And when one did, the legal mother had the final say. She alone could choose whichever couple she wanted—there was no waiting list, no way to predict who she would choose.

But right now Keira's future plans were not her concern.

"And what about this baby?" Ella knew she sounded angry. But, damn it, she *was* angry. Yevgeny made her blood bubble— even when he wasn't present. Just the mention of the man was enough! "You can't just dump it—"

"I'm not dumping it— You're the legal mother. I know you'll make the best decision for the baby." There was an imploring expression in her sister's eyes that caused the hairs at the back of Ella's neck to stand on end.

Oh, no! Keira *had* planned to leave the baby with her and come back to claim it. Panic prickled through her. "I *can't* keep the baby."

Keira's eyes teared up again. "I know I shouldn't have expected you to. But you always wanted the adoption of the baby to us to be an open one. So I hoped you would consider..."

"No!" Panic swamped Ella. "We have a surrogacy arrangement—"

Keira was shaking her head. "But Ella, you explained we can't actually adopt the baby until after you sign the consent to give her up on the twelfth day. As the legal mother, you're entitled to change your mind—but so are we."

She'd explained the legalities too well to her sister. Ella swallowed a curse. "You can't change your mind—because I can't keep this baby."

A wave of sick helplessness engulfed her.

Keira sighed. "We already have. We're not ready to raise a child. I don't even want to think about the decision you're going to have to make, but you have to do what you feel is right, Ella. It's your body, your b—"

"Don't tell me it's my baby!"

Keira looked doleful. "I think I always knew deep in my heart that you wouldn't agree to keep her, and I've made peace with that. Even though I had so hoped..." Her little sister's voice trailed away.

Dear God.

Did Keira not know how much this *hurt?* What she was asking? The pain that pierced her chest was sharp and unforgiving. And guilt made it worse. Ella wished she could burst into tears…weep and wail. But she couldn't. Instead, she fought for composure.

She'd always been the adult in their relationship. No doubt Keira had known all along she would agree to sort everything out.

Her heart was racing, and her head had started to pound. The ache in her back seemed to be growing worse by the minute. Ella knew all this couldn't be good for the baby. She had to calm down. *Think of the baby.* She drew a shuddering breath… counted to five…and exhaled slowly.

Pulling a cloak of assumed indifference around herself, Ella said with every bit of dignity she could muster, "I have a job—a demanding job. I don't have time for a pet, much less a baby." Ella would've loved a pet—a cat. But she didn't have time to care for any living thing.

Keira was staring at her again, her bottom lip quivering.

Ella refused to feel one bit guilty. She was *not* going to be left holding the baby; she couldn't keep it. That had never been the plan. The baby had been conceived for Keira—and Dmitri—to parent. This was not her baby.

Lifting her hand from her belly, she said, "Then we're in agreement. I have no choice but to give your baby up for adoption."

"If you see no other way out."

Before she could reiterate that this was not her preference, that the baby was Keira and Dmitri's responsibility, to her horror Ella felt the warm, wet flood as her water broke.

Keira's baby girl was not going to wait another week to be born.

Night had already fallen by the time Yevgeny Volkovoy strode into the waiting room set aside for family visitors on the hospital's first floor. He didn't notice the calming decor in gentle blues and creams lit up by strategically placed wall sconces, or even the soft-focus photographs of Madonna-like mothers cradling babies that hung on the wall. Instead, his focus homed in on where his brother sprawled across an overstuffed chair while watching a wide-screen television.

Fixing startlingly light blue eyes on Dmitri, he demanded, "Where is he?"

"Who?" Dmitri swung a blank look up at him.

"The child."

"It's not a boy…it's a girl," his brother corrected him even as the soccer game on the television recaptured his attention. "I told you that after the ultrasound."

Yevgeny suppressed the surge of bitter disappointment. He'd been so sure that the ultrasound had been read wrong. He should've known! For almost a century his family had produced boys…there hadn't been a girl in sight. How typical of Ella McLeod to give birth to a girl. Contrary creature.

He waved a dismissive hand. "Whatever. I want to see her."

Retracing his steps out of the family room he emerged in time to see his sister-in-law appear through the next door down the carpeted corridor. Yevgeny strode forward. Nodding at his startled sister-in-law as he passed her, he entered the private ward beyond.

Keira's icicle sister was sitting up in the bed, propped up against large cushions.

Yevgeny came to an abrupt stop. He had never seen Ella McLeod in bed before.

The sight caused a shock of discomfort to course through him. Despite the fact that she barely reached his shoulder when she was on her feet, she'd always seemed so formidable. Stern. Businesslike. Unsmiling. Even at family occasions she dressed in a sharp, formal fashion. Dark colors—mostly black dresses with neck scarves in muted shades.

Now he allowed his gaze to drift over her and take in the other differences.

No scarf. No oversize glasses. No makeup. Some sort of ivory frilly lace spilled around the top of her breasts. She looked younger…paler…more fragile than he'd ever seen her.

The icicle must be thawing.

Yevgeny shook off the absurd notion.

As though sensing his presence, she glanced up from the screen of a slim white phone she'd been squinting at. Antagonism snaked down his spine as their eyes clashed.

"What are you doing here?" she demanded.

"Where is the baby?"

He'd expected to find the child in her arms.

He should've known better. There wasn't a maternal bone in Ella McLeod's frozen body. No softness. No tender feelings. Only sharp, legal-eagle eyes that she usually disguised with a pair of glasses—and from all accounts, a steel-trap brain. According to the rumor mill her law practice did very well. No doubt her success came from divorce dollars siphoned off men with avaricious ex-wives.

Ella hadn't answered. A haunted flicker in her eye captured his attention, but then the fleeting expression vanished and her focus shifted beyond him. Wheeling about, Yevgeny spotted the crib.

Two strides and he stood beside it. The baby lay inside, snugly swaddled and fast asleep. One tiny hand curled beside her cheek, the fingers perfectly formed. Her lashes were impossibly long, forming dark curves against plump cheeks. Yevgeny's heart contracted and an unexpected, fierce rush of emotion swept him.

It took only an instant for him to fall deeply, utterly irrevocably in love.

"She's perfect," he breathed, his gaze taking in every last detail. The thatch of dark hair—the Volkovoy genes. The red bow of her pursed mouth.

A smile tilted the corners of his mouth up.

Reaching out, he gently touched the curve where chin became cheek with his index finger.

"Don't wake her!"

The strident demand broke the mood. Turning his head, Yevgeny narrowed his gaze and pinned the woman in the bed.

"I had no intention of waking her," he said softly, careful not to disturb the infant.

"It's only a matter of time before she wakens with you hovering over her like that."

"I never hover." But he moved away from the cot—and closer to the bed.

Ella didn't respond. But he'd seen that look in her eyes before. She wasn't bothering to argue...not because she'd been swayed by his denial, but because she was so damn certain of the rightness of her own opinion.

The woman was a pain in the ass.

The polar opposite of her sister, she was the least motherly woman he'd ever encountered—with the single exception of his own mother.

Maybe it was as well she wasn't cradling the baby; she'd freeze the little bundle if she got close enough. Ella was ice to the core—he'd been mistaken to imagine a thaw.

"Dmitri called to tell me you're planning to give up the child for adoption?" No discussion. No consultation. She'd made a life-changing decision that affected all of them, by herself. It was typical of the woman's arrogant selfishness.

"Then you must've heard that your brother and my sister have decided not to adopt the baby."

Was that irony buried in her voice? He couldn't read her expression. "Yes—Dmitri told me at the office."

"At the same time that Keira was visiting me."

This time he definitely detected an edge. But he was less concerned about her annoyance than discovering the fate of the oblivious newborn in the cot. "So it's true? You intend to give up the baby just like that?"

Her chin shot up three notches at the snapping sound his fingers made. "I will take care of the arrangements to find a new set of parents as soon as I can." Ella glanced down at the phone in her lap, then back at Yevgeny. "I've already left a message for the social worker who's handling the adoption proceedings for Keira and Dmitri, notifying her of their change of mind and requesting that she get in touch with me ASAP."

"Of course you have." It certainly hadn't taken her long to start the process to get rid of the baby. Anger sizzled inside him. "You never considered keeping her?" Not that he'd ever allow the child to stay in her care.

She shook her head, and the hair shrouding her face shimmered like the moonlit wisps of cloud outside the window. "Not an option."

"Of course it isn't."

She stared back at him, managing to look haughty and removed in the hospital bed. So certain of the rightness of her stance. "Identifying suitable adoptive parents from Jo Wells's records is the only feasible option."

"'Feasible option?'" Was this how his own mother had reasoned when she'd divorced his father and lied her way into sole custody, only to turn around and abandon the same sons she'd fought so hard to keep from their father? "This is a baby we're talking about—you're not at work now."

"I'm well aware of that. And my main concern now is the best interests of the child—exactly as it would be if I was at work."

Yevgeny snorted. "You're a divorce lawyer—"

"A family lawyer," she corrected him. "Marriage dissolution is only a part of my practice. Looking after the best interests of the children and—"

"Whatever." He waved an impatient hand. "I'd hoped for a little less *business* and a little more emotion right now."

From the lofty position of the hospital bed she raised an eyebrow in a way that instantly rankled. "You don't transfer skills learned from business to your home life?"

"I show a little more compassion when I make decisions that relate to the well-being of my family."

She laughed—a disbelieving sound. Yevgeny gritted his teeth and refused to respond. Okay, so he had a reputation—well-deserved, he conceded silently—for being ruthless in business. But that was irrelevant in this context. He'd always been fiercely protective of those closest to him. His brother. His father. His *babushka*.

He studied Ella's face. The straight nose, the lack of amusement in her light brown eyes—despite her laughing mouth. No, he wasn't going to reach her—he doubted she had any warmth to which he could appeal.

Giving a sharp, impatient sigh, he said, "You've got blinkered vision. You haven't considered all the *feasible* options."

For the first time emotion cracked the ice. "I can't keep the baby!"

Two

Ella's desperation was followed by a strained silence during which Yevgeny looked down his perfectly straight nose at her. Something withered inside her but Ella held his gaze, refusing to reveal the fragile grief that lingered deep in her most secret heart.

But she wasn't going to keep the baby.

And she'd hold firm on that.

For her sanity.

Finally he shook his head. "That poor baby is very fortunate that you will not be her mother."

The contempt caused Ella to bristle. "I agreed to be a surrogate—not a mother."

"Right now you're the only mother that baby has—you're the legal mother."

God.

This was never supposed to have happened. She stuck her hands under the bedcovers and rested them on the unfamiliar flatness of her belly. After so many months of having a mound, it felt so odd. Empty.

And, with the baby no longer moving inside, so dead.

Why had she ever offered to donate her eggs—and lend her womb—to create the baby her sister had so desperately wanted?

The answer was simple. She loved her sister...she couldn't bear to see Keira suffer.

Ah, damn. The road to hell was paved with good intentions. Now look where it had landed her—in an entanglement that was anything but simple. Ella knew that if she wasn't careful, the situation had the potential to cause her more pain...more hurt... than any she'd ever experienced before. The only way through the turbulent situation was to keep her emotional distance from the baby—not to allow herself to form that miraculous mother-baby bond that was so tenuous, yet had the strength of steel.

But there was no need to offer any explanation to the insensitive brute who towered over the hospital bed.

Rubbing her hand over her strangely flat stomach, Ella pursed her lips. "I'm well aware that I'm her legal mother."

Mother. Just one word and her heart started to bump roughly. She couldn't keep the baby. *She couldn't.*

Carefully, deliberately she reiterated, "It was never the plan for me to remain her mother. This. Is. Not. My. Baby."

It felt better to spell it out so firmly.

The surrogate agreement had been signed, the adoption proceedings had been started. All that needed to happen to formalize the situation had been to get through the twelve-day cooling-off period the New Zealand adoption laws provided. Once that period had passed, and the mother was still sure she wanted to give up the baby, the adoption could go ahead. But Ella had never contemplated reneging on the promise she'd made to her sister. And she'd certainly never expected Keira to be the one to back out!

"She was created for your brother and my sister—to satisfy their desire for a family. By assisting with her conception and bringing her into the world I've kept my part of the agreement." Damn Keira and Dmitri. "In fact, I've gone way beyond what was expected of me."

His mouth slanted down. "That is your opinion."

"And I'm entitled to it." Ella drew a steadying breath, felt her stomach rise under her hands, then calmness spread through her as she slowly exhaled. "You shouldn't expect me to even consider keeping the baby. Keira and Dmitri changed their minds about becoming parents—not me." She'd had enough of being blamed for something that wasn't her fault. And she was furious with Keira, and Dmitri, for landing her in this predicament—probably because the man standing beside the bed had caused it with his initial resistance to the baby in the first place.

But before she could confront him with his responsibility for this mess, he was speaking again, in that staccato rattle that hurt her head. "Stop making excuses. It tells me a lot about the kind of person you are—that even in these circumstances you can abandon the baby you've carried for nine months…the baby you've just given birth to."

What was the man's problem? Hadn't he listened to one word of what she'd been saying? She drew a shuddering breath. "Let's get this straight. Regardless of the position in law, this is Keira's baby, not mine." Where was her sister? She'd landed Ella in this mess, now Keira had disappeared. She'd been here a few minutes ago, but now Ella couldn't even hear her voice in the family room next door. The loneliness that seared her was as unexpected as it was alien. For once in her life, she could do with her younger sister's moral support. But of course, that was too much to expect. "I *never* intended to have children."

"Never?"

"That's right. Never." Under the bedcovers she clenched her hands into fists.

He shook his head and this time the look he gave her caused Ella to see red.

"And what about your precious brother?" It burst from her. "What about his part in this? He's the baby's biological father. Why don't you harangue him about his responsibilities? Why pick on me?"

For the first time, his glance slid away. "This has nothing to do with my brother."

Her anger soared at the double standard. "Of course not. He's male. He gets to donate his seed and walk away scot-free from all responsibility. It's the woman who carries the baby— and the blame, right?"

Yevgeny shot her a strangely savage look. "I'm not discussing this any further. I will absolve you from all blame and responsibility—*I* will adopt the baby."

"She will become my responsibility," continued Yevgeny, rather enjoying seeing cool, icy Ella looking uncharacteristically shaken. "And *I* do take care of my responsibilities."

Her mouth opened and closed, but no sound came out. Yevgeny's pleasure grew. How satisfying to discover that the always eloquent Icicle Ella, like other mere mortals, could suffer from loss of words.

"You…you live in a penthouse. Y…you're not married…" she finally stuttered out. "A baby ought to be adopted by a couple who will care for it."

It was a great pity she couldn't have remained speechless for a while longer.

"I can buy a house." Yevgeny was determined to ignore the jab about a wife. "And the baby is not an it," he rebuked gently.

Her brown eyes were wide, dazed. "What?"

"You said the baby should go to a couple who love *it*—she's not an it."

"Oh." A flush crept along her cheeks. "Of course she isn't. I'm sorry."

It was the first time he'd ever heard Ella McLeod apologize…and admit she was in the wrong. Yevgeny refused to acknowledge even to himself that he was secretly impressed. Or that it made him feel a little bit guilty about enjoying her confusion.

He studied her. To be truthful her eyes were luminous. Gold-brown with a hint of smoke. Like smoky honey. And the flush gave her pale cheeks a peachy warmth he'd never noticed before. She looked almost pretty—in an ethereal, fragile way that did not normally appeal to him.

In the spirit of reconciliation he felt compelled to add, "And I will care for her."

"A procession of big-bosomed careworkers is not what I had in mind."

Reconciliation was clearly not what Ella had in mind. He suppressed a knowing smirk at how quickly the fragile act had lasted and gave in to the urge to provoke her. "You have something against motherly, homely women?"

The look she gave him would've frozen the devil at fifty feet. "I wouldn't describe a Playboy centerfold model as homely."

This time he allowed himself to smile—but without humor. "I will need some help with the baby…but you may rest assured the criteria for hiring her caregivers will not be physical attributes. I will make sure that the women I employ will be capable of providing her—" he glanced at the baby and realized he didn't yet know her name "—with all the womanly affection the infant will require."

"You will need a wife."

Yevgeny forced a roar of laughter as Ella repeated the ridiculous suggestion. "The child will have far more than a young, struggling couple could ever give her—I don't need a wife to provide it."

"I'm not joking." Ella pressed her lips together. "And I'm not talking about the possessions you can give her—I'm sure you could provide a diamond-encrusted teething ring. But she deserves to have two parents who love her unreservedly."

His laughter ceased. "You're living in a dream if you think that happens simply because a child has two parents." His own mother was living proof of that. To ease the turmoil that memories of his mother always brought, Yevgeny stretched lazily, flexing his shoulders. He noticed how Ella looked away. "She will have to make do with me alone."

That brought her eyes back to him. "Forget it. It's not going to happen—I won't let it."

"It's not only your decision. Fathers have rights, too." He lifted his lips in a feral, not-very-amused grin. "I'm stepping into my brother's shoes."

"As you pointed out, I'm the mother. The legal birth mother." Did she think he'd missed her point? Yevgeny wondered. "I get to make the decisions," she was saying now. "I need only to consider the best interests of the child."

The look on her face made it clear that his solution was not what she considered in "the best interests of the child."

He froze as he absorbed what she was getting at. "How can that be true? This is the twenty-first century!"

"Quite correct. And a child is no longer a chattel of the head of the household."

The eyes he'd been admiring only minutes earlier gleamed in a way that caused his hackles to rise.

"So I have the final say in who will adopt the baby," she continued, "and it won't be an arrogant, unmarried Russian millionaire!"

"Billionaire," he corrected pointedly and watched her smolder even as his own anger bubbled.

"The amount of money you have doesn't change a darn thing. She's going to a couple—a family who wants her, who will love her. That's what I intended when I agreed to be a surrogate for Keira, and that's what I still want for her— I'll make sure the adoption agency is aware of that requirement. You're not married—and you're not getting the baby. End of story."

Her bright eyes glittered back at him with the frosty glare of newly minted gold.

A challenge had been issued. And he fully intended to meet it.

Ruthlessly suppressing his own hot rage, he murmured, "Well, then, it seems I'll just have to get married."

Yevgeny watched with supreme satisfaction as Ella's mouth dropped open.

War, Yevgeny suspected, had been declared.

* * *

Ella did a double take. "You? Get married? So that you can adopt a child?"

She hadn't thought Big Brother Yevgeny could surprise her. She'd thought she had his number. Russian. Raffish. Ruthless. But this announcement left her reeling. What would this playboy Russian billionaire want with a child, a *girl* child at that?

Which led her to say, "But you don't even want a girl."

Something—it couldn't be surprise—sparked in the depths of those light eyes. "What made you think that?"

"I heard you…" Ella thought back to that moment of tension when she'd heard his voice in the family room next door.

"When?"

"As you came in." She searched to remember exactly what he'd said. Slowly she said, "You asked where the *boy* was. You never even considered that the baby might be a girl."

"Aah." He smiled, a feral baring of teeth. "So *obviously* that meant I wouldn't welcome a girl, hmm?"

Sensing mockery, Ella frowned. "Why would you want a child? Any child?" Wasn't that going a little far—even for Yevgeny—to get his own way?

Yevgeny shrugged. "Perhaps it is time," he said simply.

"For a trophy toddler?"

"No, not a trophy."

"Not like your girlfriends?"

That dangerous smile widened, but his eyes crinkled with what appeared to be real amusement. "You yearn to be one of my trophies?" he asked softly—twisting her insides into pretzels.

An image of his latest woman leaped into Ella's mind. Nadiya. One of a breed of supermodels identified by their first names alone. Ella didn't need a surname to conjure up Nadiya's lean body and perfect face that were regularly featured in the double-page spreads of glossy fashion magazines. Barely twenty, Nadiya was already raking in millions as a face for a French perfume, which she wore in copious amounts that wafted about her in soft clouds. Six foot tall. Brunette. Beautiful. With slanting, catlike green eyes, which devoured Yevgeny as though he were a bowl of cream. Enormously desired by every red-blooded man on earth. A trophy any man would be proud to show off. So why should Ella imagine Yevgeny would be any different?

"That's a stupid question," she said dismissively.

"Is it?"

"Of course, I don't want to be any man's trophy." Ella was not about to be dragged into the teasing games he played. She gave him a cool look—mirroring the one she'd caught him giving her earlier—and let her eyes travel all the way down the length of his body before lifting them dismissively back to his face. "Anyway, you're not the kind of man I would ever date."

He was laughing openly now. "That's not an insult. From my observation, there is *no* kind of man you date."

The very idea that he'd been watching her, noting her lack of romantic attachments, caused a frisson to run along her spine. She refused to examine her unease further, and focused back on the bombshell he'd delivered. "You can't adopt this baby."

He came another step closer to the bed. "Why not?"

"I've already told you. You're not married."

"That's old-fashioned." He leaned over her. "Ella, I never expected such traditionalism from you."

His closeness was claustrophobic. He was so damn big. "Everyone knows you're a workaholic—you're never home." Yevgeny had less time for a kitten than she did.

At that, he thrust out his roughly stubbled chin. "I'll make time."

Right.

Somewhere between his twenty-hour workday and his even more hectic X-rated nightlife? The man obviously never slept— he didn't even take time to shave. His life was littered with women—even before his latest affair with Nadiya, she'd seen the pictures in the tabloids. Keira and Dmitri remained fiercely loyal and insisted the news was all exaggerated but Ella ignored their protests. They'd been brainwashed by the man himself. Ella knew his type—she'd seen it before. Powerful men who treated women like playthings. Men who kept their women at home, manacled by domesticity and diamonds, before stripping them of everything—including their self-respect—when the next fancy caught their eye.

"Sure you will."

"Damn right I'll take care of her."

As if the baby felt his insistence, she made a mewing noise and stirred. The pretzel knot in Ella's stomach tightened, yet thankfully the baby didn't wake. But at least it got rid of Yevgeny—he'd shot across to the cot and was staring down into the depths.

Ella breathed a little easier.

"Money doesn't equal care." She flung the words at the back of his dark head.

At her comment, his dark head turned. Ella resisted the urge to squirm under those unfathomable eyes.

"What's her name?"

"She doesn't have one." Ella had no intention of picking out a name—that would be a fast track to hell. Attachment to the baby was a dark and lonely place she had no wish to visit.

"Keira didn't choose one?"

"Not a final name."

It had puzzled Ella, too. Keira had spent weeks pouring over books, searching websites for inspiration. But she'd never even drawn up a short list. Now Ella knew why: Keira had been dithering about motherhood. Choosing a name would've been a tie to bind her to the baby.

To rid herself of that critical, disturbing gaze, Ella said, "I can ask Keira if there's one she particularly liked."

Yevgeny's gaze didn't relent. "You were supposed to be the baby's godmother, yet you have no idea of the names your sister might have been considering?"

She was not about to air her theory about why Keira hadn't picked a name in order to jump to her own defense. She simply stared back at him wordlessly and wished that he would take his big intimidating body, his hostile pale blue eyes and leave.

"Why don't you ask Dmitri what they planned to name the baby?" Let him go bully his brother. Ella had had enough. "Anyway, the baby's new parents will probably want to pick one out. Now, if you don't mind, it's been a long day. I'm tired, I need to rest."

The baby chose that moment to wake up.

At the low, growling cry, Yevgeny scooped her up in his arms and came toward the bed.

No. Panic overtook Ella. "Call the nurse!"

"What?"

"The baby will be hungry. Call the nurse to bring a bottle—they will feed her."

He halted. "The *nurses* will feed her? From a bottle?"

Ella swallowed. "Yes."

Disbelief glittered for an instant in his eyes, then they iced over with dislike. He thrust the waking baby at her. "Well, you can damn well hold her while I go and summon a nurse to do the job that should be yours."

"She's not my baby…" Ella's voice trailed away as he stalked out of the private ward leaving her with the infant in her arms.

Three

The baby let out a wail.

Ella stared down at the crumpled face of the tiny human in her arms and tried not to ache.

How dare Keira—and Dmitri—do this to her?

She'd barely gotten her emotions back under control when, a minute later, Yevgeny swept back into the ward with the force of an unleashed hurricane. Ella almost wilted in the face of all that turbulent energy. In his wake trailed two nurses, both wearing bemused, besotted expressions.

Did he have this effect on every woman he encountered?

No wonder the man was spoiled stupid.

At the sight of the baby in her arms, the nurses exchanged glances. Ella looked from one to the other. The baby wailed more loudly.

"Feed her," Yevgeny barked out.

Instead of rebuking him for his impatience, the shorter nurse, whom Ella recognized from the first feed after the baby's birth, scurried across to scoop the baby out of her arms, while the other turned to the unit in the corner of the room and started to prepare a bottle in a more leisurely fashion. Freed from the warm weight of the baby, Ella let out a sigh of silent relief… and closed her eyes.

They would take the baby to the nursery and feed her there. Ella knew the drill. All she needed to do was get rid of Yevgeny, then she could relax…even sleep…and build up the mental reserves she would need for when the baby returned.

"Do you want the bed back raised higher?"

That harsh staccato voice caused her eyelashes to lift. "If you'll excuse me, I plan to rest."

"No time for rest now." He gestured to the nurse holding the bundle. "You have a baby to feed."

Ella's throat tightened with dread.

"No!" Ella stuck her hands beneath the covers. She was not holding the baby again, not feeling the warm, unexpected heaviness of that little human against her heart. "I am not nursing her. She will be bottle-fed. The staff is aware of the arrangement—we've discussed it."

The nurse holding the baby was already heading for the door. "That's right, sir, we know Ms. McLeod's wishes." The other nurse followed, leaving Ella alone in the ward with the man she least wanted to spend time with.

Yevgeny opened his mouth to deliver a blistering lecture about selfish, self-centered mothers but the sound of light footsteps gave him pause. Ella's gaze switched past him to the doorway of the ward.

"Can I come in?"

The tentative voice of his sister-in-law from behind him had an astonishing effect on the woman in the bed. The tight, masklike face softened. Then her face lit up into a sweet smile—the kind of smile she'd never directed at him.

"Keira, of course you may." Ella patted the bedcover. "Come sit over here."

Yevgeny still harbored resentment toward his brother for the shocking about-face on the baby—not that he'd ever admit that to Ella—and he found it confounding to witness her warmth to her sister. He'd expected icy sulks—or at the very least, reproach. Not the concern and fondness that turned her brown eyes to burnished gold.

So Ella was capable of love and devotion—just not toward her baby.

Something hot and hurtful twisted deep inside him, tearing open scars on wounds he'd considered long forgotten.

To hide his reaction, he walked to the bed stand where a water pitcher sat on a tray. Taking a moment to compose himself, he poured a glass of water then turned back to the bed.

"Would you like some water? You must be thirsty."

Surprise lit up Ella's face.

But before she could respond, a vibrating hum sounded.

"That will be Jo Wells. I left an urgent message for her earlier." Ella's hands dived beneath the covers and retrieved her phone.

In the midst of perching herself on the edge of the bed, Keira went still.

And Yevgeny discovered that he'd tensed, too. Given Ella's reluctance to keep the child, she should've been grateful for his offer to take the baby. She could wash her hands of the infant. He'd never contemplated for a second that Ella would actually turn him down.

Her insistence on getting in touch with the social worker showed how determined she was to see through her plan to adopt the baby out. Evidently she wanted to make sure it was airtight.

The glass thudded on the bed stand as he set it down, the water threatening to spill over the lip. Yevgeny didn't notice. He was watching Ella's brow crease as she stared at the caller ID display.

"No, it's not Jo—it's my assistant," she said.

The call didn't last long. He glanced at his watch—7:00 p.m. on a Friday night. She'd be charging overtime rates. Ella's tone had become clipped, her responses revealing little. Another poor bastard was about to be taken to the cleaners.

Ella was already ending the call. "If you wouldn't mind setting up an appointment for early next week I'd appreciate that," she murmured into the sleek, white phone. "Just confirm the time with me first, please."

That caught his attention.

As soon as she'd killed the call, he echoed, "Early next week? You're not intending to go back to work that soon. Have you already forgotten that you have a newborn that needs attention?"

"Hardly." Her teeth snapped together. "But I have a practice to run."

"And a newborn baby to take care of."

"The baby wasn't supposed to arrive for another week!" Ella objected.

Keira laughed. "You can't really have expected a baby to conform to your schedule, Ella. Although, if you think about it, the baby did arrive on a Friday evening. Maybe you do already have her trained."

Ella slanted her sister a killing look.

It sank in that Ella *had* expected the baby to conform. Clearly, she rigorously ran her life by her calendar. Why shouldn't a baby comply, too? Yevgeny started to understand why Ella could be so insistent that she'd never have a baby.

Her selfishness wouldn't allow for it.

The woman never dated. She didn't even appear to have a social life—apart from her sister. Keeping the baby would mean disruption in her life by another person. Ella was not about to allow that. Everything he knew about her added up to one conclusion: Ella was the most self-centered woman he'd ever met.

Except there was one thing wrong with that picture...

Keira must have begged to get her sister to agree to be a surrogate in the first place. Ella carrying the baby for nine months was the one thing that went against the picture he'd built in his mind. Allowing her body to be taken over by a baby she had no interest in was a huge commitment.

But Yevgeny knew even that could be explained—Ella was a lawyer. She knew every pitfall. And she was such a control freak she wouldn't have wanted to risk some other surrogate changing her mind once the baby was born. This way she could make sure that Keira got the baby she and his brother had planned.

Ella was speaking again. He put aside the puzzle of Ella's motivations and concentrated on what she was saying. "Well, that's when I planned my maternity leave to begin," she was informing Keira. "Another week and everything in the office would've been totally wrapped up—I planned it that way."

"Oh, Ella!" The mirth had faded from his sister-in-law's face. "Sometimes I worry about you. You need the trip to Africa more than Dmitri and I. In fact, you should visit India, take up meditation."

"Don't be silly! I'm perfectly happy with my life."

It appeared Ella was not as calm and composed as he'd thought. The brief flare of irritation revealed she was human, after all.

From his position beside the bed stand, Yevgeny switched his attention to the younger McLeod sister. Keira was biting her lip.

"You were going to ask Keira about names." Yevgeny spoke into the silence that had settled over the ward following Ella's curt response.

"Names?" Ella's poise slipped further. "Oh, yes."

Yevgeny waited.

Keira twisted her head and glanced at him, a question in her eyes. "What names are you talking about?"

His brows jerked together. "The names you've been considering for the baby." His sister-in-law shouldn't need a prompt. The baby was so firmly in the forefront of his mind, how could it not be the same for her…and for Ella? What was wrong with these McLeod women?

"I hadn't chosen one yet."

"That's what I told him," Ella added quickly, protectively, her hand closing over her sister's where it rested on the edge of the bed. "Keira, you don't need to think about it if it upsets you.…"

Relief flooded Keira's face as she turned away from him and said, "Ella, you're the best. I knew you would take care of everything."

Those words set his teeth on edge.

Shifting away from the sisters, Yevgeny crossed the room. Foreboding filled him.

Keira's confidence in her sister didn't reassure Yevgeny one bit. Because it was clear to him that Ella couldn't wait to get rid of the baby.

And that was the last thing he wanted.

Despite all the drama of the day, Ella surprised herself by managing to get several hours sleep that night.

Yet she still woke before the first fingers of daylight appeared through the crack in the curtains. For a long while she lay staring into space, thinking about what needed to happen. Finally, as dawn arrived, filling the ward with a gentle wash of December sun, she switched on the over-bed light and reached into the drawer of the bed stand for the legal pad she'd stowed there yesterday.

By the time the day nurse bustled in to remind her that the baby would be brought in from the nursery in fifteen minutes for the appointment with the pediatrician, Ella had already scribbled pages of notes. After a quick shower, she put on a dab of makeup and dressed in a pair of gray trousers and a white T-shirt. Then she settled into one of the pair of padded visitor chairs near the window to await the doctor's arrival.

The baby was wheeled in at the same time that the pediatrician scurried into the room, which—to Ella's great relief—meant that she wasn't left alone with the wide-awake infant. The doctor took charge and proceeded to do a thorough examination before pronouncing the baby healthy.

Tension that Ella hadn't even known existed seeped away with the doctor's words. The baby was healthy. For the first

time she acknowledged how much she'd been dreading that
something might be wrong. Of course, a well baby would benefit
by having many more potential sets of adoptive parents wanting
to love and cherish her.

After the pediatrician departed, the nurse took the baby back
to the nursery, and Ella's breakfast arrived in time to stem the
blossoming regret. Fruit, juice and oatmeal along with coffee
much more aromatic than any hospital was reputed to produce.

Ella had just finished enjoying a second cup when Jo Wells
entered her room. Ella had been pleased when she'd discovered
that Jo had been assigned to processing the baby's adoption to
Keira and Dmitri. Of course, that had all changed. Now she was
even more relieved to have Jo's help.

Slight with short, dark hair, the social worker had a firm
manner that concealed a heart of gold. Ella had worked with
Jo a few times in the past. Once in a legal case where a couple
wanted to adopt their teen daughter's baby, and more recently
in a tough custody battle where the father had threatened to
breach a custody order and kidnap his children to take them
back to his home country.

"How are you doing?"

The understanding in Jo's kind eyes caused Ella's throat to
tighten. She waved Jo to the other visitor seat, reached for the
yellow legal pad on the bed stand and gave the social worker a
wry smile. "As well as can be expected in the circumstances—
This is not the outcome I'd planned."

Jo nodded with a degree of empathy that almost shredded the
tight control Ella had been exercising since Keira had dropped
her bombshell—was it only yesterday?

"I want the best for the baby, Jo."

Focusing on what the baby needed helped stem the tears that
threatened to spill. Ella tore the top three pages off the pad and
offered them to the social worker.

"I knew you'd ask. So I've already listed the qualities I'd
like to see in the couple who adopts her. It would be wonderful
if the family has an older daughter—perhaps two years older."

That way the baby would have a bond like the one Ella shared with Keira, but the age difference would be smaller. Hopefully the sisters would grow up to be even closer than she and Keira were. "If possible, I'd like for her to be the younger sister—like Keira is. But above all, I'd like her to go to a family who will love her...care for her...give her everything that I can't."

Another nod. Yet instead of reading the long wish list that had taken Ella so much soul-searching in the dark hours this morning to compile, Jo pulled the second chair up. Propping the manila folder she'd brought with her against a bent knee, she spread the handwritten pages Ella had given her on top.

Then Jo looked up. "I spoke to Keira before coming here. She and Dmitri haven't had second thoughts."

Ella had known that. From the moment Keira had told her of their decision yesterday, she'd known Keira was not going to change her mind. But deep down she must have harbored a last hope because her breath escaped in a slow, audible hiss.

"Is there anyone else in the family who would consider adopting the baby?" Jo asked.

"My parents have just reached their seventies." Ella had been born to a mother already in her forties and Keira had followed five years later. "They've just moved into a retirement village. There's no chance that they're in a position to care for a newborn."

Even if they'd wanted to adopt the child, she wouldn't allow it. Her parents had already been past parenting when she and Keira had reached their teens. She was not letting this baby experience the kind of distant, disengaged upbringing they'd experienced.

"And we have no other close family," she tacked on.

"What about the biological father's family?"

An image of Yevgeny hovering over the bed last night like some angel of vengeance flashed into Ella's mind. His pale, wolflike eyes filled with determination. His expression downright dangerous as she resisted what he wanted.

She dismissed the image immediately and said, "There's no

one to my knowledge—his parents are dead." A pang of guilt seared her. Reluctantly she found herself correcting herself. "He does have an older brother. Yevgeny. But he's far from suitable."

Jo tilted her head to one side. "In what way is Yevgeny not suitable?"

"He's single—for one thing. The adoption laws don't allow single men to adopt female babies." Ella didn't mention Yevgeny's rash vow to marry to flout her plans.

"Except in exceptional circumstances…" Jo's voice trailed away as she bent her head and made a note on the cover of the manila file resting in her lap. "The court may consider his relationship to the baby sufficient."

"It's unlikely." Ella didn't want Jo even considering Yevgeny as a candidate—or learning that he intended to get married for the baby's sake.

But Jo wasn't ready to be deflected. "Hmm. We could certainly consider interviewing him."

Jo would discover that Yevgeny was determined to adopt the baby.

Ella's heart started to knock against her ribs. *No.* This wasn't what she wanted for the baby. Even if he did marry, Yevgeny would farm the baby out to a series of stunning Russian nannies and continue with his high-flying, jet-set lifestyle. Growing up with Yevgeny would be a far worse experience than the distracted neglect she and Keira had suffered.

"He's a playboy—he has a different woman every week."

That assessment was probably a little harsh, Ella conceded silently. He'd been linked to Nadiya for several months and before that he'd been single for a while—according to Keira. Although that hadn't stopped him from dating a string of high-profile women.

"And he's a workaholic," she added for good measure just in case Jo was still considering Yevgeny. Then she played her trump card. "He certainly won't provide the kind of stable home that I always intended for the child. I don't want the baby going to him."

"Being the legal mother, your wishes will take precedence." Jo tapped her pen against her knee. "This is still going to be an open adoption, right?"

An open adoption meant keeping in touch with the new adoptive parents, watching the baby grow up, being part of her life, yet not a parent.

Ella swallowed.

This was the hard part.

"Ella?" Concern darkened Jo's eyes as she failed to respond. "Research has shown open adoptions are far more beneficial because—"

"They give the child a sense of history and belonging, and help prevent the child having identity crises as a teen and in later life," Ella finished. She knew all the benefits. She'd had a long time to ponder over all the arguments. "We'd planned an open adoption with Keira and Dmitri. The baby would always know I was her tummy mummy—" now the affectionate term for a surrogate rang false in her ears "—her birth mother…even though Keira would be her real mother."

"So it will still be an open adoption?"

Ella nodded slowly. "It's in the baby's best interests."

But dear God, it was going to kill her.

Ella was relieved that Jo hadn't asked whether she would consider keeping the baby. She'd already emphatically told both Keira and Yevgeny she couldn't do it. A third denial would've been more than she could handle at this stage.

Jo's head was bent, eyes scanning the wish list Ella had given her.

Finally she looked up. "I have several sets of IPs—intending parents—" Jo elaborated, "who might fit your requirements. I'll pull their profiles out and bring them back for you to look through."

"Thank you." Gratitude flooded Ella. "You have no idea how much of a help it is knowing you are here for support."

"It's my job." But Jo's warm eyes belied the words. "When will you be going home?"

"Probably tomorrow."

"And the baby?"

"The baby will go to a foster carer." Ella was determined not to allow any opportunity for a maternal bond to form.

"I know you probably don't want to hear this, but you should reconsider your decision not to have counseling after you sign the final consent to give the baby up." Without looking at her, Jo shuffled the wish list into the manila file. Getting to her feet she pushed the visitor chair back against the wall before turning to face Ella. "I know you said previously that you didn't feel you'd need counseling because she was never intended to be your baby—that it was your gift to Keira and Dmitri. But given that circumstances have changed, I think it would be a serious mistake. You'll be experiencing a lot of emotions, which you never expected."

Ella resisted the urge to close her eyes and shut out the world. Signing the consent could only be done on the twelfth day. She didn't want to even think about the approaching emotional maelstrom.

So she gave Jo a small smile. "I'll think about it," she conceded. "But I don't think it will be necessary. I'm tougher than I look."

Before Jo could reply, footsteps echoed outside the ward.

A moment later, Yevgeny appeared in the doorway.

Ella's heart sank.

"This is Dmitri's brother, Yevgeny." She made the introduction reluctantly, and hoped that Jo would depart quickly.

To her dismay Jo and Yevgeny took their time sizing each other up. Only once they'd taken each other's measure, shaken hands and exchanged business cards, did Jo finally walk to the door. Ella let out the breath she'd been holding. Neither had even mentioned the baby's adoption.

Disaster averted.

For now.

"We'll talk again," the social worker said from her position in the doorway, giving Ella a loaded look over her shoulder. "I'll be back."

* * *

This morning Yevgeny was wearing a dark gray suit that fitted beautifully.

Towering over the chair she sat on, with the light behind him, Ella could see that his dark hair was still a touch damp—evidence of a recent shower, perhaps.

It was only as he tilted his head to look down at her that she noticed the stubble shadowing his jawline. A dazzling white shirt with the top button undone stood in stark contrast to his dark face.

Ella was suddenly desperately glad that she was not in bed.

Yesterday she'd felt at a terrible disadvantage as he'd towered over her while she'd been clad in a nightdress. She'd felt exposed...vulnerable. Even now, seated, his height was intimidating. But at least she could rectify that...

She rose to her feet. "The baby is in the nursery."

"I know—I have already been to visit her."

Annoyance flared. She had not been consulted. "They let you in?"

The staff would have to be told he was not welcome in the future—she wouldn't put it past him to try and take the baby. This was a man accustomed to getting his own way. But not this time.

Some indefinable emotion glimmered deep in the deceptively clear depths of his eyes. "Keira and Dmitri were with me—they vouched for me."

"Keira's here?"

Had her sister had second thoughts since Jo had spoken to her?

Yevgeny was shaking his head. "They've gone. Dmitri has quite a bit to finalize before I can release him to fly across the world."

All Ella could think of was that Keira hadn't even bothered to come past and say good morning. Hurt stabbed her. Then she set it aside. No doubt Keira was avoiding her because deep

down her sister must be experiencing some guilt for the decision
she and Dmitri had made.

Ella decided she wasn't going to let herself dwell on the
turmoil that Keira's choice had created.

It was done.

Now there was the baby to think about....

But Yevgeny's response caused her to realize that she hadn't
even asked her sister when they planned to leave for Africa.
She'd been too busy trying to cope with the magnitude of the
shock. Keira had said she and Dmitri had already booked the
tickets but that's all she knew.

"Do you have any idea when they plan to leave?" It rankled
to have to depend on Yevgeny for information but she needed
to know.

"I believe they leave the day after tomorrow."

"That soon?"

Ella was still absorbing this new upset when he asked, "What
will you be thinking about?"

"Pardon?" For a moment Ella thought Yevgeny had picked up
on her earlier hurt at Keira's failure to come say good morning
and was asking about her thoughts.

"You told the social worker you'd think about it." Yevgeny
had moved up beside her, causing the space in the ward to
shrink. "What will you be thinking about?"

Ella frowned as she realized he'd overheard the last part of
her discussion with Jo. She had no intention of revealing that Jo
thought she needed counseling. The good thing was at least he
hadn't detected her hurt over Keira. "It's nothing important,"
she said dismissively. "It wasn't about the baby."

"Did you tell her I am going to adopt the baby?"

"But you're not." Inside, her stomach started to twist into a
pretzel. Ella pursed her lips. "I told her you weren't suitable."

"You did not!"

"Yes, I did."

His gaze blitzed into her. "Because I'm single?"

Ella didn't glance away from his hard stare. "Among other things."

"But once I'm married that will change," he said softly and came another step closer. "You know that."

Ella blinked. And found herself inhaling the warm scent of freshly showered male. This close she could see the crisp whiteness of his ironed shirt.

What was he up to now?

"You should've seen her." His voice took on a husky, intimate tone. "She's so beautiful—"

Ella recoiled. "I don't care what your wife-to-be looks like!"

At her interruption, he looked puzzled, then he smiled. A smile filled with a burst of charm and humor that Ella hadn't wanted to recognize in Yevgeny Volkovoy. It made him all too human. And irresistibly appealing. This wouldn't do at all. She wanted—no, needed—to keep thinking of him as Keira's overbearing, bullying brother-in-law.

"No, not my wife-to-be. The baby." He chuckled. "She was awake...waving her hands and watching them. Smart *and* beautiful. You've seen her this morning."

It was a statement—rather than a question.

Ella squirmed, reluctant to admit that she'd barely glanced at the baby while she was in the ward during the pediatrician's consultation. Then she told herself she had no reason to feel guilty. Keira and Dmitri's actions were not her fault.

Rather than answering his question, she changed the subject. "So you're going through with it? You're really going to get married?"

He nodded. "I want that baby."

God, the man was stubborn. Didn't he ever accept no for an answer? Time for him to learn he couldn't always get what he wanted in life. Sometimes someone else's needs came first.

This time, the baby's best interests were paramount. Not his.

Letting out the breath she'd been unconsciously holding since that first whiff of his male essence, Ella said, "Well, you need to know that you're sacrificing yourself for nothing. I'm not going to change my mind. And it's still my decision. As the legal mother, I get to choose the parents the baby will go to."

He went deadly still. "You will choose me—and my wife."

Was that a threat?

Ella carefully assessed his motionless body, the face with the high Slavic cheekbones, skin stretched taut across them. Yevgeny needed to know she wasn't going to let him bully her.

"Unlikely. This morning I gave Jo a list of the qualities I'm seeking in the prospective parents. Nothing you can offer meets the criteria. She's going to bring me portfolios of prospective parents to look at—and I'll choose a couple from there."

The tension in the air became electric. "When?"

"Shouldn't you be at work doing whatever it is that high-powered billionaires do?" Ella knew she was being deliberately provocative, but she'd never expected him to be this concerned about the baby.

"When?" he repeated, his face tight.

He wasn't going to relent, she realized. "As soon as I'm back home—tomorrow probably."

"And then what happens?"

"The couples have already been interviewed and screened. Police checks have been done. Once I choose a couple and the consent is signed, then the paperwork for the adoption can be filled in and submitted."

"The consent?"

"Yes." Ella explained further, "The legal mother can only sign the consent—that's the formal document where she agrees to give up the baby—on the twelfth day. And yesterday, the day the baby was born, counts as the first day."

From where she stood Ella could sense the intensity of his gaze. He wasn't smiling anymore. He was watching her, his head tipped slightly to one side, his brain working overtime. Yevgeny was busy hatching a fiendish plot. She was certain of it.

There was something curiously exhilarating about being the focus of all that raw, brilliant energy. He might come in a devastatingly well-groomed, freshly scented and well-built male package, but it was his mind that Ella found fascinating. That ability to concentrate with such single-minded intensity. The ability to conjure up solutions no one had come up with before.

She could kind of understand why women might be attracted to that....

"So you can change your mind anytime up until that twelfth day?" he asked.

Ella blinked—and wrenched herself away from her fancies. "In theory. But I wouldn't do it. It wouldn't be very fair to do that to a couple once I've told them they've been chosen."

Determination fired in his eyes. "This baby will be mine—I will do everything in my power to make sure that happens."

Despite the morning sunshine spilling through the windows of the ward, Ella shivered.

It was evening.

The sun was setting beyond the distinctive silhouette of the Auckland Bridge transforming the Waitemata Harbour to liquid gold. Turning his head away from the magnificent view, Yevgeny dropped down onto the king-size bed in Nadiya's hotel suite and gazed contemplatively across at the woman standing in front of the dresser, the woman he planned shortly to reduce to screaming satisfaction.

Yet instead of dwelling on the pleasures of seduction, his mind was already elsewhere.

It was the end of day two. He had only ten days left. Yevgeny knew he needed to act—and fast.

He had to get engaged—and he needed to convince Ella to change her mind about his suitability to be a father.

That was going to take some doing.

It was enough to make him grind his teeth with frustration. Yet he was a long way from conceding defeat. He'd never been the kind of man to back away from a challenge—and this was the most important challenge of his life.

Now or never.

Taking a deep breath, he gave Nadiya his most practiced

smile and patted the bedcover beside him. "Come make yourself comfortable."

Nadiya glided across the room. Kicking off her high heels, she settled herself on the bed beside him. Long fingertips reached for the buttons of her silk shirtdress, and she gave him a pout.

"How do you feel about children?"

"Children?"

Nadiya's eyes widened, and her fingers stilled in the act of undressing. Her lips, still plump with gloss, parted. Yevgeny could identify with her shock. *He* was shocked. This was a discussion he had never before conducted with a woman. It was breaking new ground. But not only had he always desired Nadiya, he'd always liked her, too—even though, for the first time, he struggled to focus on their approaching lovemaking.

She hesitated, and then said, "I've always wanted children."

This was good.

Coming up on his elbow, he propped his hand under his head. "I am pleased to hear that."

From across the pale pink satin comforter, with her long legs folded beneath her, she watched him through those catlike eyes. "So you want children?"

What choice did he have? There was a child…and he couldn't walk away from her. But he wasn't ready to reveal more. So he gave Nadiya the same answer he'd given Ella. "The time has come."

She said, "I do have contractual obligations."

This wasn't what he needed to hear. Talk of contracts reminded him too much of…Ella.

He rolled away and lay back. She, too, was proving to be like the woman he tried never to think about. Keeping his voice level, he said, "You don't have time for children."

"No, no. I'm not saying that!" Nadiya edged closer and placed her hand over his. "But I never expected you to offer—"

She broke off.

Sensing opportunity, he turned his head. "You never expected me to offer...what?"

"What *are* you offering, Yevgeny? You haven't actually said."

This was another thing he liked about Nadiya—she was direct. He chuckled softly, secure that he was about to get what he wanted. The sensation that shot through him was familiar; the dart of adrenaline that signified the successful conclusion of a deal. "I'm offering a diamond ring to the mother of my child."

"Marriage?"

He nodded. For one uncertain instant he considered telling her about the baby girl he planned to adopt...but before he could speak, Nadiya let out a breathy little gasp and started to bounce on the bed. "Yes! Yes! Yes!"

A wave of euphoria swept him. The first step of his plan had been accomplished. Ella McLeod would stand no chance....

But why was he thinking about *her* when he should be focused on Nadiya? Tightening his fingers around his fiancée's, he prompted, "And what about your contract?"

"We will work something out—I do want a baby."

Yevgeny studied her from under hooded eyelids. It might be a good idea to wait...to see how she reacted to the baby before he showed his hand entirely. The brief moment of uncertainty passed. Nadiya was beautiful, no doubt about that. Sexy, too. And beneath the model-perfect exterior she was likable. Everything a man could ever want. Everything he should be desiring....

So why did he keep remembering a pair of outraged honey-gold eyes?

Four

Yevgeny returned to the hospital late the following afternoon—with his supermodel in tow. His face wore no expression as the pair entered the family waiting room where Ella had just met with Jo, and now she tried desperately to match his insouciance. All day, she'd found herself wondering when he would arrive.

Now he was here.

And he hadn't come alone.

Sitting on one of the two-seater love seats, her overnight bag already packed and ready to go, Ella couldn't help wishing that she'd taken the time to blow-dry her hair straight after breakfast instead of wasting time staring out the hospital-ward window for thirty soul-searching minutes. Now, at the end of the day, her hair hung like rats' tails around her face while Nadiya looked absolutely fabulous. Not that Ella should care... but unaccountably she did.

Maybe she couldn't look as if she'd stepped out the pages of *Vogue,* but she wanted to look capable and together—like someone out of a feature on successful women in *Cosmo.*

Brisk. Businesslike. A woman who had achieved every

career goal she'd ever set for herself; not the quivering mass of Jell-O–like uncertainty that she was right now.

Nadiya was glancing around the family room with interest—taking in the large black-and-white photos of mothers cradling babies that decorated the walls. Ella wondered if she'd ever seen inside a maternity unit before. Given the model's whippet-slim figure, pregnancy was not something Ella could imagine the supermodel contemplating with glee.

"Where's the baby?"

Ella managed not to roll her eyes skyward. Of course the baby would be the first thing that Yevgeny asked about.

"Her diaper is being changed."

"The birth went well?" asked Nadiya.

Ella could've hugged the woman for unwittingly preventing Yevgeny from venting the criticism that hovered unspoken on his lips. Clearly he thought *she* should be attending to the baby.

"Yes, very well." She gave the supermodel a small smile. "I've already been discharged."

"That's good. How much does she weigh?"

Ella told her.

"Your sister must be thrilled—she's changing her now?"

Did Nadiya not know that Keira had pulled out of the adoption? Ella's questioning gaze slid to Yevgeny. Perhaps the two weren't as close as she'd assumed…perhaps Nadiya was not the bride he intended to sucker into marriage.

"I—"

"I brought Nadiya to meet the baby," he cut in before Ella could respond. "She has agreed to marry me." He lifted Nadiya's hand to flash a gigantic diamond, and smirked at Ella.

"No!" She realized she'd said it out loud as Nadiya's face reflected shock. "I mean…what a surprise."

The other woman's eyes had narrowed and she was studying Ella in a way that made her feel decidedly uncomfortable. Nadiya's gaze flashed back and forth between Ella and Yevgeny. Her discomfort increased. The conclusion the other woman was drawing about Ella's hasty objection was wrong.

She hastened to correct her. "You don't understand—"

"Let's go visit the baby." Nadiya smiled up at Yevgeny as her fingers walked up his arm then spread out and rested against his suit-clad biceps in an unmistakably possessive gesture. The diamond sparkled. The model turned her head, and her gaze glittered *mine* at Ella.

Nadiya was welcome to the man!

As the pair exited the ward, Ella glared at Yevgeny's retreating back. He was the most devious, cold-bloodedly scheming man she'd ever come across—and she'd seen enough. He'd gone out to find the first woman to marry him—and proposed—without bothering to explain *why* he wanted to marry her.

He was using the young woman.

Deep down, Ella knew she was being unfair. Nadiya might be young but she was far from naive. And what man wouldn't want to marry Nadiya?

But at the back of her mind, worry raged for the baby. Given a choice, a fashion model was hardly the kind of mother she would've picked out. Together, as a couple, Yevgeny and Nadiya were so far removed from her notion of ideal parents. This was a train crash waiting to happen…and the baby would be the biggest victim.

Even as anxiety noodled her stomach into a tangle of nerves, one of the caregivers bustled in. "I've changed the baby. Mr. Volkovoy and his friend are with her in the nursery. The baby is looking well. She'll be fine to leave." She stopped beside Ella and said in a tone of inquiry, "Jo said the adoption is still some time away from being finalized."

Not if Yevgeny had his way….

But Ella was far from convinced that the Russian billionaire and his supermodel fiancée were the kind of parents the baby deserved. The last thing she wanted was to read about the baby in the tabloids and gossip magazines as so often happened with celebrities who seemed to care little for their offspring.

She might not be in a position to keep the baby. But she could damn well make sure it got the best start in life—and that meant the best parents possible.

And she'd told Jo that in as many words.

The five profiles she'd gone through with Jo earlier before rejecting them all had confirmed Jo's statement that there were many parents anxiously waiting to adopt. But Ella had a sinking feeling that Yevgeny's insistence to adopt might still prove a hindrance.

"The baby will stay with a foster family until I choose the final adoptive parents," Ella answered at last.

"That will be one very happy set of parents," the caregiver said, drawing the curtains farther back to let more light into the room.

There was nothing more to say.

Ella knew it was time to pick up the overnight bag she'd packed hours ago and for her to leave the place where she'd given birth—and leave the baby behind.

But before Ella got a chance to gather up her overnight bag and make her escape, Yevgeny and Nadiya returned—with the baby. Wheeling the cot into the middle of the room, Yevgeny bent forward to lift her out.

Ella closed her eyes. Every muscle tensed. *Don't give her to me. Don't give her to me.* The frantic refrain echoed through her head. She hadn't wanted to see the baby before she left. Ella had hoped that the next time she saw her, the baby would be securely in her new parents' home.

A gurgling sound broke into her desperation.

"She's grinning!"

Ella opened her eyes. Yevgeny was holding the baby up, one big hand cradling the back of her neck. Face-to-face with the baby, his strong masculine profile provided a sharp contrast to the baby's swaddled softness. She looked tiny against this big hulk. Ella tensed further. What if he dropped her?

"Careful!"

He didn't even look at her; all his attention was focused on the baby.

"Look, she's laughing."

Nadiya leaned in toward the two of them, resting long slim fingers on Yevgeny's arm, her silky sable hair spilling over his shoulder. "Babies that young don't laugh. She's yawning."

A jab pierced Ella's heart at the sight of the three dark heads so close together. To her horror she felt her throat tighten. She swallowed. The tightness swelled more.

She couldn't have said anything even if she hadn't felt so awful.

"No, that's not a yawn—it's laughter," the billionaire insisted.

Nadiya moved even closer, and Ella was sure that Yevgeny and the baby would be asphyxiated by Nox Parfum fumes.

"This is something I know a lot about," Nadiya said. "I've handled many babies… I've got four sisters and about a dozen nieces and nephews." Nadiya took the baby from him with an easy competence that Ella found herself envying.

Maybe Yevgeny hadn't made such a mistake in picking the supermodel to marry. Clearly Nadiya knew something about babies—despite her glamorous exterior.

Loneliness swamped Ella, dismaying her. To ward it off, she said, "You're happy to adopt her?"

Startled eyes met hers. "Adopt her?"

Yevgeny moved. All too soon he stood between Ella and his bewildered fiancée like some oversize sentinel. He shot Ella a fulminating look.

"Nadiya and I have yet to discuss the specifics."

No…it wasn't possible, he couldn't have been that… arrogant…that dumb. Could he?

Over the head of the oblivious baby, the supermodel's attention shifted to her fiancé. "The specifics of what?"

Yes, he'd been that dumb.

He hadn't told Nadiya.

Now he looked hunted. Then he smiled at his fiancée—a

slow, deliberate smile that oozed intimacy. "We will talk later. In private."

Ella watched as he gave the supermodel a slow once-over that was clearly intended to turn her legs to water. She knew she should've experienced distaste at the obvious sexual manipulation he was using on the young woman. Instead, to her utter dismay, her own stomach started to churn at the blatant sensuality in that hard-boned face. What would it feel like to be the object of this man's desire? To have him gaze at *her* with such unwavering intensity?

Heat, wanton—no, *unwanted*—blazed through her.

To rid herself of the emotional storm she didn't want, Ella said with a coolness she was far from feeling, "Yevgeny intends to adopt the baby."

Nadiya stared down at the wrapped infant in her arms. "This baby?" She lifted her head and turned her attention to her fiancé. "But why?"

"He didn't explain it to you—that I told him he needed a wife?"

Ella couldn't stem the words.

Pity for the younger woman filled her. Yevgeny hadn't taken Nadiya's wishes into account. He'd simply assumed she would fall in with what he wanted. Once again he was putting what he wanted first, not thinking of anyone else. What arrogance! The dislike Ella already felt toward him escalated, not helped by that surge of awareness that he had unwittingly aroused.

But to Ella's surprise, Nadiya was glaring at him. "You asked me if I wanted children…" As her voice trailed away, the frown marring her forehead deepened. "You weren't talking about the future, you were talking about now. About this baby."

"Nadiya—"

But Nadiya held up a hand, interrupting whatever he'd been about to say. A couple of quick steps brought her to Ella's side and she deposited the baby into Ella's lap. The baby started to cry—a gruff, growly sound that caused Ella to freeze. She stared down at the crumpled, red face and panic pierced her.

What the hell was she supposed to do now?

From a distance she could hear Nadiya angrily saying something to Yevgeny, but Ella was in no state to listen. She stroked the baby with a tentative hand. The cries continued. Awkwardly she patted the baby's back…then rocked her a little. There was a pause. The tightly pressed eyelids opened. The baby's eyes were a dark shade of midnight. Ella stared, transfixed.

"You need to support her neck."

The voice came from far off. The words were repeated and a hand with a flashing diamond appeared in Ella's peripheral vision. It cupped her own.

"There. Like that," said Nadiya.

Ella looked up. "Thank you."

But Nadiya had already spun to confront Yevgeny. Ella couldn't look away as Nadiya hissed, "Why this child?" Her hands were on her hips. She shot a quick look over her shoulder at Ella, then moved her attention back to the Russian. "Is it your child?"

"Nadiya—"

"Answer me!"

Holding the now quiet infant, Ella wanted to cheer.

But before she could make any sound, Nadiya's gaze arced to her "…and yours?"

That was taking it too far. It was one thing to needle Yevgeny, but Ella didn't want anyone thinking she'd slept with this bully.

"No!" said Ella. "This is not his child—it's Dmitri's child!"

Confusion misted Nadiya's eyes. "So where is Dmitri?" Her attention swung to Yevgeny. "And why are you talking about adopting your brother's child?"

He really hadn't told Nadiya anything at all.

"Because my brother and his wife have decided they no longer want a baby. She's of my blood. How can I let her go to strangers?"

There lay the key to his behavior—he was prepared to

sacrifice his own freedom for the baby's sake to prevent a person he believed belonged to his family from going to strangers.

Nadiya's gaze moved back to Ella. "And you are the mother, right? Not your sister?"

Why did Nadiya have to put it like that? Ella rocked the baby a little more. "I'm *not* the planned mother—Keira is. Or was supposed to be," she amended. "I'm only a surrogate."

She couldn't help feeling the stab of a traitor's guilt.

"You only carried the baby?"

Ella wriggled uncomfortably before conceding, "The eggs are mine, too."

"So you are the mother." Nadiya cut to the heart of it.

Ella shifted again. The baby mewed. A quick glance revealed that the baby's face had puckered up. Oh, no, she was about to cry again. Ella rocked harder; the puckers relaxed a little. She risked raising her head. "Biologically, yes. Legally, yes. Morally, no."

Over the baby's head, Nadiya gave her a long, searching look. Then she turned to Yevgeny. "You should have told me. You knew I believed you were asking me to have *my* baby."

"It makes a difference?" Yevgeny's gaze was hooded.

"Yes. My career is demanding right now, but I would take time off for my baby. My baby—and yours."

"But not for this baby?"

Nadiya looked tormented.

"That's not fair!" Unable to keep quiet at his hectoring, Ella rose to the younger woman's defense. In her arms the soft body of the baby stiffened. Ella made a mental note to keep her voice level.

"You've already caused enough trouble. You stay out of this," he snarled.

"But she's right. You're not being fair—and I'm not going to do this." Nadiya was tugging the great glittering ring off her finger.

"Wait—"

"No, this isn't going to work. I thought you loved me...that you were talking about us having a baby together. But you were using me!" Fury sparkled in her green eyes. She thrust the ring at him, her fingers shaking. "Take it."

The baby carefully cradled on her lap, Ella drew back into the chair and tried to make herself invisible. Some things deserved privacy. And it was uncomfortable to watch Nadiya's pain as moisture glimmered in her eyes. There was hurt…and anger… and something else that made Ella wince.

It startled her to realize that the model had loved the ruthless Russian. The revelation made Ella furious. Poor, hoodwinked Nadiya.

A woman would have to be incredibly shortsighted to fall in love with him. Yet Nadiya clearly had. Being beautiful and successful hadn't saved her from being devastated by his effortless manipulation.

The tableau playing itself out in front of her brought back old hurts…humiliations…that Ella had hoped were long forgotten.…

She never intended to feel like that about any man ever again.

Particularly not a man like Yevgeny Volkovoy.

Nadiya tossed back her head, and her hair rippled like black silk in the light. "No one uses me."

Yevgeny didn't respond. He simply stood there staring down at the woman he'd so recently announced was his fiancée.

"Pah…you're not even prepared to deny it. I feel sorry for you, Yevgeny. You don't recognize the importance of love. But one day you're going to fall in love with someone—real love— and she's going to rip your heart out, just like you've ripped mine out." Wiping the tears away, the supermodel straightened to her glamorous full height. "You're not worth crying over."

"You did that deliberately!" Yevgeny blew out a pent-up breath as the rapid tap-tap of Nadiya's skyscraper heels receded down the corridor.

Ella didn't even flinch at his accusation. "What do you mean?"

Her voice was softer than he expected.

It gave him a strange feeling to see her holding the baby that he already adored. So he looked away from the infant and pinned the most irritating woman he'd ever met under his gaze. "You caused that scene you just witnessed."

"*I* caused it?" Her eyes widened. "I simply told the poor woman the truth. Don't blame me. You should've explained things to her."

Perhaps Ella had a point.

But he'd wanted to assess Nadiya's reaction to the baby first—and it had been more than he'd hoped for. He and Nadiya had never talked much about family...or children. They hadn't shared that kind of relationship. Yet when Nadiya had taken the baby into her arms like a woman created for motherhood, and revealed she was used to her sister's children, Yevgeny had been overcome by relief. He couldn't have gotten a better outcome if he'd planned it for a month. And he'd thought the baby would be safe....

Then Ella had interfered.

He stared blankly at the woman he despised as she moved the baby to and fro in small motions.

Nadiya had made it clear she wasn't prepared to raise someone else's child. In seconds his plan had started to unravel and he could do nothing but watch impotently. It was all Ella's fault. Yet she didn't even want the baby. He could understand Nadiya's stance. It was more acceptable than the distinct lack of warmth that Ella exhibited toward a child she'd carried for nine months. That coldness, that lack of feeling, he would never grasp.

And Ella already had the next step planned—to identify a couple to adopt the child.

Which raised another thought. He'd seen Jo Wells waiting at the elevator when he and Nadiya had arrived. Had the social worker been to see Ella to discuss prospective parents?

Didn't Ella realize it was a waste of time choosing other parents? He was going to adopt the baby. What Ella didn't appear to get was that he was a man of immense financial reserves and infinite patience. Those attributes had made him into the mega-wealthy man he was today. He studied the fake Madonna-child tableau in front of him through narrowed eyes.

From her hesitation, it was clear that Ella had had little to do with babies. She knew as little about them as he did. But he was willing to learn—she wasn't. He wanted this baby...and he wasn't about to let her win this round.

The sooner she got that into her stubborn head, the better.

"Well, I no longer have the prospective wife you considered I need. But I still intend to adopt the baby." He was proud of the lack of emotion in his voice.

Ella's chin came up in a gesture he was starting to recognize. Instantly his muscles tensed.

"I've been looking at portfolios of couples who've already been screened. You have not been interviewed or checked yet."

That answered his unasked question. Jo *had* been here to discuss the baby's future parents. And it was equally obvious that his own proposal had not been on the agenda—because of Ella's prejudice against him.

"Then I'll have to remedy that," he said quietly. "This baby carries the blood of generations of Volkovoys in her veins—she is not leaving my family."

"Not even if it would be better for her?"

"You don't know that." He glanced down at the baby. Her mouth was moving up and down, tempting him to smile. But now was not a time to smile. "You could be letting the baby in for a life of hell."

"That's unlikely. The couples have been assessed and police checks carried out—"

"Who really knows what happens in the privacy of a couple's home? And do you really want to take that risk?"

That silenced Ella.

As color drained from her face, leaving it a pasty shade of white, Yevgeny realized he'd overdone it. Of course, he didn't even believe his own alarmist statement—he and Dmitri might have been better off adopted by a loving couple than ordered by a bamboozled judge to stay with his mother after his parents' divorce. But if his scaremongering changed Ella's mind, then it would be worth it.

The end justified the means; he'd always lived his life by that creed.

Yet unexpectedly, shame lingered within him as unhappiness and worry clouded her eyes. Her fingers had clenched, whitening her knuckles against the Disney print of the baby's swaddling wrap. He glanced away—and caught sight of Ella's overnight bag.

After a beat, he said, "Your bags are packed. You're leaving."

Ella nodded.

"The baby will be going with you."

He told himself she wouldn't walk away now that she'd held…engaged with…the baby. He waited for her affirmation of what he hoped to hear.

She shook her head. "No."

Ella intended to go through with her vow not to keep the baby. She would leave her daughter behind. What kind of woman would do that? Yevgeny still found it hard to believe she could be so callous. "You will leave the baby here?"

"The baby will go to a specially trained foster mother who will look after her until I pick the right family out for her. Jo and I discussed the foster mother earlier—she knows the baby is coming."

Two thoughts filled his head. *She* was made of ice, and how could she not understand that *he* was the right family!

Anger rose like a tidal wave.

Yevgeny reached for his wallet to retrieve the business card Jo Wells had given him the day before. His hands trembled at the emotion swamping him. "That will not happen. I am taking the baby home with me. I will call your social worker and tell her so."

"No!" yelled Ella from behind him. "If you take her, I'll have you arrested for kidnapping."

The baby started to cry.

Yevgeny stopped in his tracks at the sound and whipped around to face them. Ella was frantically rocking the baby—even uttering hoarse hushing sounds.

When the baby quieted, she met his gaze and said in a more even tone, "You need to think about the baby. It's not fair on her to form an attachment with you if she's going to be given to another family."

Angered and frustrated, he snapped, "If you would stop being so goddamned stubborn, you would know that she should stay with me—be my daughter."

"And how will that work?" A note he'd never heard from Ella before filled her voice. "You're never home. You work like a demon—don't deny it. Keira's told me all about how Dmitri's always exhausted."

He bit back the surge of irritation at his sister-in-law. "I'll rearrange my schedule."

"You really believe that?" Ella gazed at him from pitying eyes. "You're a type-A, high-achieving success junkie… You need your daily fix. Staying home with a baby will drive you crazy. You wouldn't last more than two days."

"What makes you think that?"

"Because I know." Her shoulders drooped as she blew out a breath, yet she didn't lower the baby; she continued to rock the bundle back and forth. She gave him a sad smile. "I am exactly the same—and people like us are not made to have children. Babies should be placed in families where they will have a better chance of being loved and living fruitful lives. Taking the baby would be a selfish thing to do. Why not be selfless and allow her the chance to be happy?"

The woman didn't know what she was talking about. He and she were nothing alike. Yevgeny refused to listen to what she was saying.

Yet instead of challenging her claim, he countered, "And you think you're any less selfish?"

"What do you mean?"

"Christmas is coming." He gestured to the small tree standing in the corner of the waiting room. "And you're going to send the baby you gave birth to away to a foster home? Her first Christmas will be spent as an orphan. Alone. I will not allow it. I am calling Jo Wells now—I don't care how she arranges it, but that baby in your arms is going home with me. No baby should be alone at Christmas."

Five

Bringing the baby home was the most ill-considered thing she'd ever done, Ella decided ruefully the following morning.

She'd given up trying to get the baby to sleep an hour ago—after a night spent mixing formula and warming bottles and not a wink of sleep. A glance at the large white clock on the ivory-patterned wallpaper revealed it was already seven-thirty Monday morning. Normally she'd be in the office already, her emails read and answered. She'd be about to fetch the single cup of coffee she'd allowed herself each day during her pregnancy. Made from a fragrant, specially ground blend she favored, it was a must to kick-start her day.

This morning she hadn't even fired up her laptop…much less thought about coffee.

Ella was exhausted.

But it was worth it.…

She'd refused to allow Yevgeny to all but kidnap the baby and take it away with him. Once that happened he would never let the baby go. She knew that. The only way to stop that from happening had been to take the baby home herself…and the sacrifice was probably going to kill her.

At the very least, it was going to break what was left of her heart.

She gazed wearily at the tiny girl-monster lying on the plump couch beside her.

"Don't you think it's time for a nap?"

The baby stared back at her with round, wide-awake eyes.

Ella sighed.

She had no idea what she was doing but the few tips from a willing nurse that she'd scribbled down on the legal pad before leaving the maternity unit had been a godsend. At least the baby wouldn't starve—she'd just finished a bottle. Yet it had only reinforced how much Ella didn't know. After all, she hadn't attended parenting classes or read any books on child rearing during the pregnancy because that had been Keira's department. She'd only read the manuals about the dos and don'ts for the period the baby was growing in her stomach, none of which were of any help now.

Thank heavens she'd called an agency to engage a nanny before leaving the hospital yesterday. The agency hadn't been able to send someone at once, and Ella had wished she hadn't been so hasty in telling Yevgeny that she was taking the baby home, but pride hadn't let her back down.

How much trouble could a baby be?

She closed her eyes, thinking about the night past…trouble didn't even begin to describe the experience!

And after today there were still eight days to go before she could sign the adoption consent.

Ella didn't even want to contemplate it.

Opening her eyes, she gazed down at the baby, who was now wiggling her legs. Ella knew her biggest challenge was going to be maintaining a healthy distance from this child. What she didn't need was to form an attachment to a baby she had no intention of keeping. She'd hoped that the baby would spend most of the time asleep—after all, that was what had happened at the maternity unit.

But it certainly hadn't played out like that last night....

Since they'd gotten home to Ella's cozy town house, most of the baby's waking time had been spent in her arms. It seemed to have forgotten what sleep was. Ella had walked her up and down for what seemed like the whole night...to no avail.

Her cell phone beeped.

Ella reached for it and squinted at the hi-tech screen.

The messages had started early this morning—from colleagues and clients who had no idea of the baby's arrival on Friday evening, and thought this would be a normal work Monday. Ella knew she faced a flood of calls and emails...and that she ought to divert them to Peggy, her assistant...but right now she was too tired to move—or to think of anything.

Except sleep...

The baby chose that moment to burp.

As tired as she was, it was impossible not to smile. Ella forced her face straight. This was not the way to maintain a healthy distance. She shifted her attention back to the cell phone. Another message beeped through.

Then it rang.

It was the childcare agency she'd contacted yesterday to let her know the nanny had been dispatched.

Ella sighed with relief as she killed the call. Wrinkling her nose at the child, she said, "Sleep is on its way."

She'd have to summon the energy to call the office, check that Peggy had canceled all her meetings for the day, and then she could crawl into bed. It was the stuff fantasies were made of....

The nanny turned out to be a short, energetic woman named Deb Benson. Within half an hour she'd restored order, unexpectedly leaving Ella feeling inadequate. She was used to making decisions, doing deals, dispensing advice, but as far as babies were concerned, she was a rookie. It was hard to accept how inept she was. Explaining the situation to Deb had also proved to be difficult—so, too, the fact that the baby didn't yet have a name. Yet Deb hadn't even blinked.

It made Ella wonder what it would take to faze her.

A lot more than a baby created for a couple who'd decided to give her up...and a surrogate mother who avoided cuddling her.

But it was for her own protection, Ella reminded herself as she made her way to the sleek white-and-silver home office where she spent much of her out-of-office time. Yet once barricaded in the familiar space, Ella struggled to concentrate. It wasn't the fact that she felt different—heck, it would've been impossible not to! Her stomach felt soft—no more gym-hard abs. Her breasts were swollen, tight and aching.

Having the baby had changed her body—and now, little as Ella wanted to admit it, the infant was changing her life.

Her silver laptop sat on the smooth, white desk. Ella flipped it open. She forced herself to call Peggy.

When she put the phone down she found that her ears were straining to hear what Deb was doing. She stared blindly at the screen in front of her. Against her will she found herself using Google to search "baby names" and faced with pages of websites. Most popular girls' names of the seventies...eighties... nineties...noughties...and beyond.

There were websites for flower names, for foreign names. Her mind boggled.

Lily. Rose. Petunia.

With a click of the mouse the next webpage opened.

Manon. Jeanne.

Another click.

Eleni. Roshni.

Ella clicked back to the first website with the botanical girls' names.

Or Holly.

The sound of the doorbell was an unwelcome interruption. Scant seconds later the door to her office burst open, and an even more unwelcome male presence filled the doorway.

"You've hired a nanny!"

Determined not to give Yevgeny more advantage than surprise had already afforded him, Ella shut the computer lid and rose to her feet. He dwarfed her. She swore silently. Next time she would wear heels.

"Of course I have." She met his outraged gaze as calmly as she was able. "I have a job to get back to."

"You're due maternity leave."

Ella shook her head. "I work for myself, so any leave I take is scheduled long in advance. This time I only allowed myself a few days off." And that had been next week. When the baby was supposed to arrive—not long before Christmas. "Anyway, I wasn't keeping the baby, remember? So I certainly didn't need maternity leave." And now, since Keira's bombshell, Ella knew she definitely didn't want to be sitting around with time to think.

His eyes glittered with disbelief. "And none of that has changed since bringing the baby home?"

She struggled with another wave of weariness and searched for words to explain her feelings to the man watching her as though she were some two-headed alien.

"How can it? I have to work." She stared back at him. *Attack was the best form of defense.* "You employ women—some of them might even be executives." Although she doubted it. Men like Yevgeny Volkovoy didn't take women seriously enough to give them significant responsibility. One only had to look at the women he dated—models, socialites—to see that. Although she had to admit that Nadiya had shown more spunk than Ella would've expected from one of his conquests—certainly more than Yevgeny wanted. "I can only imagine what you'd say about a woman who planned to be back at work, then decided to take several months off instead."

He blinked, and Ella saw the truth of her argument register. He shrugged.

"Maybe." Then he added, "But I would've understood. Eventually." Putting his hands on his hips, he tilted his head to one side. "And that argument doesn't apply here—you are your own boss."

"Which means I can't just disappear from the office—I need to carefully plan the times away and arrange for someone to cover for me." And most important, she wanted to avoid becoming too attached to the child. "I *want* to go back to work."

"So when do you plan to do that?"

"As soon as I can." Ella didn't say "tomorrow," which was what she fully intended—so long as her body obliged and the fatigue that was starting to make her feel dizzy wasn't too much of a factor.

"And dump the child you haven't even given a name on the nanny?"

Ella stifled a yawn. "Holly will be perfectly happy."

"Holly? *Holly?*" He reared back. "You've named the baby?"

"Obviously."

He looked surprised. "Just now? To prove me wrong?"

"Not to prove you wrong! I picked her name earlier." She wasn't admitting to those minutes of scouring websites—after all, she couldn't even fathom what had driven her to do a Google search for baby names. It was all too uncomfortable to absorb. And why did he think she'd done it merely to prove him wrong? Let him think it had been an arbitrary name plucked out of the air. "You shouldn't assume an importance you don't have in my life."

But instead of causing Yevgeny to puff up with annoyance as she'd intended, her comment made him laugh.

"Bravo," he said.

Ella stared. Tiredness must be befuddling her. Because with his white teeth flashing and laugh lines—which she'd never noticed before—crinkling around his eyes, he caused her breath to hook in her throat. In the wickedly sparkling eyes, Ella got a glimpse of his appeal. This must be the reason women hung around him like bees around a honeypot.

The man looked devastating.

And all because she'd tried to put him in his place!

She couldn't help smiling back.

But his next words wiped the smile off her face.

"I came expecting to find you ready to beg me to take her away." His light eyes grew cloudy. "I should've known you'd hire a nanny."

He'd expected her to fail at the first hurdle.

That stung!

Because even though she'd hired a nanny to keep the baby at a distance, deep in her heart she knew he was right. She *had* failed. She was dangerously ignorant about babies, and it didn't help that her ignorance came because she'd never intended to have children of her own. It only served to underscore her secret, deeply held conviction that she would make a terrible parent.

Mostly his criticism stung because the truth of it was Ella wasn't accustomed to failure. Whatever task she undertook she saw through to the bitter end.

And arranging for the baby's adoption would be no different—once she'd had a good-night's sleep and gotten herself back to normal.

But Yevgeny only saw a woman he didn't particularly like, so he wrote her off as useless—like he'd written most of her sex off. He was definitely archaic… She'd dearly love to see him taught a lesson. Tempting as it was to daydream that she might be the woman to do that, Ella knew it wouldn't—couldn't—be her. Some other woman would have to have the pleasure of taking him down a peg or two…one day. How she'd love to see the arrogant Yevgeny grovel.

"Didn't you come to see Holly?" she asked, too exhausted to get drawn into another of their fiery exchanges.

"Thanks to the nanny, she's probably been fed at least."

Annoyance surfaced, exacerbated by the mind-numbing weariness. Did he believe she would neglect the baby? Just because she didn't want a child didn't mean that she'd ever see it harmed. No, not *it…her.* Holly was a little girl. Ella sighed inwardly. It was hard enough to keep her distance to stop an attachment forming; she didn't need his cruel barbs. "I looked after her all night. The nanny only just arrived."

"Then I'd better go check on her."

Ella ground her teeth, and turned her head to stare blindly at her computer screen. Unable to help herself she blurted out, "None of the intending parents' profiles Jo Wells left at the hospital fit what I'm looking for."

It got so quiet, she thought Yevgeny must've already gone, that he hadn't heard her.

That might be for the best.

She turned her head, glanced over her shoulder.

Yevgeny stood as unmoving as a marble statue on the office's threshold, his pale eyes hungry and intent.

Waiting.

This was what he'd wanted to know, wasn't it? But Ella refused to hold out false hope. "Jo has already brought another batch of portfolios for me to look at. There should be at least one set of suitable parents there."

"You're choosing them tonight?"

She shook her head, flinching inwardly at the thought of what lay ahead. Glimpses into the lives of strangers desperate for a baby. And not just any baby—the baby she had helped create.

More hopeful faces would smile out of the pages at her— with carefully picked words detailing their dreams. Each set of parents hoping they would be the chosen ones. And if she liked more than one set, it would only get harder. After meeting the couples, she'd have to choose one couple over the other. Right now she couldn't face the mountain that lay ahead.

"I'll do it tomorrow." She turned away from the intensity that radiated from him, back to her laptop.

A moment later his footsteps receded. After the door closed softly behind him, Ella's shoulders sagged. She could barely concentrate on the letters on the screen in front of her. Giving in, she rose and went to sit on the love seat beneath the window, her computer perched on her stomach. Much more comfortable.

For the next few minutes, she'd see what appointments she could reschedule…then…then, she'd go see what Yevgeny was doing. See if she could hurry him along. Once Yevgeny had departed, she'd be able to relax. She'd go lie down in her bedroom.

And welcome the sleep her body craved.

Yevgeny pushed the door to Ella's office open with the flat palm of his hand and reentered the room. One glance caused him to pause.

The icicle had fallen asleep.

He crossed the room with silent steps, his footfalls muffled by the pile of the pale gray carpet until he stood beside the sofa.

Yet, instead of an icicle's cold clinical perfection, Ella's skin held a very feminine rosy flush. Her hair feathered across her forehead, the sharp-angled bob nowhere in evidence.

She looked younger. Prettier. *Softer.*

Yevgeny shrugged the illusion away.

Her laptop, angled across her midriff, was in danger of toppling off. She'd been working. Of course she had.

What had he expected?

That she'd been mothering? He suppressed a snort of disgust. The baby was where he'd just left her—in the arms of the nanny. His mouth compressing, he lifted the computer gently off Ella's stomach and set it down on her desk. Turning back, he took in the uncomfortable way she was draped over the small couch. Her feet, one hooked over the other, dangled over the edge and her body was skewed so that her bottom cheek was pressed against the white leather cushions. It definitely didn't look comfortable.

Bending over, he lifted her feet and laid them straight along the couch. Instantly they slid back over the edge. He stilled, fearing she might waken. But she didn't stir.

The way her body was twisted suggested she was going to wake with a God-Almighty crick in her neck for sure. Yevgeny didn't know why it was bothering him, but he couldn't leave her like this. When he'd first arrived, she'd looked tired with gray shadows rimming her expressive eyes. Leaving aside her lack of motherly instincts, Ella had been through a lot in the past few days. She'd given birth to the baby that her sister had given up. She'd had to cope with deciding the baby's future.

She must be worn out.

The first flicker of unwilling sympathy for her stirred within him.

He might not agree with the decisions she was planning, but he could appreciate how stressful it must be. He knelt and scooped her up against his chest. She made a tiny mewing sound, and her lashes fluttered. Then she burrowed in against his shoulder.

She smelt of a soft, old-fashioned scent.

Lilacs...

Yevgeny bit back a curse.

Straightening to his full six-foot, three-inch height, he strode out of the glossy white-and-gray office. At the end of the carpeted corridor a door stood ajar. With one foot, he knocked it wide to reveal what was clearly the main bedroom in the town house.

What a difference.

While white once again dominated, it wasn't the glossy white of leather and lacquer that he'd seen in the rest of the house. No reflective glass and silver mirrors in here. This was...

Holding her against him, he let his eyes travel around.

A bed decked out with snowy-white linen was the centerpiece of this pretty, feminine room. In his peripheral vision Yevgeny caught sight of a French-style dressing table with a collection of antique, glass perfume bottles and a set of silver-backed hairbrushes. His gaze stopped on two pairs of ballet shoes suspended by faded pink satin ribbons from an ornately carved brass hook. He started to smile. On the opposite wall hung a large acrylic painting of a dancer in a style reminiscent of Degas.

It was a bedroom filled with nostalgia and romance.

Not quite what he would've expected, given the brisk business exterior Ella McLeod presented to the world.

He entered the bedroom.

Instantly he was enveloped in a mist of that flowery, feminine scent—the scent he was fast coming to associate with the essence of Ella. Gently he laid her down on the pristine white linen of the bed, then stepped back. He could hear her breathing. Deep and even through slightly parted pale pink lips. Pale pink lips that held him enthralled.

Just one kiss…and she could waken.

The idea was ridiculous, but it persisted. Sense warred with temptation. Until, at last, he succumbed to the tantalizing temptation and bent forward. He placed the softest of kisses on her lips then straightened, his color high, feeling unaccountably foolish.

Ella didn't stir.

He'd gotten the legend wrong—she was not Sleeping Beauty—and instead of waking, the Ice Queen slept on.

It was already Tuesday. Keira and Dmitri had departed for Africa—without changing their minds about the baby. It had taken all Ella's willpower not to scream at her sister that she was making the biggest mistake of her life.

To Ella's intense relief, Holly had already survived four full days and nights, and Ella herself had managed to keep from becoming too attached to the newborn.

But this evening Deb was leaving to go to a friend's housewarming party. The party had been planned long before the agency had sent her, and Ella waved aside her apologies.

"Go, enjoy yourself," she said. Holly was sleeping peacefully in her cot upstairs. The speaker for the baby monitor lay on top of a pile of magazines on the low, wide coffee table beside the collection of shopping bags that had been delivered not long ago.

With Deb gone, Ella shut the front door and took advantage of the solitude. She was busily manhandling the huge, cut-pine Christmas tree into the corner of the living room, when the doorbell chimed.

She bit back a curse. No choice but to set the tree down… and undo all the progress she'd made in the past few minutes.

Impatient, she wrenched open the door.

Yevgeny stood on the doorstep, every inch the city billionaire, immaculate in a dark, conservative business suit and a white shirt that still managed to look crisp at the end of the day.

"May I come in?"

Before she could respond, he'd brushed past her. Irritation spiked through her at his high-handedness.

Her voice heavy with irony, she muttered, "Sure you can."

He turned and grinned. "Thank you."

The flash of that wolfish smile, the gleam of wicked laughter in his eyes, indicated that he was fully mindful of her irritation. Ella couldn't halt the unfurling awareness that blossomed through her, starting deep in her chest, near her heart and spreading outward in a glow of warmth. Like a flower following the path of the sun.

The man was dynamite.

And she didn't even *like* him. He was obnoxious, arrogant, inconsiderate. So why the melting heat in the pit of her stomach? Why wasn't she recoiling? What on earth was wrong with her? Didn't she have any sense of self-preservation? Ella drew in a deep breath and was instantly flooded with the woody aroma of his aftershave.

God help her if he ever set himself the task of trying to charm her—she'd be in serious trouble!

With a toss of her head, she blew out the breath she was holding and brushed aside the absurd notion.

No threat from him.

Never.

"Holly is sleeping," she said finally as he brushed past her into the living room.

His response had nothing to do with the baby. "You're putting up a Christmas tree."

Did he have to sound so surprised?

"Yes."

Guilt stabbed Ella. She wasn't about to reveal that it was the first time in the five years she'd lived here that she'd done so. Or

that most of the reason why she'd ordered a tree to be delivered
stemmed from his barbed comments about Holly enduring her
first Christmas alone. Becoming aware of the lack of festive
cheer in her home had not been a welcome discovery.

"I almost had it in position…but then the doorbell rang."
She gestured to where the tree lay. "Now I'll have to start all
over again."

He strode across to where the tree lay. "I'll give you a hand
and we'll have it up in minutes."

"Shouldn't you still be at work?" She bit off the bit about
"making your next million."

He'd walked around to the far side of the tree. Now he shot
one immaculate shirt cuff back to glance at a flat watch on
his wrist. "Five o'clock. I've had enough for one day—boss's
prerogative. I wanted to see Holly."

She refused to let that sentiment tug at her heartstrings.

Instead, she inspected the dark, formal suit he wore and
decided it must be French, while she tried to ignore the effect
the broad shoulders tapering down to a narrow male waist had
on her. "What about your suit? You'll get resin all over it."

He'd reek of a pine forest for months to come. Ella doubted
dry cleaning would get rid of the overpowering smell of pine.
It would kill that sexy, seductive scent Yevgeny wore so well.

Her lips tilted up in secret amusement.

"What are you smiling at?"

He sounded so suspicious that her smile broadened. He'd find
out soon enough. She slanted him an impish look. "Nothing."

"Somehow I don't believe that. You're plotting."

"Gosh, but you have a suspicious mind."

"Do you blame me? I know exactly what you are."

Her smile vanished and her eyes narrowed.

"There's no point in your staying. Holly's sleeping." Ella had
had enough of his unwarranted opinions. Now she just wanted
him to leave. Before he tempted her to laugh with him…and
then he wounded her again. She wanted him gone.

But before she could turn and walk to the front door to show him on his way, he asked, "Have you reached a decision on the new set of portfolios Jo Wells showed you?"

He'd only come to influence—make that sabotage—her decision.

It was her own fault for giving in and revealing she hadn't selected any parents from the first batch of candidates. She'd been overtired…not thinking properly…reacting with her emotions rather than her head. And look where it had gotten her—Yevgeny hounding her.

Ella headed for the door and opened it. "Once I reach a final decision I'll let you know. Then you can decide if you want to stay in touch with the baby and her new family. Thank you for visiting."

Even from across the room, she saw his face fall.

He really had wanted to see the baby, she realized.

The considerations that had led her to update him about progress on the adoption proceedings yesterday returned. Yevgeny was the only blood relative who was showing any interest in the baby; he deserved to be kept in the picture. This would be an open adoption. Jo was insistent that adoptive children needed ties with their birth relatives. Those ties to family helped children grow up secure, with a healthy sense of self and identity.

Ella recognized that she needed to set aside her own antagonism toward the man…and think only of the baby.

As much as Holly needed contact with her birth mother, it would be to her advantage to know her birth father…and her uncle. Having a clear sense of identity would help her to stay intact as an individual as she grew up.

Even though Ella considered Yevgeny Volkovoy to be the most arrogantly selfish man on the face of the planet, for Holly's sake, she had to recognize that his desire to visit Holly was a blessing.

From her position at the door, Ella relented a little. "You can come back when Holly is awake."

But Yevgeny showed no sign of hearing. He'd already

shrugged off his jacket and put it on the sofa. "I said I'd help you with the tree."

So he was determined to stay—and ignore her wishes. Why had she ever imagined she might persuade him otherwise? He was accustomed to riding roughshod over other people's opinions.

She didn't want to be stuck alone with Yevgeny making small talk. Nor did she want him putting up the Christmas tree she'd bought for Holly. And she certainly didn't want to start thinking that he was helpful. Or, God help her, indispensable.

"You know, I really don't need—" *nor want* "—your help." All too aware of how much more defined the breadth of his shoulders was with his jacket off, Ella didn't dare to allow her suddenly treacherous eyes to linger on the lean narrow hips, the broad chest clad only in the soft, finest cotton shirt with the top button unbuttoned. Far too tempting. "And don't forget to take your jacket with you when you go."

The sooner he put it back on, the sooner she'd be able to visualize him as a corporate Russian bully.

Leaning on the door handle, Ella shut her eyes to block out the image of him standing in her living room rolling up his shirt sleeves. How was it possible to be attracted to a man she detested?

What the hell is wrong with me?

Six

With her eyes shut and her shoulders bowed, Ella looked more vulnerable than Yevgeny had ever seen her as she leaned against the doorjamb of the front entrance waiting for him to leave.

The last time he'd seen her she'd looked exhausted…but this was worse.

Nothing of the Ella he so disliked remained.

No black suit. Instead, she wore a white, sleeveless T-shirt that clung to curves he'd never known she had, while cropped jeans hugged her legs tapering to slim ankles. The simple outfit only served to underline her fragility.

Yevgeny forgot that he'd come to find out whether she'd looked at the portfolios she'd told him Jo would be dropping off today. He even forgot about his plan to convince her that every parent would be wrong for Holly. Except him.

Instead, driven to comfort her, he padded across the room on silent feet to stand beside her.

She hadn't heard his approach—or, if she had, she showed no sign of it. Yevgeny hesitated. Silky blond hair fell onto her shoulders, the style softer, less sharply defined than he remembered. Her scent surrounded him. Lilacs. Sweet...and elusive.

Slowly, oh, so slowly, he reached out a hand and touched the fine strands where they brushed her shoulder.

She started.

Then her head turned. Behind the large spectacles, her eyes had widened, and the summer sun streaming in through the door transformed the light brown irises to lustrous topaz.

As he stared, her lips parted.

He groped for words that made some kind of sense to fill the electric silence. "What do you want me to do first?"

"Do first?"

From this close he could see her pupils darkening.

All thoughts of offering comfort had rushed out of his mind.

Desire—dark and disturbing—grabbed him by the throat. He tried to respond, but his voice wouldn't—couldn't—work. But his body was working...in ways he didn't even want to think about. Whoa, this was Ella McLeod of all people. He didn't like her. *And* the woman had given birth to a child last Friday... He couldn't be feeling desire...where was his sense of perspective?

"What do you want me to do with the tree?" he managed at last in a gravelly rasp.

"The tree?" The dazed, startled look in her eyes faded. With her index finger she pushed her glasses up her nose. "Oh. The *tree*."

"I told you I'd help. It's too big for you to try and set up by yourself—and you had a baby not so long ago. You shouldn't be straining yourself."

Her shoulders squared. The veil of fragility fell away from her. "I was doing just fine until the doorbell rang."

Yevgeny pressed his lips together.

That was Ella.

Determinedly independent.

Making it clear she didn't need comfort—or help. Maybe she wasn't quite as vulnerable as he'd thought.

"Do you ever accept help from anybody?" he asked with

more than a touch of exasperation, letting his hand drop away. He should be relieved that she'd returned to her usual independent and icy self. At least he could breathe again—and speak. That curious immobilizing spell that had seized his body and paralyzed his vocal cords had started to lift.

Yet he felt a whisper of regret that the moment had passed. God! Had he actually *wanted* to kiss Ella McLeod?

Yes.

The answer shocked him.

He *had* wanted to kiss her, to taste her mouth, to lose himself in her womanliness. Yes, womanliness. There was no doubt about it, Ella was every inch a woman. He would never again be fooled by the lawyer in the black suit again. He'd caught a glimpse of the person—the woman—who lurked behind the legal facade. The lacy night attire. Two pairs of well-used ballet slippers hanging in her bedroom. Even the way she'd held the baby and rocked her in her arms after she'd refused to even look at Holly at first.

She intrigued the hell out of him.

If anyone had told him he'd be hot as a mink in season for lawyer Ella McLeod a few weeks ago he would've howled with scorn. Ridiculous. But now the joke was on him. Only minutes ago he'd been ready to devour her with a desperation that stunned him.

Had he lost all reason?

Could Ella the Icicle really be Ella the Enchantress?

Yevgeny turned away, lest his face reveal the turmoil of his thoughts. Ella was sharp, and he didn't want her recognizing any chinks in his armor that would render him vulnerable to her.

"My parents—when I was younger."

He realized she'd finally answered his question. "They're the only people you accept help from?"

A frown creased her brow. "Probably."

He could see her thinking, trying to come up with other names…and failing. "How about your sister?"

"Keira?" She gave a laugh of astonishment. "She's too young."

"I'm sure you were making decisions at her age."

She shrugged. "Maybe. But Keira always needs help from *me*."

Yevgeny hoarded that nugget of information away, to retrieve and examine later. "What about a mentor…or something?"

Ella immediately shook her head.

He stared then. It was inconceivable to him that she'd never asked for—never needed—help. Even he, who prided himself on his self-made success, had relied on mentors to get where he had so rapidly. How much harder would it have been without the men who had advised him…guided him…helped him?

From slitted eyes he gazed at her with fresh respect. She'd cleaved a way out for herself—amidst fierce competition—and she'd gained a good reputation. He'd seen the recognition and wary respect her name produced. Ella had done it all by herself.

Without anyone to hold her hand.

"Your parents must be proud of you," he said at last.

"They're very much older."

She'd mentioned that before….

And it didn't answer his question. But it prompted another thought. "Don't tell me you look after them, too?"

In response, Ella inclined her head slightly.

"You do!" He blinked in disbelief. She shouldered the burden of her entire family. "And your sister still comes running to you for everything she needs."

"She always has, but I don't mind. We're sisters, after all." She came instantly to Keira's defense. "Your brother does it, too. I know because Keira told me."

Yevgeny bristled. "I don't have your patience. I told him to make a man of himself." And that decision had probably cost him dearly. For a time Dmitri had torn through the Volkovoy fortune while Yevgeny could only watch. He'd been wild—and irresponsible. A spendthrift and a wastrel. He'd run through everything that was handed to him—and then come back to demand more.

That's when Yevgeny had put his foot down—he'd refused… and demanded that Dmitri come with him to Auckland to set up the new headquarters for Volkovoy cruises.

Dmitri had argued that it was a job for a menial manager. But Yevgeny had refused to bow. Do a job, earn a salary or get out.

They'd quarreled. Dmitri had chosen to get out, screeching off to the smell of burnt rubber and Yevgeny had shuddered with fear and regret. For four days his brother had not returned home. Yevgeny had held vigil and waited for news of the worst.

On the fifth day Dmitri had called and sullenly said he was on his way to Auckland. Yevgeny had thanked the gods and hoped his brother wouldn't do anything recklessly stupid.

Yevgeny later learned he had Keira to thank for Dmitri's success in New Zealand.

Meeting Keira had saved his brother—or maybe it had been being cut off from funding for his lavish lifestyle and being forced to work, to be accountable for his actions for the first time in his overindulged life.

Whatever it was, Dmitri had finally started to grow up.

"I'm very proud of what he's done in Auckland. He's hired premises and sourced some excellent staff."

Behind her glasses, Ella rolled her eyes. "Keira said anyone could've done it. That Dmitri felt it was an insult to be given such a menial task to do."

"At least he didn't screw it up." He flashed her a smile.

"You expected him to," she said after a long moment.

"Honestly?" Her eyes demanded the truth, so he gave it. "Yes, I did."

"How could you think he would fail?"

"I didn't think he'd see it through. He's never had any firm idea of what he wants from life." He paused, then turned the focus back on Ella and her sister. "How can you talk. You don't expect anything of Keira. You still take care of her, sort out all her messes. She never needs to take accountability for anything.

You're even sorting out the adoption for a baby she wanted then discarded."

For once Ella had nothing to say. He watched as her mouth opened and closed. Finally she turned away and crossed to where three large store bags sat on the floor. She reached into the closest one and took out a box. She opened it, revealing a tray containing about a dozen shiny, red ornamental balls.

It was a moment of utter emotional devastation.

And Yevgeny felt like a complete toad. It was almost Christmas. It was a time for faith…and family. He'd insisted on helping Ella decorate a tree to celebrate the festivities for Holly—and now he was upsetting her.

That wasn't right. Yevgeny couldn't help thinking that his dearly loved *babushka* would be ashamed of him for ruining Ella's moment of pleasure and forcing her to accept unwanted assistance. She'd already told him to leave—that was what she wanted. If he behaved with the honor that his *babushka* would expect of him, Yevgeny knew he was left with no choice: he must leave….

He came to a decision. "You don't want me to stay and help you with the tree, so I will leave and come back later when Holly is awake."

With an inward sigh of disappointment, Yevgeny made his way to where he'd abandoned his jacket. But before he could lean down to pick it up, Ella spoke from behind him. "You can stay—if you want."

Yevgeny jerked around in surprise.

She wasn't even looking at him, nor did she sound particularly welcoming, yet his heart lifted.

"Thank you." Gratitude welled up inside him. Before she could change her mind, he moved to the tree and hoisted it up with enthusiasm. "The Christmas tree will look good over here, hmm?"

Ella tucked her hair behind one ear, and shifted her glance to where he indicated. "Yes, I think you're right—that's the perfect spot."

His lips curved in a smile and he shot her an amused look through the gap between two branches. "Good. For once we're in agreement."

She met his gaze. Then, after a moment, she grinned back. "Yes. It would appear we are."

Ella McLeod had dimples in both cheeks.

To avoid the confusion the discovery aroused, Yevgeny ducked down and secured the base of the tree. When he'd safely assured himself that noticing Ella had dimples didn't change anything of great consequence, he finally raised his head again.

"Have you got lights for the tree?" he asked. "They will need to go up first."

Ella dove back into the shopping bags and emerged, waving a box of brand-new Christmas lights with a triumphant flourish. Another smile...and her dimples flashed again.

Blood pumped through his veins.

Yevgeny averted his gaze, and busied himself with taking the box from her hands. Her slender fingers brushed against his large ones—an electric connection. He didn't dare look at her as he broke the seal. Once the lid was open, he lifted the coiled rope of lights out. Immediately Ella crowded closer.

He inhaled deeply.

Lilacs.

Yes, he was in danger of becoming addicted to the subtle scent....

Shaking his head in rejection of that craziness, Yevgeny started to weave the lights through the branches while Ella worked alongside him, making adjustments. He'd never been this close to her for any length of time. It felt curiously—he searched for the right word—exhilarating. When she stepped away to shake out the remaining cable and then went to plug it into the wall socket, he found himself sharply aware of the gray void left in her wake.

A flick of the switch and color lit up the room.

Even Ella's white, cropped T-shirt reflected the rainbow wash of Christmas lights. It looked magical. Yevgeny found himself chuckling at the pretty picture she made.

Ella reached down and switched the lights off. "Now we know they work!"

"Are you always so prosaic?"

She glanced at him through the fan of hair that shielded her face. "Always."

Despite her reply, Yevgeny couldn't halt the spreading of awareness. He considered himself a connoisseur of beautiful women—he'd dated some of the world's best. So why hadn't he noticed how well proportioned her features were? The straight nose, the short delicate arch of her upper lip, and the uptilted curve of her smile all combined to create a striking face.

But he hadn't noticed it.

Until now.

He hadn't bothered to look beyond the dark suits, oversize glasses and abrasive manner.

What else had he missed?

"You have lovely eyes, you know," he said abruptly. "But those hideous glasses you wear do nothing to show them off."

Shock flickered in her eyes, and then a flush stained her cheeks. "Thank you…I think."

"It was a compliment—you shouldn't hide your assets."

Without replying, she pushed her glasses up, then tucked her head down and scrabbled around in the shopping bags again. "I bought decorative balls to hang on the tree."

Ella had changed the subject.

His mouth slanted. Had he really expected a different response? Or was it so hard for her to accept a compliment? He was growing more and more curious about a woman whom he wouldn't have glanced at twice a week ago.

He refrained from pointing out that she'd already opened one box and smiled at her as she continued, "I ordered red-and-silver balls from an online catalog." Ella drew out the second box. "They should look very pretty against the dark green foliage."

He let her off the hook. "My grandmother had a collection of antique glass balls."

That garnered her interest. "Your grandmother? Is she still alive?"

Yevgeny shook his head. "Unfortunately not. She passed away two months ago."

Behind those ugly glasses, Ella's eyes were perceptive. "You miss her."

"Very much—she was a loving woman." Unlike her daughter, his mother. But Yevgeny had no intention to brood about the past.

"She was Russian?" Ella was asking.

"No. She was English." He picked up one of the red balls and hooked the silver ribbon securing it over a branch. After a pause during which he could sense Ella bursting to ask more, he said, "She married my very Russian grandfather after the Second World War—and taught him to speak English. In the process, she became more Russian than he was. The handblown glass decorations she treasured belonged to his family."

"Did she ever return to England?"

"No." But his mother had, taking him and Dmitri with her....

"Was she happy living so far from home?"

It took him a moment to shift his thoughts back to their conversation, and pick up the thread again. Ella was talking about his grandmother.

"She loved my grandfather. Her home was with him." And she'd loved him and Dmitri. *Babushka* had brought some degree of normality into their lives, normality that had vanished once his mother had ripped them away from their father. Without *Babushka* their lives had been barren of feminine affection—because his beautiful mother had had little to spare. Every day Yevgeny remembered his *babushka's* legacy of kindness. "She was one in a million."

His words hung in the air as they continued to loop decorations onto the branches.

After a few minutes he added, "My *babushka* collected

wooden decorations, too. She used to say she liked her tree to be a true *yolka*."

"*Yolka?*"

Yevgeny smiled as Ella tried the unfamiliar word out.

"The traditional tree is called the *yolka*," he told her. "The first Christmas tree was brought back to Russia by Peter the Great after his travels. The tradition became very popular, until Christmas was outlawed after the 1917 Revolution. It became known as a New Year's Tree."

"That's sad."

"For most of my life Christmas celebrations have been allowed," he said quickly, lest she feel pity for him, "although people had gotten used to celebrating on the first of January, so changing back to Christmas day came slowly at first." Yevgeny changed the subject. "Your family celebrated Christmas?"

Ella hesitated. "Well, we always decorated a tree—and my parents gave us Christmas gifts each year. But they didn't believe in perpetuating the myth of Santa Claus. They were older," she said with a touch of defensiveness when he stared. "And when Keira was young I used to wrap something of mine for her to find on Christmas morning. I'd tell her it was from Santa."

"My grandmother always made sure the family celebrated Christmas," he said, "even in the Iron Curtain years when it wasn't allowed. Although I don't remember that time—I was very young when the prohibition against Christmas was lifted. We would put our tree up earlier than New Year's Day so that we could have a Christmas tree, and we would decorate it with my grandmother's collection of ornaments and tangerines and walnuts carefully wrapped in tinfoil."

When he'd lived in London, even his mother had followed Western tradition and Santa Claus had visited each year. He and Dmitri had at least had the memories of finding gifts under the Christmas tree on Christmas morning—whatever else his mother had done, she had allowed them that small pleasure. What would life have been like for Ella and Keira? To be deprived of such simple joys? Especially when all their friends must've been visited by Santa's sleigh and his reindeer.

And this Christmas Keira would be on the other side of the world.

"Will you be getting together with your parents this Christmas?"

Ella shook her head. "No, we haven't celebrated together for a number of years."

Yes, Ella would be alone.

Not wanting her to see the compassion in his eyes, he turned away and started to hang the silver balls on the tree. But his mind couldn't let go of the image of Ella stoically wrapping her treasures to give to her sister—so that Keira wouldn't miss out on all the fun that went along with Santa. Was that part of the reason Ella seemed so humorless? Had all the fun been sapped out of her young life?

Perhaps...

All the more reason why this Christmas would be different for Holly.

As he made that vow, Yevgeny hung the last silver ball on the tree then stood back to admire their efforts. "Not bad," he declared. "Let's put the lights back on."

"Before I switch the lights on, there's one more item to go on the tree." Ella was unwrapping dark green tissue paper from the object she held in her hands. "The ornament for the top."

The wrapping fell away.

Yevgeny found himself staring at an angel. His first thought was that he would've expected Ella to choose a shiny silver star for the top of the tree. Nothing as personal—and as touchingly humorous—as this angel.

He reached out a hand to touch the angel.

"She's even more beautiful than I thought she would be from the online picture." Ella placed the angel in his hands, then hit the wall switch so that the tree lights came back on again. "She's handmade," continued Ella, as she straightened up. "What do you think?"

The angel wore a long robe of some kind of shimmery silver fabric. But, as Yevgeny held her up to the light, it was her face that captured his attention. Not beautiful. But full of childlike joy. Chubby and cherubic, the angel's face was brightened by a mischievous smile.

"She's perfect," he replied.

As he reached up and perched the angel on the apex of the tree, Yevgeny couldn't help thinking that in a few years' time, Holly would be itching to be the one to put the angel on top of the Christmas tree.

But Holly wouldn't be here…if Ella got her way.

Green. Yellow. Red.

The wash of light over his face didn't offer any assistance with making Yevgeny's expression easier to read. A mix of pensiveness…and some other emotion that Ella couldn't identify clouded his face.

She hesitated, then blurted out, "Would you like to look through the adoptive parent portfolios that Jo dropped off with me?"

Almost at once she regretted the offer. Already he was frowning. She must be going soft in the head to believe she and Yevgeny could do this without coming to blows. They were polar opposites. They never agreed on anything—this was going to end up in one big battle.

But before she could cast about for a reason to retract the invitation, the cloud cleared from his face, and he said, "Oh, yes! Perhaps I can finally make you see sense."

He flung himself down on the couch beneath the window and stretched his long legs out in front of him. Crossing his arms behind his head as he leaned back, he looked far too sure of himself.

Taking in the picture he made in his suit pants and white business shirt, together with the stubbled chin and rumpled dark hair, Ella wasn't sure whether to be exasperated or amused.

He looked quite at home…and it would probably take a bulldozer to move him out again.

But the truth of it was, if Yevgeny could see what some of these families had to offer a baby, he might even have second thoughts about his rash and selfish demand to keep the baby himself.

If Yevgeny reconsidered his standpoint, and accepted that adopting the baby out would be in Holly's best interests, it would be so much easier for them all. *If* he was involved in choosing a family for the baby, Holly would come out the winner.

Buoyed up with fresh optimism, Ella collected the five profile files Jo Wells had delivered from the dining table, then seated herself beside Yevgeny.

"Those look heavy." Unlocking his arms from behind his head, he bent forward to lift all but the bottom portfolio from her lap and set the stack on the coffee table in front of the couch.

"They are! They hold the whole life story—or at least the pertinent parts—of each couple." Ella opened the first folder. "This is the hardest part for me, the first photo of the couple together. Look at their eyes. They want this baby, they want Holly."

She paused.

Then, when Yevgeny remained silent, she added, "It's the same with each profile. Every time I have to conquer a surge of guilt before I turn the page."

When he slanted her a questioning glance, she said, "In case I don't choose them."

"I see."

From the look on his face, she could tell that he didn't get it.

"In case I didn't see the plea in their eyes, the desperation on their faces," she said to make it clear.

This time he got it.

She knew it by the shock in his eyes.

Maybe it was the word "desperation" that did it.

Ella turned the page. Then the next…and the next…until she reached the end. "This couple has two sons…they live in an

apartment in Auckland City. Both parents are professionals—
like me." She looked up to find Yevgeny's eyes already fixed on
her. Shock jolted through her. She swallowed, then continued
in a slightly husky voice. "Being professionals is good—I want
Holly to have a career. But I visualized her having an older
sister—and a garden growing up. Kids need space to roam. Two
boys and an apartment? *And* their parents working long hours?
I don't know. It might mean good money and a comfortable
existence, but will the parents be able to give Holly—all of
them—enough time?"

Yevgeny shook his head.

She set the portfolio aside and reached for the next one.
Leaning back she discovered that Yevgeny had rested his arm
along the back of the couch, bringing him so much closer.
Tingles danced over her skin as her nerve endings went on
high alert. A deep, steadying breath only made her more aware
of the musky male scent that clung to him.

Hurriedly, Ella flipped open the folder and concentrated on
the first photo.

This time the decision was easy. *No.* The family just was
not right. But the following profile was much tougher to look
through. The family seemed to tick off all the boxes that
Ella could ask for, yet she didn't find herself overcome with
enthusiasm.

"They do look lovely—they have a daughter already." She
tried to fake enthusiasm as she paged through the file. "A
garden. And two dogs."

"Her mouth is too set—she's a witch." Yevgeny arched
forward and pointed at the mother with the hand that was not
settled on the back of the couch.

"Nonsense! She's not a witch. She's smiling!" Glancing up
to protest, Ella could see the dark stubble on his chin, the hard
angles of his cheekbones.

Yevgeny turned his head. Their gazes tangled. "But her eyes
are not. And that dog looks like it can't wait to get off her lap."

Ella couldn't breathe!

Feeling crowded, she glanced away...down...and focused on the photo in front of her.

The little girl wasn't smiling at all.

Ella's heart sank. Did that matter? Was it really significant? With a confused sigh she said, "We may be seeing things that don't even exist."

The instant Yevgeny removed his arm from behind her, the twisted mix of excitement and apprehension that had been fluttering in her stomach like a caged butterfly eased. She watched Yevgeny reach for the previous two portfolios, page through them and jab a finger at the family portraits. "In both of these the parents are touching each other."

Ella looked closer—it was true. She glanced back at the third portrait in the folder still open on her lap. The parents sat far apart—a gaping space yawned between them. Despite their smiles neither of them looked terribly happy. "Perhaps it's the pressure—they know how important this is."

"They're supposed to be selling themselves."

"No!" Ella pulled away a few inches to put some distance between them. "They're trying to adopt a baby."

"All the more reason to put the best—the happiest—picture forward."

She wanted to tell him that he was cynical, that he was oversimplifying the matter. But when Ella stared hard at the three faces in the photo, she realized that it didn't work for her. There was no vibe of joy or intimacy.

Ella made her decision and shut the folder with a snap.

She wasn't letting Holly go to this family. "They may be wonderful people. It may have been a tense day when the photos were taken. But that's a no."

She couldn't take that very remote chance of sending Holly to an unhappy home.

A smile lit up Yevgeny's face.

Was that a glint of triumph? Ella stilled. Suddenly his closeness took on a new aspect. Was the enforced intimacy deliberate? Had his comments been staged?

Was she being manipulated by an expert?

She rejected the suspicion almost instantly. She was no pushover.

Then she paused.

Who had the most to gain if she rejected all the families?

The answer came at once.

Yevgeny.

Ella tipped her head to one side and studied him, measuring and resisting the magnetic pull of that sexy bottom lip, the sculpted masculine features and the clear piercing eyes.

Had he deliberately tried to put her off that last family? "You're not asking me if I'm going to change my mind and keep the baby?"

"I know you won't."

The speed of his response took her aback. Ella realized she'd half expected him to try and persuade her not to give up on the child. "Why've you finally decided that?"

His eyes narrowed. Reaction bolted like lightning forks through her. His gaze drifted over her…down…down…sending shivers in its wake…then returned to her face.

Was *that* calculated, too? A deliberate attempt to ratchet up her awareness of him?

Or was she simply far too suspicious?

Ella forced herself to hold his gaze.

"You're not cut out for motherhood." There was distance between them—as wide as the Pacific and many times as deep. He shrugged. "Some women simply aren't."

All the frisson of awareness froze. The delicious moments of understanding beside the Christmas tree evaporated.

She tensed.

The dismissal implicit in his words, in that careless shrug, needled her.

How dare Yevgeny judge her when he didn't even know what made her tick? How dare he assume who she was…and what she wasn't? But she bit back the fierce tide of anger and said instead with quiet force, "What's that supposed to mean?"

Beneath the question lay a vast sea of unspoken pain.

He looked startled at the challenge. "That your career is too important. That you have other priorities." He shrugged again, in that way that was starting to seriously rile her. "It's not unusual not to want to be a mother. I've known other women like you."

He had?

And had he been as clueless about what made those women tick?

Carefully, through tight-pressed lips, Ella said, "I'm starting to think Nadiya had a very lucky escape."

Yevgeny rolled his eyes to the ceiling. "Of course you do."

Then he reached forward and picked the last profile off the coffee table in front of them. "Let's see if this couple is any more suitable than the rest."

Ella let out the breath trapped in her lungs. This time she was determined to open to the front page and fall in love with the family revealed within. This would be it. Then the search would be over, and Yevgeny would have to live with her decision.

But it didn't happen.

The text accompanying the photo indicated that couple had no children. And they requested a closed adoption.

That request unexpectedly rattled Ella.

Badly.

For the first time she realized what it would mean to never see Holly again—or at least not until her baby was all grown up and legally an adult who could request information about the identity of her birth mother contained in the sealed adoption records. To not know what color her baby's eyes turned out to be. To miss out on news about her first day at school. To never see photos of her first school dance.

Ella hadn't contemplated how much comfort having an open adoption gave her. Until now.

She didn't need to read any further. "No."

In the silence that followed, the thud of the folder landing on the coffee table sounded overloud. Ella flinched.

"At this rate you aren't going to find a family for Holly." Yevgeny sounded faintly smug. "You might find I'll be the only choice left."

"Never!" she vowed. That was not an option.

He smirked. "Never is a very long time."

"I'll ask Jo for the next set of files."

"And when all of those families fall short of your rigorous demands, what then?"

Was Yevgeny right? Was it possible that his manipulation had nothing to do with it, that she had set her standards too high? Ella looked away from him and studied the mountain of portfolios through blank eyes, then dismissed his theory.

No, she knew exactly what kind of parents she wanted for Holly.

They were out there.

Somewhere…

Drawing a steadying breath, she pushed her glasses up her nose and glanced across the couch at Yevgeny. "I'll find a family—and you're right, they will be perfect, absolutely perfect, for the baby."

Instead of the usual cocksure arrogance, there was a glint of something close to sympathy in his eyes. Slowly he shook his head from side to side. "You're not going to find what you're looking for."

"How can you say that?"

"Because I know you, Ella. Better than you know yourself."

Ella rejected that instantly. The man was delusional—he didn't know her. At all. So much for thinking she'd recognized sympathetic understanding in his eyes. All it had been was a different kind of arrogance.

"You're mad," she said.

Yet instead of flaring up in anger as she'd half expected at her accusation, he laughed, showing off dazzling white teeth. His mood had changed again.

"It's day five today. Do you really think you're going to

allow yourself to find a family before Christmas if you carry on being this picky?"

It had nothing to do with "allowing" herself. He had that all wrong. When she saw the right couple…she would know deep in her heart that they were the ones. Ella was utterly certain of that.

"I'm not being unreasonably picky," she argued. "I want the right family. I'm not going to rush this."

Even as she spoke Ella could feel the tension starting to rewind tightly in her stomach. Time was of essence. No one understood that better than she did.

She *had* to find Holly a family.

A week from today would be day twelve, the day she could finally sign the consent to adoption. The sooner Holly could start to bond with her family, the better. Yevgeny was right—if she carried on picking apart every family she would only delay letting Holly go to a family who would love and cherish her.

But on the other hand…it *was* almost Christmas.

How could she push the baby away before Christmas? She paused.

Why not…

Before she could stop herself her mind traveled down the forbidden path. The anguish she'd expected didn't come.

Yes, why not?

Ella came to a decision.

"I don't have to find a family before Christmas. I'm going to wait until after Christmas. That way Holly can spend her first Christmas here." Fearing the blaze of triumph she was certain Yevgeny's face would reflect, her gaze flicked to the corner dominated by the giant tree with its merry flashing lights.

The red-and-silver balls gleamed warmly.

The right family would emerge after Christmas.

Once she'd taken down the Christmas tree that Yevgeny had helped her put up this evening…and finally said goodbye to the baby…she would have plenty of time to reflect—and come to terms with how her life had been unexpectedly changed. And perhaps she would even follow Jo's advice and attend grief counseling.

For now she would take it one day at a time.

In the meantime, she'd take photos—make an album for the baby to take with her to her new life. That way Holly would one day be able to look back and see where her life had started.

And Ella would be satisfied that she'd done everything she could for the baby.

Because Yevgeny was right: she wasn't the kind of woman who wanted to be a mother. She was enough like his own mother to terrify him.

She was determined to choose someone better for Holly.

Seven

Seated behind the desk in her office, a legal pad open in front of her, Ella gazed sympathetically at the young, heavily pregnant woman on the other side of the desk. When Peggy had arrived to start work early this morning, she'd discovered a pregnant, tearful Pauline Patterson waiting in the lobby for the law offices to open. Taking in Pauline's red-rimmed eyes, Ella could see why her paralegal had been worried about the young woman and why Peggy had wasted no time in summoning Ella back to work.

"You're certain divorce is the course of action you want to take?" she asked Pauline.

"I can't afford a lawyer, but my sister said if I didn't retain one my husband would take me to the cleaners."

A few more questions elicited the fact that Pauline Patterson's sister seemed to have a lot of opinions about the marriage—yet some of the problems that were plaguing the couple didn't sound insurmountable to Ella. Especially given the sadness in Pauline's eyes when she spoke of leaving her husband.

Carefully Ella asked, "Have you tried couples counseling?"

Pauline shook her head. "No. My sister said I needed a lawyer—to show Ian I meant business."

Ella ignored the sister's views and explained, "Through the courts you're entitled to six free sessions. I strongly recommend that you try counseling first." Ella couldn't stop herself from glancing down at Pauline's swollen stomach. "It's a good idea to exhaust all alternatives first. Divorce is stressful for everyone… and it can be very final. Sometimes there is no going back."

Fear flared in Pauline's eyes. "I still love Ian. I don't really want to get a divorce—I want to sort this out. My sister says this is the best way to get his attention."

"He's not listening to you?"

"His friends are more important to him than me or the baby." There was a doleful note in the young woman's voice. "I miss my mother—she's back in England. Now that I'm pregnant, I need help." Tears rolled down Pauline's cheeks.

"Have you told your husband you need more help—that you miss your mother?"

Pauline shook her head. "No. His mother and my mother both said we were too young to get married. I've been determined to prove them all wrong. To show everyone—even Ian—that I wasn't too young."

Ella asked a few more questions that revealed that money wasn't a problem. Although both Pauline and Ian seemed to shop more than they should, Ian had a good job with prospects of another promotion soon. Nor, to Ella's relief, was he verbally or physically abusive. It appeared this was a case of both of them needing to grow up quickly now that they had a baby on the way, and learning to talk and listen to each other better.

Coming to a decision, Ella said, "Before you go further down the road with a divorce, why don't you talk to Ian about your unhappiness? I suggest that you both go to counseling and visit a budgeting service. If Ian refuses to go, I think you should take advantage of the sessions for yourself."

Ella reached into a drawer for business cards for a couple of counselors who worked with the court, and another card for a local budgeting service.

She smiled at the young woman as she handed the cards to her. "Sometimes, when you spend more than you earn, financial worries can put a lot of pressure on a marriage—particularly if there's a baby on the way. And if Ian is out with friends all hours of the night when you're tired and pregnant, resentment can breed. These people may be able to help you. If they can't, and you still feel certain that dissolving your marriage is the only way forward, come and see me again. We will put a plan into action."

Pauline glanced down at the business cards she held. "You really think this will work?"

This was a question to which Ella never had a good enough answer. "There are no guarantees. But at least you will know in your heart that you tried everything before you decided that divorce was the only solution. And that will help you when you start the road to recovery. You'll have fewer regrets."

Over the years Ella had learned that often parties who consulted with her determined to secure a divorce wanted nothing more than to be pointed in the right direction to save their marriage. Not in all cases, but enough for her to know that six sessions of counseling were worth trying first.

As Pauline thanked her, tears of hope sparkling in her eyes, Ella's lips curved up into a small smile, and she couldn't help wondering what Yevgeny would say if he saw her now—hardly the hotshot lawyer out to destroy every marriage in town for an outrageous fee.

Yevgeny took in the tearstained face of the young woman exiting Ella's office as he stood aside to let her pass. Then he entered Ella's workspace, shut the door behind him—and pounced. "You're doing her divorce?"

"That's none of your business!"

Ella's light brown eyes were cool. She stood behind the

barrier of a highly polished wooden desk, clad in one of those black power suits he'd come to hate.

"She's pregnant!" The angry words ripped from him.

"That doesn't mean anything. There are times when divorce is the right thing—even for a pregnant woman."

"And what about the baby's father? What if it's not the right thing for him?" Blood pounded in his head. Everything he'd come here to say had evaporated from his mind. Now he could only think about another divorce…another father deprived of his sons. *His* father. "What about the father's rights?"

"Everything in a divorce is negotiated."

"Not if the woman lies." It was a snarl. "Not if she manipulates everything and everyone to get sole custody, and bars her husband from ever seeing the children…I mean, the child," he corrected himself quickly, as he stalked to the front edge of the wooden desk. Ella still stood on the other side. She didn't seem to have noticed his slip of tongue, as she watched him, unmoved. "Both father and child lose then. I ask you, is that right? Is it fair?"

"Yevgeny, it's my job to make certain—"

"Your job is to be a divorce lawyer."

"Family lawyer," she corrected.

"You broker agreements, which keep boys from their fathers and wait like a vulture over a kill."

"What?"

She drew herself up, which wasn't much higher than his shoulder, Yevgeny knew. Her eyes blazed gold fire at him across the expanse of the polished desk.

"I don't do anything of the kind! Divorce is hard on everyone. It's my job to make the arrangements workable after a marriage ends. And that means taking the children's needs into consideration from the very beginning. Sure, the spouses are often furious with each other, but it's part of my responsibility to make sure that the party I'm representing is aware that their children take priority. I don't try to prevent the father's access to his kids—unless there's reason to do so. Violence. A history of abuse." She shrugged. "My job is not always pleasant."

"I'm not talking about instances of domestic violence." Yevgeny refused to back down. "I'm talking about women who manipulate you—and the judge." His voice was thick, his Russian accent pronounced. He drew a deep, shuddering breath and forced himself to relax.

He'd arrived at Ella's house earlier to visit Holly—and discovered Ella had abandoned the baby to return to work. He'd been outraged. He'd come here to tell Ella what he thought of her—not to be dragged into the past.

Her brow wrinkled. "Are we talking about a specific case here?"

He looked away. His stomach tightened. For a moment he could smell the long-forgotten musty smell of another legal office with its wooden-paneled walls and leather chairs. He could see the never-forgotten triumph in his mother's smile as she rose to her feet to shake the lawyer's hand. It had been three years until he'd seen his father again, and only because his mother had walked out of the fancy house his father paid a fortune to maintain, leaving her two sons alone in it. The housekeeper had called his father to advise that his mother had gone—she couldn't have cared less.

When he looked back at Ella, her head was tipped to one side as she inspected him. The brown eyes no longer flamed, they'd warmed to the pale gold of honey behind her glasses. "Did you have a child taken from you in the past?"

He'd never heard that soft, sweet tone from her before.

My God. She felt pity for him! No one ever felt that kind of emotion for him. *Never.* It rocked Yevgeny. He shook his head in a jerky motion, rejecting the very idea. "This is not about me!"

"Isn't it?" Ella stepped around the desk and came toward him. "Are you sure?"

This wasn't about him…this was about…about—

His Holly.

He could feel every muscle in his body growing increasingly

taut with every step that brought Ella closer. He wanted her to stop. He didn't want her coming near enough for him to pick up on her lilac scent. He didn't want her kindness. Not until he could examine why her sympathy caused him to crack wide open inside.

Yevgeny struggled to marshal the anger and outrage that had driven him here. He'd rather remember the side of her he detested—the human icicle, the mother who wanted to send the child she'd given birth to away and abandon her without a second thought.

That was the woman he never wanted near him. And he knew the easiest way to keep that woman—and her questions—at bay....

"What did you advise your young client?" he barked out. "To wangle as much from her husband as she can? To lie to get sole custody?"

Pausing, one foot in front of the other, Ella halted, and Yevgeny exhaled a silent sigh of relief.

Mission accomplished.

Then she said, "You can't expect me to answer that. Any advice I give is subject to legal privilege. But I can tell you that before proceeding with divorce action, I often suggest to clients that they try counseling—"

"Airy-fairy stuff." Yevgeny waved a dismissive hand. "No help at all."

"Or get budgeting advice," she continued evenly as if he hadn't interrupted. But her eyes sparkled behind her spectacles. "I'm sure a financially savvy man like you would appreciate the wisdom of that."

One dark eyebrow shot up. "Budgeting advice so that these women can afford your usurious fees?"

"No!" For the first time Ella sounded annoyed. "Budgeting advice to help them save their marriages!"

He took in the anger on her face. He was angry, too. This was not going to help his position with Holly. Yevgeny let out his breath. "This is not why I came. I will call you when we both have had a chance to simmer down."

Given their previous confrontation, the last person Ella wanted to see when she walked into her home the following evening was Yevgeny. She still had not "simmered down" as he had put it.

To make matters worse, he looked totally at ease sprawled across the carpet of her living room, his gray satin tie loosened, shirtsleeves rolled up and his hair ruffled. Holly lay on her back beside him, looking perfectly content, her bare legs kicking in the air, while the Christmas tree sparkled merrily in the background.

It was all very cozy and festive…a scene from a Christmas card…and Ella felt like a complete outsider in her own home.

"Where's Deb?" she demanded, stopping in front of Yevgeny.

"I told her to take a break while I'm here."

His high-handedness annoyed Ella. Deb reported to her, not to her nemesis. It was something she would have to discuss with the nanny.

Then Ella told herself to lighten up. It was Friday evening, she wanted to relax…but his presence nixed any chance of that.

Holly gave a squeak, and Ella instantly dropped to her knees beside her. The baby appeared to be fascinated with her own hands. She gave another high-pitched shriek.

Ella's heartbeat steadied.

Of course there was nothing wrong!

Except that she was hovering too close to the baby….

She shifted and glanced away.

Straight into Yevgeny's curious eyes.

It was a good time to remember that she hadn't forgiven him for likening her to a vulture circling a kill yesterday.

Which led her to one of the many questions that his visit to her offices had raised….

"I never did find out what you were doing at my offices

yesterday. I take it you didn't simply arrive planning to call me a vulture?" Ella raised a questioning eyebrow.

He looked discomforted. Sitting up, he said, "I ordered in dinner—I thought you might enjoy not having to cook tonight. You could give Deb the entire evening off."

"Then I'd have to look after the baby instead of cook," she pointed out, not sure that she liked the fact that he'd walked in here and taken over her life. She held her breath, waiting for him to accuse her of all the motherly shortcomings he usually did.

A furrow creased his brow, and she tensed. He surprised her by saying, "I intended to play with the baby. I thought you might want to relax. Keira once said you like to take Friday evenings easy."

Ella blinked.

He was trying to be considerate?

Was that possible? Her gaze slid to Holly. The baby was wriggling her fingers and making cooing sounds. She looked wonderfully content. It shouldn't be too difficult for Yevgeny to look after her.

"You ordered dinner in?" she asked in case she'd misunderstood.

"Yes, Italian."

That really got her attention. She loved Italian food. How did he know that? Had he pumped Peggy for information about her yesterday? Or had he been cross-examining Deb? Another thought struck her....

"Should I consider this an apology for your rudeness yesterday?"

A flush seared the high, Slavic cheekbones. "The food is from La Rosa."

The diversion worked. "I didn't know La Rosa does takeout—much less that they deliver."

"They don't."

So he was pulling out all the stops. "But you convinced them?" His sheepish nod confirmed it. "Who told you it's my favorite restaurant?"

"Keira."

"You spoke to Keira today?"

"No—she mentioned it a while ago."

"Before they left?"

"Yes." The word was dragged out of him.

What interpretation was she supposed to put on his reluctant confession that he'd remembered—and acted on—something Keira had most likely mentioned in passing?

Ella grew impatient with herself. It probably meant nothing more than that Yevgeny Volkovoy had a frighteningly good memory.

Something she'd be wise to keep in mind.

True to his word, Yevgeny tended to Holly. He even helped Deb bathe and change the baby before the nanny left. He played with the baby, waving toys and rattles to stimulate her interest. Before she could become too caught up in watching Holly interacting with her uncle, Ella excused herself to express milk from her aching breasts for the baby's next feed and to enjoy a soak in a bubble bath before the meal arrived.

By the time she emerged, dressed in comfortable skinny jeans and a T-shirt, wonderfully relaxed and scented from her fragrant hot bath, Yevgeny had set her dining table for two and, more miraculously, gotten Holly off to sleep. The handset from the baby monitor lay on the table.

Ella was impressed by his efforts—even though her eyes lingered on the second place setting.

Yevgeny intercepted her gaze. "I am staying. I want to assess whether La Rosa's cuisine lives up to your high recommendation. And I have something I wish to ask you. But I think I hear the food arriving. Let's eat first."

To Ella's delight the meal was excellent—well up to La Rosa's high standards, even without the ambience of the restaurant setting. Even better, Yevgeny graciously declared it to be among the best Italian he'd eaten in a long time.

"As an apology, that meal was most certainly acceptable."

Ella set down her dessert spoon after savoring the last spoonful of tiramisu and smiled at him.

Rather than take umbrage at her gentle ribbing, he laughed, but once his laughter died away, an awkward silence settled over the table.

Ella broke it first. Pushing her spectacles up her nose, she said, "Are you ready to tell me why you came to see me yesterday?"

He picked up his half-full glass of red wine and sat back in his chair. "I was annoyed that you'd gone back to work. I intended to confront you."

"You have no right to question my decision. My practice is my livelihood. I don't meddle in your business." Ella leaned forward, determined not to allow him to push her around. For once, the big Russian had the grace to look abashed. "Besides, I made it clear from the outset that I wouldn't look after the baby. I'm giving Holly up for adoption. I don't want to make what is already a difficult situation more difficult by bonding with her." Even by expressing her milk to feed the baby, Ella suspected she was becoming closer than she'd ever meant to be to Holly. Inside she could feel her muscles tensing and the all too familiar anxiety that she took such pains to conceal rising. The sense of well-being that the soak in the tub and the delicious meal had instilled was rapidly ebbing.

"I understand."

"Then why your annoyance yesterday?"

He didn't answer, instead swirling the glass and appearing to be enraptured by the deep ruby glow of the wine. Then he looked up, and the illusion of contentment shattered. His eyes were full of turmoil. "I understand now. I spoke to Jo Wells earlier."

What had Jo said? Ella sought his eyes for answers. But found none to justify the panic that flared inside her.

Jo couldn't have told him anything. Because not even Jo knew.

Unless Keira had told her…

Ella blocked out the possibility of such a devastating betrayal.

"The way Jo explained your decision not to bond with the baby made me realize that it wasn't an act of neglect or selfishness."

Her teeth snapped together. She'd been trying to get that through to him. But he listened to a stranger? "Thanks!"

"She also said that you wouldn't be forsaking Holly—that you intend to keep in close contact with her. She told me that you were always adamant—even when Keira and Dmitri planned to adopt her—that Holly should know that you were her tummy mummy."

Despite her outrage, it was so incongruous to hear him use that term for surrogacy that Ella almost smiled. "It's always been important to me that there should be no deception in this kind of situation—it only hurts the child." She shuddered inwardly as she looked away.

If he only knew...

When she glanced back, it was to find that Yevgeny was swirling the wine again, staring into the rich, red depths.

It must be hard for him to face the fact that he'd seriously misjudged her—and admit it. Many men would've shirked this. Maybe it was time to cut him a little slack.

"You can drink it," she assured him to lighten the mood. "It's a good wine—gold medalist, in fact."

That brought his gaze back to her. "I didn't think you would poison me."

This time it was Ella who laughed. "What makes you so sure?"

"You uphold the letter of the law. I don't see you as breaking it. I'm starting to realize you have plenty of integrity."

The unexpected compliment warmed her.

Her lips tilting up, she said, "Flatterer!"

He shook his head. "No, it's the truth...which I appear to have managed to miss."

"While we're on the topic of truth, what was really going on in my office yesterday? I asked you if you'd lost custody of a child in the past. Tell me about your child, Yevgeny," she invited softly.

A mask dropped into place.

He smiled. But no hint of humor lit his eyes. It was as though a dark thundercloud hung over him. Ella shivered, no longer sure she should pursue this line of questioning. There was pain there…and something else.

"What child? I've never been married."

Ella slanted him an old-fashioned look to lighten the mood. "I didn't think you of all people would believe you had to be married to get someone pregnant."

He chuckled. "Very funny!"

She wrinkled her nose at him, and decided to probe a little more. "So what was it all about?"

"What do you mean?" he stalled.

"There was something else going on."

"You're imagining things."

She stared at him for a long moment. His mouth was flat, there was no hint of the humor that had lit his eyes only seconds before she'd started pushing. "I don't think I am. What's more…I think it has to do with a lawyer—but not me." She thought about her own life, about what had caused her to develop her prickly, reserved shell. "Did a woman do a real number on you?"

He laughed, and she detected a palpable tension beneath the careless sound. "Never!"

"She was a lawyer, wasn't she?"

He laughed again.

This time with relief, Ella suspected. Okay, so she wasn't quite there yet, but she was definitely on the right track. She was certain of it when Yevgeny said, "You're making too much of this—"

"Because you never let anyone in," she interrupted. "No one gets close enough."

His reaction was recognizable. She did the same thing. It was what she'd been doing ever since she was nineteen. She guarded her emotions zealously, only letting Keira past the barricade of her defenses.

"What did she do?"

"Stop trying to psychoanalyze me."

"Why?" She leaned across the dining table, and rested a hand on his arm. Beneath her fingers his flesh was firm, the muscle taut. For a moment she marveled at her brazenness. "Am I getting warm?"

"Warm?" He recoiled from her touch. Ella let her hand fall. The skin stretched across his cheekbones until his face resembled a death mask. "You're as cold as ice."

She got the double meaning at once. Yevgeny considered her cold. It hurt.

Ella swallowed and looked away, determined not to let him see what his words had done to her.

What did it matter that he thought that she was as cold as ice? He wasn't the first to think so, and he wouldn't be the last. It was what she'd wanted, wasn't it? She'd cultivated a cool, distant manner to keep men like him at bay. She certainly didn't want him to feel she was approachable, or God help her, receptive to his compliments and flattery and the advances that would inevitably follow.

Or did she?

That thought was the most horrifyingly painful of all.

Escape became a necessity for survival.

"I think I'll go and check to make sure the baby is sleeping." She stumbled to her feet before he could comment on her sudden maternal urge. "I'm sure you're ready to go. You can close the front door behind you."

It was only after she heard the front door softly close long minutes later that Ella realized that she hadn't discovered what Yevgeny had wanted to ask of her.

Eight

Yevgeny wasn't certain of his reception when he rang the doorbell to Ella's home on Sunday morning. So when she finally opened the door and the warm summer sun fell on her face, he experienced an unfamiliar, giddy surge of relief.

"You never did say what you wanted to ask me on Friday night." Behind her spectacles, her honey-brown eyes were wide with wariness. "I expect that's why you're here today. Or have you come to see Holly?"

It shouldn't surprise him that she'd guessed what he was doing here. But it did. The way in which she was so attuned to his thoughts, his actions, should've driven a stake into his heart. He didn't need Ella of all people possessing the ability to read his mind. There was too much that was private—and some information was not his alone to share.

Yet, instead of bolting in fear as he had on Friday night, he stood his ground.

Nor did he take refuge in half-truths and claim that he'd only come to visit Holly, although the baby did play a big role in his presence here today. But, to be fair, he'd played with her when he'd passed by yesterday. Ella had been out. "I wanted to ask you if you would come with me to look at a house I'm thinking of buying," he said, deciding that directness would be the best policy.

Whatever she'd been expecting, clearly, it hadn't been that. "You're buying a house?"

He nodded. More than a house, a home. For him…and Holly.

With the sun playing across her features Ella looked warm and approachable. For a moment he had a vision of…

Then he pulled himself together.

What was he considering? Was he mad?

He tried to get a grasp on his thoughts…and answer her so that she wouldn't get a whiff of the crazy notion he'd experienced. "It's time. The penthouse apartment has never been more than a place to sleep after a long day's work. I want a building with space around it. A garden. And I'd like a woman's opinion on the house I've seen."

Ella rested one arm against the doorjamb, blocking his entry. "Why not take Nadiya— Why me?"

He gave her a disbelieving look. "Do you think Nadiya would want to come and look at houses with me after the humiliation of our last encounter?"

He didn't want to take Nadiya—or any other woman. It had to be Ella. No one else would understand….

"You haven't seen her since?"

The question jolted him. "Nadiya?"

"Yes, Nadiya."

He shook his head.

Ella hesitated. "I suppose I could join you. Now would be better than later. I'd planned to prepare for a meeting on Monday. So, as long as you give me a few minutes to get ready, I'll come. Holly is taking a nap. I'll need to tell Deb we're going out so that she can get her ready."

"It might be a good idea to leave Holly here."

At the surprised look she shot him, he added reluctantly, "My Porsche is a two-seater." It was becoming clear to him that, along with a new home, he was going to have to purchase a new car, too.

"We can take my car…it's a station wagon," she said wryly.

That amused Yevgeny. Ella didn't have dogs or children yet she drove a station wagon? He kept the observation to himself. "We'll take my car and leave Holly at home. That way the visit will take less time." And as much as he adored the baby, this morning he wanted Ella's undivided attention. It would be easier to assess her gut response to the house without the baby around to distract her. "I'll call the Realtor to arrange access."

"You'd better come in while I get ready." She stepped away from the doorjamb to let him pass, and tossed him a prim smile. "I won't be long."

As Yevgeny followed Ella indoors he told himself it was going to be okay—everything would work out. The sunny morning. Her smile. The fact that Christmas was fast approaching.

All augured well.

He could sense that Ella was beginning to weaken.

As Yevgeny pulled the Porsche to a stop, Ella's breath caught in her throat.

Nestled amidst sprawling gardens, the house was not a multimillion-dollar sculpture comprised of a series of post-modern boxes.

It was a jewel of a home.

With wide lawns and big leafy trees, it cried welcome to a family—not a bachelor billionaire.

Yevgeny unclipped his seat belt and turned to her. "I like the feel of this place. What do you think?"

What did she think? She loved it. But…

Ella stared through the tinted windshield trying—and failing—to imagine Yevgeny living here all by himself. "It looks…big."

"Three stories, garage for half a dozen cars, several reception rooms, a home cinema, an indoor heated pool, staff quarters—and six bedrooms," he recited. "But that's not what interests me."

He climbed out the sports car and came around to open her door before she could ask what *did* interest him—if not the sheer impressive scale of the residence.

"Come."

Ella followed Yevgeny along the path that led up to the house.

Her emotions were all over the place. Why was Yevgeny considering buying such a house? He already had a penthouse apartment—from what she'd heard it was extremely luxurious. Why did he need a house, too?

Unless…

For Holly?

But Ella was not ready to face what the answer to that might mean. For the baby. For her. For everyone. Instead, she paused under the spreading, twisted branches of an old pohutukawa tree, and said, "Ah, a real, live New Zealand Christmas tree. It's made for a tree house."

His gaze followed hers to the beautiful branches loaded with bunches of red flowers. "I'm afraid I know little about tree houses—Dmitri and I never had one."

"This calls out for one." Squinting upward, Ella continued, "In fact, there's enough space for a playhouse up there. It would need to be furnished. Chairs. A table. Kid-size crockery. Keira and I had a tree house growing up—we spent hours in ours."

"What did you do?"

"We held tea parties. And played dress-up. And one summer we even made lemonade from the lemons that grew in the garden and opened a stall." She turned her head to discover a slightly stunned expression in Yevgeny's eyes.

Finally he said, "Then I'll know who to call on to attend to the decor when the time is ripe."

She smiled, but didn't acknowledge the burgeoning certainty that the playhouse would be for Holly. Yevgeny had no intention of disappearing from the baby's life.

It seemed like a huge amount of trouble to go to for a child he would only see for periods agreed to by her adoptive parents. Unless…unless he still believed he could convince her otherwise?

No.

She'd made her position crystal clear—she wanted the baby to go to a family…. Yevgeny would have to accept that once she found the right parents for Holly.

And it was her choice.

Not his.

Hers.

This house was for him—not Holly. Although Ella recognized it would be lovely for Holly to have such a fantasy place to visit from time to time.

He was looking past her at the old tree with its low, sweeping branches crowned with red flowers. "Now, I can see that that bough would be perfect to support a swing."

"A swing?"

Switching his attention back to her, Yevgeny gave her a crooked smile. "Holly would love it."

So it *was* about Holly…not just him.

For a moment Ella allowed herself to imagine him pushing Holly on the swing on a warm summer's eve…she could even hear Holly's laughter ringing out.

Then she pulled herself up short.

No.

This house wasn't for Holly…it was for Yevgeny. Primarily because his penthouse apartment had grown too small for his requirements. Better she keep her mind on task.

"Let's look inside," she said briskly.

The Realtor waited in front of the white front door at the top of the stairs. A smartly dressed woman with dark hair and hungry eyes, she smiled at Ella. "Mrs. Volkovoy?"

Good grief! "No." Ella felt herself flushing. She shouldn't be here. She was starting to feel like an imposter. "I'm not his wife—I'm a lawyer."

The Realtor's gaze arced to Yevgeny. "You didn't mention you were bringing your lawyer."

"Ella is not my lawyer," said Yevgeny through clenched teeth

"Oh." The Realtor's curious eyes darted between them. To Ella's relief the woman didn't ask any of the questions that were clearly burning to escape. "Perhaps I should let you browse— and we can talk afterward?"

"Perfect." Yevgeny gave a grim smile. "We'll catch up later."

Ella couldn't help wondering what the hell she was doing here as she rushed to keep up with Yevgeny's long stride.

"Oh, wow."

Yevgeny stopped at the sound of Ella's breathy exclamation. She was standing in the middle of the living room, staring out the wall of glass sliders leading to a long veranda with a backdrop of verdant gardens and sea beyond.

"One could spend the entire summer living on that veranda," she said, transfixed. Then she gestured to the sleek fireplace in the end wall. "But in winter the fire would make it warm and welcoming inside."

"There's a hot spa at the end of the veranda to make winter even more pleasant," Yevgeny told her.

"How fabulous."

"And a kitchen and dining area made for entertaining on the other side of the dividing wall," he added. "The home theater and wine cellar are downstairs. But come and look upstairs." He wanted her opinion on the bedroom and playroom where Holly would spend most of her time.

"This one. What do you think?" Upstairs he led Ella eagerly to the second bedroom.

As Ella scanned the bedroom from the doorway, taking in the bright sunny light spilling through the high arched windows, he saw her surprise register.

"But this isn't the master bedroom. You wouldn't occupy this room." Her eyes held a question as they met his. "This is for a…" Her voice trailed away.

Yevgeny could see the realization dawning as she entered. He headed in after her.

The room was decorated in shades of rich cream and pale blue. A bed with an intricate white ironwork bedstead was piled high with a collection of soft toys on a patchwork comforter, setting the girlish tone. Overhead, a chandelier winked in the sunlight. There was a window seat beneath the arched windows with space for picture books.

He could imagine Holly seated there paging through her favorite book as she grew up. Perhaps he could even ask Ella to help him furnish the room in a similar style once the house was his.

"This…this room is for Holly, right?" Ella sounded choked up.

Yevgeny came to a stop in front of her. "Yes. Do you like it?"

She shrugged her shoulders helplessly. "What can I say? It's perfect."

For that heartbeat they were in perfect accord, no hint of the animosity that had dogged their relationship since their first meeting. Yevgeny held his breath, loath to say anything lest the instant of harmony shatter into jagged shards of discontent. Seconds passed, and they stood drenched in warm sunlight in the house Yevgeny wanted for a home.

Deep in his chest hope started to build. Ella was starting to see things his way….

At last he moved.

Her eyes squeezed shut.

"Ella?"

At the questioning lilt of his voice, her lids lifted. And she looked straight into his eyes. Yevgeny felt a physical jolt. He was so close that he could see the shades of velvet brown and glittering gold. Desire flared. And something more…something new and fresh.

Again the crazy vision he'd glimpsed on her doorstep earlier and dismissed rose up. It was cemented with how right…how happy…Ella appeared to be in this setting.

Ella fit this place…

He bent his head. His lips met hers…pressed…waiting.

Hers parted.

The kiss deepened.

Closing his own eyes he sank into the softness that was Ella, a softness he'd never expected to discover, and concentrated on imprinting the instant in his memory to pull out and analyze later. To make sense of the inexplicable. For now, he simply absorbed the feel of her body against his. The warmth. The womanliness. The sweet, lilac scent that was the unique essence of Ella.

Finally, when his head lifted, his breath was ragged and he felt dazed and disoriented.

To his enormous dismay, Ella recovered first.

"Well," she said, the bright flush on her cheeks already starting to fade, "I don't think we need to take a look at the master suite after that."

Ella glanced at her watch.

They were back downstairs, standing on the spacious veranda protected from the sea breeze that ruffled the tops of the great trees that flanked the house.

"Need to be somewhere else?" Yevgeny drawled. He leaned against the balustrade, blocking her view of the well-kept gardens below. "Or are you in a hurry to leave?"

Ella looked up at him.

The sun splintered in the gold of her eyes, blinding him for an instant.

Yevgeny blinked.

Ella was speaking, and he struggled to focus on what she was saying.

"No, I was simply thinking that if this was a weekday I'd be in my office working." She made a sweeping gesture with her arm. "Solving other people's problems and missing out on all this beauty."

It was a relief to break away from the spell of her golden

eyes, to swing around and follow where her arm indicated, out over the vista of the gardens to the azure sea and the hazy horizon beyond.

The crazy feeling was back. *Affinity.* A vision of him and Holly and…

He drew a deep, shaky breath.

"I have a proposition for you."

"A proposition?"

Ella lifted a hand and nudged her glasses up. If he'd known better he might have thought she was apprehensive. But this was Ella—she didn't have an apprehensive bone in her body. "Play hooky with me tomorrow."

That gave him twenty-four hours to decide how to broach the topic they most needed to discuss.

Holly…

"Pardon?" She blinked at him.

"Take the day off—we can take Holly out for the day." It would be easier with the baby there. "And enjoy the December sun and fresh summer air. It's almost Christmas, take some time out."

Her brow creased in a frown. "I have a meeting."

"Can you postpone it?"

She shook her head slowly. "It's important."

"Holly is important—nothing else comes close. In five years' time will you even remember what this meeting is about? Because Holly will still be important then."

Ella pushed her glasses up her nose. "I can't—not tomorrow."

"No one else can do it?" he persisted, frustrated. This was important—too important to be overshadowed by work.

Ella shook her head again. "I'm the only one who knows all the fine details."

His frustration bubbled over. "Then you have a problem—you need to learn how to delegate."

"To whom? No one else—"

"Can do the job as well as you?" He raised an eyebrow.

Ella nodded slowly. "I suppose that's what I mean."

"Then you have two problems—maybe more. You've surrounded yourself with the wrong people, you've failed to train them adequately, you don't empower your staff by giving them responsibility. Or all of the above."

"None of the above." Ella's teeth snapped shut. She gave him a "take that" look.

Yevgeny narrowed his gaze. "Then you're guilty of bad planning."

She made a peculiar sound, and stalked to the end of the veranda, where she stood with her back to him, looking out over the garden. Her shoulders were stiff. In the pause that followed Yevgeny found himself watching her…anticipating her next volley. Until he caught himself.

He padded to where she stood, and her shoulders stiffened. This was not what he wanted. "Ella—" He broke off as heels clicked on the tiles behind him.

The Realtor had returned.

Ella still hadn't responded. Yevgeny sighed. "You go to your meeting. I'll take Holly to the park."

To his surprise, she didn't object.

"Are you going to put an offer in on this house?" Ella asked too softly for the Realtor to hear, her back still to him.

He nodded, suddenly tired of the dance around the truth, and then realized she couldn't see his acknowledgement. "Yes," he said. "This will be my home."

Once back at her town house, Ella made a hasty escape on the pretext of checking on the baby, the memory of his unexpected kiss in that wonderful house still numbing her mind.

Ella was in turmoil. Joining Yevgeny for a romp in the park with Holly had been beyond her.

Ella knew that Yevgeny was going to pressure her again.

To try and convince her that he would be the best thing for Holly. She was so confused. Yevgeny offered none of the qualities she wanted in the family who'd adopt Holly.

He was a bachelor. A type-A billionaire. He wasn't even

in a stable relationship. Sure he had a stable full of centerfold supermodels at his disposal, but that was hardly the same thing....

Yet, as she entered the nursery, Ella found herself wondering whether she'd leaped from the frying pan into the fire.

Holly was awake, gurgling happily to herself in the white cot.

Coping with Yevgeny was child's play compared to this....

"She's just woken," Deb told her from the depths of the rocker where she sat surrounded with the Sunday newspapers. "I swear she knew you'd come home. I might go to the kitchen and warm a bottle for her."

"Thank you." Moving slowly across the room, Ella paused beside the cot and glanced down at the baby inside.

Holly moved her head...then chuckled.

Ella told herself it wasn't possible. The baby was too young to be laughing. And she hadn't spent enough time with Ella to form a bond. The baby couldn't possibly recognize her...could she?

Yet Ella couldn't resist.

She bent down and laughed with the baby, an ache in her heart. Her breasts felt hot and tight. Ella tried to convince herself that Deb's mention of the milk bottle had stimulated the need to express. That was better than the danger of the instinctive age-old maternal response at the sight of her child.

Holly kicked her bare legs in the air, and Ella grasped the perfectly shaped little foot. Her fingertips brushed the soles, and the baby crowed with delight.

"You're ticklish! I've discovered your secret." She leaned closer and whispered, "Never fear, it will be safe with me."

Warmth rose within her, fierce and unfamiliar. What spell was Holly weaving about her? Why could she no longer think of the baby without a smile curving her lips? How was she ever going to let the baby go?

This was precisely what she'd fought so desperately to avoid. This...this emotional tug that went all the way to her womb.

As if feeling her straying attention, the baby gurgled and

pumped her legs. Ella smiled again but this time there was a tinge of sadness in the smile.

She would not be privy to all Holly's secrets as she grew up. That would be a role taken by someone else…a woman who could love Holly with all her heart, a mother who wasn't crippled by fear—and pain.

"I'm going to find you the best mother in the world, I promise."

She was so intent on the exchange with the baby, that she didn't sense the arrival of the man in the doorway. Nor did she see him hesitate before exiting, a stormy frown darkening his face.

The Porsche purred as it swept through the bends along Tamaki Drive. On the right, white sails fluttered in the wind in the bay as locals enjoyed the Sunday summer evening, while across the sea the menacing volcano of Rangitoto Island slumbered.

So Ella was going to find his baby the best mother in the world?

Yevgeny braked and geared down for the next curve. He slowed as a pack of cyclists came into sight, throttling back the powerful engine to a throaty roar.

Ella was still determined to give Holly away to strangers. Despite everything he had done to show her that Holly belonged with him.…

Watching as one cyclist cut to the center lane, he dropped farther back. A moment later the bikes were bunched up together again, the cyclists in their bright attire pedaling furiously.

Maybe not *everything*.

The time had come to use all the weapons in his armory.

And that meant confronting his brother.

It was not the path he had ever intended to take—for his brother's sake. But Ella's talk of transparency on Friday night had set him thinking.

Ella was right about one thing: Holly came first. The bond—

because that's what it was, a fast, blood bond—that tied him to the baby was as vital to him as breathing. He would not risk losing her.

Tonight, when he announced to his brother what he was going to do, there was a very good chance it was going to cost him their relationship. But Dmitri had Keira.

And Holly had no one…except him.

He already knew his actions were going to alienate Ella. He'd hoped to gain her cooperation by letting her see how much the baby meant to him, but it was finally starting to sink in that Ella would never be swayed from her viewpoint. She was not prepared to recognize what he had to offer Holly.

He had a claim to the baby—one that would secure his place in her life. He had the money and resources to fight Ella and win temporary custody. Up until now, the only thing that had stood in his way of using the brute force of legal muscle had been his brother—or, more accurately, his brother's pride.

The Porsche swung easily into the next curve. Ahead, the group of cyclists had spread into a single file, and he nosed past.

In the previous ten days he'd grown to know and love Holly. He could not walk away. Yevgeny was all too conscious that tomorrow was D-Day, as he'd come to think of it. It would be his last chance to convince Ella that Holly belonged with him. Because the day after tomorrow, Ella would be legally able to sign a consent to allow Holly to be adopted by another couple. Once that was done, the decision would be final.

Sure, she'd said she was going to wait until after Christmas. But Yevgeny could not risk the danger that Ella might change her mind.

Then all would be lost.

Holly would be lost to him.

Forever.

Tomorrow was his best chance.

Tonight he would contact Dmitri far away in Africa to let his brother know of the decision he had made. Because he could not do what he had to do without letting his brother know. He'd left it too long already—because of his misguided confidence in his ability to convince Ella to come round to his point of view.

Time was fast running out....

Nine

The meeting dragged on.

Ella doodled on the legal pad in front of her and wondered what Yevgeny and Holly were doing in the park. Yevgeny had taken Holly alone, giving Deb a sizable block of time off for the first time in over a week. Now Ella was fretting. Had she done the right thing letting Yevgeny take the baby out alone? Of course she had. He was the baby's uncle—he deserved some sort of relationship with Holly. The next worry popped up. Had Deb packed the bag? Would Yevgeny have remembered to take a bottle? To put sunscreen onto the baby's fair skin? Her gaze slid to where her cell phone sat on the conference table beside her legal pad.

She could call him....

"What do you think, Ella?"

The question wrenched her out of her reverie. Ella set her pen down and forced herself to focus. This was important. *But would it be important five years from now?* Yevgeny's lecture came back to her.

Ella gazed around the table. Two unsmiling executives

dressed in pin-striped black suits stared at her. The older executive was the CFO, the younger was the corporation's legal advisor.

Would the outcome of this meeting be important in five years? She considered the radical thought. Work—any work—had always been important. But this time? Ella wasn't so sure. Originally she'd viewed this meeting as an opportunity to gain a toehold in bankruptcy law, and add another specialty to her expertise. But it didn't fit with the rest of her family law practice. She was no longer sure she wanted to do the company's work—she didn't even like the CFO. She'd handled his sister's divorce and received the referral. It had sounded like a great opportunity.

But she didn't want to spend her days filing bankruptcy suits.

So what was she doing wasting precious time on this? Where had her ideals of building a quality practice doing work she loved gone? What was she doing representing corporate sharks? And for what? More money? More prestige? Longer hours?

Was it worth bargaining her soul for?

"Will you be able to do the work?"

"Sorry?" Ella struggled to grasp the implication of the CFO's question. Was he doubting her legal ability? Both men were watching her across the polished expanse of the table. Her stomach knotted. She'd missed a crucial part of the dialogue. Now she was floundering. "I missed the last bit."

"I heard you had a baby." The CFO's tone was patronizing. His gaze dropped to the legal pad in front of her, then lifted to meet hers. His expression said it all. She was losing her edge; her femininity was the problem.

Ella found herself flushing. She resisted the urge to cover the doodles, to deny every thought she read in his face. Then she caught herself.

Why should I feel ashamed?

She had been daydreaming…imaging Holly and Yevgeny out in the sunshine, then fretting about all the things—important things—Yevgeny might forget.

It had taken Holly less than twelve days to change her life.

For the first time in years she was focusing on what she wanted. Evaluating. Choosing.

What had happened to her dreams? When had her desire to only take on work she wanted to do become hijacked by visions of wealth and power? That had been the whole reason she'd left the large, city practice where she'd been a rising star. She'd wanted to be able to take cases that interested her—refuse those she didn't wish to do. Not have her days…weeks…years dictated by billable hours.

It had worked out. She earned a good living…she had a retirement plan…her town house was paid off…she worked for herself and was answerable to no one.

She wanted for nothing.

But along the way she'd become more ambitious. Her schedule had become crowded.

There was no time left for…Ella.

When had she last taken a vacation? She'd always loved movies. When had she last taken the night off and gone to watch a movie and share a tub of popcorn with Keira or a friend? And, for that matter, when had she last actually met up with any of her friends? Ella couldn't even remember. Most of the people she socialized with these days were her work colleagues.

"I don't think I'm the right person for the job," Ella found herself saying. "But I have a colleague who might be a perfect fit. Let me call your office later with his contact details." There was immense satisfaction in watching the CFO sputter for words. Ella rose to her feet, and gave the pair her most gracious smile. "Thank you so much for considering me. I do appreciate it, but I think Mark Stanley will be a much better fit for your company."

And she was going to rewrite her business plan to focus on the work she did best—and enjoyed most. But first she was going to see if she could find Yevgeny and Holly.

She was going out to play in the park.

* * *

Yevgeny spotted Ella approaching long before she reached them. There was something about the way she moved that had clued him in that it was Ella when she'd still been a speck in the distance.

"You were worried about the baby. You thought I'd screw up." Partly annoyed by Ella's inability to give up control but also pleased that she'd been worried enough about the baby to come to the park, Yevgeny grinned at her from where he was sprawled on a picnic blanket on the grass in the shade of an ancient oak.

"I wasn't worried."

Yevgeny didn't believe that for one minute. "So why did you come?"

She glanced away. "I thought it would be nice to be outside on such a lovely day."

He snorted in disbelief.

"I did. Honestly! I—"

She was talking so fast that Yevgeny found his grin growing wider. "Slow down!"

Ella stopped talking abruptly and gave him a sheepish smile. Her dimples appeared. Then she sank down beside Holly, who was sound asleep on the blanket. She touched the baby's cheek with one finger and Holly made a snuffling sound.

Ella quickly withdrew her finger. "I don't want to wake her just yet."

"How did the meeting go?" he asked.

"Fine." Her face tightened.

Not fine, then. His good humor faded. "There was a problem?" He couldn't help remembering his criticism of her priorities. It made him feel guilty.

"No." She paused. "Not really."

"There was a problem." There was no doubt in his mind.

She turned to face him. The bright gold eyes were dulled by specks of unhappiness. Something was bothering Ella. And Yevgeny was surprised by the wave of protectiveness that swamped him.

"What went wrong?"

She hesitated. "Nothing. The meeting went fine. *I* was the problem."

Stretching out beside Ella and the baby, he propped himself on his elbows. Keeping his eyes intent on her face, he asked, "What do you mean?"

"It's hard to explain." She shrugged.

"Try," he prompted, sensing quicksand ahead.

"I'm not sure I understand myself." She looked away.

Yevgeny sensed this was not the time to push her. Above them the wind rustled through the leaves. He could hear blackbirds chirruping.

"Something has changed."

The admission surprised him. "You were treated different than usual?"

She shook her head. "That's not it. It's me—I've changed."

He studied her, seeking signs of the change she was talking about.

The wind caught at her hair. One hand brushed a recalcitrant strand back behind her ear. Except for a mussing from the wind's touch her hair was sleek and styled. The black business suit Ella wore was smart—even though by virtue of sitting on the picnic blanket she was showing far more leg than the designer had ever intended to be revealed in the office.

His eyes traveled down the length of leg encased in sheer stockings. Until he reached her feet. She'd kicked her shoes off. Already scraps of grass clung to the stockinged soles of her feet.

She might look the same…

But he would never have imagined that Ella he'd known before sprawled across a picnic blanket in a suit, her hair wind-tousled, her shoes abandoned.

She *had* changed.

"If you want the truth, I like the change."

Her eyes widened. "You can see it?"

He found himself leaning forward. "You're more relaxed—not so uptight."

"Uptight?" She drew away. "I'm not uptight!"

The quicksand deepened. He drew a measured breath. "I meant that as a compliment, not a criticism."

The look she flicked him was laden with uncertainty. An uncertainty that bothered him far more than he cared to admit. Had he been so critical of her? That she had to examine everything he said for hidden motive? Yevgeny didn't like that thought at all. He always considered Ella opinionated and judgmental. Had he been every bit as bad?

Leaning forward, he brushed the grass cuttings from her stockings.

She wiggled her toes and jerked away. "Don't!"

Acting on instinct, he grasped her foot and pulled it back to him. Then, on a wicked suspicion, he tickled the sole of the foot now resting against his leg.

She gave a shriek of laughter that she quickly bit off.

"You're ticklish." The discovery delighted him.

"Very." She glanced at the still sleeping baby, then mock frowned at him. "Don't you dare!"

"I never could resist a dare."

Or the temptation of revealing this unexpected side of Ella....

She convulsed with laughter as his fingers descended. "I haven't even begun," he protested.

"No, no." But she was laughing.

So he tickled more.

She writhed on the blanket, breathless with mirth. Her body rolled up against him, and Yevgeny went still. He had only a moment to make the decision…it was no decision. His fingers trailed away from her foot, his touch firming as he stroked along her leg.

Her laughter faltered, and her head turned. She must have glimpsed the intent in his eyes because her breath hooked in her throat.

The sudden silence was deafening.

Her lips moved. "Yev—"

Before she could protest he shifted his body and slanted his mouth across hers.

Then he waited.

She made no sound, no move rejecting him.

She gave a little gasp beneath his lips. Then her mouth opened like a flower.

Then a growling wail broke the tension.

"It's Holly, she's awake!" Ella pushed at his shoulders. "Let me up."

Yevgeny rolled away onto his back, one arm flung across his eyes. The baby sure picked her moments....

"My God. Anyone could have seen us." Ella's breath was coming in shallow gasps. "What was I thinking?"

"You weren't thinking...." Yevgeny lowered his arm to gauge her response "You were feeling."

"What's that supposed to mean?" Ella picked up the baby. "That I don't feel? That's what you believe?" She clasped the baby to her chest, rocking her. "That I have no feelings?"

It was hardly the time to confess that he'd considered all her feelings to be entombed in ice. Nor could he lie. He settled for, "I didn't know you."

"So you jumped to conclusions instead of trying to find out more."

There was nothing he could say to refute her statement.

"So much for being someone who doesn't react on impulse."

Having his own words flung back at him was no more than he deserved. He tried not to flinch. "I still believe that is the best way—even though I am perhaps not the best example."

"Well, at least you're honest."

"And you're generous to concede that. Thank you." Her shoulders sagged as she let out a deep breath. She hitched the baby higher.

He reached awkwardly forward. "Let me take her. She must be heavy."

"I can manage."

His arms fell away. For the first time he took in how comfortable Ella looked holding the baby. This wasn't a picture of a woman who couldn't wait to get rid of the child in her arms. Ella looked...maternal.

Surprise jolted Yevgeny.

He blinked. Looked again. Ella still looked perfectly at home. He waited for Holly to regurgitate the bottle he'd given her before she'd gone to sleep over Ella's formal suit. But that didn't happen. Instead, Ella continued looking down at the baby cradled in the crook of her arm with a curiously content expression.

Yevgeny couldn't concentrate on anything except Ella.

Every time he turned his head, those golden eyes ensnared him. The rose-tinted mouth that was so much softer than he'd ever envisaged. The Ella he was discovering behind the professional dark suits and efficient manner was very different from what he'd built her into.

So much more.

Her humor. Her rounded, infectious laugh. The love for her sister. The way her eyes softened like melting honey when she looked at Holly and thought no one was watching.

She even possessed a degree of sensitivity and self-awareness he'd never expected—she knew she was changing.

Like one of his *babushka's matryoshka* dolls where every layer opened to reveal something different. Something unexpected and new. Another layer that entranced him even further.

His chest tightened.

Yevgeny shook his head to clear the confusion. He must be dreaming...having such thoughts, such feelings about Ella.

But Ella was right about one thing: he knew far too little about her. And that was something he intended to remedy.

Starting now.

"What's your star sign?"

Her head lifted, and her attention switched from Holly to him. "My what?"

"Your star sign."

"I heard you, but I can't figure out why you'd want to know. Surely you don't follow astrology?"

He shrugged. "All women know their star signs." Some that he'd dated consulted their horoscopes every day. He couldn't understand why she was fussing about it.

"Because they hope that some vague prediction of good fortune will get them something that usually takes plenty of work."

His mouth quirked up. He suspected that assessment fit a couple of women he had known. "You're talking about finding a husband?"

"No! I'm talking about career and the financial benefits that come with hard work."

"Ah, I should've known." He had known. Of course that's what she meant. But he couldn't resist teasing her. She rose to the bait so beautifully. Every time.

She cast him a suspicious look. "I don't read my daily horoscope."

He didn't grin. "I imagine you read the financial pages."

"What's wrong with that? At least I have a better idea where the real financial advantages lie."

He held his hands up in surrender. "I'm not arguing with that logic."

"Really?" She tipped her head to one side. "Are you saying you actually agree with me?"

"You're surprised?"

Her lips curved up into a smile that attracted his attention to her mouth—her very kissable mouth, a mouth he was rapidly becoming addicted to. But with Holly now awake he had no chance of exploring that new obsession anytime soon.

Better to focus on getting to know what other surprises Ella had in store....

Holly chose that moment to squeak and reach out a hand to tug at Ella's bracelet. As soon as she had Ella's full attention the baby started trying to blow raspberries.

"Oh, Yevgeny, look!"

She laid the baby back down on the blanket and spent the next few minutes playing peekaboo. Holly was wide-eyed with interest.

Ella was laughing.

And Yevgeny knew he needed to get to know this woman better.

"What's your favorite color?"

She stopped giggling at Holly's attempts to blow raspberries and blinked at him. "Why?"

"Just answer."

"Why do you want to know?"

The familiar frustration rose. "Are you always this suspicious?"

"Of you? Yes."

"Why?"

"Because you're not the kind of man who engages in careless conversation. There's always a reason behind everything you say. But I can't figure out why you'd want to know what my favorite color is."

He lowered his voice to a purr. "If you tell me gold, I can tell you it matches your eyes. Or if you say rose, I could compare it to the flush on your cheeks."

Her cheeks flamed. "Why would you want to say such things?"

"You are a beautiful woman—when you allow yourself to be."

"Is this part of the same conversation about my not having feelings?"

He took her hand in his and turned it over. "Rounded nails. Your nails are carefully tended."

She snatched her hand away.

"Wait. I haven't finished." He retrieved it from where she'd laid it back in her lap. "No nail color."

"I'm sorry that displeases you."

"It doesn't displease me, but it tells me plenty about you."

"What? That I'm not trying to capture a man's attention?"

"There are many ways to capture a man's attention. Painted nails are only one." He stroked the back of her hand. "Your skin is soft. That's very attractive. You take care of it."

Her lips parted, but she didn't utter the words that he could see bubbling. Instead, her breathing quickened.

God. He was only touching her hand....

Yevgeny let it go. "When is your birthday?"

"Why? Do you want to read my horoscope? Or do you want to buy me a present?"

"Perhaps—but it would be difficult to choose. I don't know you very well."

"You don't get your assistant to pick out gifts for all your women?"

There was a buzzing in his ears. "Are you saying you're one of my women?"

She paled. "Of course not!" She fussed with the bottle that Holly had discarded. "I can think of nothing worse."

"Nothing?"

Her gaze dropped to the baby and he knew she'd gotten his point. Giving Holly up for adoption was far, far worse than being his woman—or the next step, having a child with him.

Then he spelled it out, "It would be easier to give Holly away, would it?"

Ella went white, and for the first time he noticed the sprinkling of bronze freckles across her nose. "It won't be giving her away. She'll be going to a family who desperately wants a baby to love—and I still intend to see her from time to time." She paused. There was a peculiar light in her eyes. "If you really want to know, my birthday was Friday before last."

It took him only a moment to make the connection. "The day Holly was born."

There was no way in hell he could say any more.

Ella didn't look at the baby on the blanket beside her. Instead, she wrapped her arms around herself. "I better get back to work. I have one more appointment before I'm done for the day."

* * *

"What do you mean you don't care?" Frustration soared as Yevgeny changed the cell phone to his other ear and tried to ignore the crackle that distorted his brother's voice. Yes, it must be the crack of dawn in Africa. Without a doubt, he'd woken his brother out of a deep sleep. But he wasn't sorry. He was too relieved he'd finally made contact, after almost twenty-four hours of trying. He'd pulled the Porsche over to try calling—and gotten lucky. "But you never wanted anyone to know you're sterile. You swore me to secrecy."

Dmitri mumbled something to the effect that Keira already knew—and that was all who really mattered.

Of course Keira knew!

How else had Holly been conceived with Yevgeny's donated sperm?

Which Ella didn't know. She still believed Dmitri was Holly's biological father. And Yevgeny had been so confident that she'd ultimately allow him to adopt Holly without the need to air Dmitri's tragic secret.

He'd sure been wrong about that.

Yevgeny was relieved that the baby wasn't here to experience his raised voice. He never wanted her associating her daddy with anger. He'd left her with Deb only ten minutes ago; soon he would be back at his penthouse.

"But you were so adamant about it," Yevgeny gritted out. Hell, if he'd known his brother had become so casual about who knew about his sterility he'd have told Ella yesterday at that bewitching house. Or earlier today at the park.

He'd had the opportunity.

A year ago it had been a different story altogether…then Dmitri hadn't wanted anyone—except Keira—to know the truth. He appeared to have forgotten all about that.

"Yevgeny, it was you who was so uptight about it." Even over the distorted line he could hear his brother's protest.

"Me?"

That wasn't true. His brother had always been deeply

embarrassed about the sterility that had resulted from his contracting mumps when he was young. During his teen years it had been a shameful secret as he roared around wildly with gangs of girls to prove his virility. Even now the memory of those days, the fights he'd had as Dmitri leaped from one disaster to the next made Yevgeny shudder.

"Yes. You thought it made me less of a man. A sissy."

"I *never* said that!" He struggled with an impotent sense of growing outrage.

"But you thought it."

Never! "Where the hell did you get that screwed-up idea from?" he growled.

"You."

Yevgeny sucked in a breath, counted to ten. Outside the Porsche the street was alive with people hurrying home at the end of the day. "Then you read me wrong."

"*You* were terrified about it getting into the papers. You didn't want anyone to know you'd donated sperm in case *Babushka* found out."

That part was true.

"Maybe I overreacted about that." It was a huge admission to make. Again he was guarding his brother. His grandmother's one shortcoming in life was that she'd always been very conservative—and tended to be too outspoken and hurtful at times. "*Babushka* was probably a lot tougher than I give her credit for being. But it was more than that. I was terrified of the paparazzi stalking you. The stories in the gossip rags would emasculate you." And shame his brother further.

Too late he realized what he'd said. Silence crackled down the line.

"Dmitri?" No answer. More loudly he demanded, "Dmitri?" He was thankful that the Porsche was soundproof. The woman wheeling a pram past the passenger side didn't even turn her head.

An angry grunt told him his brother hadn't hung up.

"I'm sorry." The words came with difficulty. "That was

tactless." And that instinct to protect his brother had been there all his life, started by his mother calling Dmitri a crybaby.

"Tactless?" This time he heard a laugh. His shoulders sagged with relief as Dmitri continued. "My never-wrong brother admits he has been tactless?"

"That's how you see me? Never wrong?" Yevgeny knew he sounded incredulous, but dammit, he'd never heard Dmitri going on like this. Like a sullen child. How long had this resentment been simmering?

"You've always taken charge of everything—there was never any space for me to do anything—you had it all under control."

It sure as hell didn't sound like he had it all under control now! "Dmitri, is everything okay?"

"I'm fine. Better than I've ever been in my life."

"What does that mean?"

"I'm discovering what it means to be myself."

"But you always were yourself." Yevgeny couldn't understand any of this. It was starting to feel as if he'd barged into one of those online gaming sites his brother habitually frequented—a dark, confusing alien parallel universe.

"No." His brother denied. "I was drifting. I wasn't myself. I was living in your shadow."

Yevgeny started to take issue with that, and then stopped to consider what Dmitri was saying. Perhaps he had tried to force choices on his brother, but he'd done it for Dmitri's own good. He had worried Yevgeny with his wild behavior, spendthrift ways, fast cars and equally fast women. Had he unconsciously adopted his mother's attitude that his brother was weak?

His brother was talking again. Yevgeny forced himself to concentrate—to really listen. "Keira's calling. I have to go help in the clinic."

"The clinic?"

"It's a health clinic. Run by volunteers. A nurse comes once every second week—mostly to attend to vaccinations and refer more serious cases to the nearest doctor two hundred miles away. I did a first-aid course in Auckland, so I'm working there."

"You've done a first-aid course?" Yevgeny couldn't keep the surprise out of his voice. "I didn't know."

Dmitri said, "You also don't know that I'm tossing around the idea of going to university to study to become a doctor."

"A doctor?" Yevgeny decided that he must be dreaming.

A laugh came down the line. "There's a whole wide world out there, *braht*—you should see it one day."

But right now Yevgeny needed permission from his brother. "So I can tell Ella?"

"Yes. Keira never wanted to keep it from her. But I thought you didn't want anyone to know your brother was less than a whole man. So I convinced her it was better this way."

Oh, Christ. "I've made a right mess of it, haven't I?"

It didn't matter what he had or hadn't thought. His relationship with his brother was clearly far from healthy.

After a moment his brother came back with, "It's not your fault alone. We always seem to talk at cross-purposes."

"That's going to change," Yevgeny vowed. And his brother wasn't the only person with whom he had a communication issue.

The realization, as he ended the call, was not a pleasant one.

But it had to be faced. His interaction with Ella had been based on quick judgments and half-assed opinions from the start.

No wonder he'd stood no chance of gaining her consent to adopt Holly. But he intended to change that. It was time he put all his cards on the table, and told Ella the truth.

Ella's last appointment took longer than she'd scheduled.

When her cell phone rang, Ella glanced at the caller ID. Yevgeny. Her fingers hovered over the face of the phone. Finally she pressed the button to kill the call and let it divert to voice mail, then looked back at the man sitting in front of her.

Jerry Foster was at the end of his tether.

Two weeks ago he'd received divorce papers. Like many of Ella's clients, he hadn't even known his wife had been unhappy.

Yes, Lois had nagged him to change his workaholic habits a couple of years ago; and, yes, she'd asked him to join the tennis club and play doubles two nights a week but he'd been too busy with the business. He'd told her to find another doubles partner. He'd thought the problem was solved.

Until two weeks ago.

Now he was in a spin. His wife was demanding custody… occupation of the marital home…and worst of all, Jerry was starting to suspect that her new doubles partner was more to her than a fellow tennis player. What Jerry wanted, he'd told Ella, was not a divorce. What he wanted was to keep his wife and kids.

Jerry wanted his life back.

He was ready to do whatever it took to restore his marriage. But his wife wasn't playing ball.

"Why won't she talk to me?" He jabbed his fingers through messed curls, the gold of his wedding ring glinting in the office lighting. "I was doing this for her—for us," he amended.

Jerry owned a multimillion-dollar investment company. It generated enough income to more than meet the family's needs for years to come.

"I wanted her—our family—to be cared for," Jerry was saying. "Not like my mother. My father died when I was ten, a heart attack, and my mother had to scrub toilets to put food on the table."

"Did you ever explain this to Lois?" Ella asked gently.

Jerry looked at her as if she were an alien from another planet. "Of course not. I didn't want her to feel sorry for me. I always played down my roots. My mother died the year before I met Lois—there was no need for her to know all that sordid stuff."

"Do you think she would've loved you less if she'd known about your background?" Ella wasn't a therapist but she'd seen similar versions of this sorry tale played out too many times to count.

A feeling of déjà vu settled over her.

"No!" He looked shocked. "She's not like that. She's the kindest woman I ever met. That's why I love her so much."

The confusion in his eyes made Ella feel like crying.

Jerry didn't need a lawyer—he needed someone who could teach him how to communicate with his wife!

A knock sounded on the door. A moment later Peggy peered around the door frame.

"I have Mr. Volkovoy on the line. He says it's urgent."

Ella gave her cell phone a sideways glance. There were three new messages since she'd killed that call a few minutes ago. Her heartbeat picked up. Holly. Had something happened to the little girl? And if so, wouldn't she have heard from Deb first? Drawing a deep breath she told herself not to jump to conclusions. "Do you know what the matter is?"

"He wouldn't say. But he did admit it wasn't a medical emergency."

Holly was okay!

Ella silently blessed her assistant's unflappable common sense.

"Tell him I'm with a client. I'll call him back in about ten minutes when our meeting is done."

Peggy nodded. "I'll let Mr. Volkovoy know."

Yevgeny found himself pacing the vast black marble floor of his penthouse as he waited for Ella to call him back.

He wasn't sure what childish urge had compelled him to insist it was an emergency. He wasn't used to women not being available to take his calls—and being left to cool his heels. Yet he suspected he'd behaved badly. How often had he been annoyed by women calling and insisting that trivial matters were crises that needed his immediate attention? How often had that led to him backing out of the relationship?

He didn't like the idea that he was acting in a similar, irrational fashion.

In truth, the very idea scared the hell out of him.

Not that he was in any kind of relationship with Ella....

When Ella's call finally came, it came through on his cell phone. He leaped on it.

"You were looking for me?"

Her voice sounded warm and welcoming. He stopped pacing. Something in him responded and he felt the tension that had ratcheted up during his conversation with Dmitri slowly uncoiling. "Yes, I was." He searched for words.

"I called Deb. She says Holly is fine. Is it Keira—has something happened?"

There was a note of fear in her voice now. Yevgeny squeezed his eyes shut. God. Why hadn't he foreseen that his stupidity might cause her to worry needlessly? He opened them again and stared out the wall of glass but, for once, the spectacular view failed to register. "No, no, nothing to do with Keira."

He hesitated.

No, filling her in over the phone about his conversation with his brother was precipitate. He'd talk to her…face-to-face… as he'd planned. Now wasn't the time to go off half-cocked; too much was at stake.

"Then what's wrong?"

"Nothing's wrong."

He shifted his feet. He could feel himself coloring. He felt like a total idiot. It was not a familiar feeling. Against this backdrop he was going to break the news of what he planned to do? He had to pull himself together, or else he was going to end up alienating Ella forever. And that would not be in Holly's best interests.

But the edginess wouldn't leave him. "Uh—I have to go to a charity function tomorrow night."

Today was D-Day.

Was he taking too much of a risk, leaving it until tomorrow? Even though Ella had said she'd only make a decision about Holly after Christmas?

"Yes?"

There was confusion in Ella's voice.

"I accepted several weeks ago." While he'd still been dating

Nadiya. "For myself and a partner. I was wondering whether you would be prepared to come with me?"

His grip on the cell phone tensed.

"You want me to go on a date with you?"

Yevgeny couldn't tell whether she was annoyed or amused. Nor did he want to point out that technically they'd been on two dates already—one he'd orchestrated at her home with food from La Rosa and the second at the park earlier.

"That's what was so urgent?"

The disbelief in her tone made him writhe.

Because he wasn't being truthful.

Turning away from the glass wall, he started to pace again. "The organizer called me to get my partner's name for the table lists— I needed to let her know."

"Urgently?" she asked pointedly.

"Yes— The function is tomorrow." He'd forgotten all about taking a date. Hell, finding a woman had been far from his thoughts these past couple of weeks. The only female that filled his head had been Holly—and Ella. But she didn't really count.

"Why me?"

He hesitated again. He'd reached the silver-and-black open-plan kitchen. He swung around. Then stopped. He drew a deep breath, and let it out slowly. Then he leaned back against the kitchen counter.

God, he was becoming more and more tangled in this deception—even though he'd planned to be honest and put an end to it all.

"Because I can't believe you haven't got someone else in your little black book you could call," she blurted out when he didn't answer.

Yevgeny found himself grinning. "I don't have a little black book."

She clicked her tongue. "The contacts list in your phone, then."

How to admit that none of them stirred his interest enough? His mind skittered away from the terrifying specter that thought raised—the only person he wanted to ask was Ella. Because that had to be wrong. It could never be true.

She was prickly and defensive. Not his type.

She reminded him of his mother.

Or did she? Flashes of Ella laughing with Holly. Of how she looked at the baby. Of her gentle cloying concern for her sister. Of her care for her elderly parents.

For the first time he realized that his assumption was quite untrue: Ella was nothing like the woman who had given birth to him—and then deserted him.

Ella would never desert Holly.

She planned to stay in touch with a baby who was never meant to be hers. She only wanted what she considered the very best for Holly—even though Yevgeny didn't share her views.

"Why me?" she asked again.

"Because you would probably have held it against my proposed adoption if I turned up with a beauty queen from my contacts list."

There was a silence in response to his facetious reply.

Then she said, "I don't think—"

"Please," he said abruptly, kicking himself for not holding his tongue.

"You could go alone, you know."

"I probably will. It's a charity event—I'd feel bad not showing up." With a sigh, he said, "You would've enjoyed the ballet."

"Ballet?"

Yevgeny held his breath.

"Which ballet?"

A vision of two pairs of ballet slippers with faded satin ribbons danced before his eyes. He had her! A smile curved his lips up. *"Giselle."*

He heard as she sucked her breath in. Finally she said, "I'd love to come with you to the ballet."

Ella set the phone down, terminating the connection to Jo Wells.

The day she'd been waiting for had arrived. Yevgeny was

due to pick her up in—Ella glanced at her watch—two hours. She still had to beat the rush-hour traffic home, see that Deb had handed Holly over to the night caregiver, express milk for Holly's night bottle, shower and glam herself up. Now Jo was on her way, too.

Of course, everything always did happen at once.

The social worker had identified a couple whom she believed met every one of Ella's criteria. A professional couple who'd already adopted a two-year-old girl, they had a very good relationship with their daughter's biological parents and grandparents. Their home was located in a rural suburb of Auckland, less than forty minutes drive from where Ella lived. The property abounded with pets and ponies, with a garden that led down to the sea.

They'd flown through the police checks. The family offered everything and more.

Jo was ecstatic. She was bringing the profile file for Ella to view immediately.

The family was so perfect that Jo's biggest concern was that the biological mothers of two other babies currently waiting for adoption might choose this family. But Jo had said that the family was more than happy to let Holly spend Christmas with Ella—if that was what Ella wanted.

Ella knew she should be experiencing profound joy. But she could only feel the heaviness of dread.

When she examined the dark source of that heaviness she concluded that deep down she'd been secretly hoping that Keira would come to her senses and contact Ella to claim the baby. Was that why she'd been stalling? Was that why she'd vetoed every other couple?

Why she'd been so critical of every other solution available to Holly? Even the option Yevgeny offered? She closed her eyes. She didn't even want to think about the house Yevgeny was going to buy. Every nook and cranny of her memory of that place was infused with imaginary visions of Holly running across the lawns, Holly playing on the swing Yevgeny intended to build, Holly curled up in the window seat while a fuzzy feminine figure read her a story—

But this would be an open adoption. No reason why Holly would not still have that… She would visit Yevgeny. This family clearly welcomed full participation for the biological family.

There was no reason to hesitate. Ella knew she had to breach the barrier and take the final, irrevocable step.

But she had to face that it wasn't a case of Keira coming to her senses—Keira had made her own choice. She wanted to find herself—she wasn't ready to become a mother. Keira was a grown-up. Ella could no longer make her decisions—live her life—for her. Keira had already had twelve days to change her mind.

But she hadn't.

Ella knew it was time to stop clinging to a thread of hope that had already snapped.

She had to stop putting roadblocks up. This state of limbo was stressful for everyone. And it was unfairest of all to Holly— Every day that passed was taking away the opportunity for the baby to form a strong relationship with her new mother. Ella knew she had to finally let go of the secret dreams she'd been harboring and start working with Jo Wells to finalize the adoption.

For Holly's sake.

She would look at the profile that Jo was bringing with an open mind…and try not to compare the home with the dream home she'd visited with Yevgeny on the weekend.

Then she would have to face up to Yevgeny himself when he collected her tonight, and tell him what she'd decided.

Applause thundered around the theatre.

The dramatic stage curtains came down as the first act of *Giselle* reached its dramatic conclusion. The lights came up. Around them the audience was already swarming up the aisles to take advantage of the intermission. Yevgeny was in time to

catch the transfixed glow on Ella's face, before she blinked
rapidly.

"Glad you came?"

Ella shivered. "Good grief, of course! Thank you. It's
incredibly powerful."

As Yevgeny got to his feet, Ella gave herself a shake. He
could see her starting to come back down to earth.

"How can they possibly top that performance in the second
act?" she asked as she rose. Her delicate chiffon wrap dropped
from her shoulders, exposing the deep V-shaped back of her
fitted black dress.

Yevgeny tucked his arm around her waist and ushered her
into the aisle ahead of him. She didn't shake his hand away, so
he left it there. Nudged from behind, he pressed up against her,
all at once aware of the warm softness of her body against his.
His gaze lingered on the soft skin exposed by the dress.

He ached to touch that skin, run a finger down her spine, see
the frisson of desire convulse her.

The emotions that had played out on stage in the first act
had heightened all his senses. The love. The despair. And the
intense passion.

His awareness of Ella leaped higher, blazing through him.

Yevgeny swallowed.

This was truly crazy!

As they emerged from the theater into the lobby he murmured, "Let me fetch us a couple of glasses of wine."

She hesitated, then nodded.

In relief he swung away. Surrounded by the din of chatter,
he took a moment to assemble his thoughts, to deal with his
fascination for Ella. A waiter bearing a tray filled with tall,
slim champagne glasses was coming toward him. Yevgeny took
two glasses.

At a touch on his arm, he glanced sideways—and broke
into a smile.

"Jerry, how are you?" Then his smile faded as he remembered

the gossip. Jerry's wife had left him for another man. Awkwardly he held up the glasses. "Sorry, no free hand to shake yours."

An uncomfortable pause followed, and then Yevgeny caught sight of Ella's blond head on the other side of the room. "Good to see you again, Jerry."

"Call me—perhaps we can play golf sometime," Jerry said.

Yevgeny nodded. "I'll do that." Then he made his way over to Ella and handed her a glass.

After a few minutes the bell signaling the end of intermission sounded.

Ella turned away and handed her still-full flute to a passing waiter.

Yevgeny sensed a black hole opening between them. Widening with every second that passed. Yet he couldn't find the words to bridge it.

What to do? To say? Yevgeny wasn't used to floundering for words. He was decisive. A leader.

He wasn't accustomed to this rudderless uncertainty.

Carefully he inched forward. He rested his fingers on her arm. She jumped. He let her go at once.

"Time to see what the second act holds." Ella threw the comment back over one pale exposed shoulder as she made her way back to the theater. "Let's see what the ghosts of jilted brides intend to do to the lying, faithless Albrecht."

That jolted him back to the present.

What was Ella going to say when she learned about the deception Keira, Dmitri and he had been engaged in?

The baby deserved honesty from all the adults around her. Not just from Ella. Holly was the innocent in this situation. Yet, ultimately she would suffer most from any deception.

Shame smothered him.

Ten

"You've booked a table for dinner?" Inside the confines of the cockpit of the stationary Porsche, Ella stared at Yevgeny in horror.

What to do now? How could she possibly tell him about the couple who wanted to adopt Holly amidst a room full of diners having a wonderful time? How could she kill his hopes in such a public arena?

It seemed too callous.

But if she asked him to take her home, and invited him in for a nightcap back at her town house, the night nanny—and Holly—would be waiting....

They needed somewhere private.

"Aren't you hungry?"

"A little." But she wasn't up to enduring two hours of polite pretense in a high-society restaurant while she sat on new information that involved Holly's adoption.

Maybe she should simply insist he take her home...and wait until tomorrow, then ask him to meet at her office? That would

be appropriate. Yet Ella didn't want to leave this any longer—
Yevgeny deserved to know of her decision.

Holly.

It was all for Holly.

Her chest ached, and she felt quite ill. Ella knew her heart
was breaking. Her glasses had misted up. She couldn't possibly
be crying?

Ella ducked her head and fished in her purse for a tissue.
Removing her glasses, she gave them a perfunctory polish then
put them back on. The mist had cleared.

Yevgeny was watching her.

"Don't you feel like going out? Would you prefer to have
something light to eat at my apartment? With a glass of wine?
I have a fabulous cellar."

That was a solution, although wine might not be such a good
idea—not now that Holly was drinking breast milk.

And Ella discovered she was curious to see where he lived,
to find out what lifestyle he would be shedding when he moved
into his new home. The next wave of pain washed over her.

Goodness, she was behaving like a goose.

"That sounds like a good idea—but I had a late lunch so
don't go to any trouble. I'm not that hungry."

"Hold on." The Porsche growled. They started to nose
forward out of the theater's parking lot. "Won't be long now."

Ella pulled out her cell phone to text Holly's night nurse not
to wait up for her.

The talk to come might take a while.

Yevgeny's penthouse apartment was perched high above
Auckland City like an eagle's nest.

From the private elevator, Ella alighted onto a steel mezzanine
bridge spanning the length of the penthouse. Two steps down,
and Ella found herself in the living area with Yevgeny right
behind her.

Black marble floors gleamed under blindingly bright track-
mounted spotlights. The immense space stretched miles to the

left and right. In front of her a wall of glass framed the unfolding cityscape like an enormous, dramatic work of art.

"This is awesome."

Yevgeny touched a panel on the wall and music swelled.

One end of the vast living space was filled with a high-tech kitchen dominated by jet-black marble and the brash shine of stainless steel. In the center of the space, a slab of glass suspended on white marble blocks and surrounded with designer ghost chairs gave a highly luminous, yet strangely floating, transparent take on a dinner table. To her left, a sitting area was furnished with sofas constructed of blocks of black and gray leather artfully arranged to take advantage of the view beyond.

"There's no television." Ella was surprised by the absence of electronics.

"Oh, it's here—you just can't see it."

Yevgeny walked to the sitting area and picked up a sleek object that, had Ella given it a second glance, she would've assumed to be a modern artifact. He pointed it at the glass wall in front of the sofas. With a soft click a narrow panel alongside the window slid open. A second click and the largest, slimmest wide-screen television Ella had ever seen rose out of the floor.

The mind boggled. "Very James Bond."

Amusement flashed in Yevgeny's eyes. "The theater sound system has been built into the walls and ceilings." He moved a finger and the television came on. "There are blinds that roll down to block out the light. Then this becomes a home cinema. The security system is also wired in."

The picture on the television changed and the screen split into a grid of images. As her eyes flicked from one image to the next, Ella could see the Porsche parked underground, the entrance to the private elevator where they'd been minutes before, the concierge desk in the lobby as well as images of rooms she had not yet seen. A huge bedroom with a scarlet bed clearly designed to reflect the passion of the occupant, caused her to glance away.

"There must be cameras everywhere in this apartment. Don't you ever feel...watched?"

"There are no cameras in the guest washroom."

Ella shot him a wary look to see if he was joking. His face appeared to be perfectly straight. With an edge she said, "How very fortunate for your female…guests."

Yevgeny gave her a lazy smile. "All my guests deserve a modicum of privacy."

This…this was a playboy's pad, jam-packed with boy-toys. Ella searched the screen. "What about the guest bedroom? Any cameras in there?"

"There is no guest bedroom—only the master bedroom and bathroom—and a study. I'll show you around if you like."

"The ultimate bachelor's dream," she said, not ready to acknowledge his offer to show her his bedroom. Although her heart had picked up at the thought of standing with Yevgeny in the same space as that wildly passionate scarlet bed.…

Her eyes roamed the living area, seeking a distraction.

Minimalist. Glossy hard surfaces. Hardly the kind of place that a child could visit. It belonged on the pages of interior-design magazines and was far removed from the house Ella had visited with Yevgeny on Sunday.

That place—while big—was meant for a family.

"I see why you wanted to go house hunting," she said.

A pang of guilt stabbed her. Ella knew she was procrastinating. It was time to talk to Yevgeny about Holly's future.

The bubble of hope he'd been fantasizing about was about to burst. And it was an unrealistic fantasy— Ella had only to look at the kind of place he lived in to know that his lifestyle was totally unsuited to a child. Buying that dream house wasn't going to change who Yevgeny was.

Even though she'd discovered he was capable of patience and enormous devotion toward Holly, it was not enough.

He could not provide the family Holly needed.

But, Ella told herself, that didn't mean he could have no relationship with Holly. An open adoption allowed that. They would both be able to be part of Holly's life.

Holly would have it all. A wonderful family and plenty of

support from both sides of her biological family. They were all giving Holly the best chance of success in the circumstances.

Yevgeny had opened a panel in the end wall to reveal a bar complete with a fridge below the counter. "Would you like a glass of Merlot? Or I can offer Sauvignon Blanc—or what about a flute of chilled Bollinger?"

About to ask for a glass of mineral water, Ella changed her mind. What the hell, a woman didn't have the chance to drink Bollinger in this kind of place too often in her life. And the effervescence of champagne might clear the sadness that was settling around her like smog at the end of a winter's workday.

With a determined smile, she said, "Bollinger, please."

"Have a seat."

Yevgeny turned back to the bar fridge and extracted a frosted jeroboam. A moment later he popped the cork. Perched on a sofa, Ella listened to the sound of the champagne being poured into two tall flutes and tried to tell herself that everything was working out for the best.

Crossing to where she sat, he handed her a glass, then settled down beside her.

Ella felt her pulse pick up. Partly due to anxiety, she knew, because of the discussion to come about Holly's new family. But there was more to it. Sadness—obviously—because the time with Holly was drawing to an end. And beneath that was another layer: the unsettling edginess that Yevgeny always aroused in her.

She focused on that layer of restlessness. When she'd first met Yevgeny, she'd have identified this feeling as…animosity. Now it had metamorphosed into something else. Still unsettling—but far from unpleasant.

There was excitement…anticipation…and a hint of apprehension, too.

Ella took a small sip of the bubbly liquid then set it down on the highly reflective glass side table. Mistake. Without the drink to focus on, all her awareness centered on Yevgeny.

Her skin prickled and shivers spread through her.

Oh, God.

She shut her eyes.

The music danced along her senses. Sweet. Pleasurable. Ella tried to focus only on that.

It didn't work…because listening to the music led to thoughts of the ballet earlier…which led her to think about the man who had invited her.

Opening her eyes, she found herself impaled by Yevgeny's startling stare. Her heart stopped, then resumed with a jolt.

The silence between them had swelled to an expectant readiness.

When Yevgeny reached forward and cupped her face with one hand, her lashes feathered down and Ella sighed softly.

To Yevgeny's astonishment, the hand that cupped Ella's cheek was shaking.

White-hot emotions chased through him. Emotions so intense, so charged, he did not know what they signaled.

All he knew was that it seemed right to kiss Ella.

With great care he removed her glasses and set them down on the table beside them. Then, moving slowly, he leaned forward. His lips closed over hers. He tasted her gasp, and deepened the kiss. Ella gave a husky, raw moan and relaxed back on the sofa.

Desire burned him.

His heart thundered in his ears as he shifted his body across hers on the black leather and slanted his head to seal their mouths together. Beneath him Ella was soft, incredibly feminine. Still cupping her head, he feasted on the lushness of her mouth, devouring her. He could feel her heart thudding against his chest, and he knew she felt the intensity of this as much as he did.

Ending the kiss, he slid his lips down along the skin of her neck, tracing the V neckline of the sexy dress with open-mouthed caresses until he stopped at the hollow between her breasts. He nuzzled at the lilac-scented valley.

Under him, Ella shivered.

And Yevgeny reacted.

His thigh sank between hers, causing her dress to ruche up.

The temptation was too much. He ran one hand along the soft skin of her inner thigh until he found the lace edge of her panties. He eased his fingers beneath the lace. Lifting his head, he watched her as his fingers roamed closer...closer.

Ella was breathing quickly now, in soft, shallow gasps.

He touched her.

She was slick and already wet. Her back arched off the leather, and her eyes closed tight.

It was his turn to moan.

Withdrawing his hand, Yevgeny shifted off the sofa, so that he kneeled beside her.

"Why are you stopping?" she whispered, her eyes still tightly shut.

"You want me to carry on?"

Gold eyes glinted at him through dark lashes. "Yes!"

Sliding his arms beneath her, he hoisted her up and rose to his feet in one smooth move.

Ella grabbed at his shoulders. "What are you doing?"

"Taking you someplace more comfortable," he murmured. Then he bent his head and licked her ear, his tongue exploring the spiral shape. The moan that broke from her this time sounded wild.

In the softly lit bedroom, he let her slide down his body and as soon as her feet found the carpeted floor, he unzipped her dress. He drew her out of the dress and lifted her onto the bed.

He tore off his shirt and trousers in record time. A moment later, clad only in underpants, he joined her on the bed.

Ella was wearing only wisps of black lace.

Against the red satin of his bedcover, with her blond hair and pale skin, and the skimpy bits of black lace, she looked provocatively sensual.

The low-cut cups of her wicked bra revealed curves he hadn't known she possessed. Until now.

He touched the indent of her waist, and traced the flaring

outline of her hip. His hand rested on the rounded flesh of her bottom, then he stroked up along the groove of her spine. Her skin was like silk. Just touching her aroused him.

"You are lovely."

For a moment uncertainty glittered in her eyes. "Hardly a supermodel. You've dated—"

"Hush." He placed his index finger on her lips to silence her. "Now there is only you. No one else."

It stunned him how right speaking those words felt.

Only Ella?

But he wasn't ready to consider why it felt so right. Not yet. And not now.

He stroked her stomach where only a few weeks ago a baby had rested. The emotions that flooded him were too complex to name.

All he knew was that somewhere in that cocktail was gratitude. He sank his head down and kissed her belly, paying homage to her fertility and femininity.

Then, slipping a hand under her, he unclipped her bra with a deft flick and brushed the lace aside.

His breath caught.

Ella's breasts were full and high. The dark nipples stood proud. He touched them with reverent fingers. "Are they tender?" he asked.

She shook her head.

His index finger traced a light blue vein beneath the taut, pale skin. This was life. This was the very essence of womanhood— and Ella's nurturing of Holly.

Her hands were on him now, stroking up his chest, along the apex of his shoulders and down his arms with soft, feathery caresses.

Immediately he became aware of his body's response to her touch. He was hard and quivering. Ella placed a hand on either side of his hips and pushed his underpants down his legs.

As the full aroused length of him was revealed, he heard her breath catch.

He flung his head back.

Her fingers were sure and clever. She touched him in ways that drove him to the end of madness…then summoned him back.

When he could take no more, he fell back on the bed and pulled her with him, the satin smooth against his skin. Pushing off the last remaining bit of lace, he gently eased two trembling fingers into her slick warmth. Her flesh stretched around him. He moved his fingers, fluttering them, seeking the hard nub that made her breath stop.

When her breathing was ragged, her eyes wild, he shifted over her. With great care, he sank into her, then withdrew. Entered again. And pulled away.

Her arms came round his back, and her fingers dug into his buttocks. "Don't go," she pleaded. "Stay with me."

"Show me what you want," he demanded as passion ripped his heart apart.

Ella didn't hesitate. Within minutes she'd torn any control he'd had to shreds. He felt himself going…going…

As Ella's body clenched around him, he felt the first shudder. She arched beneath him, bucking and twisting, and he could no longer hold on as pleasure flooded them both in a torrent of sensation.

"Will you marry me?"

Whatever Ella had expected him to say on opening her eyes this morning, it was not this.

Her mouth dropped open. "M-marry you?"

His face filled her vision as Yevgeny nodded slowly.

She rolled away from him and dropped her legs out over the edge of the bed. Her naked back to him, she pressed the scarlet cover over her bare breasts and scanned the floor frantically for some sort of clothing.

"This proposal is a bit sudden."

Was this the point of the invitation to the ballet…and the romantic restaurant dinner he'd planned afterward? Had the whole evening been nothing but a staged seduction to get her to do what he wanted?

Except a date to the ballet followed by dinner need not have ended up in bed. *She'd* been the one to veto dinner. In all fairness to Yevgeny, he'd only invited her to his penthouse at her prompting. Ella shook her head to clear the confusion and struggled to focus.

Why had he asked her to marry him?

"Why?"

He didn't answer. But she sensed a distance between them that hadn't been there a moment ago.

The idyll had been shattered.

It had been such a beautiful night.... Ella had felt transported. From the moment the ballet had begun the magic had wound itself around her. As though she'd entered a hidden, undiscovered world of possibilities she'd never imagined. As for the night that had followed...

Not once but twice he'd made love to her.

The beauty of it had called to her. That feeling of exploring an intimate link she'd never dared dream existed. A moment of pure, blistering ecstasy. Then freedom. She'd encountered a facet of herself that she had never known—a facet that fitted perfectly, in fairy-tale fashion with—

She shook her head again, her hair whipping around her face.

There was no such thing as fairy tales—she of all people should know that.

Behind her he spoke in a low voice that breached all the barriers she was rebuilding. "Come back to bed."

Oh, she was tempted. To give in, to give up all her tightly held defenses and surrender to pleasure.

To the vision he offered.

"Say yes, Ella. Come lie with me again. Make love. We have time."

That seductive purr...

Then reality snapped in.

He had time. She didn't.

She was supposed to be meeting Jo Wells and the family who hoped to adopt Holly in—she squinted at the clock beside the bed struggling to make out the numbers without her glasses— an hour. And all she had to wear was a skimpy black cocktail dress, which she couldn't even find.

She would also have to explain to the night nurse and to Deb—who would be arriving at her town house by now—why she hadn't come home last night. The round-the-clock care she'd hired for Holly would mean the baby was fine.

But she wasn't.

Ella fought the urge to bury her head in her hands and burst into uncharacteristic tears as shame swamped her.

She'd almost fallen for it— This request to marry her could be nothing more than another ploy to get Holly.

This was not about intimate connections. Or profound pleasure. Or even about any feeling for her. This was about Yevgeny getting what he wanted in any way possible.

She'd do well to remember that.

Still clutching the covers to her chest, she leaned forward and scanned the carpet. Finally she caught sight of a puddle of black. Her dress. Her bra and briefs were nowhere to be seen. Ella had a distant memory of Yevgeny taking off her glasses last night; she'd have to retrieve them from the living room in order to locate her underwear.

For now she snagged the black dress with the tips of her fingers. In a smooth movement she pulled it over her head and shimmied it over her torso. It seemed absurd to protect her modesty now, but she no longer wanted to be naked in front of Yevgeny. Not until she'd worked out his motives.

Turning her head, she looked at him, fully looked at him, and her heart contracted.

He reclined against the pillows, the sun slanting through the window revealed his lips curved up in a sensual smile, while lazy appreciation still lingered in those glittering wolf eyes.

Lust bolted through her.

She wanted him.

Again.

Even though she suspected his motives.

How *could* she still desire him?

What kind of black magic had he unleashed on her? How had he managed to reduce her to…this? Never had anything interfered with her ability to think…to reason clearly…until now. He had her tied up in knots.

And no doubt he knew it.

It had been his plan.

Suspicion cooled her ardor like a bucket of icy water.

"No."

"No?" He raised a dark brow. "You don't want to stay?"

She flushed. "No—I can't marry you."

Ella emerged from the master bathroom, her purse under her arm. The transformation from siren to icicle was complete. Her makeup was perfect—and no doubt her underwear was back in place, too.

Instead of looking at him where he lounged in the big bed, she pushed her glasses up her nose and glanced down at her watch. "It's late—I have to go."

"Work. I suppose." Yevgeny resisted the urge to roll his eyes skyward.

"My work is important to me." Her voice cooled. Finally she looked at him. "But this time it's about Holly."

He started to pay attention. "Holly?"

Ella was fiddling with pulling the neckline of the black dress straight. He bit back the urge to tell her it was fine. "I intended to tell you about it last night. But I got…distracted." Her chin lifted a notch, signaling that he wouldn't like what was about to follow.

"Yes?"

"Jo Wells found a couple she thinks will be a perfect fit to adopt Holly."

Yevgeny stiffened at that revelation. "*I'm* the perfect fit to adopt Holly," he said unequivocally.

"I saw their profile yesterday. They offer everything I asked for." Ella swept her hair back behind her ear. "I'm meeting them this morning—" She broke off and glanced at her watch again. "In an hour."

Her stubbornness infuriated him. Fixing his gaze on her, he said softly, "I am absolutely committed to adopting Holly."

"It won't work. We've been through this before." She was talking so fast he didn't even try to get a word in. "You're a billionaire playboy. What do you want with a baby? You haven't thought this through. What will you do with a growing girl? How will you provide the mothering model she requires? What do you know about the needs of teenage girls? This feeling of responsibility will pass."

"I will learn. Whatever Holly needs I will provide," he said fiercely. "Whoever adopts her will also have to develop and learn about the needs she has—no one is a perfect parent from the start." He paused for an instant. "Parenting is about committing to learn about the needs of children." Something his own selfish mother had never made any effort to do.

But Ella was already turning away. "I've got to get to this appointment—and I need to stop by my town house to collect some suitable clothes first."

He could not risk Ella allowing a couple to get their hopes up about adopting Holly—he was taking Holly. Nor could he take the chance that Ella would get it into her head to sign the consent to adoption. Twelve days had passed. She could do it now.

"Then I will have to come with you."

She swung around, her face tight and closed—a world away from the woman who had responded so passionately to him last night...all through the night. A tight band settled around his chest.

"I don't want you to come. This is going to be hard enough without you there making it more difficult for me."

Yevgeny got out of the bed. Ella recoiled. Impatiently he reached for a pair of jeans slung over the blanket box at the end of the bed and dragged them on. Buttoning the fly, he said,

"My intention is not to make it more difficult—but to make it easier—"

"You're not doing that!"

"Ella, you should consider my proposal—"

"No!" She warded off his reaching hands. "No. No. *No.* I'm not marrying you!"

He wished she would stop interrupting him, stop rejecting him and stop pushing him away. She was making it so much more difficult...for both of them.

"Ella. *Listen to me.* I am Holly's father."

Eleven

"*What?*"

Ella's eyes stretched wide with shock. Finally, anger set in.

"What kind of stunt is this?" He'd tried persuasion, coercion—all with no luck. So last night he'd taken her to bed and, while she still basked in the warm, golden glow of his lovemaking, he'd asked her to marry him. *Now this.* Ella marched toward the bedroom door. "I don't believe you."

His hand closed around her arm.

"Wait!"

Fury broke over her. She yanked her arm loose.

"Don't touch me!"

He put his hands up in a gesture of surrender. "This is no stunt. I am Holly's biological father...I donated the sperm."

Frantically Ella searched his face, seeking something—anything—that would prove his claim a lie. Instead, she saw only calm, unwavering certainty.

Her shoulders sagged.

Holly's father. Not her uncle...

The dizzying discovery changed everything. And explained so much.

Like exactly why he'd slept with her last night. And why he'd asked her to marry him…and why he just refused to give up in his pursuit to adopt Holly.

A heavy weight sank over Ella, until it settled deep in her belly. He wanted Holly so badly—because she was his daughter.

The queasy feeling in Ella's stomach grew. Churned. Nausea rolled over her in turbulent, battering waves.

Vivid images flashed through her mind. Yevgeny demanding to know where the baby was that first day in the hospital. Yevgeny bending over Holly's cot, entranced. Yevgeny producing Nadiya as his fiancée so Holly would have the mother Ella demanded. Yevgeny's fury whenever she'd tried to roadblock his efforts. And the picture that hurt most of all? Yevgeny kissing her…loving her…to get want he most wanted….

Holly.

The next realization struck her.

Yevgeny wasn't going to give up. Ever. Last night's seduction had already proved just how far he would go to get Holly.

As Holly's biological father, he would be eligible to adopt the baby. The prohibition against a single man adopting a girl child did not apply to a father.

Ella's lawyerly brain went into overdrive. Hell, he might already be contemplating the first step: applying for guardianship. Ella knew she could challenge that. After all, Yevgeny had not been married to her—or even in a relationship with her. But there was a chance that a judge would grant the order because Holly's best interests were a stake. Once he'd been appointed joint guardian along with her, Ella suspected he'd waste no time seeking temporary custody of the baby. He was Holly's biological father; the court might look favorably on it. Unless she fought him. When Holly had been born, Ella would have done anything she could to stop Yevgeny getting the baby.

But now?

Ella bit her lip. He loved Holly. How could she stand in his way?

There would be some formalities to go through—paternity tests—not that Ella doubted that what he'd said was the truth. She could hear it in his voice, see it in his eyes. He was Holly's father. Even the hard-nosed, skeptical-lawyer part of her believed it. The court would, of course, demand incontrovertible evidence. But Ella knew the tests would prove beyond doubt he was Holly's father.

And once he'd secured temporary care of Holly he'd launch a formal application to adopt the baby.

"You're going to use the courts to get Holly," she breathed. "This is not—"

"You're not going to give up, are you? Why didn't you tell me this before?"

"I hoped to convince you without having to reveal this."

"You're ashamed of being Holly's father?" But that didn't make sense.

His eyes caught fire. "Never!"

"Of being involved in sperm donation?"

"I'm not ashamed of that—but to be honest, I don't think my grandmother would have been too keen on the idea." He shrugged. "But with her recent death that's not relevant anymore. If Keira and Dmitri had adopted the baby as planned no one else need ever have known the truth."

"Not me." Ella made it a statement. "And not even the person who needed most in the world to know the truth—Holly."

"Of course I knew Holly would have to know one day. Ella—"

She warded him off with blank, blind eyes. "But when Keira and Dmitri decided they didn't want Holly—why didn't you tell me then?" An instant pulsed past.

He took two long steps closer to her, and when she shuddered, he halted. "I was as shocked by the situation as you were. The first day I couldn't think straight." He'd expected Ella to do the motherly thing and keep the baby. But he didn't want to say that now. He wasn't prepared to risk extinguishing the burgeoning understanding that was forming between them. "We were always at such loggerheads. And I couldn't tell you... immediately."

"So when did you intend to tell me?"

By the time it had sunk in that he'd have to tell her, Keira and Dmitri had already flown off to Africa. In his arrogance, he'd believed Ella would be grateful for his offer to take the baby from her unwilling arms; he'd never expected her feisty resistance to his proposition. Well, he'd sure discovered how mistaken he was.

"Once I'd spoken to my brother—"

Ella laughed, a high, hopeless sound that sounded wild and desperate, cutting off his clumsy attempt at an explanation. "Sure. Now you need your brother's permission? You've never waited for anyone else in your life before you act, Yevgeny. Now you want me to believe you needed your brother's permission?"

Strangely enough he could understand her pain, her anger. She'd stood so firm in her conviction to be transparent, to do the very best for Holly. To the point where she was prepared to keep in touch with the baby as she grew older so that Holly would have a fully developed sense of her own identity.

"And why you? Why not Dmitri's sperm?"

The first wave of shock had passed. He could see her brain starting to process the information. "I'm trying to explain."

"Then get on with it."

God, this was hard. Even though he now knew how it must hurt her, Ella had been determined to be honest with the baby to whom she'd given birth.

He'd been less honorable.

Regret ate at him. But he couldn't change his actions, couldn't make them more honest. All he could do was explain what had driven his deception. And be totally honest in his relationship with Holly from now on. "Ella, you need to understand..."

Ella focused on him and the pain in her eyes caused the

words to trail away and his heart to clench. Then she raised her eyebrows in a way that brought his feisty Ella back. "*I* need to understand?"

He had to make her understand. "I needed to clear it with Dmitri—because it involves him."

"Does it? I'd say that the essence of the situation is that it doesn't involve him—he played no part in Holly's conception." She dropped her head into her hands. "And all the time I thought—" Ella broke off and lifted her face. "Keira lied to me, then—she was part of it."

Ella had gone white.

Yevgeny started toward her, but stopped when she glared at him.

"Keira had no choice," he told her. "Dmitri didn't want anyone to know—although he disputes that now."

"I don't believe that she kept this…this…from me. I'm her sister—I offered to carry the baby she wanted. She owed me some loyalty…she *and* Dmitri." Her mouth twisted in a rictus of a smile. "Or perhaps Dmitri never wanted a baby—and he was just stringing Keira along."

"That's not true!"

"Isn't it? Then why the elaborate charade?"

"Because my brother is sterile!" he announced.

There was a deathly silence.

Then Ella said, "Oh." After a moment she said, "But why such a big secret? Everyone knew from the outset Keira couldn't have babies. There was no big secret about that."

"It seems that it is my fault."

That got her attention. "Your fault?"

He sighed and rubbed a hand over his hair. "Yes."

"Was there an…accident?" she asked carefully.

It took Yevgeny a moment to realize that she'd taken him literally. "I didn't cause my brother's sterility," he said broodingly. "But apparently I caused him to be ashamed of his lack of manhood."

Ella stared at him without responding.

He laughed without humor. "So it would appear you are right. I am the big-brother bully. My brother didn't want anyone to know because he feared I would be angry—while I thought he didn't want anyone to know because he would feel…awkward."

"You were trying to protect him."

Yevgeny shrugged. "Except he doesn't see it that way."

"Of course he doesn't. He only sees it from his side—because that's what you've allowed him to do all his life. You've allowed him to be selfish. You created a monster."

He opened his mouth to object to the attack on his brother.

But Ella was already speaking. "Don't worry—I've done the same thing." She lifted her hands and shrugged. "I've indulged Keira so much that she doesn't need to take responsibility for anything. She simply needs to dump it on me and swan off secure in the knowledge that I will take care of it." Ella hitched her purse up. "Whatever 'it' happens to be at the moment."

"And right now it is Holly."

"Exactly."

It took a minute of silence for that to sink in. Yevgeny found himself smiling at her as a newfound sense of truce surrounded them. "We're a fine pair, aren't we?"

Ella glanced at her watch. "Good grief, the meeting. I need to fly."

"I am coming with you—don't even try to keep me away."

Ella was relieved that today was over.

Jo Wells had dropped her home. Ella had been extremely grateful. She had a headache and it had taken all her energy to persuade Yevgeny that she didn't want him taking her home. She needed nothing more than to sleep—which she'd done, while Deb had tended to Holly.

Now she sat curled up in the rocking chair in Holly's nursery, watching the baby sleep in her cot while the night nurse took a coffee break in the kitchen.

This morning's meeting had been unspeakably difficult,

despite the fact that Yevgeny had behaved like a saint. And, to make things worse, Jo Wells had been right.

The family was delightful—everything Ella had once wanted for Holly.

Holly. It was all about Holly.

Only Holly.

Too soon Holly would be gone....

Ella knew she shouldn't be thinking about herself. About how she was going to feel once Holly had gone. But she couldn't help herself.

She'd taken all possible precautions to stop this from happening yet still it had happened. She'd grown attached to the baby lying in the cot only feet away.

One thing had become clear to Ella—Yevgeny wanted to adopt the baby with his whole heart. He might not be listed on the birth certificate as Holly's father, but she didn't need to have blood tests run to confirm his paternity claim. She believed him—even though the lawyerly side of her would force her to cross the *t*'s. His desire to keep Holly wasn't a spur-of-the-moment whim driven by impulse. He loved Holly—he was her father. Holly was his daughter, a part of him.

An ache filled Ella. Holly was a part of her, too. Her daughter. *Their* daughter.

Her heart was telling her Holly belonged with the father who already loved her...even though he was far from perfect.

Could she forget about the plans—dreams—she'd had for Holly to go to the perfect family? And give Yevgeny what all his billions would never buy him?

That way there would be no messy, turbulent court battles... no legacy of bitterness.

Ella rose to her feet and went to stand by the cot. Inside Holly slept peacefully.

"What do you want, my angel?" she asked the baby.

It was Christmas Eve.

Using the excuse that his brother and her sister were both

away in Africa, Ella had invited Yevgeny around for dinner. She hadn't been surprised when he'd leaped at the opportunity to spend time with Holly.

Ella had decorated the table with cheery green-and-red place settings for her and Yevgeny. There was a place for Holly, too, and Ella planned to draw her stroller up to the table for dinner to participate in the event.

This Christmas Eve was special.

It was Holly's first Christmas Eve. And, Ella knew, it would be the only Christmas she would ever spend with the baby. At the moment the baby was lying on her back on the carpet wearing a cute Santa's elf outfit.

She looked absolutely adorable.

Ella had spent the afternoon since returning from work taking photos. One day Holly would be able to look back through the album that Ella would put together for this day. In fact, Ella had decided to keep a duplicate copy of the album for herself…to form an invisible bond between her and Holly.

Forever.

A secret they would share.

The doorbell interrupted her musings.

That would be Yevgeny.

Opening the door, she found him standing outside in the warmth of the evening sunshine, his arms piled high with goodies and gifts.

"You shouldn't have." She laughed, ushering him in. "Put the presents under the tree. Actually, let me help unpack the top items first."

There was a bouquet of flowers, chocolates, an iced Christmas cake…and crackers.

"This wasn't necessary," she scolded.

"What? And deprive me of the opportunity to spoil Holly rotten?" He started to pack the gaily wrapped parcels under the tree. Ella couldn't help noticing how well his black jeans fit his narrow waist and long legs, and how the T-shirt clung to his muscular shoulders.

Oh, my. All he needed was a red bow and some ribbon to be someone's perfect Christmas present.

But she had to remember he wasn't intended for her.

She swallowed. "Can I get you something to drink?"

"There's a bottle of red wine somewhere in here. Or it may still be in my car— I'll go check."

"I'll find it," Ella said. "Look, here it is."

But Yevgeny had already disappeared through the front door. He returned minutes later without the wine—but this time he carried an enormous boxed gift as tall as he was.

Ella did a double take. "What is that?"

"A playhouse—one to set up inside, until I get the one in the tree built."

Ella couldn't help herself. She laughed.

They had eaten dinner. Lazy now, Ella sat on the carpet in the living room leaning against the sofa, her legs stretched out in front of her with Holly cradled in the crook of her arm sucking sleepily at the last dregs of her bottle, while Yevgeny sprawled in front of the Christmas tree with his head propped up on his elbow, watching them both through pale, wolf eyes.

"Holly is almost asleep," Ella said softly, bending her head.

The baby was heavy and relaxed in her arms.

For so long Ella had been at pains not to hold or feed Holly, to keep her distance. Yet tonight she was eager for the experience. With Deb gone home to enjoy Christmas with her family it seemed like the right time. Ella knew that she was going to spend plenty of time with Holly over the next two days, and that she'd grow fonder of the baby with every hour, making the final wrench of separation so much harder. But she'd accepted that.

With the pain came immense pleasure. The joy in watching Holly's mouth twitch as she sucked. The satisfaction of stroking a finger along the baby's velvety skin. And these precious days would give her a chance to say goodbye to the baby.

But tonight there were three of them—herself, Yevgeny and the baby.

Almost a family.

To escape that delinquent thought she glanced back at Yevgeny, and asked, "What was your first Christmas memory?"

The flickering red-and-green lights on the tree reflected in Yevgeny's colorless eyes.

"The Christmas season would run from the last day of December to around the tenth of January. When I was a boy, on New Year's Day we would hold hands and form a chain around the tree and call out for Grandfather Frost—not Santa Claus. He would hand out presents helped by his granddaughter, the Snow Maiden. There were always tables laden with food, a total contrast to the food shortages that my parents had grown up with. Things denied us during the rest of the year appeared. A goose. Cakes. Meatballs. Pineapple— My mother queued for hours to get pineapple. I'd almost forgotten about that. And no celebration would be complete without *kutya*."

"Kutya?"

"A kind of porridge made from wheat berries, honey, poppyseed and nuts. My *babushka* would make it a few days in advance because that way, she used to say, the flavors had time to develop. But the best part, the part I couldn't wait for, was watching my grandmother hurl a spoonful of *kutya* up at the ceiling in the hope that it would stick."

Ella found herself laughing. "She sounds like a character."

"Everyone did it—it was a tradition. The theory went that if the *kutya* stayed stuck to the ceiling, a successful honey harvest would follow. And that is good for everyone—because honey represents happiness and success." His mouth softened into a smile, and even the hard angles of his cheekbones disappeared as he lost himself in the memories.

"Your grandmother must've been a wonderful woman."

"Oh, she could be a tartar, too." He reached out and grasped the hand resting on Holly's cheek. His fingers tightened around hers. "But she made Christmas special."

Who would make Holly's Christmas special?

The sudden question flitted through Ella's mind with the

speed of light, causing her to stare down at the little angel in her arms. Not her—she wouldn't be around to be Holly's mother. Yevgeny had a wealth of tradition that she would never have expected. But where would the mother figure in Holly's life be?

Yes, she would visit—but would that be enough? Ella shook her head, her throat tight. Why was she worrying? Yevgeny loved the baby, and he'd clearly forged a strong bond with Holly. What did it matter that Holly would have no mother figure? She would have a father who loved her.

"Ella?"

She looked up.

"What are you thinking?" he asked softly.

The tightness in her throat made it impossible for her to speak. She shook her head instead.

"You love her, don't you?"

She hesitated, then nodded. It was true. Holly had crept into her heart against Ella's will and twisted herself around it. She bit her lip, struggling to hold back the tears that threatened.

"You've come to a decision," he prompted.

The tears spilled over. She nodded. Only once. Then her face puckered up. Ella knew she was going to disgrace herself by sobbing all over Yevgeny.

She found her voice. "I think I'll take her upstairs and put her to bed."

His hands clenched hers. "You're running away."

"No!" She simply wanted to get herself under control. Ella rose to her feet, and his hand slipped away. "I won't be long. I'll be back in a few minutes."

When Ella came back to the living room, Yevgeny's gaze fastened to her. He'd settled himself on the sofa, and she hesitated a moment before perching on the opposite end. She turned so that she was facing him, and drew her bare feet up onto the seat.

"You've decided you're going to keep the baby," he said.

Ella blinked at him. There was loneliness in his eyes. Was

he giving up? "No, I haven't changed my mind." At least not about that.

"No?"

This was so hard. "I love Holly."

There, she'd said it. Now for the next bit…

"But my keeping Holly would not be in her best interests." Ella got restlessly to her feet.

"Because you've got your mind fixed on wanting her to be raised by a family?"

Because she'd make a terrible parent. "That's part of it, but not the only reason I can't do it."

She'd reached the Christmas tree. Ella leaned forward and scooped up a wrapped scroll.

"I'd planned to give you this tomorrow, on Christmas Day. But now is as good a time as any."

She handed it to him. He took it with reluctance. "Open it," she said.

He drew out the document she'd rolled up and secured with gold ribbon. "What is this?"

Even as he pulled the ribbon loose, Yevgeny stared across at Ella.

She sighed. "It's my consent to the adoption."

He glanced down. "Why give it to me…"

The moment his voice trailed away Ella knew he'd seen his name. "It's in your favor."

When he looked up, the brilliance in his eyes made her want to cry. But this time with joy…and relief.

She was doing the right thing.

"I can't offer her a big sister—or a mother," he said. "But I can offer her a home, a garden, a place to call her own."

"I think Holly will be very fortunate to call the house we looked at together home."

"But more than a home, I can offer her every bit of love I am capable of giving. And I can offer her an aunt and an uncle—" he hesitated "—and a tummy mummy who are all her family."

The sweetness of his words caused her to smile.

"What about the other family?" he asked.

His concern caused her heart to melt. "I've already told Jo—she promised to let them know." At least she'd never told them they were getting the baby. To hold out hope then snatch it away in such circumstances was more than Ella could bear.

Mixed up with a sense of sadness at the goodbyes she needed to say to Holly once Christmas was over was relief that Yevgeny wouldn't be taking her away. He wouldn't whisk Holly away to Russia—or London. He would be working and living in Auckland. He was buying a house with Holly in mind. She'd seen the room that would be Holly's. She would be able to visualize Holly safe in her home, keep her in mind in the months—years—that lay ahead.

Ella knew she would see the baby and, thanks to Jo Wells, Yevgeny knew how important it was to her that this be an open adoption.

She shouldn't be feeling like this….

So empty.

Like her guts—her heart—had been ripped out.

Get over it. For once, Ella found the bracing words didn't work.

So she tried reason instead. Her daughter would still live in the same city, not across the ocean in another world.

And she would stay in touch with the baby.

That made Ella feel better.

While Holly would not call her mom, she would always be Holly's tummy mummy—Yevgeny had made that clear. She felt a lump forming at the back of her throat. The alternative, cutting all ties to the little girl, would be so much worse. It was not an option—not for Holly.

And not for her.

Yet the night he'd made love to her, Yevgeny had offered more. He'd asked her to marry him. She had said no in a way that had brooked no argument. For one wild, magic moment Ella considered what might have happened if she'd accepted.

Then she shrugged it away. The moment was past. He would not ask again. Why should he? He had what he wanted....

Holly.

Why would he want her? He didn't even like her....

Why could it not have been different?

She quickly stifled that thought. That would mean that she never agreed to act as surrogate for Keira and Dmitri, that Holly had never been born, that she would never have gotten to know Yevgeny better.

And those were things she could not contemplate living without now.

Because she loved Holly.

As for Yevgeny...she was so confused about the swings of emotion he aroused in her. Anger. Passion. Empathy. And something she feared to name.

So when his arms came around her, the lighted Christmas tree, the gaily colored packages, all dissolved in a blur of tears as Ella started to weep uncontrollably.

Twelve

"Hey, don't cry," Yevgeny whispered against Ella's hair, and his arms tightened around her.

She snuffled. "I'm not crying." And she felt him smile.

"Sure you're not." He pressed a kiss to the top of her head. After a moment he added, "Thank you for my Christmas gift. It is without a doubt the best present I've ever received."

"My pleasure." Ella found she meant it. With her tears stanched, she lifted her head and warned him, "But you better make Holly happy."

His expression deadly serious, he said, "My offer is still open. If you marry me and come live with us, you'll be able to gauge for yourself how happy she is."

Ella's heart leaped, and then settled into a rapid beat.

The offer was unbearably tempting. Looking away, she focused on the flickering of the Christmas lights. There was something about the powerful emotions that Yevgeny stirred in her that made her suspect she was falling in love with him. Heck, not falling…fallen.

She was in love.

It had been so long, she'd forgotten how it felt to be in love.

And back then it had been so different. Young love. This time it was deeper…less impulsive. Yet Ella knew if she accepted Yevgeny's proposal she needed to be sure that her love was strong enough for both of them. There could be no going back because Holly would suffer.

Of course, they shared that bond. She loved Holly…and Yevgeny loved the baby, too.

But, despite his proposal, Ella was under no illusion that he loved her. He never had. Could he learn to love her in the future? Was it worth taking a chance on that? Could she love enough for two?

"So what do you think?" he asked at last.

"I'm scared," she said honestly, switching her gaze back to find him still watching her with that unnerving intensity.

"Scared? *You?*" There was disbelief in his voice. "But why?"

Not ready to confess that she wasn't sure about the wisdom of going into a marriage where he didn't love her, she said instead, "I don't know that I'd make a very good mother."

He reared back and looked down at her. "What makes you think that? You're wonderful with Holly. I didn't think that at the start but you've managed to convince me. Your love for her is evident every time you look at her."

"My parents haven't provided the best template, but to be truthful, that's not the only reason I think I'd be a hopeless failure as a mother…and wife."

"Who was he?"

She gave him a startled look. "How did—" Ella broke off. Then, "What makes you think there was a man?" she hedged.

"Your reaction." Yevgeny's brow was creased in a frown of concern, and his hold loosened, giving her more space. "Tell me who he was."

Did she really want to expose herself to the possibility that he might not even understand her pain? Perhaps the time had come to reveal something more. It was the only way to discover if there was substance to this attraction that floated between them.

Her shoulders slumping, she said, "I was eighteen, he was nineteen. We were in love."

A shadow passed across his face.

"You can't imagine it, can you?" Ella pulled a face. "I was besotted. I thought it was forever."

"What happened?"

"I got pregnant."

He sighed, the sound overloud in the living room of Ella's town house. Something cold shriveled in Ella's chest. "It was perfectly predictable," she said. "He disappeared as soon as I told him. All his promises of our future together vanished as he ran for the plane to take him to a new job and new future in Australia. Within weeks I heard he had a new girlfriend, too."

"And you were left holding the baby." Ella could feel the tension that coiled through his body even before he asked, "You had an abortion?"

She gave him a sharp look and broke out of his arms, shifting to sit on the side of the sofa farthest from him. "No!"

"So what happened to the baby?"

"The baby," she said through stiff lips, "died."

This time Yevgeny brooked no resistance as he took Ella in his arms.

Her body was rigid and she felt worryingly cold. He rubbed his hands along her arms, and marveled that he'd ever considered Ella a human icicle.

She was complex, yet kind. And she'd endured more than any woman should need to.

"I'm sorry."

He brushed his lips over hers in a gesture of sympathy. Her mouth clung to his, and Yevgeny kept the contact until she finally broke it.

"Thank you."

He let the silence surround them, not pressing her to tell him more. It was curiously companionable, with no rough edges as she nestled closer. His hands stroked along her back, touching, offering wordless comfort, even as Yevgeny wished he could take the pain from her.

When she did speak, she lifted her face up to him and said, "Make love to me."

"Now?" His hands paused in their stroking. "Are you sure?"

She nodded, her honey-colored eyes pleading. "Yes. Now. Here. I want to feel alive again."

This time their loving held a well of tenderness.

Rather than passion, it was care and concern that Yevgeny expressed with every stroke and touch. Only when her body softened, became increasingly fluid, did he finally pull her over him and let her take him into her.

Then he rocked her.

Slowly and so gently. Until the sensations built to a peak and the passion broke.

When it was over, he pulled her up against him, and held her tight.

A while later, Ella straightened up. "I feel much better." She sounded surprised. "Definitely more alive."

"Good."

She sat up slowly and reached for the clothing she'd discarded. "You've been very patient."

"It's one of my less well-known qualities." He gave her a small smile and was relieved when her eyes sparkled back. After she'd pulled the garments on, Yevgeny reached out his hand and took hers. "I'm here for as long as you need me."

Astonishment flitted across her face, followed by acceptance. "Thank you."

"I'm the one who needs to say thank you," he said, "for giving me Holly."

"The other baby—" Ella broke off.

"You don't need to talk about that if you don't wish to."

"I want to." Her eyes met his bravely. "The other baby was going to be adopted out. It was a closed adoption—my parents thought it would be for the best. I never knew anything about the family she was going to—only that they couldn't have children. Once the baby was gone…I knew I would never see it again."

That's why she'd been so insistent about an open adoption this time around, he realized. "That must have been hard to deal with."

Her eyes had gone blank. She'd retreated into the world of the past. "The morning I went into labor—I changed my mind. I wanted to keep the baby. My parents wouldn't hear of it. We were still fighting when I went into labor. It was a boy."

Yevgeny waited. Nothing he could say would be adequate to comfort her.

"But something went wrong. The cord was wrapped around his neck…and he died. I felt like I'd killed him—by changing my mind and deciding to keep him."

"No!"

"I know. It's not a rational fear. But it took me a long time to come to terms with it."

Yevgeny finally understood why it had been so difficult for her to change her decision to give Holly up to a couple who could love her…to give her to him.

It had taken courage. She'd had to conquer her demons.

"You're the bravest woman I've ever met," he told her.

It was then that he realized how deeply he loved her. But now was not the time to convince her that marrying him would heal them all.

So all he said was, "Come, let me hold you."

When the doorbell rang on Christmas morning, Ella had no idea who could be outside.

She pulled open the door to find Keira and Dmitri on the doorstep, luggage piled up beside them. "You're back!"

Concern instantly settled over her. What had gone wrong? Then she gathered her scattered thoughts.

"Merry Christmas! Don't stand out on the doorstep. Come in."

Ushering the pair into her living room, while leaving the

luggage stacked in the hall, Ella asked, "What happened? Why've you left Malawi?"

Keira came to a halt in the middle of the room and exchanged glances with Dmitri.

"Ella, we've changed our minds."

Something in her sister's tense tone caused adrenaline to surge through Ella's veins. "You've changed your mind? About volunteering in Malawi?"

But she knew...

It was much, much more.

"No, about the baby." Keira's words confirmed what Ella had already sensed. Keira wore a mulish expression. "Dmitri and I have decided we're going to keep Jessica."

"Jessica?" Ella's brain was spinning. "Her name isn't Jessica, it's Holly."

"We've chosen to name her Jessica." Dmitri placed an arm around Keira's shoulders and drew her close.

This was what she'd wanted...wasn't it? Taking in their unified pose, Ella swallowed. She'd hoped for Keira to change her mind and keep the baby. Yet now confronted by the pair who had just announced that's what they wanted, Ella found the idea of losing Holly terrified her.

Then anger set in.

"But you gave her up—you told me to sort everything out."

"We made a mistake."

Her sister's eyes filled with tears. For the first time ever, Keira's tears failed to move Ella. The customary protectiveness failed to materialize. This time it was Holly she wanted to protect.

"You decided you weren't ready for a baby yet."

"That's what we thought, but the time in Malawi made us decide we're ready for parenthood."

"It's too late, Keira—"

"She's already been adopted? You've signed the consent?" Keira must've seen the answer in her eyes. "You should've let me know—"

"You walked away—you made her my problem. Remember?"

"Because I knew you would be able to give her up for adoption—you've done it before. And you did it without any trouble." Keira huddled closer to Dmitri. "I'm not as tough as you, Ella, I couldn't face the pain. I could never have done it."

Tough? A shaft of pain shot through Ella. Was that how her sister saw her? Did no one see how painful these decisions were for her? Ella swallowed. She'd lost one baby—she wasn't losing this one. "I couldn't give Holly up."

"Then why did you imply she's been adopted?"

"Wait, let me get a word in edgewise. I never said she's been given up for adoption. I'm getting married—I'm going to keep her."

"Married?" Keira gave a laugh of surprise. "To who?"

"Your sister is marrying me."

The dark voice came from behind her. Yevgeny. Relief swarmed through Ella as he enfolded her in his arms. She shut her eyes and allowed herself to lean into his strength.

Strength. Comfort. Understanding. That was what he'd offered her through this period of turmoil. He'd been there for her—and Holly—every minute. He'd never failed her or walked away.

He was a man in a million.

A man worth loving. Forever.

It would be so easy to abdicate all responsibility, to let Yevgeny take over. But it wasn't fair.

Ella forced herself to keep steady. And to think. Was this the best course for Holly? She loved Yevgeny but he didn't love her. But he was reliable. He would never leave her.... She knew from what he'd told her about his mother walking out on him and Dmitri he would never do that to his own child. Could she marry him under such circumstances, knowing there was no way out?

"We came back for the baby." Dmitri stood toe to toe with his older brother.

"Until you change your mind again next week?"

"We won't."

"Ella and I are hardly convinced. Until you turned up here today we haven't received one call from the pair of you to find out how the baby was."

"I called," objected Keira. "Only once but at least I called."

"This is true?" Yevgeny spoke into Ella's ear.

She nodded slowly, and waited for him to stiffen, to release his hold and withdraw his support.

But he stayed exactly where he was.

Before she could say anything, Keira started to speak. "Yes, Ella told me she'd hired a nanny, that she was back at work. I felt so guilty. I knew the baby was screwing up her life."

Ella closed her eyes. "Things changed."

She'd changed.

And Yevgeny had noticed the change even as she'd started becoming aware of it herself. She thought back to their visit to that magical house…the day he'd kissed her for the first time.

Ella placed her hands on his forearms, emphasizing their unity in the face of her sister and his brother. What they were doing was right. They both loved Holly.

They would make this work.

It had to.

Her resolve hardened. "I'm sorry, Keira. I got pregnant for you originally. Then you and Dmitri decided you both needed time and space for yourselves. But now I can't give her up. I'm her mother."

Saying those words freed something deep inside her. All the hurt of the past softened, eased and floated gently away.

For the first time in many years, Ella felt…whole. At peace.

"After my first baby died, I thought I'd never smile again…" Her voice trailed away.

Behind her the rise and fall of Yevgeny's chest slowed. His arms tensed into bands of steel around her.

Keira's face crumpled. "None of us could reach you."

"I'm happy now. Holly has brought me happiness. Please be happy for me— I don't want to fight you on this," she said to her sister.

There'd been enough fighting. Against Yevgeny. Against herself. But she would fight no longer.

"Keira, I haven't discussed this with Yevgeny, but why don't we talk about you and Dmitri becoming Holly's godparents? That way, you can both have a significant part in her life." When Keira's eyes brightened, Ella started to think about the old saying that it took a village to raise a child. Holly would never be short of family. She glanced from Keira to Dmitri and finally to Yevgeny. "What do you all think?"

Yevgeny nodded, his expression unfathomable.

"We'll discuss it," said Keira. "But first I want to be matron of honor at your wedding."

Ella knew she should come clean and reveal there might be no wedding—she hadn't yet given Yevgeny his answer, even though she'd told Keira and Dmitri they were getting married.

Ironically, she now desperately wanted to marry Yevgeny—but there was still a stumbling block.

He didn't love her.

Thirteen

Red. Yellow. Green.

The Christmas tree lights lit up Ella's pale face.

Holly was having her afternoon nap, and they'd finally seen Keira and Dmitri off after they'd stayed for Christmas lunch. Yevgeny had given the pair the keys to the Porsche and the freedom to stay in his penthouse. He would've done anything to get rid of them.

Because he needed to talk to Ella.

She'd announced to his brother and her sister that they were getting married—that she was keeping Holly. He should be pumped…everything he wanted was falling into place. But he didn't like the quiet air that had settled around her like a shroud. It was a far cry from the happiness expected of a bride-to-be.

"Ella, are you okay?"

Her hands paused in the act of picking up the shredded wrapping paper that lay on the carpet, left over from the orgy of unwrapping that had taken place earlier. Holly had gotten a treasure trove of gifts. The eyes that looked up at him held confusion—with none of the honey-gold tones that indicated happiness. She pushed her glasses up her nose in the way she had when she was uncertain.

"Do you think I've been too hasty?" she asked. "Holly was born for Keira and Dmitri—should I give her back to them?" The pain in her eyes was blinding. "It would give Keira the gift of happiness I intended all along."

"But what about you?"

She stared at him. "Me?"

"Yes, *you.*" This lay at the heart of the matter, he realized. He came to stand in front of her. "What do *you* want?" Ella blinked up at him. "I think, for once in your life, you need to think about what you want. And go after it."

The bewilderment faded, and a strange expression came over her face. Her eyes flicked to him, then shot away. "That would be selfish."

"You deserve to be happy, too."

"It's not just about me. There are other issues at stake here, too."

He placed his finger under her chin and tilted it so that he could see her eyes. They were guarded. "Like what?"

"Like you."

He tried to read her, started to hope. "What do you mean?"

"I don't want you to feel obliged to marry me because of what my stupid pride caused me to say to Keira."

Had it been pride that had caused her declaration? He'd thought there'd been a lot of honesty—her love for Holly had shone from her.

Yet now doubt shadowed her face.

"You're having second thoughts about giving Holly up?"

She shook her head. "No, she belongs with you."

"You could belong with us, too. If you choose." His finger trailed along her jawline and stroked her hair off her face as he'd seen her do so often in the past. He was no longer sure whether marriage for Holly's sake alone would be enough for him.

In the past few weeks his fears had changed. He no longer dreaded that Ella would abandon Holly someday, as his mother had abandoned his father, himself and his brother. He now feared that she would never be able to love him. Hell, she hadn't liked him that long ago. His own arrogance had cemented that. At least the raw antagonism had diminished. He could make her laugh. He was certain she at least liked him now.

But love?

Not yet.

He didn't want to wait for her to fall in love with him—to live in uncertainty about whether it would come to pass even as he took her to his bed each night.

He wanted her love. Now.

But he didn't want to put more pressure on her, either. This time he had to be selfless, this time he was putting Ella first.

This was about Ella. It was her choice.

"What do you want, Ella? What is your dream?"

Ella bit her lip.

How to tell Yevgeny that her dream lay at the magical home he'd bought for him and Holly. She wanted to share that home with him and Holly—she wanted to share their future.

Because she loved them both…more than anything in the world. Between the two of them, they'd taught her to love again. They'd brought her back to life.

Yevgeny's hands cupped her face.

She met his gaze…and trembled inside.

Could she risk revealing her dream to him? What if he ridiculed it? Or dismissed it? As quickly as they came the thoughts vanished. Once they'd come to an understanding about Holly, Yevgeny had shown her nothing but kindness. And passion. *That* thought swept in from nowhere and caused her cheeks to heat.

"Let me tell you what I never dared dream of." His voice broke into her thoughts. "I never dared dream that I'd one day have a family. You see, my family was a train wreck. My mother and father had a dysfunctional relationship and when my mother left, she used me and Dmitri to get what she wanted—financial support while she swanned around with her new lover."

Ella knew she should have suspected something like this; all the clues had been there. She should have worked out that he was the childhood victim of a bitter divorce.

"Your mother got custody of you both?" she asked slowly.

He nodded, his eyes vulnerable. "She took us away from Russia—to London. Until she decided she wanted to be young and unfettered again and ran off with her toyboy. My father came to fetch us—it was the first time we'd seen him in three years. She'd fed the court a bunch of lies, and he'd been barred from seeing us."

"I'm sorry," she said, and took a step forward. She wrapped her arms around this strong man, and leaned into him. She kissed his cheek.

He dropped his face into the cleft formed by her neck and shoulder, and said so softly that she had to strain her ears to hear, "I never wanted to marry—to risk that happening to my child. I was not ever going to give any woman that kind of power over me."

Ella struggled to absorb what he was telling her. But he'd asked her marry him. What did that mean? Was this regret for flouting his vow to himself?

Probably.

Ella knew exactly what to do. She had to set him free. Dropping her arms, she said, "And now I've gone and told both our families that we're getting married. I'll tell Keira it was a mistake."

"No!" He raised his head. The expression in his eyes caused her breath to catch in disbelief. "Ella, you don't understand—I *want* to marry you. That's the dream I never dared to dream. I love you."

To Ella's horror, she felt tears prick.

"Hey, I didn't mean to make you cry."

That caused her to smile through the tears. "I'm sorry. I don't normally cry this much. But these are tears of relief—and joy. You see, I love you, too."

At that, Yevgeny's arms encircled her and crushed her to his heart.

"Are you happy?"

"Me?" Ella turned her head to smile at her fiancé. Yevgeny's arm rested around her waist as they stood on the wide veranda of their dream home taking in the view they'd be seeing every day in the new year. "I'm walking on clouds—life couldn't be better."

The sale of the house had gone through. In a few days they would be moving in.

Everything in her world was going right.

Ella glanced down at the stroller beside them, where Holly was quite comfortably ensconced. For now. In years to come Ella knew Holly would tear around the gardens, explore the trees…and play on the swing Yevgeny intended to build. Perhaps there would be a younger sister. Maybe a brother, too.

A hand cupped her chin. Instantly her pulse quickened. Yevgeny bent his head and sealed her smiling lips with a kiss.

When he raised his head, she said, "Did you ever imagine this could happen between us?"

"I'll tell you a secret."

She tipped her head back, waiting for him to continue. "Yes?"

"I used to think you were an icicle. I didn't think the man had been born who could melt you."

"No secret." She laughed. "I knew what you thought of me. But you once told me you never could resist a dare. Was that how you viewed me? A challenge to defrost?"

"It never crossed my mind. I have to say that I must be incredibly blind because you're the warmest, most passionate woman I've ever known." He ran a finger over her bottom lip. "You're not angry?"

"I'd be hypocritical if I was." Ella paused, then grinned.

"You see, I thought you were a bully—I called you Bossy Big Brother."

"I'm not a bully!"

"Ah, but I thought you were. I thought you controlled every aspect of your brother's life, and that was why the poor thing was so irresponsible."

Yevgeny swung round and leaned against the balustrade. Placing his hands on her hips, he drew her closer. "What can I say? I admit it. I did pull him out of too many scrapes."

"I did the same with Keira. It was easier to sort her mistakes out for her than let her learn to do it herself." She grinned at him as she allowed her body to rest against his. "At least we won't make those mistakes with Holly."

"I have no doubt there will be others to make."

Ella looked up at him, aghast. "Good grief. I hope not."

"But don't worry. Like her mother, I know she's ticklish— under her feet."

"How long have you known that?"

He paused. "I'll tell you something else I know."

"What's that?"

"The night I discovered Holly was ticklish, I overheard your promise to our daughter that you'd find her the best mother in the world. If you ask me, I think you've done that."

Her heart stopped. "That's the nicest thing you've ever said to me."

"And it's perfectly true. Come here my wife-to-be. Let me show you again how much I love you."

This time when his mouth closed over hers, he was in no hurry to end the kiss.

* * * * *

A sneaky peek at next month...

Desire™

PASSIONATE AND DRAMATIC LOVE STORIES

My wish list for next month's titles...

In stores from 15th February 2013:

2 stories in each book - only £5.49!

☐ All or Nothing – Catherine Mann

& A Conflict of Interest – Barbara Dunlop

☐ Sunset Surrender – Charlene Sands

& Undeniable Demands – Andrea Laurence

☐ Bachelor Unclaimed – Brenda Jackson

& In His Brother's Place – Elizabeth Lane

Available at WHSmith, Tesco, Asda, Eason, Amazon and Apple

Just can't wait?

MILLS & BOON® Book Club

2 Free Stories!

Get your free stories now at
www.millsandboon.co.uk/freebookoffer

Or fill in the form below and post it back to us

THE MILLS & BOON® BOOK CLUB™—HERE'S HOW IT WORKS: Accepting your free stories places you under no obligation to buy anything. You may keep the stories and return the despatch note marked 'Cancel'. If we do not hear from you, about a month later we'll send you 2 Desire™ 2-in-1 books priced at £5.49* each. There is no extra charge for post and packaging. You may cancel at any time, otherwise we will send you 4 stories a month which you may purchase or return to us—the choice is yours. *Terms and prices subject to change without notice. Offer valid in UK only. Applicants must be 18 or over. Offer expires 31st July 2013. **For full terms and conditions, please go to www.millsandboon.co.uk/freebookoffer**

Mrs/Miss/Ms/Mr (please circle)
_____

First Name
_____

Surname
_____

Address
_____

_____

                              Postcode

E-mail
_____

Send this completed page to: Mills & Boon Book Club, Free Book Offer, FREEPOST NAT 10298, Richmond, Surrey, TW9 1BR

Find out more at
www.millsandboon.co.uk/freebookoffer

Visit us Online

0113/D3XEb